ff

HANIF KUREISHI

The Buddha
of Suburbia

faber and faber

LONDON · BOSTON

First published in 1990
by Faber and Faber Limited
3 Queen Square London WC1N 3AU
This TV tie-in paperback edition first published in 1993

Phototypeset by Wilmaset, Birkenhead, Wirral
Printed in England by Clays Ltd, St Ives plc

A CIP record for this book is available from the British Library

ISBN 0-571-17128-1

6 8 10 9 7 5

The Buddha of Suburbia

Hanif Kureishi was born and brought up in Kent. He read philosophy at King's College, London, where he started to write plays. In 1981 he won the George Devine Award for his play *Outskirts*, and in 1982 he was appointed Writer in Residence at the Royal Court Theatre. In 1984 he wrote *My Beautiful Laundrette*, which received an Oscar nomination for Best Screenplay. His second film was *Sammy and Rosie Get Laid* followed by *London Kills Me*, which he also directed. *The Buddha of Suburbia* won the Whitbread Prize for Best First Novel in 1990. The BBC is currently producing a four-part drama series for transmission in Autumn 1993.

by the same author

screenplays

MY BEAUTIFUL LAUNDRETTE
SAMMY AND ROSIE GET LAID
LONDON KILLS ME
OUTSKIRTS AND OTHER PLAYS

PART ONE

In the Suburbs

CHAPTER ONE

My name is Karim Amir, and I am an Englishman born and bred, almost. I am often considered to be a funny kind of Englishman, a new breed as it were, having emerged from two old histories. But I don't care – Englishman I am (though not proud of it), from the South London suburbs and going somewhere. Perhaps it is the odd mixture of continents and blood, of here and there, of belonging and not, that makes me restless and easily bored. Or perhaps it was being brought up in the suburbs that did it. Anyway, why search the inner room when it's enough to say that I was looking for trouble, any kind of movement, action and sexual interest I could find, because things were so gloomy, so slow and heavy, in our family, I don't know why. Quite frankly, it was all getting me down and I was ready for anything.

Then one day everything changed. In the morning things were one way and by bedtime another. I was seventeen.

On this day my father hurried home from work not in a gloomy mood. His mood was high, for him. I could smell the train on him as he put his briefcase away behind the front door and took off his raincoat, chucking it over the bottom of the banisters. He grabbed my fleeing little brother, Allie, and kissed him; he kissed my mother and me with enthusiasm, as if we'd recently been rescued from an earthquake. More normally, he handed Mum his supper: a packet of kebabs and chapatis so greasy their paper wrapper had disintegrated. Next, instead of flopping into a chair to watch the television news and wait for Mum to put the warmed-up food on the table, he went into their bedroom, which was downstairs next to the living room. He quickly stripped to his vest and underpants.

'Fetch the pink towel,' he said to me.

I did so. Dad spread it on the bedroom floor and fell on to his knees. I wondered if he'd suddenly taken up religion. But no, he placed his arms beside his head and kicked himself into the air.

'I must practise,' he said in a stifled voice.

'Practise for what?' I said reasonably, watching him with interest and suspicion.

'They've called me for the damn yoga Olympics,' he said. He easily became sarcastic, Dad.

He was standing on his head now, balanced perfectly. His stomach sagged down. His balls and prick fell foward in his pants. The considerable muscles in his arms swelled up and he breathed energetically. Like many Indians he was small, but Dad was also elegant and handsome, with delicate hands and manners; beside him most Englishmen looked like clumsy giraffes. He was broad and strong too: when young he'd been a boxer and fanatical chest-expander. He was as proud of his chest as our next-door neighbours were of their kitchen range. At the sun's first smile he would pull off his shirt and stride out into the garden with a deckchair and a copy of the *New Statesman*. He told me that in India he shaved his chest regularly so its hair would sprout more luxuriantly in years to come. I reckoned that his chest was the one area in which he'd been forward-thinking.

Soon, my mother, who was in the kitchen as usual, came into the room and saw Dad practising for the yoga Olympics. He hadn't done this for months, so she knew something was up. She wore an apron with flowers on it and wiped her hands repeatedly on a tea towel, a souvenir from Woburn Abbey. Mum was a plump and unphysical woman with a pale round face and kind brown eyes. I imagined that she considered her body to be an inconvenient object surrounding her, as if she were stranded on an unexplored desert island. Mostly she was a timid and compliant person, but when exasperated she could get nervily aggressive, like now.

'Allie, go to bed,' she said sharply to my brother, as he poked his head around the door. He was wearing a net to stop his hair going crazy when he slept. She said to Dad, 'Oh God, Haroon, all the front of you's sticking out like that and everyone can see!' She turned to me. 'You encourage him to be like this. At least pull the curtains!'

'It's not necessary, Mum. There isn't another house that can see us for a hundred yards – unless they're watching through binoculars.'

'That's exactly what they are doing,' she said.

I pulled the curtains on the back garden. The room immediately seemed to contract. Tension rose. I couldn't wait to get out of the house now. I always wanted to be somewhere else, I don't know why.

When Dad spoke his voice came out squashed and thin.

'Karim, read to me in a very clear voice from the yoga book.'

I ran and fetched Dad's preferred yoga book – *Yoga for Women*, with pictures of healthy women in black leotards – from among his other books on Buddhism, Sufism, Confucianism and Zen which he had bought at the Oriental bookshop in Cecil Court, off Charing Cross Road. I squatted beside him with the book. He breathed in, held the breath, breathed out and once more held the breath. I wasn't a bad reader, and I imagined myself to be on the stage of the Old Vic as I declaimed grandly, 'Salamba Sirsasana revives and maintains a spirit of youthfulness, an asset beyond price. It is wonderful to know that you are ready to face up to life and extract from it all the real joy it has to offer.'

He grunted his approval at each sentence and opened his eyes, seeking out my mother, who had closed hers.

I read on. 'This position also prevents loss of hair and reduces any tendency to greyness.'

That was the coup: greyness would be avoided. Satisfied, Dad stood up and put his clothes on.

'I feel better. I can feel myself coming old, you see.' He softened. 'By the way, Margaret, coming to Mrs Kay's tonight?' She shook her head. 'Come on, sweetie. Let's go out together and enjoy ourselves, eh?'

'But it isn't me that Eva wants to see,' Mum said. 'She ignores me. Can't you see that? She treats me like dog's muck, Haroon. I'm not Indian enough for her. I'm only English.'

'I know you're only English, but you could wear a sari.' He laughed. He loved to tease, but Mum wasn't a satisfactory teasing victim, not realizing you were supposed to laugh when mocked.

'Special occasion, too,' said Dad, 'tonight.'

This was obviously what he'd been leading up to. He waited for us to ask him about it.

'What is it, Dad?'

'You know, they've so kindly asked me to speak on one or two aspects of Oriental philosophy.'

Dad spoke quickly and then tried to hide his pride in this honour, this proof of his importance, by busily tucking his vest in. This was my opportunity.

'I'll come with you to Eva's if you want me to. I was going to go to the chess club, but I'll force myself to miss it if you like.'

I said this as innocently as a vicar, not wanting to stymie things by seeming too eager. I'd discovered in life that if you're too eager others tend to get less eager. And if you're less eager it tends to make others more eager. So the more eager I was the less eager I seemed.

Dad pulled up his vest and slapped his bare stomach rapidly with both hands. The noise was loud and unattractive and it filled our small house like pistol shots.

'OK,' Dad said to me, 'you get changed, Karim.' He turned to Mum. He wanted her to be with him, to witness him being respected by others. 'If only you'd come, Margaret.'

I charged upstairs to get changed. From my room, the walls decorated ceiling to floor with newspapers, I could hear them arguing downstairs. Would he persuade her to come? I hoped not. My father was more frivolous when my mother wasn't around. I put on one of my favourite records, Dylan's 'Positively Fourth Street', to get me in the mood for the evening.

It took me several months to get ready: I changed my entire outfit three times. At seven o'clock I came downstairs in what I knew were the right clothes for Eva's evening. I wore turquoise flared trousers, a blue and white flower-patterned see-through shirt, blue suede boots with Cuban heels, and a scarlet Indian waistcoat with gold stitching around the edges. I'd pulled on a headband to control my shoulder-length frizzy hair. I'd washed my face in Old Spice.

Dad waited at the door for me, his hands in his pockets. He wore a black polo-neck sweater, a black imitation-leather jacket and grey Marks and Spencer cords. When he saw me he suddenly looked agitated.

'Say goodbye to your mum,' he said.

In the living room Mum was watching *Steptoe and Son* and taking a bite from a Walnut Whip, which she replaced on the pouf in front of her. This was her ritual: she allowed herself a nibble only once every fifteen minutes. It made her glance constantly between the clock and the TV. Sometimes she went berserk and scoffed the whole thing in two minutes flat. 'I deserve my Whip,' she'd say defensively.

When she saw me she too became tense.

6

'Don't show us up, Karim,' she said, continuing to watch TV. 'You look like Danny La Rue.'

'What about Auntie Jean, then?' I said. 'She's got blue hair.'

'It's dignified for older women to have blue hair,' Mum said.

Dad and I got out of the house as quickly as we could. At the end of the street, while we were waiting for the 227 bus, a teacher of mine with one eye walked past us and recognized me. Cyclops said, 'Don't forget, a university degree is worth £2,000 a year for life!'

'Don't worry,' said Dad. 'He'll go to university, oh yes. He'll be a leading doctor in London. My father was a doctor. Medicine is in our whole family.'

It wasn't far, about four miles, to the Kays', but Dad would never have got there without me. I knew all the streets and every bus route.

Dad had been in Britain since 1950 – over twenty years – and for fifteen of those years he'd lived in the South London suburbs. Yet still he stumbled around the place like an Indian just off the boat, and asked questions like, 'Is Dover in Kent?' I'd have thought, as an employee of the British Government, as a Civil Service clerk, even as badly paid and insignificant a one as him, he'd just have to know these things. I sweated with embarrassment when he halted strangers in the street to ask directions to places that were a hundred yards away in an area where he'd lived for almost two decades.

But his naïveté made people protective, and women were drawn by his innocence. They wanted to wrap their arms around him or something, so lost and boyish did he look at times. Not that this was entirely uncontrived, or unexploited. When I was small and the two of us sat in Lyon's Cornerhouse drinking milkshakes, he'd send me like a messenger pigeon to women at other tables and have me announce, 'My daddy wants to give you a kiss.'

Dad taught me to flirt with everyone I met, girls and boys alike, and I came to see charm, rather than courtesy or honesty, or even decency, as the primary social grace. And I even came to like people who were callous or vicious provided they were interesting. But I was sure Dad hadn't used his own gentle charisma to sleep with anyone but Mum, while married.

Now, though, I suspected that Mrs Eva Kay – who had met Dad a year ago at a 'writing for pleasure' class in an upstairs room at the King's Head in Bromley High Street – wanted to chuck her arms around him. Plain prurience was one of the reasons I was so keen to go to her place, and embarrassment one of the reasons why Mum refused. Eva Kay was forward; she was brazen; she was wicked.

On the way to Eva's I persuaded Dad to stop off at the Three Tuns in Beckenham. I got off the bus; Dad had no choice but to follow me. The pub was full of kids dressed like me, both from my school and from other schools in the area. Most of the boys, so nondescript during the day, now wore cataracts of velvet and satin, and bright colours; some were in bedspreads and curtains. The little groovers talked esoterically of Syd Barrett. To have an elder brother who lived in London and worked in fashion, music or advertising was an inestimable advantage at school. I had to study the *Melody Maker* and *New Musical Express* to keep up.

I led Dad by the hand to the back room. Kevin Ayers, who had been with Soft Machine, was sitting on a stool whispering into a microphone. Two French girls with him kept falling all over the stage. Dad and I had a pint of bitter each. I wasn't used to alcohol and became drunk immediately. Dad became moody.

'Your mother upsets me,' he said. 'She doesn't join in things. It's only my damn effort keeping this whole family together. No wonder I need to keep my mind blank in constant effortless meditation.'

I suggested helpfully, 'Why don't you get divorced?'

'Because you wouldn't like it.'

But divorce wasn't something that would occur to them. In the suburbs people rarely dreamed of striking out for happiness. It was all familiarity and endurance: security and safety were the reward of dullness. I clenched my fists under the table. I didn't want to think about it. It would be years before I could get away to the city, London, where life was bottomless in its temptations.

'I'm terrified about tonight,' Dad said. 'I've never done anything like this before. I don't know anything. I'm going to be a fuck-up.'

The Kays were much better off than us, and had a bigger house, with a little drive and garage and car. Their place stood on its own in a tree-lined road just off Beckenham High Street. It also had bay windows, an attic, a greenhouse, three bedrooms and central heating.

I didn't recognize Eva Kay when she greeted us at the door, and for a moment I thought we'd turned up at the wrong place. The only thing she wore was a full-length, multi-coloured kaftan, and her hair

8

was down, and out, and up. She'd darkened her eyes with kohl so she looked like a panda. Her feet were bare, the toenails painted alternately green and red.

When the front door was safely shut and we'd moved into the darkness of the hall, Eva hugged Dad and kissed him all over his face, including his lips. This was the first time I'd seen him kissed with interest. Surprise, surprise, there was no sign of Mr Kay. When Eva moved, when she turned to me, she was a kind of human crop-sprayer, pumping out a plume of Oriental aroma. I was trying to think if Eva was the most sophisticated person I'd ever met, or the most pretentious, when she kissed me on the lips too. My stomach tightened. Then, holding me at arm's length as if I were a coat she was about to try on, she looked me all over and said, 'Karim Amir, you are so exotic, so original! It's such a contribution! It's so you!'

'Thank you, Mrs Kay. If I'd had more notice, I'd have dressed up.'

'And with your father's wonderful but crushing wit, too!'

I felt that I was being watched, and when I looked up I saw that Charlie, her son, who was at my school in the sixth form and almost a year older, was sitting at the top of the stairs, partly concealed by the banisters. He was a boy upon whom nature had breathed such beauty – his nose was so straight, his cheeks so hollow, his lips such rosebuds – that people were afraid to approach him, and he was often alone. Men and boys got erections just being in the same room as him; for others the same effect was had by being in the same country. Women sighed in his presence, and teachers bristled. A few days ago, during the school assembly, with the staff sitting like a flock of crows on the stage, the headmaster was expatiating on Vaughan Williams. We were about to hear his *Fantasia on Green-sleeves*. As Yid, the religious-education master, sanctimoniously lowered the needle on to the dusty record, Charlie, standing along the row from me, started to bob and shake his head and whisper, 'Dig it, dig it, you heads.' 'What's going down?' we said to each other. We soon found out, for as the headmaster put his head back, the better to savour Vaughan Williams's mellow sounds, the opening hisses of 'Come Together' were rattling the speakers. As Yid pushed his way past the other teachers to re-take the record deck, half the school was mouthing the words '. . . groove it up slowly . . . he got ju-ju eyeballs . . . he got hair down to his knees . . .' For this, Charlie was caned in front of us all.

9

Now he lowered his head one thirty-secondth of an inch in acknowledgement of me. On the way to Eva's I'd deliberately excluded him from my mind. I hadn't believed that he would be at home, which was why I'd gone into the Three Tuns, in case he'd popped in for an early-evening drink.

'Glad to see you, man,' he said, coming slowly downstairs.

He embraced Dad and called him by his first name. What confidence and style he had, as always. When he followed us into the living room I was trembling with excitement. It wasn't like this at the chess-club.

Mum often said Eva was a vile show-off and big-mouth, and even I recognized that Eva was slightly ridiculous, but she was the only person over thirty I could talk to. She was inevitably good-tempered, or she was being passionate about something. At least she didn't put armour on her feelings like the rest of the miserable undead around us. She liked the Rolling Stones's first album. The Third Ear Band sent her. She did Isadora Duncan dances in our front room and then told me who Isadora Duncan was and why she'd liked scarves. Eva had been to the last concert the Cream played. In the playground at school before we went into our classrooms Charlie had told us of her latest outrage: she'd brought him and his girlfriend bacon and eggs in bed and asked them if they'd enjoyed making love.

When she came to our house to pick up Dad to drive him to the Writer's Circle, she always ran up to my bedroom first thing to sneer at my pictures of Marc Bolan. 'What are you reading? Show me your new books!' she'd demand. And once, 'Why ever do you like Kerouac, you poor virgin? Do you know that brilliant remark Truman Capote made about him?'

'No.'

'He said, "It's not writing, it's typing!"'

'But Eva – '

To teach her a lesson I read her the last pages of *On the Road*. 'Good defence!' she cried, but murmured – she always had to have the last word: 'The cruellest thing you can do to Kerouac is reread him at thirty-eight.' Leaving, she opened her goody bag, as she called it. 'Here's something else to read.' It was *Candide*. 'I'll ring you next Saturday to test you on it!'

The most thrilling time was when Eva, lying on my bed and

listening to the records I wanted to play her, started to get pretty intimate and everything, telling me the secrets of her love life. Her husband hit her, she said. They never made love. She wanted to make love, it was the most ravishing feeling on offer. She used the word 'fuck'. She wanted to live, she said. She frightened me; she excited me; somehow she had disturbed our whole household from the moment she entered it.

What was she up to now with Dad? What was going on in her front room?

Eva had pushed back the furniture. The patterned armchairs and glass-topped tables were up against the pine bookshelves. The curtains were drawn. Four middle-aged men and four middle-aged women, all white, sat cross-legged on the floor, eating peanuts and drinking wine. Sitting apart from these people with his back against the wall was a man of indeterminate age – he could have been anything between twenty-five and forty-five – in a threadbare black corduroy suit and old-fashioned heavy black shoes. His trouser bottoms were stuffed inside his socks. His blond hair was dirty; his pockets bulged with torn paperbacks. He didn't appear to know anyone else, or if he did he wasn't prepared to talk to them. He seemed interested, but in a scientific way, as he sat smoking. He was very alert and nervous.

There was some chanting music going on that reminded me of funerals.

Charlie murmured, 'Don't you just love Bach?'

'It's not really my bag.'

'Fair 'nough. I think I've got something that's more your bag upstairs.'

'Where's your dad?'

'He's having a nervous breakdown.'

'Does that mean he's not here?'

'He's gone into a kind of therapy centre where they allow it all to happen.'

In my family nervous breakdowns were as exotic as New Orleans. I had no idea what they entailed, but Charlie's dad had seemed the nervous type to me. The only time he came to our house he sat on his own in the kitchen crying as he mended Dad's fountain pen, while in the living room Eva said she had to buy a motorcycle. This made Mum yawn, I remember.

11

Now Dad was sitting on the floor. The talk was of music and books, of names like Dvořák, Krishnamurti and Eclectic. Looking at them closely, I reckoned that the men were in advertising or design or almost artistic jobs like that. Charlie's dad designed advertisements. But the man in the black corduroy suit I couldn't work out at all. Whoever these people were, there was a terrific amount of showing off going on – more in this room than in the whole of the rest of southern England put together.

At home Dad would have laughed at all this. But now, in the thick of it, he looked as if he was having the highest time of his whole life. He led the discussion, talking loudly, interrupting people and touching whoever was nearest. The men and women – except for Corduroy Suit – were slowly gathering in a circle around him on the floor. Why did he save sullenness and resentful grunting for us?

I noticed that the man sitting near me turned to the man next to him and indicated my father, who was now in full flow about the importance of attaining an empty mind to a woman who was wearing only a man's long shirt and black tights. The woman was nodding encouragingly at Dad. The man said in a loud whisper to his friend, 'Why has our Eva brought this brown Indian here? Aren't we going to get pissed?'

'He's going to give us a demonstration of the mystic arts!'

'And has he got his camel parked outside?'

'No, he came on a magic carpet.'

'Cyril Lord or Debenhams?'

I gave the man a sharp kick in the kidney. He looked up.

'Come up to my pad, Karim,' said Charlie, to my relief.

But before we could get out Eva turned off the standard lamp. Over the one remaining light she draped a large diaphanous neckscarf, leaving the room illuminated only by a pink glow. Her movements had become balletic. One by one people fell silent. Eva smiled at everyone.

'So why don't we relax?' she said. They nodded their agreement. The woman in the shirt said, 'So why don't we?' 'Yes, yes,' someone else said. One man flapped his hands like loose gloves and opened his mouth as wide as he could, and thrust his tongue out, popping his eyes like a gargoyle.

Eva turned to my father and bowed to him, Japanese fashion. 'My good and deep friend Haroon here, he will show us the Way. The Path.'

'Jesus fucking Christ,' I whispered to Charlie, remembering how Dad couldn't even find his way to Beckenham.

'Watch, watch closely,' murmured Charlie, squatting down.

Dad sat down at the end of the room. Everyone looked keenly and expectantly at him, though the two men near me glanced at each other as if they wanted to laugh. Dad spoke slowly and with confidence. The nervousness he'd shown earlier appeared to have disappeared. He seemed to know he had their attention and that they'd do as he asked. I was sure he'd never done anything like this before. He was going to wing it.

'The things that are going to happen to you this evening are going to do you a lot of good. They may even change you a little, or make you want to change, in order to reach your full potential as human beings. But there is one thing you must not do. You must not resist. If you resist, it will be like driving a car with the handbrake on.'

He paused. Their eyes were on him.

'We'll do some floor work. Please sit with your legs apart.'

They parted their legs.

'Raise your arms.'

They raised their arms.

'Now, breathing out, stretch down to your right foot.'

After some basic yoga positions he had them lying on their backs. To his soft commands they were relaxing their fingers one by one, then their wrists, toes, ankles, foreheads and, peculiarly, their ears. Meanwhile Dad wasted no time in removing his shoes and socks, and then – I should have guessed it – his shirt and clean string vest. He padded around the circle of dreamers, lifting a loose arm here, a leg there, testing them for tension. Eva, also lying on her back, had one naughty, slowly enlarging eye open. Had she ever seen such a dark, hard, hairy chest before? When Dad floated past she touched his foot with her hand. The man in black corduroy couldn't relax at all: he lay there like a bundle of sticks with his legs crossed, a burning cigarette in his fingers, gazing reflectively at the ceiling.

I hissed to Charlie, 'Let's get out of here before we're hypnotized like these idiots!'

'Isn't it just fascinating?'

On the upstairs landing of the house was a ladder which led up to

Charlie's attic. 'Please remove your watch,' he said. 'In my domain time isn't a factor.' So I put my watch on the floor and climbed the ladder to the attic, which stretched out across the top of the house. Charlie had the whole space to himself. Mandalas and long-haired heads were painted on the sloping walls and low ceiling. His drum-kit stood in the centre of the floor. His four guitars – two acoustic and two Stratocasters – leaned against the wall in a line. Big cushions were flung about. There were piles of records and the four Beatles in their *Sergeant Pepper* period were on the wall like gods.

'Heard anything good lately?' he asked, lighting a candle.

'Yeah.'

After the calm and silence of the living room my voice sounded absurdly loud. 'The new Stones album. I played it at music society today and the lads went crazy. They threw off their jackets and ties and danced. I was on top of my desk! It was like some weird pagan ritual. You shoulda bin there, man.'

I knew immediately from the look on Charlie's face that I'd been an animal, a philistine, a child. Charlie threw his shoulder-length hair back, looked at me tolerantly for some time, and then smiled.

'I think it's time you bathed your ears in something really nourishing, Karim.'

He put on a record by the Pink Floyd called *Ummagumma*. I forced myself to listen while Charlie sat opposite me and rolled a joint, sprinkling a dried leaf over the tobacco.

'Your father. He's the best. He's wise. D'you do that meditation stuff every morning?'

I nodded. A nod can't be a lie, right?

'And chanting, too?'

'Not chanting every day, no.'

I thought of the morning in our place: Dad running around the kitchen looking for olive oil to put on his hair; my brother and I wrestling over the *Daily Mirror*; my mother complaining about having to go to work in the shoe shop.

Charlie handed me the joint. I pulled on it and handed it back, managing to sprinkle ash down the front of my shirt and burn a small hole in it. I was so excited and dizzy I stood up immediately.

'What's going down?'

'I have to go to the bog!'

I flew down the attic ladder. In the Kays' bathroom there were framed theatre posters for Genet plays. There were bamboo and parchment scrolls with tubby Orientals copulating on them. There was a bidet. As I sat there with my trousers down, taking it all in, I had an extraordinary revelation. I could see my life clearly for the first time: the future and what I wanted to do. I wanted to live always this intensely: mysticism, alcohol, sexual promise, clever people and drugs. I hadn't come upon it all like this before, and now I wanted nothing else. The door to the future had opened: I could see which way to go.

And Charlie? My love for him was unusual as love goes: it was not generous. I admired him more than anyone but I didn't wish him well. It was that I preferred him to me and wanted to be him. I coveted his talents, face, style. I wanted to wake up with them all transferred to me.

I stood in the upstairs hall. The house was silent except for the distant sound of 'A Saucerful of Secrets' coming from the top of the house. Someone was burning incense. I crept down the stairs to the ground floor. The living-room door was open. I peered round it into the dimly lit room. The advertising men and their wives were sitting up, cross-legged, straight-backed, eyes closed, breathing regularly and deeply. The Corduroy Suit was sitting in a chair with his back to everyone, reading and smoking. Neither Eva nor Dad were in the room. Where could they have gone?

I left the hypnotized Buddhas and went through the house and into the kitchen. The back door was wide open. I stepped out into the darkness. It was a warm evening; the moon was full.

I got down on my knees. I knew this was the thing to do – I'd gone highly intuitive since Dad's display. I crawled across the patio. They must have had a barbecue out there recently, because razor-sharp charcoal shards jabbed into my knees, but I reached the edge of the lawn without serious injury. I could see vaguely that at the end of the lawn there was a garden bench. As I crawled closer there was enough moonlight for me to see that Eva was on the bench. She was pulling her kaftan up over her head. If I strained my eyes I could see her chest. And I did strain; I strained until my eyeballs went dry in their sockets. Eventually I knew I was right. Eva had only one breast. Where the other traditionally was, there was nothing, so far as I could see.

Beneath all this hair and flesh, and virtually concealed from me, was my father. I knew it was Daddio because he was crying out across the Beckenham gardens, with little concern for the neighbours, 'Oh God, oh my God, oh my God.' Was I conceived like this, I wondered, in the suburban night air, to the wailing of Christian curses from the mouth of a renegade Muslim masquerading as a Buddhist?

With a harsh crack, Eva slapped her hand over my father's mouth. This was a touch peremptory, I thought, and I almost jerked forward to object. But, my God, could Eva bounce! Head back, eyes to stars, kicking up from the grass like a footballer, her hair flying. But what of the crushing weight on Dad's arse? Surely the impress of the bench would remain for days seared into his poor buttocks, like grill marks on steak?

Eva released her hand from his mouth. He started to laugh. The happy fucker laughed and laughed. It was the exhilaration of someone I didn't know, full of greedy pleasure and self. It brought me all the way down.

I hobbled away. In the kitchen I poured myself a glass of Scotch and threw it down my throat. Corduroy Suit was standing in the corner of the kitchen. His eyes were twitching badly. He stuck out his hand. 'Shadwell,' he said.

Charlie was lying on his back on the attic floor. I took the joint from him, removed my boots and lay down.

'Come and lie beside me,' he said. 'Closer.' He put his hand on my arm. 'Now, you're not to take this badly.'

'No, never, whatever it is, Charlie.'

'You've got to wear less.'

'Wear less, Charlie?'

'Dress less. Yes.'

He got up on to one elbow and concentrated on me. His mouth was close. I sunbathed under his face.

'Levi's, I suggest, with an open-necked shirt, maybe in pink or purple, and a thick brown belt. Forget the headband.'

'Forget the headband?'

'Forget it.'

I ripped my headband off and tossed it across the floor.

'For your mum.'

'You see, Karim, you tend to look a bit like a pearly queen.'

I, who wanted only to be like Charlie – as clever, as cool in every part of my soul – tattooed his words on to my brain. Levi's, with an open-necked shirt, maybe in a very modest pink or purple. I would never go out in anything else for the rest of my life.

While I contemplated myself and my wardrobe with loathing, and would willingly have urinated over every garment, Charlie lay back with his eyes closed and real sartorial understanding in his mind. Everyone in the house but me was practically in heaven.

I laid my hand on Charlie's thigh. No response. I rested it there for a few minutes until sweat broke out on the ends of my fingers. His eyes remained closed, but in his jeans he was growing. I began to feel confident. I became insane. I dashed for his belt, for his fly, for his cock, and I took him out into the air to cool down. He made a sign! He twitched himself! Through such human electricity we understood each other.

I had squeezed many penises before, at school. We stroked and rubbed and pinched each other all the time. It broke up the monotony of learning. But I had never kissed a man.

'Where are you, Charlie?'

I tried to kiss him. He avoided my lips by turning his head to one side. But when he came in my hand it was, I swear, one of the pre-eminent moments of my earlyish life. There was dancing in my streets. My flags flew, my trumpets blew!

I was licking my fingers and thinking of where to buy a pink shirt when I heard a sound that was not the Pink Floyd. I turned and saw across the attic Dad's flaming eyes, nose, neck and his famous chest hoiking itself up through the square hole in the floor. Charlie swiftly put himself away. I leapt up. Dad hurried over to me, followed by smiling Eva. Dad looked from Charlie to me and back again. Eva sniffed the air.

'You naughty boys.'

'What, Eva?' Charlie said.

'Smoking home-grown.'

Eva said it was time for her to drive us home. We all climbed backwards down the ladder. Dad, being the first, trod on my watch at the bottom, trampling it to pieces and cutting his foot.

At the house we got out of the car and I said goodnight to Eva and walked away. From the porch I could see Eva trying to kiss Dad, while he was trying to shake her hand.

Our house was dark and cold as we crept in, exhausted. Dad had to get up at six-thirty and I had my paper-round at seven. In the hall Dad raised his hand to slap me. He was drunker than I was stoned and I grabbed the ungrateful bastard.

'What the hell were you doing?'

'Shut up!' I said, as quietly as I could.

'I saw you, Karim. My God, you're a bloody pure shitter! A bum-banger! My own son – how did it transpire?'

He was disappointed in me. He jumped up and down in anguish as if he'd just heard the whole house had been burned to the ground. I didn't know what to do. So I started to imitate the voice he'd used earlier with the advertisers and Eva.

'Relax, Dad. Relax your whole body from your fingers to your toes and send your mind to a quiet garden where – '

'I'll send you to a fucking doctor to have your balls examined!'

I had to stop him yelling before we had Mum out and the neighbours round. I whispered, 'But I saw you, Dad.'

'You saw nothing,' he said, with utter contempt. He could be very arrogant. It must have been his upper-class background. But I had him.

'At least my mum has two tits.'

Dad went into the toilet without shutting the door and started to vomit. I went in behind him and rubbed his back as he threw up his guts. 'I'll never mention tonight again,' I said. 'And nor will you.'

'Why did you bring him home like this?' said Mum. She was standing behind us in her dressing-gown, which was so long it almost touched the floor, making her look square. She was tired. She reminded me of the real world. I wanted to shout at her: Take that world away!

'Couldn't you have looked after him?' she said. She kept plucking at my arm. 'I was looking out of the window and waiting for you for hours. Why didn't you ring?'

Eventually Dad stood up straight and pushed right past us.

'Make up a bed for me in the front room,' she said. 'I can't sleep next to that man stinking of sick and puking all night.'

When I'd made the bed and she'd got herself into it – and it was far too narrow and short and uncomfortable for her – I told her something.

'I'll never be getting married, OK?'

'I don't blame you,' she said, turning over and shutting her eyes.

I didn't think she'd get much sleep on that couch, and I felt sorry for her. But she angered me, the way she punished herself. Why couldn't she be stronger? Why wouldn't she fight back? I would be strong myself, I determined. That night I didn't go to bed but sat up listening to Radio Caroline. I'd glimpsed a world of excitement and possibility which I wanted to hold in my mind and expand as a template for the future.

For a week after that evening Dad sulked and didn't speak, though sometimes he pointed, as at salt and pepper. Sometimes this gesticulation got him into some complicated Marcel Marceau mime language. Visitors from other planets looking in through the window would have thought we were playing a family guessing game as my brother, Mum and I gathered around Dad yelling clues to each other as he tried, without the compromise of friendly words, to show us that the gutters had become blocked with leaves, that the side of the house was getting damp and he wanted Allie and me to climb up a ladder and fix it, with Mum holding the ladder. At supper we sat eating our curled-up beefburgers, chips and fish fingers in silence. Once Mum burst into tears and banged the table with the flat of her hand. 'My life is terrible, terrible!' she cried. 'Doesn't anyone understand?'

We looked at her in surprise for a moment, before carrying on with our food. Mum did the washing-up as usual and no one helped her. After tea we all dispersed as soon as possible. My brother Amar, four years younger than me, called himself Allie to avoid racial trouble. He always went to bed as early as he could, taking with him fashion magazines like *Vogue*, *Harper's and Queen*, and anything European he could lay his hands on. In bed he wore a tiny pair of red silk pyjamas, a smoking jacket he got at a jumble sale, and his hair-net. 'What's wrong with looking good?' he'd say, going upstairs. In the evenings I often went to the park to sit in the piss-stinking shed and smoke with the other boys who'd escaped from home.

Dad had firm ideas about the division of labour between men and women. Both my parents worked: Mum had got a job in a shoe shop in the High Street to finance Allie, who had decided to become a ballet dancer and had to go to an expensive private school. But Mum did all the housework and the cooking. At lunchtime she shopped, and every evening she prepared the meal. After this she watched television until ten-thirty. The TV was her only area of absolute authority. The unspoken rule of the house was that she always watched what she wanted; if any of us wanted to watch anything else, we had no chance at all. With her last energy of the day she'd throw such a fit of anger, self-pity and frustration that no one dared interfere with her. She'd die for *Steptoe and Son*, *Candid Camera* and *The Fugitive*.

If there were only repeats or political programmes on TV, she liked to draw. Her hand flew: she'd been to art school. She had drawn us, our heads, three to a page, for years. Three selfish men, she called us. She said she'd never liked men because men were torturers. It wasn't women who turned on the gas at Auschwitz, according to her. Or bombed Vietnam. During this time of Dad's silence she drew a lot, putting her pad away behind the chair, with her knitting, her childhood diary of the war ('Air-raid tonight') and her Catherine Cookson novels. I'd often tried to oppress her into reading proper books like *Tender is the Night* and *The Dharma Bums*, but she always said the print was too small.

One afternoon, a few days into the Great Sulk, I made myself a peanut-butter sandwich, put the Who's *Live at Leeds* under the needle at full volume – the better to savour Townshend's power chords on 'Summertime Blues' – and opened Mum's sketch pad. I knew I would find something. I flipped through the pages until I came to a drawing of my father naked.

Standing next to him, slightly taller, was Eva, also naked, complete with one large breast. They were holding hands like frightened children, and faced us without vanity or embellishment, as if to say: This is all that we are, these are our bodies. They looked like John Lennon and Yoko Ono. How could Mum be so objective? How did she even know they'd fucked?

No secrets were safe from me. I didn't restrict my investigations to Mum. That's how I knew that although Dad's lungs were quiet his eyes were well exercised. I peeped into his briefcase, and pulled out books by Lu Po, Lao Tzu and Christmas Humphreys.

I knew that the most interesting thing that could happen in the house would be if the phone rang for Dad, thereby testing his silence. So when it rang late one evening at ten-thirty, I made sure I got there first. Hearing Eva's voice, I realized that I too had been very keen to hear from her again.

She said, 'Hallo, my sweet and naughty boy, where's your dad? Why haven't you called me? What are you reading?'

'What do you recommend, Eva?'

'You'd better come and see me, and I'll fill your head with purple ideas.'

'When can I come?'

'Don't even ask – just show.'

I fetched Dad, who just happened to be standing behind the bedroom door in his pyjamas. He snatched up the receiver. I couldn't believe he was going to speak in his own house.

'Hallo,' he said gruffly, as if unaccustomed to using his voice. 'Eva, it's good to talk to you, my love. But my voice has gone. I suspect bumps on the larynx. Can I ring you from the office?'

I went into my room, put the big brown radio on, waited for it to warm up and thought about the matter.

Mum was drawing again that night.

The other thing that happened, the thing that made me realize that 'God', as I now called Dad, was seriously scheming, was the queer sound I heard coming from his room as I was going up to bed. I put my ear against the white paintwork of the door. Yes, God was talking to himself, but not intimately. He was speaking slowly, in a deeper voice than usual, as if he were addressing a crowd. He was hissing his s's and exaggerating his Indian accent. He'd spent years trying to be more of an Englishman, to be less risibly conspicuous, and now he was putting it back in spadeloads. Why?

One Saturday morning a few weeks later he called me to his room and said mysteriously, 'Are you on for tonight?'

'Tonight what, God?'

'I'm appearing,' he said, unable to reduce the pride in his voice.

'Really? Again?'

'Yes, they've asked me. Public demand.'

'That's great. Where is it?'

'Location secret.' He patted his stomach happily. This was what he really wanted to be doing now, appearing. 'They are looking forward to me all over Orpington. I will be more popular than Bob Hope. But don't mention anything to your mother. She doesn't understand my appearances at all, or even, for that matter, my disappearances. Are we on?'

'We're on, Dad.'

'Good, good. Prepare.'

'Prepare what?'

He touched my face gently with the back of his hand. 'You're excited, eh?' I said nothing. 'You like all this getting-about business.'

'Yes,' I said, shyly.

'And I like having you with me, boy. I love you very much. We're growing up together, we are.'

He was right – I was looking forward to this second appearance of his. I did enjoy the activity, but there was something important I had to know. I wanted to see if Dad was a charlatan or if there was anything true in what he was doing. After all, he'd impressed Eva and then done the difficult thing – knocked Charlie out. His magic had worked on them and I'd given him the 'God' moniker, but with reservations. He wasn't yet fully entitled to the name. What I wanted to see was whether, as he started to blossom, Dad really did have anything to offer other people, or if he would turn out to be merely another suburban eccentric.

CHAPTER TWO

Dad and Anwar lived next door to each other in Bombay and were best friends from the age of five. Dad's father, the doctor, had built a lovely low wooden house on Juhu beach for himself, his wife and his twelve children. Dad and Anwar would sleep on the veranda and at dawn run down to the sea and swim. They went to school in a horse-drawn rickshaw. At weekends they played cricket, and after school there was tennis on the family court. The servants would be ball-boys. The cricket matches were often against the British, and you had to let them win. There were also constant riots and demonstrations and Hindu–Muslim fighting. You'd find your Hindu friends and neighbours chanting obscenities outside your house.

There were parties to go to, as Bombay was the home of the Indian film industry and one of Dad's elder brothers edited a movie magazine. Dad and Anwar loved to show off about all the film-stars they knew and the actresses they'd kissed. Once, when I was seven or eight, Dad told me he thought I should become an actor; it was a good life, he said, and the proportion of work to money was high. But really he wanted me to be a doctor, and the subject of acting was never mentioned again. At school the careers officer said I should go into Customs and Excise – obviously he thought I had a natural talent for scrutinizing suitcases. And Mum wanted me to go into the Navy, on the grounds, I think, that I liked wearing flared trousers.

Dad had had an idyllic childhood, and as he told me of his adventures with Anwar I often wondered why he'd condemned his own son to a dreary suburb of London of which it was said that when people drowned they saw not their lives but their double-glazing flashing before them.

It was only later, when he came to England, that Dad realized how complicated practical life could be. He'd never cooked before, never washed up, never cleaned his own shoes or made a bed. Servants did that. Dad told us that when he tried to remember the house in Bombay he could never visualize the kitchen: he'd never been in it. He remembered, though, that his favourite servant had been sacked for kitchen misdemeanours; once for making toast by lying on his back and suspending bread from between his toes over a flame, and on a second occasion for cleaning celery with a toothbrush – his own brush, as it happened, not the Master's, but that was no excuse. These incidents had made Dad a socialist, in so far as he was ever a socialist.

If Mum was irritated by Dad's aristocratic uselessness, she was also proud of his family. 'They're higher than the Churchills,' she said to people. 'He went to school in a horse-drawn carriage.' This ensured there would be no confusion between Dad and the swarms of Indian peasants who came to Britain in the 1950s and 1960s, and of whom it was said they were not familiar with cutlery and certainly not with toilets, since they squatted on the seats and shat from on high.

Unlike them, Dad was sent to England by his family to be educated. His mother knitted him and Anwar several itchy woollen vests and waved them off from Bombay, making them promise never to be pork-eaters. Like Gandhi and Jinnah before him, Dad would return to India a qualified and polished English gentleman lawyer and an accomplished ballroom dancer. But Dad had no idea when he set off that he'd never see his mother's face again. This was the great undiscussed grief of his life, and, I reckon, explained his helpless attachment to women who would take care of him, women he could love as he should have loved the mother to whom he never wrote a single letter.

London, the Old Kent Road, was a freezing shock to both of them. It was wet and foggy; people called you 'Sunny Jim'; there was never enough to eat, and Dad never took to dripping on toast. 'Nose drippings more like,' he'd say, pushing away the staple diet of the working class. 'I thought it would be roast beef and Yorkshire pudding all the way.' But rationing was still on, and the area was derelict after being bombed to rubble during the war. Dad was amazed and heartened by the sight of the British in England, though. He'd never seen the English in poverty, as roadsweepers, dustmen, shopkeepers and barmen. He'd never seen an Englishman stuffing bread into his mouth with his fingers, and no one had told him the English didn't wash regularly because the water was so cold – if they had water at all. And when Dad tried to discuss Byron in local pubs no one warned him that not every Englishman could read or that they didn't necessarily want tutoring by an Indian on the poetry of a pervert and a madman.

Fortunately, Anwar and Dad had somewhere to stay, at Dr Lal's, a friend of Dad's father. Dr Lal was a monstrous Indian dentist who claimed to be a friend of Bertrand Russell. At Cambridge during the war, a lonely Russell advised Dr Lal that masturbation was the answer to sexual frustration. Russell's great discovery was a revelation to Dr Lal, who claimed to have been happy ever after. Was his liberation one of Russell's more striking achievements? For perhaps if Dr Lal hadn't been so forthright about sex with his two young and sexually rapacious lodgers, my father wouldn't have met my mother and I wouldn't be in love with Charlie.

Anwar was always plumper than Dad, with his podgy gut and round face. No sentence was complete without the flavouring of a few noxious words, and he loved the prostitutes who hung around Hyde Park. They called him Baby Face. He was less suave, too, for as soon as Dad's monthly allowance arrived from India, Dad visited Bond Street to buy bow-ties, bottle-green waistcoats and tartan socks, after which he'd have to borrow money from Baby Face. During the day Anwar studied aeronautical engineering in North London and Dad tried to glue his eyes to his law books. At night they slept in Dr Lal's consulting room among the dental equipment, Anwar sleeping in the chair itself. One night, enraged by the mice running around him, by sexual frustration too, and burning with the itching of his mother's woollen vests, Dad dressed himself in Lal's pale blue smock, picked up the most ferocious drill and attacked Anwar as he slept. Anwar screamed when he awoke to find the future guru of Chislehurst coming at him with a dentist's drill. This playfulness, this refusal to take anything seriously, as if life didn't matter, characterized Dad's attitude to his studies. Dad just couldn't concentrate. He'd never worked before and it didn't suit him now. Anwar started to say of Dad, 'Haroon is called to the Bar every day – at twelve o'clock and five-thirty.'

Dad defended himself: 'I go to the pub to think.'

'No, not think – drink,' Anwar replied.

On Fridays and Saturdays they went to dances and smooched blissfully to Glenn Miller and Count Basie and Louis Armstrong. That is where Dad first laid eyes and hands on a pretty working-class girl from the suburbs called Margaret. My mother told me that she loved him, her little man, from the first moment she saw him. He was sweet and kind and utterly lost-looking, which made women attempt to make him found-looking.

There was a friend of Mum's whom Baby Face walked out with, and apparently even walked in with, but Anwar was already married, to Jeeta, a princess whose family came on horseback to the wedding held in the old British hill station of Murree, in the north of Pakistan. Jeeta's brothers carried guns, which made Anwar nervous and want to head for England.

Soon Princess Jeeta joined Anwar in England, and she became Auntie Jeeta to me. Auntie Jeeta looked nothing like a princess, and I mocked her because she couldn't speak English properly. She was very shy and they lived in one dirty room in Brixton. It was no palace and it backed on to the railway line. One day Anwar made a serious mistake in the betting shop and won a lot of money. He bought a short lease on a toy shop in South London. It was a miserable failure until Princess Jeeta made him turn it into a grocer's shop. They were set up. Customers flocked.

In contrast, Dad was going nowhere. His family cut off his money when they discovered from a spy – Dr Lal – that he was being called to the Bar only to drink several pints of rough stout and brown ale wearing a silk bow-tie and a green waistcoat.

Dad ended up working as a clerk in the Civil Service for £3 a week. His life, once a cool river of balmy distraction, of beaches and cricket, of mocking the British, and dentists' chairs, was now a cage of umbrellas and steely regularity. It was all trains and shitting sons, and the bursting of frozen pipes in January, and the lighting of coal fires at seven in the morning: the organization of love into suburban family life in a two-up-two-down semi-detached in South London. Life was thrashing him for being a child, an innocent who'd never had to do anything for himself. Once when I was left with him all day and I shat myself, he was bewildered. He stood me naked in the bath while he fetched a cup from which, standing on the other side of the bathroom as if I had the plague, he threw water at my legs while holding his nose with his other hand.

I don't know how it all started, but when I was ten or eleven he turned to Lieh Tzu, Lao Tzu and Chuang Tzu as if they'd never been read before, as if they'd been writing exclusively for him.

We continued to visit Baby Face and Princess Jeeta on Sunday afternoons, the only time the shop closed. Dad's friendship with Anwar was still essentially a jokey one, a cricket-, boxing-, athletics-, tennis-watching one. When Dad went there with a library copy of *The Secret of the Golden Flower* Anwar snatched it from him, held it up and laughed.

'What's this bloody-fool thing you're playing with now?'

Dad promptly started up with, 'Anwar, *yaar*, you don't realize the great secrets I'm uncovering! How happy I feel now I'm understanding life at last!'

Anwar interrupted, stabbing at Dad with his roll-up. 'You bloody Chinese fool. How are you reading rubbish when I'm making money! I've paid off my bastard mortgage!'

Dad was so keen for Anwar to understand that his knees were vibrating. 'I don't care about money. There's always money. I must understand these secret things.'

Anwar raised his eyes to heaven and looked at Mum, who sat there, bored. They both had sympathy for Dad, and loved him, but in these moods love was mixed with pity, as if he were making some tragic mistake, like joining the Jehovah's Witnesses. The more he talked of the Yin and Yang, cosmic consciousness, Chinese philosophy, and the following of the Way, the more lost Mum became. He seemed to be drifting away into outer space, leaving her behind; she was a suburban woman, quiet and kind, and found life with two children and Dad difficult enough as it was. There was at the same time a good chunk of pride in Dad's Oriental discoveries, which led him to denigrate Anwar's life.

'You're only interested in toilet rolls, sardine tins, sanitary pads and turnips,' he told Anwar. 'But there are many more things, *yaar*, in heaven and earth, than you damn well dream of in Penge.'

'I haven't got time to dream!' interrupted Anwar. 'Nor should you be dreaming. Wake up! What about getting some promotion so Margaret can wear some nice clothes. You know what women are like, *yaar*.'

'The whites will never promote us,' Dad said. 'Not an Indian while there is a white man left on the earth. You don't have to deal with them – they still think they have an Empire when they don't have two pennies to rub together.'

'They don't promote you because you are lazy, Haroon. Barnacles are growing on your balls. You think of some China-thing and not the Queen!'

'To hell with the Queen! Look, Anwar, don't you ever feel you want to know yourself? That you are an enigma to yourself completely?'

'I don't interest anyone else, why should I interest myself?' cried Anwar. 'Get on with living!'

On and on these arguments went, above Anwar and Jeeta's shop, until they became so absorbed and hostile that their daughter, Jamila, and I could sneak away and play cricket with a broom handle and a tennis ball in the garden.

Beneath all the Chinese bluster was Dad's loneliness and desire for internal advancement. He needed to talk about the China-things he was learning. I often walked to the commuter station with him in the morning, where he caught the eight-thirty-five to Victoria. On these twenty-minute walks he was joined by other people, usually women, secretaries, clerks and assistants, who also worked in Central London. He wanted to talk of obtaining a quiet mind, of being true to yourself, of self-understanding. I heard them speak of their lives, boyfriends, agitated minds and real selves in a way, I'm sure, they never talked to anyone else. They didn't even notice me and the transistor radio I carried, listening to the Tony Blackburn Show on Radio One. The more Dad didn't try to seduce them, the more he seduced them; often they didn't leave their houses until he was walking by. If he took a different route for fear of having stones and ice-pops full of piss lobbed at him by schoolboys from the secondary modern, they changed their route too. On the train Dad would read his mystical books or concentrate on the tip of his nose, a large target indeed. And he always carried a tiny blue dictionary with him, the size of a matchbox, making sure to learn a new word every day. At the weekends I'd test him on the meaning of analeptic, frutescent, polycephalus and orgulous. He'd look at me and say, 'You never know when you might need a heavyweight word to impress an Englishman.'

It wasn't until he met Eva that he had someone to share his China-things with, and it surprised him that such mutual interest was possible.

*

Now, I presumed, on this Saturday night, God was going to meet Eva again. He gave me the address on a piece of paper and we caught a bus, this time towards what I considered to be the country. It was dark and icy when we got off in Chislehurst. I led Dad first one way and then, speaking with authority, in the opposite direction. He was so keen to get there he didn't complain for twenty minutes; but at last he became poisonous.

'Where are we, idiot?'

'I don't know.'

'Use the brains you've inherited from me, you bastard!' he said, shivering. 'It's bloody cold and we're late.'

'It's your fault you're cold, Dad,' I said.

'My fault?'

It was indeed his fault, for under his car coat my father was wearing what looked like a large pair of pyjamas. On top was a long silk shirt embroidered around the neck with dragons. This fell over his chest and flew out at his stomach for a couple of miles before dropping down to his knees. Under this he had on baggy trousers and sandals. But the real crime, the reason for concealment under the hairy car coat, was the crimson waistcoat with gold and silver patterns that he wore over the shirt. If Mum had caught him going out like that she would have called the police. After all, God was a Civil Servant, he had a briefcase and umbrella, he shouldn't be walking around looking like a midget toreador.

The houses in Chislehurst had greenhouses, grand oaks and sprinklers on the lawn; men came in to do the garden. It was so impressive for people like us that when our families walked these streets on Sunday visits to Auntie Jean we'd treat it as a lower-middle-class equivalent of the theatre. 'Ahhh' and 'oohh', we'd go, imagining we lived there, what times we'd have, and how we'd decorate the place and organize the garden for cricket, badminton and table tennis. Once I remember Mum looking reproachfully at Dad, as if to say: What husband are you to give me so little when the other men, the Alans and Barrys and Peters and Roys, provide cars, houses, holidays, central heating and jewellery? They can at least put up shelves or fix the fence. What can you do? And Mum would stumble into a pothole, just as we were doing now, since the roads were deliberately left corrugated with stones and pits, to discourage ordinary people from driving up and down.

As we crunched up the drive at last – with a pause for God to put his thumbs together and do a few minutes' trance practice – God told me that the house was owned by Carl and Marianne, friends of Eva, who'd recently been trekking in India. This was immediately obvious from the sandalwood Buddhas, brass ashtrays and striped plaster elephants which decorated every available space. And by the fact that Carl and Marianne stood barefoot at the door as we entered, the palms of their hands together in prayer and their heads bowed as if they were temple servants and not partners in the local TV rental firm of Rumbold & Toedrip.

As soon as I went in I spotted Eva, who had been looking out for us. She was wearing a long red dress which fell to the floor and a red turban. She swooped down upon me, and after twelve kisses she pressed three paperbacks into my hand.

'Smell them!' she urged me.

I dipped my nose between the foxed leaves. They smelled of chocolate.

'Second-hand! Real discoveries! And for your dad, this.' She gave me a new copy of the *Analects* of Confucius, translated by Arthur Waley. 'Please hold on to it for him. Is he OK?'

'Dead nervous.'

She glanced around the room, which contained about twenty people.

'They're a sympathetic lot. Pretty stupid. I can't see he'll have any problems. My dream is to get him to meet with more responsive people – in London. I'm determined to get all of us to London!' she said. 'Now, let me introduce you to people.'

After shaking a few hands I managed to get comfortably settled on a shiny black sofa, my feet on a furry white rug, with my back to a row of fat books handtooled in plastic – abridged versions (with illustrations) of *Vanity Fair* and *The Woman in White*. In front of me was what seemed to be an illuminated porcupine – some kind of clear bulb with hundreds of different coloured waving quills which stuck out of it and shimmered – an object, I'm sure, designed to be appreciated with the aid of hallucinogenics.

I heard Carl say, 'There are two sorts of people in the world – those who have been to India and those who haven't,' and was forced to get up and move out of earshot.

Beside the double-glazed french windows, with their view of the long garden and its goldfish pond glowing under purple light, was a bar. Not many people were drinking on this big spiritual occasion, but I could easily have put back a couple of pints. It wouldn't have looked too good, though, even I knew that. Marianne's daughter and an older girl in tight hotpants were serving lassi and hot Indian nibbles, guaranteed, I knew, to make you fart like a geriatric on All-bran. I joined the girl in hotpants behind the bar and found out her name was Helen and she was at the high school.

'Your father looks like a magician,' she said. She smiled at me and took two quick sidesteps into the circle of my privacy so she was beside me. Her sudden presence surprised and aroused me. It was only a minor surprise on the Richter surprise scale, a number three and a half, say, but it registered. At that moment my eyes were on God. Did he look like a magician, a wonder-maker?

He was certainly exotic, probably the only man in southern England at that moment (apart, possibly, from George Harrison) wearing a red and gold waistcoat and Indian pyjamas. He was also graceful, a front-room Nureyev beside the other pasty-faced Arbuckles with their tight drip-dry shirts glued to their guts and John Collier grey trousers with the crotch all sagging and creased. Perhaps Daddio really was a magician, having transformed himself by the bootlaces (as he put it) from being an Indian in the Civil Service who was always cleaning his teeth with Monkey Brand black toothpowder manufactured by Nogi & Co. of Bombay, into the wise adviser he now appeared to be. Sexy Sadie! Now he was the centre of the room. If they could see him in Whitehall!

He was talking to Eva, and she had casually laid her hand on his arm. The gesture cried out. Yes, it shouted, we are together, we touch each other without inhibition in front of strangers. Confused, I turned away, to the matter of Helen.

'Well?' she said gently.

She desired me.

I knew this because I had evolved a cast-iron method of determining desire. The method said she desired me because I had no interest in her. Whenever I did find someone attractive it was guaranteed by the corrupt laws which govern the universe that the person would find me repellent, or just too small. This law also guaranteed that when I was with someone like Helen, whom I didn't desire, the chances were they would look at me as she was looking at me now, with a wicked smile and an interest in squeezing my mickey, the thing I wanted most in the world from others, provided I found them attractive, which in her case I didn't.

My father, the great sage, from whose lips instruction fell like rain in Seattle, had never spoken to me about sex. When, to test his liberalism, I demanded he tell me the facts of life (which the school had already informed me of, though I continued to get the words uterus, scrotum and vulva mixed up), he murmured only, 'You can always tell when a woman is ready for sex. Oh yes. Her ears get hot.'

I looked keenly at Helen's ears. I even reached out and pinched one of them lightly, for scientific confirmation. Warmish!

Oh, Charlie. My heart yearned for his hot ears against my chest. But he had neither phoned since our last love-making nor bothered to turn up here. He'd been away from school, too, cutting a demo tape with his band. The pain of being without the bastard, the cold turkey I was enduring, was alleviated only by the thought that he would seek more wisdom from my father tonight. But so far there was no sign of him.

Eva and Marianne were starting to organize the room. The candle industry was stimulated, Venetian blinds were lowered, Indian sandalwood stinkers were ignited and put in flowerpots, and a small carpet was put down for the Buddha of suburbia to fly on. Eva bowed to him and handed him a daffodil. God smiled at people recognized from last time. He seemed confident and calm, easier than before, doing less and allowing the admirers to illuminate him with the respect that Eva must have been encouraging in her friends.

Then Uncle Ted and Auntie Jean walked in.

CHAPTER THREE

There they were – two normal unhappy alcoholics, her in pink high heels, him in a double-breasted suit, dressed for a wedding, almost innocently walking into a party. They were Mum's tall sister Jean and her husband, Ted, who had a central heating business called Peter's Heaters. And they were clapped in the eyeballs by their brother-in-law, known as Harry, lowering himself into a yogic trance in front of their neighbours. Jean fought for words, perhaps the only thing she had ever fought for. Eva's finger went to her lips. Jean's mouth closed slowly, like Tower Bridge. Ted's eyes scoured the room for a clue that would explain what was going on. He saw me and I nodded at him. He was disconcerted, but not angry, unlike Auntie Jean.

'What's Harry doing?' he mouthed.

Ted and Jean never called Dad by his Indian name, Haroon Amir. He was always 'Harry' to them, and they spoke of him as Harry to other people. It was bad enough his being an Indian in the first place, without having an awkward name too. They'd called Dad Harry from the first time they'd met him, and there was nothing Dad could do about it. So he called them 'Gin and Tonic'.

Uncle Ted and I were great mates. Sometimes he took me on central heating jobs with him. I got paid for doing the heavy work. We ate corned-beef sandwiches and drank tea from our thermos flask. He gave me sporting tips and took me to the Catford dog track and Epsom Downs. He talked to me about pigeon racing. Ever since I was tiny I'd loved Uncle Ted, because he knew about the things other boys' fathers knew about, and Dad, to my frustration, didn't: fishing and air rifles, aeroplanes, and how to eat winkles.

My mind was rapidly working as I tried to sort out how it was that Ted and Jean had turned up here, like characters from an Ealing Comedy walking into an Antonioni film. They were from Chislehurst too, but worlds away from Carl and Marianne. I concentrated until things started to get clear in my mind. How had all this happened? I began to see. What I saw didn't cheer me.

Poor Mum must have fallen into such unhappiness that she'd spilled out Dad's original guru exploit in Beckenham to her sister. Jean would have been apopleptic with outrage at her sister's weakness in allowing it to happen. Jean would have hated Mum for it.

When God had announced – or, rather, got me to announce, just a few hours before – that he was making a comeback as a visionary, Mum would have rung her young sister. Jean would have tautened, turning into the steely scheming knife she really was. Into action she went. She must have told Mum she knew Carl and Marianne. Their radiators had perhaps been installed by Peter's Heaters. And Ted and Jean did live in a newish house nearby. That would be the only way a couple like Carl and Marianne would know Ted and Jean. Otherwise Carl and Marianne, with their books and records and trips to India, with their 'culture', would be anathema to Ted and Jean, who measured people only in terms of power and money. The rest was showing off, an attempt to pull a fast one. For Ted and Jean, Tommy Steele – whose parents lived round the corner – was culture, entertainment, show business.

Meanwhile, Eva had no idea who Ted and Jean were. She just waved irritably at these late and oddly respectable intruders.

'Sit down, sit down,' she hissed.

Ted and Jean looked at each other as if they'd been asked to swallow matchsticks.

'Yes, you,' Eva added. She could be sharp, old Eva.

There was no choice. Ted and Jean slid slowly to the floor. It must have been years since Auntie Jean had been anywhere near the ground, except when she fell over drunk. They certainly couldn't have expected the evening to be this devout, with everyone sitting admiringly around Dad. We would be in big trouble later, no doubt about that.

God was about to start. Helen went and sat down with the others on the floor. I stood behind the bar and watched. Dad looked over the crowd and smiled, until he discovered himself smiling at Ted and Jean. His expression didn't change for a moment.

Despite calling Ted and Jean Gin and Tonic, he didn't dislike Jean and he did like Ted, who liked him in return. Ted often discussed his 'little personal difficulties' with Dad, for although it was perplexing for Ted that Dad had no money, Ted sensed that Dad understood life, that Dad was wise. So Ted told Dad about Jean's heavy drinking, or her affair with a young local councillor, or how his life was beginning to seem futile, or how unsatisfied he felt.

Whenever they had these truth sessions Dad took care to take advantage of Ted. 'He can talk and work at the same time, can't he?' said Dad as Ted, sometimes in tears, inserted rawl-plugs into brick as he made a shelf for Dad's Oriental books, or sanded a door, or tiled the bathroom in exchange for Dad listening to him from an aluminium garden chair. 'Don't commit suicide until you've finished that floor, Ted,' he'd say.

Tonight Dad didn't linger over Gin and Tonic. The room was still and silent. Dad went into a silence too, looking straight ahead of him. At first it was a little silence. But on and on it went, becoming a big silence: nothing was followed by nothing, which was followed quite soon by more nothing as he sat there, his eyes fixed but full of care. My head started to sweat. Bubbles of laughter rose in my throat. I wondered if he were going to con them and sit there for an hour in silence (perhaps just popping out one mystical phrase such as, 'Dried excrement sits on the pigeon's head') before putting his car coat on and tramping off back to his wife, having brought the Chislehurst bourgeoisie to an exquisite understanding of their inner emptiness. Would he dare?

At last he started out on his rap, accompanying it this time with a rattling orchestra of hissing, pausing and gazing at the audience. And he hissed and paused and gazed at the audience so quietly the poor bastards had to lean forward to hear. But there was no slacking; their ears were open.

'In our offices and places of work we love to tell others what to do. We denigrate them. We compare their work unfavourably with our own. We are always in competition. We show off and gossip. Our dream is of being well treated and we dream of treating others badly . . .'

Behind Dad the door slowly opened. A couple stood there – a tall young man with short, spiky hair dyed white. He wore silver shoes and a shiny silver jacket. He looked like a spaceman. The girl with him was dowdy in comparison. She was about seventeen, wearing a long hippie smock, a skirt that trailed to the ground, and hair to her waist. The door closed and they were gone; no one was disturbed. Everyone listened to Dad, apart from Jean, who tossed her hair

35

about as if to keep him away. When she glanced at Ted for a sign of support she received none: he was absorbed too.

Like a stage-manager pleased that his production is going well and knowing there is no more to be done, I slipped out of the room through the french windows. The last words I heard were, 'We must find an entirely new way of being alive.'

It was Dad's presence that extracted the noise from people's heads, rather than anything in particular he said. The peace and calm and confidence he exuded made me feel as if I were composed of air and light as I drifted through Carl and Marianne's silent, perfumed rooms, sometimes sitting down and staring into the distance, other times just strolling around. I became more intensely aware of both sounds and silence; everything looked sharper. There were some camellias in an art nouveau vase, and I found myself staring at them in wonderment. Dad's repose and concentration had helped me find a new and surprising appreciation of the trees in the garden as I looked at objects without association or analysis. The tree was form and colour, not leaves and branches. But, slowly, the freshness of things began to fade; my mind speeded up again and thoughts crowded in. Dad had been effective and I was pleased. Yet the enchantment wasn't over: there was something else – a voice. And the voice was speaking poetry to me as I stood there, in Carl and Marianne's hall. Every word was distinct, because my mind was so empty, so clear. It went:

> ' 'Tis true, 'tis day; what though it be?
> O wilt thou therefore rise from me?
> Why should we rise? because 'tis light?
> Did we lie downe, because 'twas night?
> Love which in spight of darkness brought us hither,
> Should in despight of light keepe us together.'

It was a rich, male voice, which came, not from above me, as I first thought – I was not being directly addressed by an angel – but from one side. I followed it until I came to a conservatory where I could see the boy with the silver hair sitting with the girl on a swing seat. He was talking to her – no, he was reading to her, from a small leather-bound book he held in one hand – and leaning into her face, as if to press the words into her. She sat impassively, smelling of

36

patchouli, twice pulling a strand of hair out of her eyes while he went on:

> 'The serpent is shut out from Paradise.
> The wounded deer must seek the herb no more
> In which its heart-cure lies . . .'

The girl, bored to death, became more lively and nudged him when she saw me, always the voyeur, peeping at them.

'Sorry,' I said, turning away.

'Karim, why are you ignoring me?'

I could see now it was Charlie.

'I'm not. I mean, I don't want to. Why have you gone silver?'

'To have more fun.'

'Charlie, I haven't seen you for ages. What have you been doing? I've been worried and everything, about you.'

'No reason to worry, little one. I've been preparing for the rest of my life. And everything.'

This fascinated me.

'Yeah? What kind of thing is the rest of your life going to be? D'you know already?'

'When I look into the future I see three things. Success. Success – '

'And success,' the girl added, wearily.

'I hope so,' I said. 'Right on, man.'

The girl looked at me wryly. 'Little one,' she giggled. Then she nuzzled her lips in his ear. 'Charlie, can't you read to me some more?'

So Charlie started up again, reading to both of us, but I didn't feel too good by now. To be honest, I felt a fool. I needed a fast dose of God's head-medicine right now, but I didn't want to leave Charlie. Why had he gone silver? Were we entering a new hair era that I'd completely failed to notice?

I forced myself back into the living room. Dad's gig consisted of half an hour's sibilant instruction plus questions, half an hour's yoga and some meditation. At the end, when everyone had got up and they were chatting sleepily, Auntie Jean said hallo, pretty curtly. I could see she wanted to leave, but at the same time she had her eyes fixed on a relieved and smiling Dad at the other side of the room. He had Eva beside him, and several people wanted more information about his teaching. Two of them asked if he'd go to their house and hold sessions there. Eva had become proprietorial, leading him away from bores while he nodded regally.

Before I left, Helen and I exchanged addresses and phone numbers. Charlie and the girl were arguing in the hall. Charlie wanted to take her home but she insisted on going her own way, the little fool. 'But why don't you want me?' he said. 'I really want you. I love you now.'

What was he being so uncool for? Yet I wondered if, when the day came that I wanted someone and they didn't want me, I'd be able to remain indifferent. I snorted in derision in his direction and waited outside for Dad and Eva.

So there it was. Helen loved me futilely, and I loved Charlie futilely, and he loved Miss Patchouli futilely, and no doubt she loved some other fucker futilely. The only unfutilely loving couple were God and Eva. I had a bad time just sitting in the car with them, with Eva putting her arms around Dad everywhere. Dad had to raise one authoritative finger to warn her away – which she bit. And I sat there like a good son, pretending not to exist.

Was Dad really in love with Eva? It was difficult for me to accept that he was, our world seemed so immutable. But hadn't he gone public? At the end of the gig he had given Eva a smacking kiss that sounded as if he were sucking an orange, and he'd told her he could never had done it without her. And she'd had her hand in his hair while Carl and Marianne were in their hands-together praying position, and Ted and Jean just stood there watching, in their stupid coats, like under-cover police. What was wrong with Dad?

Mum was waiting for us in the hall, her face partly hidden in the telephone. She was saying little, but I could hear the tinny sound of Jean on the other end. No time had been wasted. Dad scarpered into his room. I was about to run upstairs when Mum said, 'Wait a minute, smart-arse, someone wants to talk to you.'

'Who?'

'Come here.'

She shoved the phone at me and I heard Jean say just one thing. 'Come and see us tomorrow. Without fail. Do you understand?'

She always shouted at you, as if you were stupid. Fuck you, I thought. I didn't want to go near her in that mood. But, of course, I was the nosiest person I'd ever met. I'd be there – that I knew for sure.

So the next morning I cleaned my bike and was soon bumping along the unmade roads, following the route Dad and I had taken the previous evening. I rode slowly and watched the men hoovering, hosepiping, washing, polishing, shining, scraping, repainting, discussing and admiring their cars. It was a lovely day but their routine never changed. Women called out that dinner was on the table. People in hats and suits were coming back from church and they carried Bibles. The kids had clean faces and combed hair.

I wasn't quite ready to be brought down by Ted and Jean, so I decided to drop in and see Helen, who lived nearby. Earlier that morning I'd popped into Dad's room and whipped one of his dusty Durex Fetherlites – just in case.

Helen lived in a big old place set back from the road. Everyone I knew, Charlie and the rest, seemed to live in big places, except for us. No wonder I had an inferiority complex. But Helen's place hadn't been painted in aeons. The bushes and flowerbeds were overgrown, there were dandelions coming out of the path. The shed had half collapsed. Uncle Ted would have said it was a crying shame.

I parked the bike outside, chaining it to the fence. When I tried to open the gate I discovered it was jammed. I couldn't fiddle about; I climbed over. In the porch I pulled the bell and heard it ring somewhere deep in the house. It was spooky, I can tell you. There was no reply, so I strolled around the side.

'Karim, Karim,' Helen said quickly, in an anxious voice, from a window above my head.

'Hiya,' I called. 'I just wanted to see you.'

'Me too, yeah?'

I got irritated. I always wanted everything to happen immediately. 'What's wrong, then? Can't you come out? What's this Juliet business you're doing?'

At this her head seemed to have been jerked back into the house. There was some muffled arguing – a man's voice – and the window banged down. Then the curtains were drawn.

'Helen, Helen!' I called, suddenly feeling quite attached to her.

The front door opened. Helen's dad stood there. He was a big man with a black beard and thick arms. I imagined that he had hairy shoulders and, worst of all, a hairy back, like Peter Sellers and Sean Connery. (I kept a list of actors with hairy backs which I constantly updated.) And then I went white, but obviously not white enough, because Hairy Back let go of the dog he was holding, a Great fucking Dane, and it padded interestedly towards me, its mouth hanging open like a cave. It looked as though a jagged wedge had been ripped from the lump of its head to form its yellow-toothed, string-spittled mouth. I put my arms out in front of me so the dog wouldn't rip my hands off. I must have looked like a sleepwalker, but as I wanted my hands for other purposes I didn't care about this Baroque pose, though as a rule I cared fanatically about the way I looked, and behaved as if the entire world had nothing better to do than constantly observe me for slips in a very complicated and private etiquette.

'You can't see my daughter again,' said Hairy Back. 'She doesn't go out with boys. Or with wogs.'

'Oh well.'

'Got it?'

'Yeah,' I said sullenly.

'We don't want you blackies coming to the house.'

'Have there been many?'

'Many what, you little coon?'

'Blackies.'

'Where?'

'Coming to the house.'

'We don't like it,' Hairy Back said. 'However many niggers there are, we don't like it. We're with Enoch. If you put one of your black 'ands near my daughter I'll smash it with a 'ammer! With a 'ammer!'

Hairy Back slammed the front door. I took a couple of steps back and turned to go. Fucking Hairy Back. I badly wanted to piss. I looked at his car, a big Rover. I decided to let his tyres down. I could do it in a few seconds, piss in the window, and if he came out I'd be over the fence quicker than a cat through a window. I was moving towards the Rover when I realized that Hairy Back had left me alone with the dog, which was sniffing at turds only a few yards away. It started to move. I stood there pretending to be a stone or a tree until, gingerly, I turned my back on the dog and took a couple of steps, as if I were tip-toeing across a dangerous roof. I was hoping Helen would open the window and call my name, and call the dog's name too. 'Oh, Helen, Helen,' I murmured.

My soft words obviously affected the dog, for suddenly there was a flurry and I felt something odd on my shoulders. Yes, it was the dog's paws. The dog's breath warmed my neck. I took another step and so did the dog. I knew by now what the dog was up to. The dog was in love with me – quick movements against my arse told me so. Its ears were hot. I didn't think the dog would bite me, as its movements were increasing, so I decided to run for it. The dog shuddered against me.

I flew to the gate and climbed over, catching my pink shirt on a nail as I jumped. Safely over, I picked up some stones and let the dog have a couple of shots. One cracked off its nut but it didn't seem bothered. As I climbed on to my bike I took off my jacket and discovered dog jissom.

I was fucking bad-tempered when I finally pedalled up Jean's front path. And Jean always made everyone take off their shoes at the front door in case you obliterated the carpet by walking over it twice. Dad said, when we went in once, 'What is this, Jean, a Hindu temple? Is it the shoeless meeting the legless?' They were so fastidious about any new purchase that their three-year-old car still had plastic over the seats. Dad loved to turn to me and say, 'Aren't we just in clover in this car, Karim?' He really made me laugh, Dad.

That morning when I set off I'd been determined to be suave and dismissive, a real Dick Diver, but with dog spunk up the back of my tonic jacket, no shoes, and dying for a piss, I found the Fitzgerald front an effort. And Jean led me straight into the living room, sat me down by the innovative method of pressing on my shoulders, and went out to find Ted.

I went to the window and looked out over the garden. Here, in the summer, in the heyday of Peter's Heaters, Ted and Jean had magnificent parties, or 'do's, as Ted called them. My brother Allie, Ted and I would put up a big marquee on the lawn and wait breathlessly for the arrival of all South London and Kent society. The most important builders, bank managers, accountants, local politicians and businessmen came with their wives and tarts. Allie and I loved running among this reeking mob, the air thick with aftershave and perfume. We served cocktails and offered strawberries and cream and gâteaux, and cheese and chocolates, and sometimes, in exchange, women pinched our cheeks, and we tried to stick our hands up their daughters' skirts.

Mum and Dad always felt out of place and patronized on these grand occasions, where lives were measured by money. They were of no use to anyone and there was nothing they sought from any of the guests. Somehow they always seemed to wear the wrong clothes and look slightly shabby. After a gallon of Pimms Dad usually tried to discuss the real meaning of materialism, and how it was thought that we lived in a materialistic age. The truth was, he said, we didn't genuinely appreciate the value of individual objects, or their particular beauty. It was greed our materialism celebrated, greed and status, not the being and texture of things. These thoughts were not welcomed at Jean's parties, and my mother would covertly mouth and flap at Dad to shut up: he became rapidly depressed. Mum's ambition was to be unnoticed, to be like everyone else, whereas Dad liked to stand out like a juggler at a funeral.

Ted and Jean were a little king and queen in those days – rich, powerful, influential. Jean excelled in the business of introductions, both business and romantic. She was a local monitor of love, mediating in numerous affairs, warning, advising, cajoling and shoring up certain marriages while ripping unsuitable liaisons to shreds. She knew what was happening everywhere, on account sheets and under bed-sheets.

Jean seemed invulnerable until she pursued and started an affair with a pallid twenty-eight-year-old Tory councillor from an old and well-regarded middle-class Sevenoaks family. He was a virtual virgin, naïve and inexperienced, and with bad skin, but she was far outclassed. Oh yes, his parents stomped on it within six months and he never saw her again. She mourned for two years, Ted day by day seeming the more wretched in comparison with her long-gone Tory boy. The parties stopped and the people went away.

Now Auntie Jean came into the room with Uncle Ted. He was a born coward, and nervous as hell. He was shit-scared of confrontations or arguments of any kind.

'Hallo, Uncle Ted.'

'Hallo, son,' he said miserably.

Auntie Jean started up right away. 'Listen, Karim – '

'How's football?' I asked, overriding her and smiling at Ted.

'What?' he asked, shaking his head.

'Spurs doing well, aren't they?'

He looked at me as if I were mad. Auntie Jean had no idea what was going on. I clarified. 'About time, isn't it, that we went to another match, eh, Uncle Ted?'

Ordinary words indeed, but they did the trick with Uncle Ted. He had to sit down. I knew that after I mentioned football he would at least be neutral in this dispute about Dad, if not entirely on my side. I knew this because I had some serious shit on Ted that he would not want Auntie Jean to hear, just as I had the garden bench incident locked in my mind against Daddio.

I began to feel better.

This is the dirt.

At one time I really wanted to be the first Indian centre-forward to play for England and the school sent me for trials with Millwall and Crystal Palace. Spurs were our team, though, and as their ground was far away in North London, Ted and I didn't get to see them often. But when they were at home to Chelsea I persuaded Ted to take me. Mum tried to stop me going, convinced that the Shed boys would ensure me a sharpened penny in the skull. Not that I was too crazy about live matches. You stood there in the cold with icicles on your balls, and when someone was about to score the entire ground leapt in the air and all you could see were woolly hats.

The train took Ted and me and our sandwiches up through the suburbs and into London. This was the journey Dad made every day, bringing keema and roti and pea curry wrapped in greasy paper in his briefcase. Before crossing the river we passed over the slums of Herne Hill and Brixton, places so compelling and unlike anything I was used to seeing that I jumped up, jammed down the window and gazed out at the rows of disintegrating Victorian houses. The gardens were full of rusting junk and sodden overcoats; lines of washing criss-crossed over the debris. Ted explained to me, 'That's where the niggers live. Them blacks.'

On the way back from the match we were squashed into the corner of the carriage with dozens of other Spurs fans in black and white scarves. I had a football rattle I'd made at school. Spurs had won. 'Tottenham, Tottenham!' we chanted.

The next time I looked at Ted he had a knife in his hand. He jumped on to his seat and smashed the lightbulbs in the carriage. Glass flew into my hair. We all watched as Ted carefully unscrewed the mirrors from the carriage partitions – as if he were removing a radiator – and lobbed them out of the train. As we moved around the carriage to make way for him – no one joined in – Ted stabbed the seats and tore the stuffing out of them. Finally he thrust an unbroken lightbulb at me and pointed at the open window.

'Go on, enjoy yourself, it's Saturday.'

I got up and flung the lightbulb as far as I could, not realizing we were drawing into Penge Station. The lightbulb smashed against a wall where an old Indian man was sitting. The man cried out, got up and hobbled away. The boys in the train jeered racist bad-mouth at him. When Ted brought me home Mum pointed at me and asked Ted if I'd behaved myself.

Now Auntie Jean fixed the full searchlight of her eyes on me.

'We've always quite liked your dad, and we never had no objections to him marrying Margaret, though some people didn't like her marrying a coloured – '

'Auntie Jean – '

'Duck, don't interrupt. Your mum's told me all about what a caper your dad's been leading over in Beckenham. He's been impersonating a Buddhist – '

'He is a Buddhist.'

'And carrying on with that mad woman, who everyone knows – because she's told them – is disfigured.'

'Disfigured, Auntie Jean?'

'And yesterday, well, we couldn't believe our eyes, could we, Ted. Ted!'

Ted nodded to indicate that he couldn't believe his eyes.

' 'Course, we presume this madness is going to stop right now.'

She sat back and waited for my reply. I tell you, Auntie Jean really knew how to give you frightening looks, so much so that I found myself struggling to suppress a fart that needed to be free. I crossed my legs and pressed down into the sofa as hard as I could. But it was no use. The naughty fart bubbled gaily out of me. Within seconds the rank gas had risen and was wafting towards Auntie Jean, who was still waiting for me to speak.

'Don't ask me, Auntie Jean. It's none of our business, what Dad does, is it?'

'I'm afraid it's not just his bloody business, is it? It affects all of us! They'll think we're all bloody barmy. Think of Peter's Heaters!' she said, and turned to Uncle Ted, who was holding a cushion over his face. 'What are you doing, Ted?'

I asked as innocently as I could, 'How will Dad's behaviour affect your livelihood, Auntie Jean?'

Auntie Jean scratched her nose. 'Your mum can't take no more,' she said. 'It's your job to stop the rot right now. If you do that nothing more will be said. God's honour.'

' 'Cept at Christmas,' added Ted. He loved to say the wrong thing at the wrong time, as if some self-respect came from rebellion.

Jean got up and walked across the carpet in her high heels. She opened a window and sniffed the fresh garden air. This tonic turned her thoughts to Royalty.

'Anyway, your dad's a Civil Servant. What would the Queen say if she knew what he was up to?'

'Which queen?' I murmured to myself. Aloud I said, 'I don't answer rhetorical questions,' and got up and went to the door. As I stood there I realized I was trembling. But Jean smiled at me as if I'd agreed with everything she said.

'There's a good boy, duck. Now give me a kiss. And what's that mess on the back of your coat?'

I heard nothing more from either Gin or Tonic for a few weeks, and during that time I didn't run to Dad and urge him, on my knees, to give up the Buddha business just because Jean didn't like it.

As for Eva, there was no word from her. I began to think the whole affair was over, and I rather regretted this, as our life returned to dull normalcy. But one evening the phone rang and Mum answered it. She immediately replaced the receiver. Dad was standing at the door of his room. 'Who was it?' he asked.

'No one,' said Mum, with a defiant look.

CHAPTER FOUR

It was clear in other ways that Eva wasn't going to leave our lives now. She was present when Dad was withdrawn and preoccupied – every night, in fact; she was there when Mum and Dad watched *Panorama* together; she was there when he heard a sad record or anyone mentioned love. And no one was happy. I had no idea if Dad was meeting Eva on the sly. How could that have been possible? Life for commuters was regulated to the minute; if trains were delayed or cancelled there were always others soon after. There were no excuses to be made in the evenings: no one went out, there was nowhere to go, and Dad never socialized with anyone from the office. They too fled London as quickly as they could after work. Mum and Dad went to the pictures maybe once a year, and Dad always fell asleep; once they went to the theatre to see *West Side Story*. We didn't know anyone who went to pubs, apart from Uncle Ted: pubbing was lower class, and where we lived the toothless and shameless tended to sing 'Come, come, come and make eyes at me, down at the old Bull and Bush' to knackered pianos.

So the only time Dad could have got to see Eva was at lunchtimes, and maybe she did meet him outside his office for an arm-in-arm lunch in St James's Park, just like Mum and Dad when they were courting. Whether Dad and Eva were making love or not, I had no idea. But I found a book in his briefcase with illustrations of Chinese sexual positions, which included Mandarin Ducks Entwined, the complicated Dwarfed Pine Tree, Cat and Mouse Share a Hole, and the delightful Dark Cicada Clings to a Branch.

Whether the Dark Cicada was clinging to a branch or not, life was tense. But on the surface, at least, it was straightforward, until one Sunday morning two months after I'd visited Gin and Tonic's house I opened our front door and Uncle Ted was standing there. I looked at him without a smile or greeting, and he looked at me back, getting uncomfortable until he managed to say, 'Ah, son, I've just popped round to look at the garden and make sure them roses have come out.'

'The garden's blooming.'

Ted stepped over the threshold and sang, 'There'll be blue birds over, the white cliffs of Dover.' He asked, 'How's yer old dad?'

'Following up on our little discussion, eh?'

'Keep that to yerself as previously agreed,' he said, striding past me.

' 'Bout time we went to another football match, Uncle Ted, isn't it? By train, eh?'

He went into the kitchen, where Mum was putting the Sunday roast in the oven. He took her out into the garden, and I could see him asking her how she was. In other words, what was happening with Dad and Eva and all the Buddha business? What could Mum say? Everything was OK and not OK. There were no clues, but that didn't mean crimes were not being committed.

Having dealt with Mum, still in his businessman mode, Ted barged into the bedroom, where Dad was. Nosy as ever, I followed him, even as he tried to slam the door in my face.

Dad was sitting on the white counterpane of his bed, cleaning his shoes with one of my tie-dyed vests. Dad polished his shoes, about ten pairs, with patience and care, every Sunday morning. Then he brushed his suits, chose his shirts for the week – one day pink, the next blue, the next lilac and so on – selected his cufflinks, and arranged his ties, of which there were at least a hundred. Sitting there absorbed, and turning in surprise as the door banged open, with huge puffing Ted in black boots and a baggy green turtle-neck filling the room like a horse in a prison cell, Dad looked small and childlike in comparison, his privacy and innocence now violated. They looked each other, Ted truculent and clumsy, Dad just sitting there in white vest and pyjama bottoms, his bull neck sinking into his tremendous chest and untremendous guts. But Dad didn't mind at all. He loved it when people came and went, the house full of talk and activity, as it would have been in Bombay.

'Ah, Ted, please, can you have a look at this for me?'

'What?'

A look of panic invaded Ted's face. Every time he came to our place he determined not to be manoeuvred into fixing anything.

'Just glance at one gone-wrong damn thing,' Dad said.

He led Ted around the bed to a shaky table on which he kept his record-player, one of those box jobs covered in cheap felt with a small speaker at the front and a brittle cream turntable, with a long spindle through it for stacking long-players. Dad waved at it and addressed Ted as I'm sure he used to speak to his servants.

'I'm heart-broken, Ted. I can't play my Nat King Cole and Pink Floyd records. Please help me out.'

Ted peered at it. I noticed his fingers were thick as sausages, the nails smashed, the flesh ingrained with filth. I tried to imagine his hand on a woman's body. 'Why can't Karim do it?'

'He's saving his fingers to be a doctor. Plus he's a useless bastard.'

'That's true,' said Ted, cheered by this insult.

'Of course, it's the useless that endure.'

Ted looked suspiciously at Dad after this uncalled-for mysticism. I fetched Ted's screwdriver from his car and he sat on the bed and started to unscrew the record-player.

'Jean said I should come and see you, Harry.' Ted didn't know what to say next and Dad didn't help him. 'She says you're a Buddhist.'

He said 'Buddhist' as he would have said 'homosexual' had he cause to say 'homosexual' ever, which he didn't.

'What is a Buddhist?'

'What was all that funny business with no shoes on the other week up in Chislehurst?' Ted countered.

'Did it disgust you, listening to me?'

'Me? No, I'll listen to anyone. But Jean, she definitely had her stomach turned queer.'

'Why?'

Dad was confusing Ted.

'Buddhism isn't the kind of thing she's used to. It's got to stop! Everything you're up to, it's got to stop right now!'

Dad went into one of his crafty silences, just sitting there with his thumbs together and his head humbly bent like a kid who's been told off but is convinced, in his heart, that he's right.

'So just stop, or what will I tell Jean?'

Ted was getting stormy. Dad continued to sit.

'Tell her: Harry's nothing.'

This took the rest of the puff out of Ted, who was, failing everything else, in need of a row, even though he had his hands full of record-player parts.

Then, with a turn of speed, Dad switched the subject. Like a footballer passing a long low ball right through the opposition's defence he started to ask Ted how work was, work and business. Ted sighed, but he brightened: he seemed better on this subject.

'Hard work, very hard, from mornin' till night.'

'Yes?'

'Work, work, damn work!'

Dad was uninterested. Or so I thought.

Then he did this extraordinary thing. I don't think he even knew he was going to do it. He got up and went to Ted and put his hand on the back of Ted's neck, and pulled Ted's neck towards him, until Ted had his nose on Dad's chest. Ted remained in that position, the record-player on his lap, with Dad looking down on to the top of his head, for at least five minutes before Dad spoke. Then he said, 'There's too much work in the world.'

Somehow Dad had released Ted from the obligation to behave normally. Ted's voice was choked. 'Can't just stop,' he moaned.

'Yes, you can.'

'How will I live?'

'How are you living now? Disaster. Follow your feelings. Follow the course of least resistance. Do what pleases you – whatever it is. Let the house fall down. Drift.'

'Don't be a cunt. Got to make an effort.'

'Under no circumstances make an effort,' said Dad firmly, gripping Ted's head. 'If you don't stop making an effort you'll die soon.'

'Die? Will I?'

'Oh yes. Trying is ruining you. You can't try to fall in love, can you? And trying to make love leads to impotence. Follow your feelings. All effort is ignorance. There is innate wisdom. Only do what you love.'

'If I follow my fucking feelings I'll do fuck-all,' said Ted, I think. It was hard to be sure, what with his nose pressed into Dad and this honking noise come out. I tried to take up a grandstand position to see if Uncle Ted was in tears, but I didn't want to jump around all over the place and distract them.

'Do nothing, then,' said God.

'The house will fall down.'

'Who cares? Let it drop.'

'The business will collapse.'

'It's on its arse anyway,' Dad snorted.

Ted looked up at him. 'How d'you know?'

'Let it collapse. Do something else in a couple of years' time.'

'Jean will leave me.'

'Oh, but Jean's left you.'

'Oh God, oh God, oh God, you're the stupidest person I've ever met, Harry.'

'Yes, I think I am quite stupid. And you're suffering like hell. You're ashamed of it, too. Are people not allowed even to suffer now? Suffer, Ted.'

Ted was suffering. He sobbed generously.

'Now,' said Dad, readjusting his priorities, 'what's wrong with this fucking record-player?'

Ted emerged from Dad's room to find Mum coming up the hall with a full plate of Yorkshire puddings. 'What have you done to Uncle Ted?' she said, clearly shocked. She stood there as Uncle Ted's endless legs buckled and he sank down on the bottom of the stairs like a dying giraffe, still holding Dad's turntable, his head against the wall, rubbing Brylcreem against the wallpaper, the one thing certain to incense Mum.

'I've released him,' said Dad, rubbing his hands together.

What a weekend it was, with the confusion and pain between Mum and Dad virtually tangible; if it had had physical substance, their antipathy would have filled our house with mud. It was as if only one more minor remark or incident were required for them to murder each other, not out of hatred but out of despair. I sat upstairs in my room when I could, but kept imagining they were going to try and stab each other. And I panicked in case I wouldn't be able to separate them in time.

The following Saturday, when we were all together again with hours of proximity ahead of us, I cycled out of the suburbs, leaving that little house of turmoil behind me. There was another place I could go.

When I arrived at Uncle Anwar's shop, Paradise Stores, I could see their daughter, Jamila, filling shelves. Her mother, the Princess Jeeta, was on the till. Paradise Stores was a dusty place with a high, ornate and flaking ceiling. There was an inconvenient and tall block of shelves in the centre of the shop, around which customers shuffled, stepping over tins and cartons. The goods seemed to be in no kind of order. Jeeta's till was crammed into a corner by the door, so she was always cold and wore fingerless gloves all the year round. Anwar's chair was at the opposite end, in an alcove, from which he looked out expressionlessly. Outside were boxes of vegetables. Paradise opened at eight in the morning and closed at ten at night. They didn't even have Sundays off now, though every year at Christmas Anwar and Jeeta took a week off. Every year, after the New Year, I dreaded hearing Anwar say, 'Only three hundred and fifty-seven days until we can rest freely again.'

I didn't know how much money they had. But if they had anything they must have buried it, because they never bought any of the things people in Chislehurst would exchange their legs for: velvet curtains, stereos, Martinis, electric lawnmowers, double-glazing. The idea of enjoyment had passed Jeeta and Anwar by. They behaved as if they had unlimited lives: this life was of no consequence, it was merely the first of many hundreds to come in which they could relish existence. They also knew nothing of the outside world. I often asked Jeeta who the Foreign Secretary of Great Britain was, or the name of the Chancellor of the Exchequer, but she never knew, and did not regret her ignorance.

I looked through the window as I padlocked my bike to the lamppost. I couldn't see Anwar. Maybe he'd gone out to the betting shop. His absence struck me as odd, because usually at this time, unshaven, smoking, and wearing a rancid suit that Dad gave him in 1954, he was nosing around the backs of possible shoplifters, whom he referred to as SLs. 'Saw two bad SLs today,' he'd say. 'Right under my bloody nose, Karim. I chased their arses like mad.'

I watched Jamila, and pressed my nose to the glass and made a range of jungle noises. I was Mowgli threatening Shere Khan. But she didn't hear me. I marvelled at her: she was small and thin with large brown eyes, a tiny nose and little wire glasses. Her hair was dark and long again. Thank Christ she'd lost the Afro 'natural' which had so startled the people of Penge a couple of years ago. She was forceful and enthusiastic, Jamila. She always seemed to be leaning forward, arguing, persuading. She had a dark moustache, too, which for a long time was more impressive than my own. If anything it resembled my eyebrow – I had only one and, as Jamila said, it lay above my eyes, thick and black, like the tail of a small squirrel. She said that for the Romans joined eyebrows were a sign of nobility; for the Greeks they were a sign of treachery. 'Which will you turn out to be, Roman or Greek?' she liked to say.

I grew up with Jamila and we'd never stopped playing together. Jamila and her parents were like an alternative family. It comforted me that there was always somewhere less intense, and warmer, where I could go when my own family had me thinking of running away.

Princess Jeeta fed me dozens of the hot kebabs I loved, which I coated with mango chutney and wrapped in chapati. She called me the Fire Eater because of it. Jeeta's was also my favourite place for a bath. Although their bathroom was rotten, with the plaster crumbling off the walls, most of the ceiling dumped on the floor and the Ascot heater as dangerous as a landmine, Jeeta would sit next to the bath and massage my head with olive oil, jamming her nifty fingers into every crevice of my skull until my body was molten. In return Jamila and I were instructed to walk on her back, Jeeta lying beside her bed while Jammie and I trod up and down on her, holding on to each other while Jeeta gave orders: 'Press your toes into my neck – it's stiff, stiff, made of iron! Yes, there, there! Down a bit! Yes, on the bulge, on the rock, yes, downstairs, upstairs, on the landing!'

Jamila was more advanced than I, in every way. There was a library next to the shop, and for years the librarian, Miss Cutmore, would take Jamila in after school and give her tea. Miss Cutmore had been a missionary in Africa, but she loved France too, having suffered a broken heart in Bordeaux. At the age of thirteen Jamila was reading non-stop, Baudelaire and Colette and Radiguet and all that rude lot, and borrowing records of Ravel, as well as singers popular in France, like Billie Holliday. Then she got this thing about wanting to be Simone de Beauvoir, which is when she and I started having sex every couple of weeks or so, when we could find somewhere to go – usually a bus shelter, a bomb-site or a derelict house. Those books must have been dynamite or something, because we even did it in public toilets. Jammie wasn't afraid of just strolling straight into the Men's and locking the cubicle behind us. Very Parisian, she thought, and wore feathers, for God's sake. It was all pretentious, of course, and I learned nothing about sex, not the slightest thing about where and how and here and there, and I lost none of my fear of intimacy.

Jamila received the highest-class education at the hands of Miss

Cutmore, who loved her. Just being for years beside someone who liked writers, coffee and subversive ideas, and told her she was brilliant had changed her for good, I reckoned. I kept moaning that I wished I had a teacher like that.

But when Miss Cutmore left South London for Bath, Jamila got grudging and started to hate Miss Cutmore for forgetting that she was Indian. Jamila thought Miss Cutmore really wanted to eradicate everything that was foreign in her. 'She spoke to my parents as if they were peasants,' Jamila said. She drove me mad by saying Miss Cutmore had colonized her, but Jamila was the strongest-willed person I'd met: no one could turn her into a colony. Anyway, I hated ungrateful people. Without Miss Cutmore, Jamila wouldn't have even heard the word 'colony'. 'Miss Cutmore started you off,' I told her.

Via the record library Jamila soon turned on to Bessie and Sarah and Dinah and Ella, whose records she'd bring round to our place and play to Dad. They'd sit side by side on his bed, waving their arms and singing along. Miss Cutmore had also told her about equality, fraternity and the other one, I forget what it is, so in her purse Jammie always carried a photograph of Angela Davis, and she wore black clothes and had a truculent attitude to schoolteachers. For months it was Soledad this and Soledad that. Yeah, sometimes we were French, Jammie and I, and other times we went black American. The thing was, we were supposed to be English, but to the English we were always wogs and nigs and Pakis and the rest of it.

Compared to Jammie I was, as a militant, a real shaker and trembler. If people spat at me I practically thanked them for not making me chew the moss between the paving stones. But Jamila had a PhD in physical retribution. Once a greaser rode past us on an old bicycle and said, as if asking the time, 'Eat shit, Pakis.' Jammie sprinted through the traffic before throwing the bastard off his bike and tugging out some of his hair, like someone weeding an overgrown garden.

Now, today, Auntie Jeeta was serving a customer in the shop, putting bread and oranges and tins of tomatoes into a brown-paper bag. Jamila wasn't acknowledging me at all, so I waited by Auntie Jeeta, whose miserable face must, I was sure, have driven away thousands of customers over the years, none of them realizing she was a princess whose brothers carried guns.

'How's your back, Auntie Jeeta?' I asked.

'Bent like a hairpin with worries,' she said.

'How could you worry, Auntie Jeeta, with a thriving business like this?'

'Hey, never mind my mouldy things. Take Jamila on one of your walks. Please, will you do that for me?'

'What's wrong?'

'Here's a samosa, Fire Eater. Extra hot for naughty boys.'

'Where's Uncle Anwar?' She gave me a plaintive look. 'And who's Prime Minister?' I added.

Off Jamila and I went, tearing through Penge. She really walked, Jamila, and when she wanted to cross the road she just strode through the traffic, expecting cars to stop or slow down for her, which they did. Eventually she asked her favourite question of all time. 'What have you got to tell, Creamy? What stories?'

Facts she wanted, and good stories, the worse the better – stories of embarrassment and humiliation and failure, mucky and semen-stained, otherwise she would walk away or something, like an unsatisfied theatre-goer. But this time I was prepared. Spot-on stories were waiting like drinks for the thirsty.

I told her all about Dad and Eva, about Auntie Jean's temper and how she pressed down on my shoulders, which made me fart. I told her about trances, and praying advertising executives, and attempts in Beckenham to find the Way on garden benches. And I told her nothing about Great Danes and me. Whenever I asked her what she thought I should do about Dad and Mum and Eva, or whether I should run away from home again, or even whether we should flee together to London and get work as waiters, she laughed louder.

'Don't you see it's fucking serious?' I told her. 'Dad shouldn't hurt Mum, should he? She doesn't deserve it.'

'No, she doesn't. But the deed has been done, right, in that Beckenham garden, while you were watching in your usual position, on your knees, right? Oh, Creamy, you do get in some stupid situations. And you do realize it's absolutely characteristic of you, don't you?'

Now she was laughing at me so hard she had to stop and bend forward for breath, with her hands on her thighs. I went on. 'But shouldn't Dad restrain himself, you know, and think about us, his family? Put us first?'

It was talking about it now for the first time that made me realize how unhappy the whole thing was making me. Our whole family was in tatters and no one was talking about it.

'Sometimes you can be so bourgeois, Creamy Jeans. Families aren't sacred, especially to Indian men, who talk about nothing else and act otherwise.'

'Your dad's not like that,' I said.

She was always putting me down. I couldn't take it today. She was so powerful, Jammie, so in control and certain what to do about everything.

'And he loves her. You said your dad loves Eva.'

'Yes, I s'pose I did say that. I think he loves her. He hasn't exactly said it all over the place.'

'Well, Creamy, love should have its way, shouldn't it? Don't ya believe in love?'

'Yes, OK, OK, theoretically. For God's sake, Jammie!'

Before I knew it, we were passing a public toilet beside the park and her hand was pulling on mine. As she tugged me towards it and I inhaled the urine, shit and disinfectant cocktail I associated with love, I just had to stop and think. I didn't believe in monogamy or anything old like that, but my mind was still on Charlie and I couldn't think of anyone else, not even Jammie.

It was unusual, I knew, the way I wanted to sleep with boys as well as girls. I liked strong bodies and the backs of boys' necks. I liked being handled by men, their fists pulling me; and I liked objects – the ends of brushes, pens, fingers – up my arse. But I liked cunts and breasts, all of women's softness, long smooth legs and the way women dressed. I felt it would be heart-breaking to have to choose one or the other, like having to decide between the Beatles and the Rolling Stones. I never liked to think much about the whole thing in case I turned out to be a pervert and needed to have treatment, hormones, or electric shocks through my brain. When I did think about it I considered myself lucky that I could go to parties and go home with anyone from either sex – not that I went to many parties, none at all really, but if I did, I could, you know, trade either way. But my main love at the moment was my Charlie, and even more important than that, it was Mum and Dad and Eva. How could I think about anything else?

I had the brilliant idea of saying, 'And what's your news, Jammie? Tell me.'

She paused. It worked remarkably well. 'Let's take another turn around the block,' she said. 'It's seriousness squared, Creamy Jeans. I don't know what's happening to me. No jokes, all right?'

She started at the beginning.

Under the influence of Angela Davis, Jamila had started exercising every day, learning karate and judo, getting up early to stretch and run and do press-ups. She bowled along like a dream, Jamila; she could have run on snow and left no footsteps. She was preparing for the guerrilla war she knew would be necessary when the whites finally turned on the blacks and Asians and tried to force us into gas chambers or push us into leaky boats.

This wasn't as ludicrous as it sounded. The area in which Jamila lived was closer to London than our suburbs, and far poorer. It was full of neo-fascist groups, thugs who had their own pubs and clubs and shops. On Saturdays they'd be out in the High Street selling their newspapers and pamphlets. They also operated outside the schools and colleges and football grounds, like Millwall and Crystal Palace. At night they roamed the streets, beating Asians and shoving shit and burning rags through their letter-boxes. Frequently the mean, white, hating faces had public meetings and the Union Jacks were paraded through the streets, protected by the police. There was no evidence that these people would go away – no evidence that their power would diminish rather than increase. The lives of Anwar and Jeeta and Jamila were pervaded by fear of violence. I'm sure it was something they thought about every day. Jeeta kept buckets of water around her bed in case the shop was fire-bombed in the night. Many of Jamila's attitudes were inspired by the possibility that a white group might kill one of us one day.

Jamila tried to recruit me to her cadre for training but I couldn't get up in the morning. 'Why do we have to start training at eight?' I whined.

'Cuba wasn't won by getting up late, was it? Fidel and Che didn't get up at two in the afternoon, did they? They didn't even have time to shave!'

Anwar didn't like these training sessions of hers. He thought she was meeting boys at these karate classes and long runs through the city. Sometimes she'd be running through Deptford and there, in a doorway with his collar turned up, his hairy nose just visible, would be Baby Face watching her, turning away in disgust when she blew Daddy a kiss.

Soon after Daddy's hairy nose had been blown a kiss that didn't reach its destination, Anwar got a phone installed and started to lock himself in the living room with it for hours on end. The rest of the time the phone was locked. Jamila had to use a phone-box. Anwar had secretly decided it was time Jamila got married.

Through these calls Anwar's brother in Bombay had fixed up Jamila with a boy eager to come and live in London as Jamila's husband. Except that this boy wasn't a boy. He was thirty. As a dowry the ageing boy had demanded a warm winter overcoat from Moss Bros., a colour television and, mysteriously, an edition of the complete works of Conan Doyle. Anwar agreed to this, but consulted Dad. Dad thought the Conan Doyle demand very strange. 'What normal Indian man would want such a thing? The boy must be investigated further – immediately!'

But Anwar ignored Dad's feeling. There had been friction between Anwar and Dad over the question of children before. Dad was very proud that he had two sons. He was convinced it meant he had 'good seed'. As Anwar had only produced one daughter it meant that he had 'weak seed'. Dad loved pointing this out to Anwar. 'Surely, *yaar*, you have potentially more than one girl and one girl only in your entire lifetime's seed-production, eh?'

'Fuck it,' Anwar replied, rattled. 'It's my wife's fault, you bastard. Her womb has shrivelled like a prune.'

Anwar had told Jamila what he'd decided: she was to marry the Indian and he would come over, slip on his overcoat and wife and live happily ever after in her muscly arms.

Then Anwar would rent a flat nearby for the newly-weds. 'Big enough for two children,' he said, to a startled Jamila. He took her hand and added, 'Soon you'll be very happy.' Her mother said, 'We're both very glad for you, Jamila.'

Not surprisingly for someone with Jamila's temper and Angela Davis's beliefs, Jamila wasn't too pleased.

'What did you say to him?' I asked, as we walked.

'Creamy, I'd have walked out there and then. I'd have got the Council to take me into care. Anything. I'd have lived with friends, done a runner. Except for my mother. He takes it out on Jeeta. He abuses her.'

'Hits her? Really?'

'He used to, yes, until I told him I'd cut off his hair with a carving knife if he did it again. But he knows how to make her life terrible without physical violence. He's had many years of practice.'

'Well,' I said, satisfied that there wasn't much more to be said on the matter, 'in the end he can't make you do anything you don't want to do.'

She turned on me. 'But he can! You know my father well, but not that well. There's something I haven't told you. Come with me. Come on, Karim,' she insisted.

We went back to their shop, where she quickly made me a kebab and chapati, this time with onions and green chillis. The kebab sweated brown juice over the raw onions. The chapati scalded my fingers: it was lethal.

'Bring it upstairs, will you, Karim?' she said.

Her mother called through to us from the till. 'No, Jamila, don't take him up there!' And she banged down a bottle of milk and frightened a customer.

'What's wrong, Auntie Jeeta?' I asked. She was going to cry.

'Come on,' Jamila said.

I was about to wedge as much of the kebab as I could into my gob without puking when Jamila pulled me upstairs, her mother shouting after her, 'Jamila, Jamila!'

By now I wanted to go home; I'd had enough of family dramas. If I wanted all that Ibsen stuff I could have stayed indoors. Besides, with Jamila's help I'd wanted to work out what I thought of Dad and Eva, whether I should be open-minded or not. Now there was no chance of contemplation.

Half-way up the stairs I smelled something rotten. It was feet and arseholes and farts swirling together, a mingling of winds which hurried straight for my broad nostrils. Their flat was always a junk shop, with the furniture busted and fingerprints all over the doors and the wallpaper about a hundred years old and fag butts sprinkled over every surface, but it never stank, except of Jeeta's wonderful cooking, which went on permanently in big burnt pans.

Anwar was sitting on a bed in the living room, which wasn't his normal bed in its normal place. He was wearing a frayed and mouldy-looking pyjama jacket, and I noticed that his toenails rather resembled cashew nuts. For some reason his mouth was hanging open and he was panting, though he couldn't have run for a bus in the last five minutes. He was unshaven, and thinner than I'd ever seen him. His lips were dry and flaking. His skin looked yellow and his eyes were sunken, each of them seeming to lie in a bruise. Next to the bed was a dirty encrusted pot with a pool of piss in it. I'd never seen anyone dying before, but I was sure Anwar qualified. Anwar was staring at my steaming kebab as though it were a torture instrument. I chewed speedily to get rid of it.

'Why didn't you tell me he's sick?' I whispered to Jamila.

But I wasn't convinced that he was simply sick, since the pity in her face was overlaid with fury. She was glaring at her old man, but he wouldn't meet her eyes, nor mine after I'd walked in. He stared straight in front of him as he always did at the television screen, except that it wasn't on.

'He's not ill,' she said.

'No?' I said, and then, to him, 'Hallo, Uncle Anwar. How are you, boss?'

His voice was changed: it was reedy and weak now. 'Take that damn kebab out of my nose,' he said. 'And take that damn girl with you.'

Jamila touched my arm. 'Watch.' She sat down on the edge of the bed and leaned towards him. 'Please, please stop all this.'

'Get lost!' he croaked at her. 'You're not my daughter. I don't know who you are.'

'For all our sakes, please stop it! Here, Karim who loves you – '

'Yes, yes!' I said.

'He's brought you a lovely tasty kebab!'

'Why is he eating it himself, then?' Anwar said, reasonably. She snatched the kebab from me and waved it in front of her father. At this my poor kebab started to disintegrate, bits of meat and chilli and onion scattering over the bed. Anwar ignored it.

'What's going on here?' I asked her.

'Look at him, Karim, he hasn't eaten or drunk anything for eight days! He'll die, Karim, won't he, if he doesn't eat anything!'

'Yes. You'll cop it, boss, if you don't eat your grub like everyone else.'

'I won't eat. I will die. If Gandhi could shove out the English from India by not eating, I can get my family to obey me by exactly the same.'

'What do you want her to do?'

'To marry the boy I have selected with my brother.'

'But it's old-fashioned, Uncle, out of date,' I explained. 'No one does that kind of thing now. They just marry the person they're into, if they bother to get married at all.'

This homily on contemporary morals didn't exactly blow his mind.

'That is not our way, boy. Our way is firm. She must do what I say or I will die. She will kill me.'

Jamila started to punch the bed.

'It's so stupid! What a waste of time and life!'

Anwar was unmoved. I'd always liked him because he was so casual about everything; he wasn't perpetually anxious like my parents. Now he was making a big fuss about a mere marriage and I couldn't understand it. I know it made me sad to see him do this to himself. I couldn't believe the things people did to themselves, how they screwed up their lives and made things go wrong, like Dad having it away with Eva, or Ted's breakdown, and now Uncle Anwar going on this major Gandhi diet. It wasn't as if external circumstances had forced them into these lunacies; it was plain illusion in the head.

Anwar's irrationality was making me tremble, I can tell you. I know I kept shaking my head everywhere. He'd locked himself in a private room beyond the reach of reason, of persuasion, of evidence. Even happiness, that frequent pivot of decision, was irrelevant here – Jamila's happiness, I mean. Like her I wanted to express myself physically in some way. It seemed to be all that was left to us.

I kicked Uncle Anwar's piss-pot quite vigorously so that a small wave of urine splashed against the overhanging bed-sheets. He ignored me. Jamila and I stood there, about to walk out. But now I was making my uncle sleep in his own piss. Suppose he later clutched that piece of sheet to his nose, to his mouth. Hadn't he always been kind to me, Uncle Anwar? Hadn't he always accepted me exactly as I was, and never told me off? I bolted into the bathroom and fetched a wet cloth, returning to soak the pissy sheet until I was sure it wouldn't stink any more. It was irrational of me to hate his irrationality so much that I sprayed piss over his bed. But as I scrubbed his sheet I realized he had no idea what I was doing on my knees beside him.

Jamila came outside while I unlocked my bike.

'What are you going to do, Jammie?'

'I don't know. What do you suggest?'

'I don't know either.'

'No.'

'But I'll think about it,' I said. 'I promise I'll come up with something.'

'Thanks.'

She started unashamedly to cry, not covering her face or trying to stop. Usually I get embarrassed when girls cry. Sometimes I feel like clouting them for making a fuss. But Jamila really was in the shit. We must have stood there outside Paradise Stores for at least half an hour, just holding each other and thinking about our respective futures.

CHAPTER FIVE

I loved drinking tea and I loved cycling. I would bike to the tea shop in the High Street and see what blends they had. My bedroom contained boxes and boxes of tea, and I was always happy to have new brews with which to concoct more original combos in my teapot. I was supposed to be preparing for my mock A levels in History, English and Politics. But whatever happened I knew I would fail them. I was too concerned with other things. Sometimes I took speed – 'blues', little blue tablets – to keep me awake, but they made me depressed, they made my testicles shrivel up and I kept thinking I was getting a heart attack. So I usually sipped spicy tea and listened to records all night. I favoured the tuneless: King Crimson, Soft Machine, Captain Beefheart, Frank Zappa and Wild Man Fisher. It was easy to get most of the music you wanted from the shops in the High Street.

During these nights, as all around me was silent – most of the neighbourhood went to bed at ten-thirty – I entered another world. I read Norman Mailer's journalism about an action-man writer involved in danger, resistance and political commitment: adventure stories not of the distant past, but of recent times. I'd bought a TV from the man in the chip shop, and as the black-and-white box heated up it stank of grease and fish, but late at night I heard of cults and experiments in living, in California. In Europe terrorist groups were bombing capitalist targets; in London psychologists were saying you had to live your own life in your own way and not according to your family, or you'd go mad. In bed I read *Rolling Stone* magazine. Sometimes I felt the whole world was converging on this little room. And as I became more intoxicated and frustrated I'd throw open the bedroom window as the dawn came up, and look across the gardens, lawns, greenhouses, sheds and curtained windows. I wanted my life to begin now, at this instant, just when I was ready for it. Then it was time for my paper-round, followed by school. And school was another thing I'd had enough of.

Recently I'd been punched and kicked to the ground by a teacher because I called him a queer. This teacher was always making me sit on his knee, and when he asked me questions like 'What is the square root of five thousand six hundred and seventy-eight and a half?', which I couldn't answer, he tickled me. Very educational. I was sick too of being affectionately called Shitface and Curryface, and of coming home covered in spit and snot and chalk and wood-shavings. We did a lot of woodwork at our school, and the other kids liked to lock me and my friends in the storeroom and have us chant 'Manchester United, Manchester United, we are the boot boys' as they held chisels to our throats and cut off our shoelaces. We did a lot of woodwork at the school because they didn't think we could deal with books. One day the woodwork teacher had a heart attack right in front of our eyes as one of the lads put another kid's prick in a vice and started to turn the handle. Fuck you, Charles Dickens, nothing's changed. One kid tried to brand my arm with a red-hot lump of metal. Someone else pissed over my shoes, and all my Dad thought about was me becoming a doctor. What world was he living in? Every day I considered myself lucky to get home from school without serious injury.

So after all this I felt I was ready to retire. There was nothing I particularly wanted to do. You didn't have to do anything. You could just drift and hang out and see what happened, which suited me fine, even more than being a Customs Officer or a professional footballer or a guitarist.

So I was racing through South London on my bike, nearly getting crushed several times by lorries, head bent over the dropped handlebars, swiftly running through the ten Campagnola gears, nipping through traffic, sometimes mounting the pavement, up one-way streets, breaking suddenly, accelerating by standing up on the pedals, exhilarated by thought and motion.

My mind was crawling with it all. I had to save Jamila from the man who loved Arthur Conan Doyle. She might have to run away from home, but where could she go? Most of her friends from school lived with their parents, and most of them were poor; they couldn't have Jamila with them. She definitely couldn't stay with us: Dad would get in shit with Anwar. Who could I discuss it with? The only person I knew who'd be helpful and objective and on my side was Eva. But I wasn't supposed to like her because her love for my father was buggering up our entire family. Yet she was the only sane grown-up I knew now that I could cross Anwar and Jeeta off my list of normals.

It was certainly bizarre, Uncle Anwar behaving like a Muslim. I'd never known him believe in anything before, so it was an amazing novelty to find him literally staking his life on the principle of absolute patriarchal authority. Through her mother's staunch and indulgent love (plus the fibbing extravagances of her wonderful imagination), but mainly because of Anwar's indifference, Jamila had got away with things some of her white counterparts wouldn't dream of. There had been years of smoking, drinking, sexual intercourse and dances, helped by there being a fire escape outside her bedroom and the fact her parents were always so exhausted they slept like mummies.

Maybe there were similarities between what was happening to Dad, with his discovery of Eastern philosophy, and Anwar's last stand. Perhaps it was the immigrant condition living itself out through them. For years they were both happy to live like Englishmen. Anwar even scoffed pork pies as long as Jeeta wasn't looking. (My dad never touched the pig, though I was sure this was conditioning rather than religious scruple, just as I wouldn't eat horse's scrotum. But once, to test this, when I offered him a smoky bacon crisp and said, as he crunched greedily into it, 'I didn't know you liked smoky bacon,' he sprinted into the bathroom and washed out his mouth with soap, screaming from his frothing lips that he would burn in hell.)

Now, as they aged and seemed settled here, Anwar and Dad appeared to be returning internally to India, or at least to be resisting the English here. It was puzzling: neither of them expressed any desire actually to see their origins again. 'India's a rotten place,' Anwar grumbled. 'Why would I want to go there again? It's filthy and hot and it's a big pain-in-the-arse to get anything done. If I went anywhere it would be to Florida and Las Vegas for gambling.' And my father was too involved with things here to consider returning.

I was working on all this as I cycled. Then I thought I saw my father. As there were so few Asians in our part of London it could hardly have been anyone else, but the person had a scarf over most of his face and looked like a nervous bank robber who couldn't find a bank. I got off my bicycle and stood there in Bromley High Street, next to the plaque that said 'H. G. Wells was born here'.

The creature with the scarf was across the road in a crowd of shoppers. They were fanatical shoppers in our suburbs. Shopping was to them what the rumba and singing is to Brazilians. Saturday afternoons, when the streets were solid with white faces, was a carnival of consumerism as goods were ripped from shelves. And every year after Christmas, when the sales were about to begin, there'd be a queue of at least twenty idiots sleeping in the winter cold outside the big stores for two days before they opened, wrapped in blankets and lying in deckchairs.

Dad normally wouldn't have been out in such madness, but there he was, this grey-haired man just over five feet tall, going into a phone-box when we had a working telephone in our hall. I could see he'd never used a public phone before. He put on his glasses and read through the instructions several times before putting a pile of coins on top of the box and dialling. When he got through and began to speak he cheered up as he laughed and talked away, before becoming depressed at the end of the call. He put the phone down, turned, and spotted me watching him.

He came out of the phone-box and I pushed my bicycle beside him through the crowds. I badly wanted to know his opinion on the Anwar business, but obviously he wasn't in the mood for it now.

'How's Eva?' I asked.

'She sends her love.'

At least he wasn't going to pretend he hadn't been talking to her.

'To me or to you, Dad?' I said.

'To you, boy. Her friend. You don't realize how fond she is of you. She admires you, she thinks – '

'Dad, Dad, please tell me. Are you in love with her?'

'Love?'

'Yes, in love. You know. For God's sake, you know.'

It seemed to surprise him, I don't know why. Maybe he was surprised that I'd guessed. Or maybe he hadn't wanted to raise the lethal notion of love in his own mind.

'Karim,' he said, 'she's become close to me. She's someone I can talk to. I like to be with her. We have the same interests, you know that.'

I didn't want to be sarcastic and aggressive, because there were certain basic things I wanted to know, but I ended up saying, 'That must be nice for you.'

He didn't appear to hear me; he was concentrating on what he was saying.

He said, 'It must be love because it hurts so much.'

'What are you going to do, then, Dad? Will you leave us and go away with her?'

There are certain looks on certain faces I don't want to see again, and this was one of them. Confusion and anguish and fear clouded his face. I was sure he hadn't thought much about any of this. It had all just happened in the random way things do. Now it surprised him that he was expected to declare the pattern and intention behind it all in order that others could understand. But there wasn't a plan, just passion and strong feeling which had ambushed him.

'I don't know.'

'What do you feel like?'

'I feel as if I'm experiencing things I've never felt before, very strong, potent, overwhelming things.'

'You mean you never loved Mum?'

He thought for a while about this. Why did he have to even think!

'Have you ever missed anyone, Karim? A girl?' We must have both been thinking of Charlie, because he added kindly, 'Or a friend?'

I nodded.

'All the time I am not with Eva I miss her. When I talk to myself in my mind, it is always her I talk to. She understands many things. I feel that if I am not with her I will be making a great mistake, missing a real opportunity. And there's something else. Something that Eva just told me.'

'Yeah?'

'She is seeing other men.'

'What sort of men, Dad?'

He shrugged. 'I didn't ask for specifications.'

'Not white men in drip-dry shirts?'

'You snob, I don't know why you dislike drip-dry shirts so much. These things are very convenient for women. But you remember that beetle Shadwell?'

'Yeah.'

'She is with him often. He is in London now, working in the theatre. He will be a big shot one day, she thinks. He knows those artistic types. She loves all that art-fart thing. They come to her

66

house for parties.' Here Dad hesitated. 'She and the beetle don't do anything together in that way, but I am afraid that he will romantically take her away. I will feel so lost, Karim, without her.'

'I've always been suspicious of Eva,' I said. 'She likes important people. She's doing it to blackmail you, I know she is.'

'Yes, and partly because she's unhappy without me. She can't wait for me for years and years. Do you blame her?'

We pushed through the throng. I saw some people from school and turned my head away so as to avoid them. I didn't want them to see me crying. 'Have you told Mum all this?' I said.

'No, no.'

'Why not?'

'Because I'm so frightened. Because she will suffer so much. Because I can't bear to look at her eyes as I say the words. Because you will all suffer so much and I would rather suffer myself than have anything happen to you.'

'So you'll be staying with Allie and me and Mum?'

He didn't reply for a couple of minutes. Even then he didn't bother with words. He grabbed me and pulled me to him and started to kiss me, on the cheeks and nose and forehead and hair. It was crazy. I nearly dropped my bike. Passers-by were startled. Someone said, 'Get back in yer rickshaw.' The day was closing in on me. I hadn't bought any tea and there was an Alan Freeman radio programme on the story of the Kinks that I wanted to listen to. I pulled away from Dad and started to run, wheeling my bike beside me.

'Wait a minute!' he shouted.

I turned. 'What, Dad?'

He looked bewildered. 'Is this the right bus stop?'

It was strange, the conversation Dad and I had, because when I saw him at home later and over the next few days he behaved as if it had never happened, as if he hadn't told me he'd fallen in love with someone else.

Every day after school I rang Jamila, and every day the reply to my question, 'How are things?' was always, 'The same, Creamy,' or, 'The same but worse.' We agreed to have a summit meeting in Bromley High Street after school, where we'd make a decision on what to do.

But that day I was leaving the school gates with a group of boys when I saw Helen. It was a surprise because I'd barely thought of her since I was fucked by her dog, an incident with which she had become associated in my mind: Helen and dog-cock went together. Now she was standing outside my school in a black floppy hat and long green coat, waiting for another boy. Spotting me, she ran over and kissed me. I was being kissed a lot lately: I needed the affection, I can tell you. Anybody could have kissed me and I'd have kissed them right back with interest.

The boys, the group I hung around with, had stinking matted hair down to their shoulders and wore decomposing school jackets, no ties, and flares. There had been some acid, some purple haze, going round the school recently, and a couple of boys were tripping. I'd had half a tab at prayers in the morning but it had worn off by now. Some of the boys were exchanging records, Traffic and the Faces. I was negotiating to buy a Jimi Hendrix record – *Axis: Bold as Love* – from a kid who needed money to go to an Emerson, Lake and Palmer concert at the Fairfield Hall, for fuck's sake. I suspected this fool was so desperate for money that he'd concealed the bumps and scratches on the disc with black shoe polish, so I was examining its surface with a magnifying glass.

One of the boys was Charlie, who'd bothered to turn up to school for the first time in weeks. He stood out from the rest of the mob with his silver hair and stacked shoes. He looked less winsome and poetic now; his face was harder, with short hair, the cheekbones more pronounced. It was Bowie's influence, I knew. Bowie, then called David Jones, had attended our school several years before, and there, in a group photograph in the dining hall, was his face. Boys were often to be found on their knees before this icon, praying to be made into pop stars and for release from a lifetime as a motor-mechanic, or a clerk in an insurance firm, or a junior architect. But apart from Charlie, none of us had high expectations; we had a combination of miserable expectations and wild hopes. Myself, I had only wild hopes.

Charlie ignored me, as he was ignoring most of his friends since he'd appeared on the front page of the *Bromley and Kentish Times* with his band, Mustn't Grumble, after an open-air gig in a local sports ground. The band had been playing together for two years, at school dances, in pubs and as support at a couple of bigger concerts, but they'd never been written about before. This sudden fame impressed and disturbed the whole school, including the teachers, who called Charlie 'Girlie'.

Charlie brightened at the sight of Helen and came over to us. I had no idea that he knew her. On tip-toe she kissed him.

'How are the rehearsals?' she asked, her hand in his hair.

'Great. And we're doing another gig soon.'

'I'll be there.'

'If you're not, we won't play,' he said. She laughed all over the place at this. I intervened. I had to get a word in.

'How's your dad, Charlie?'

He looked at me with amusement. 'Much better.' He said to Helen, 'Dad's in the head hospital. He's coming out next week and keeps saying he's going home to Eva.'

'Really?'

Eva living with her own husband again? That surprised me. It would surprise Dad too, no doubt.

'Is Eva pleased?' I said.

'As you well know, you little pouf, she nearly died. She's interested in other things now. Other people. Right? I reckon Dad'll be getting the bum's rush to his mum as soon as he steps in our door. And that'll be that between them.'

'Oh God.'

'Yeah, but I don't like him too much anyway. He's sadistic. There'll be room in our house for someone else. Everything in our lives is going to change pretty soon. I love your old man, Creamy. He inspires me.'

I was flattered to hear this. I was about to say, If Eva and Dad get married you'll be my brother and we'll have committed incest, but I managed to shut my trap. Still, the thought gave me quite a jolt of pleasure. It meant I'd be connected to Charlie for years and years, long after we left school. I wanted to encourage Dad and Eva to get together. Surely it was up to Mum to get on her feet again? Maybe she'd even find someone else, though I doubted it.

Suddenly the suburban street outside the school was blasted by an explosion louder than anything heard there since the Luftwaffe bombed it in 1944. Windows opened; grocers ran to the doors of their shops; customers stopped discussing bacon and turned; our teachers wobbled on their bicycles as the noise buffeted them like a violent squall; and boys sprinted to the school gates as they came out of the building, though many others, cool boys, shrugged or turned away in disgust, gobbing, cursing and scuffling their feet.

The pink Vauxhall Viva had quadrophonic speakers from which roared the Byrds's 'Eight Miles High'. In the back were two girls, driven by Charlie's manager, the Fish, a tall, straight-backed and handsome ex-public school boy whose father was rumoured to be a Navy admiral. They said his mother was a Lady. The Fish had short hair and wore uninspired clothes, like a white shirt, crumpled suit and tennis shoes. He made no concessions to fashion, yet somehow he was hip and cool. Nothing confused that boy. And this enigma was all of nineteen, not much older than us, but he was posh, not common like us, and we considered him to be superior, just the right boy to be in charge of our Charlie. Almost every afternoon when Charlie was at school he turned up to take him to the studio to rehearse with his band.

'Want a lift anywhere?' Charlie shouted to Helen.

'Not today! See you!'

Charlie strolled to the car. The closer he got the more agitated the two girls became, as if he'd sent a wind on before him which made them flutter. When he climbed in beside the Fish they leaned forward and kissed him enthusiastically. He was rearranging his hair in the rear-view mirror as the monster moved out into the traffic, scattering small boys who'd gathered at the front of the car to try and open the bonnet, for God's sake, and examine the engine. The crowd dispersed quickly as the vision floated away. 'Wanker,' boys said despondently, devastated by the beauty of the event. 'Fucking wanker.' We were going home to our mothers, to our rissoles and chips and tomato sauce, to learn French words, to pack our football gear for tomorrow. But Charlie would be with musicians. He'd go to clubs at one in the morning. He'd meet Andrew Loog Oldham.

But at least for now I was with Helen.

'I'm sorry about what happened when you came to the house,' she said. 'He's usually so friendly.'

'Fathers can get moody and everything.'

'No, I mean the dog. I don't approve of people being used just for their bodies, do you?'

'Look,' I said, turning sharply on her and utilizing advice I'd been given by Charlie about the treatment of women: Keep 'em keen, treat 'em mean. 'I've got to walk to the bus stop. I don't want to stand here all afternoon being laughed at like a cunt. Where is the person you're waiting for?'

'It's you, silly.'

'You came to see me?'

'Yes. D'you have anything to do this afternoon?'

'No, 'course not.'

'Be with me, then?'

'Yeah, great.'

She took my arm and we walked on together past the schoolboy eyes. She said she was going to run away from school and go to live in San Francisco. She'd had enough of the pettiness of living with parents and the irrelevance of school was smothering her head. All over the Western world there were liberation movements and alternative life-styles – there had never been a kids' crusade like it – and Hairy Back wouldn't let her stay out after eleven. I said the kids' crusade was curdling now, everyone had overdosed, but she wouldn't listen. Not that I blamed her. By the time we had heard of anything you could be sure it was over. But I hated the idea of her going away, mainly because I hated the idea of staying behind. Charlie was doing big things, Helen was preparing her escape, but what was I up to? How would I get away?

I looked up and saw Jamila hurrying towards me in black T-shirt and white shorts. I'd forgotten that I'd agreed to meet her. She ran the last few yards and was breathing heavily, but more out of anxiety than exhaustion. I introduced her to Helen. Jamila barely glanced at her but Helen kept her arm in mine.

'Anwar's getting worse and worse,' Jamila said. 'He's going the whole way.'

'D'you want me to leave you two together?' Helen asked.

I quickly said no and asked Jammie if I could tell Helen what was happening.

'Yes, if you want to expose our culture as being ridiculous and our people as old-fashioned, extreme and narrow-minded.'

So I told Helen about the hunger-strike. Jamila butted in to add details and keep us up to date. Anwar hadn't compromised in the slightest, not nibbling a biscuit or sipping a glass of water or smoking a single cigarette. Either Jamila obeyed or he would die

71

painfully, his organs failing one by one. And if they took him to hospital he'd just do the same thing again and again, until his family gave in.

It was starting to rain, so the three of us sat in a bus shelter. There was never anywhere to go. Helen was patient and attentive, holding my hand to calm me. Jamila said, 'What I've agreed with myself is that it's going to be tonight, at midnight, when I decide what to do. I can't carry on with this indecision.'

Every time we talked about Jamila running away from home, where she could go and how we could get money to help her survive, she said, 'What about my mother?' Anwar would blame Jeeta for everything Jamila did. Jeeta's life would be living death and there was nowhere she could escape to. I had the brilliant idea that both Jamila and Jeeta should run away together, but Jeeta would never leave Anwar: Indian wives weren't like that. We went round and round until Helen had a brain-wave.

'We'll go and ask your father,' she said. 'He's a wise man, he's spiritual and – '

'He's a complete phoney,' said Jamila.

'Let's at least try it,' Helen replied.

So off we went to my house.

In the living room, with her almost translucent white legs sticking out of her dressing-gown, Mum was drawing. She closed her sketch-book quickly and slipped it behind her chair. I could see she was tired from her day in the shoe shop. I always wanted to ask her about it but could never bring myself to say something as ridiculous as, 'How was your day?' Consequently she never discussed her work with anyone. Jamila sat down on a stool and stared into space as if happy to leave the subject of her father's suicide to others.

Helen didn't help herself or increase the possibility of peace on earth by saying she'd been at Dad's Chislehurst gig.

'I didn't see it,' said Mum.

'Oh, what a shame. It was profound.' Mum looked self-pitying but Helen went on. 'It was liberating. It made me want to go and live in San Francisco.'

'That man makes me want to go and live in San Francisco,' said Mum.

'But then, I expect you've learned everything he has to teach. Are you a Buddhist?'

72

It seemed pretty incongruous, the conversation between Mum and Helen. They were talking about Buddhism in Chislehurst, against a background of mind-expansion, freedom and festivals. But for Mum the Second World War was still present in our streets, the streets where she'd been brought up. She often told me of the nightly air-raids, her parents worn out from fire-watching, houses in the familiar streets suddenly plunged into dust, people suddenly gone, news of sons lost at the Front. What grasp of evil or the possibilities of human destruction could we have? All I materially knew of the war was the thick squat block of the air-raid shelter at the end of the garden which as a child I took over as my own little house. Even then it contained its rows of jam-jars and rotten bunk-beds from 1943.

'It's simple for us to speak of love,' I said to Helen. 'What about the war?'

Jamila stood up irritably. 'Why are we discussing the war, Karim?'

'It's important, it's – '

'You idiot. Please – ' And she looked imploringly at Mum. 'We came here for a purpose. Why are you making me wait like this? Let's get on with the consultation.'

Mum said, indicating the adjoining wall, 'With him?'

Jamila nodded and bit her fingernails. Mum laughed bitterly.

'He can't even sort himself out.'

'It was Karim's idea,' Jamila said, and swept out of the room.

'Don't make me laugh,' Mum said to me. 'Why are you doing this to her? Why don't you do something useful like clearing out the kitchen? Why don't you go and read a school book? Why don't you do something that will get you somewhere, Karim?'

'Don't get hysterical,' I said to Mum.

'Why not?' she replied.

When we went into his room, God was lying on his bed listening to music on the radio. He looked approvingly at Helen and winked at me. He liked her; but then, he was keen for me to go out with anyone, as long as they were not boys or Indians. 'Why go out with these Muslims?' he said once, when I brought a Pakistani friend of Jamila's home with me. 'Why not?' I asked. 'Too many problems,' he said imperiously. 'What problems?' I asked. He wasn't good at being specific; he shook his head as if to say there were so many problems he didn't know where to begin. But he added, for the sake of argument, 'Dowries and all.'

'Anwar is my oldest friend in the world,' he said sadly when we told him everything. 'We old Indians come to like this England less and less and we return to an imagined India.'

Helen took Dad's hand and patted it comfortingly.

'But this is your home,' she said. 'We like you being here. You benefit our country with your traditions.'

Jamila raised her eyes to heaven. Helen was driving her to suicide, I could see that. Helen just made me laugh but this was sober business.

I said, 'Won't you go and see him?'

'He wouldn't listen to Gandhi himself,' Jamila said.

'All right,' said Dad. 'You come back in ninety-five minutes, during which time I will have meditated. I'll give you my answer at the end of this thought.'

'Great!'

So the three of us left the cul-de-sac which was Victoria Road. We walked through the gloomy, echoing streets to the pub, past turdy parks, past the Victorian school with outside toilets, past the numerous bomb-sites which were our true playgrounds and sexual schools, and past the neat gardens and scores of front rooms containing familiar strangers and televisions shining like dying lights. Eva always called our area 'the higher depths'. It was so quiet none of us wanted to hear the sound of our own embarrassing voices.

Here lived Mr Whitman, the policeman, and his young wife, Noleen; next door were a retired couple, Mr and Mrs Holub. They were socialists in exile from Czechoslovakia, and unknown to them their son crept out of the house in his pyjamas every Friday and Saturday night to hear uncouth music. Opposite them were another retired couple, a teacher and his wife, the Gothards. An East End family of birdseed dealers, the Lovelaces, were next to them – old Grandma Lovelace was a toilet attendant in the Library Gardens. Further up the street lived a Fleet Street reporter, Mr Nokes, his wife and their overweight kids, with the Scoffields – Mrs Scoffield was an architect – next door to them.

All of the houses had been 'done up'. One had a new porch, another double-glazing, 'Georgian' windows or a new door with brass fittings. Kitchens had been extended, lofts converted, walls removed, garages inserted. This was the English passion, not for self-improvement or culture or wit, but for DIY, Do It Yourself, for bigger and better houses with more mod cons, the painstaking accumulation of comfort and, with it, status – the concrete display of earned cash. Display was the game. How many times on a visit to families in the neighbourhood, before being offered a cup of tea, had we been taken around a house – 'The grand tour again,' sighed Dad – to admire knocked-through rooms, cunning cupboards and bunk-beds, showers, coal bunkers and greenhouses.

In the pub, the Chatterton Arms, sat ageing Teddy Boys in drape coats, with solid sculpted quiffs like ships' prows. There were a few vicious Rockers too, in studded leather and chains, discussing gang-bangs, their favourite occupation. And there were a couple of skinheads with their girls, in brogues, Levi's, Crombies and braces. A lot of them I recognized from school: they were in the pub every night, with their dads, and would be there for ever, never going away. They were a little startled to see two hippies and a Paki walk in; there was some conversation on the subject and several glances in our direction, so I made sure we didn't eyeball them and give them reason to get upset. All the same, I was nervous they might jump on us when we left.

Jamila said nothing and Helen was eager to talk about Charlie, a subject on which she was obviously preparing for an advanced degree. Jamila wasn't even contemptuous, as she abstractedly poured pints of bitter into herself. She'd met Charlie a couple of times at our house and wasn't thrilled by him, to say the least. 'Vanity, thy name is Charlie', was her conclusion. Charlie made no effort with her. Why should he? Jamila was no use to him and he didn't want to fuck her. Jamila saw right through old Charlie: she said there was iron ambition under the crushed-velvet idealism which was still the style of the age.

Helen gladly confirmed that not only was Charlie a little star at our school but he was illuminating other schools too, especially girls' schools. There were girls who followed Mustn't Grumble from gig to gig just to be near the boy, recording these concerts on reel-to-reel tape-recorders. Rare photographs of Charlie were passed around until they were in tatters. Apparently he'd been offered a record contract which the Fish had turned down, saying they weren't good enough yet. When they did get good they'd be one of the biggest bands in the world, the Fish predicted. I wondered if Charlie really knew this, felt this, or whether his life as he lived it from day to day was as fucked-up and perplexed as everyone else's.

Later that night, with Jammie and Helen behind me, I rapped on the door of Dad's room. There was no response.

'Perhaps he's still on another level,' said Helen. I looked at Jammie and wondered if she, like me, could hear Dad snoring. Obviously: because she banged loudly and impatiently on the door until Dad opened it, his hair standing on end, looking surprised to see us. We sat around his bed and he went into one of the formidable silences which I now accepted as the concomitant of wisdom.

'We live in an age of doubt and uncertainty. The old religions under which people lived for ninety-nine point nine per cent of human history have decayed or are irrelevant. Our problem is secularism. We have replaced our spiritual values and wisdom with materialism. And now everyone is wandering around asking how to live. Sometimes desperate people even turn to me.'

'Uncle, please – '

Dad raised his index finger a fraction of an inch and Jamila was reluctantly silent.

'I've decided this.'

We were all concentrating so much that I almost giggled.

'I believe happiness is only possible if you follow your feeling, your intuition, your real desires. Only unhappiness is gained by acting in accordance with duty, or obligation, or guilt, or the desire to please others. You must accept happiness when you can, not selfishly, but remembering you are a part of the world, of others, not separate from them. Should people pursue their own happiness at the expense of others? Or should they be unhappy so others can be happy? There's no one who hasn't had to confront this problem.'

He paused for breath and looked at us. I knew he was thinking of Eva as he said all this. I suddenly felt desolate and bereft, realizing he would leave us. And I didn't want him to leave, because I loved him so much.

'So, if you punish yourself through self-denial in the puritan way, in the English Christian way, there will only be resentment and more unhappiness.' Now he looked only at Jamila. 'People ask for advice all the time. They ask for advice when they should try to be more aware of what is happening.'

'Thanks a lot,' said Jamila.

It was midnight when we took her home. Her head was bowed as she went in. I asked her if she'd made her decision.

'Oh yes,' she said, starting up the stairs to the flat where her parents, her tormentors, were lying awake in separate rooms, one trying to die, the other no doubt wishing for death. The meter in the hall which regulated the lights was ticking loudly. Helen and I stared at Jamila's face in the gloom for a clue as to what she was going to do. Then she turned, was shrouded in darkness, and went up to bed.

Helen said Jamila would marry the boy. I said no, she'd turn him down. But it was impossible to tell.

Helen and I climbed into Anerley Park and lay down on our backs on the grass by the swings, and looked at the sky, and pulled our clothes down. It was a good fuck, but hurried, as Hairy Back would be getting anxious. I wondered if we were both thinking of Charlie as we did it.

CHAPTER SIX

The man walking towards England, towards our curious eyes, and towards the warm winter overcoat that I held in my hands, was not Flaubert the writer, though he had a similar grey moustache, two double chins, and not much hair. Not-Flaubert was smaller than me, about the same size as Princess Jeeta. But unlike her – and the exact shape of her body was difficult to determine because of her roomy *salwar kamiz* – Changez had a stomach that rode out before him, with a dark-red stringy knitted jumper stretched over it. The hair that God had left him was sparse, dry and vertical, as if he brushed it forward every morning. With his good hand he shoved a trolley loaded with two rotting suitcases, which were saved from instant disintegration only by thin string and fraying pyjama cord.

When Not-Flaubert spotted his name on the piece of cardboard I was holding, he simply stopped pushing the trolley, left it standing among the shoving airport crowd and walked towards Jeeta and his wife-to-be, Jamila.

Helen had agreed to help us out on this day of days, and she and I rescued the trolley and staggered around, heaving Changez's junk into the back of the big Rover. Helen wouldn't hold on to anything properly in case mosquitoes jumped out of the suitcases and gave her malaria. Not-Flaubert stood by us, not getting into the car until, sanctioned by his regal nodding approval, I finally locked the boot, ensuring his sacred suitcases were safe from dacoits and thuggees.

'Maybe he's used to servants,' I said to Helen in a loud voice, as I held the door open for him to slide in next to Jeeta and Jamila. Helen and I got in front. This was a delicious moment of revenge for me, because the Rover belonged to Helen's dad, Hairy Back. Had he known that four Pakis were resting their dark arses on his deep leather seats, ready to be driven by his daughter, who had only recently been fucked by one of them, he wouldn't have been a contented man.

The actual wedding was to be held the next day, and then

Changez and Jamila would stay at the Ritz for a couple of nights. Today there would be a small party to welcome Changez to England.

Anwar was standing anxiously at the window of Paradise Stores as the Rover turned into the street, stopping outside the library. Anwar had even changed his suit; he was wearing a late 1950s job, as opposed to the usual early 1950s number. The suit was pinned and tucked all over, for he was bony now. His nose and cheekbones protruded as never before, and he was paler than Helen, so pale that no one could possibly call him a darkie or black bastard, though they might legitimately have used the word bastard. He was weak and found it difficult to pick up his feet as he walked. He moved as if he had bags of sugar tied to his ankles. And when Changez embraced him in the street I thought I heard Anwar's bones cracking. Then he shook Changez's hand twice and pinched his cheeks. This effort seemed to tire Anwar.

Anwar had been extraordinarily exuberant about Changez's arrival. Perhaps it was something to do with his not having a son and now having gained one; or perhaps he was pleased about his victory over the women. Whatever the extent of his self-inflicted frailty, I'd never seen him as good-tempered as he had been recently, or as nervously loquacious. Words weren't his natural medium, but these days, when I went to help out in the shop, he inevitably took me aside – blackmailing me with samosas, sherbet fountains and the opportunity not to work – for an extended ear-bashing. I'm convinced he drew me aside, away from Jeeta and Jamila, into the store-room, where we sat on wooden boxes like skiving factory workers, because he was ashamed, or at least bashful, about his unsweet victory. Recently Princess Jeeta and Jamila had been in funereal moods, not for a second allowing Anwar to enjoy the pleasure of his tyranny. So all he could do, poor bastard, was celebrate it with me. Would they never understand the fruits of his wisdom?

'Things are really going to change round here with another man about the place,' he told me jubilantly. 'The shop needs decorating. I want some boy who can climb a ladder! Plus I need someone to carry boxes from the wholesaler. When Changez arrives he can run the shop with Jamila. I can take that woman' – he meant his wife – 'out somewhere beautiful.'

'Where beautiful will you take her, Uncle, to the opera? I heard there's a good production of *Rigoletto* on at the moment.'

'To an Indian restaurant that a friend of mine owns.'

'And where else beautiful?'

'To the zoo, dammit! Any place she wants to go!' Anwar became sentimental, as unfeeling people often do. 'She has worked so hard all her life. She deserves a little break. She has given us all so much love. So much love. If only the women could grasp my points of view. They will begin to understand only when the boy gets here. Then they will see, eh?'

I also learned in the store-room-of-secrets that Anwar was looking forward to having grandchildren. According to Anwar, Jamila would become pregnant immediately, and soon there'd be little Anwars running all over the place. Anwar would attend to the kids' cultural upbringing and take them to school and mosque while Changez was, presumably, redecorating the shop, moving boxes and impregnating my girlfriend Jamila again. As Anwar and I had these conversations Jamila liked to open the door to the store-room and just point the black barrel-ends of her eyes at me as if I were sitting with Eichmann.

Upstairs in the flat, Jeeta and Jamila had prepared a steaming, delicious feast of keema and aloo and all, and rice, chapatis and nan. There was Tizer and cream soda and beer and lassi to drink, all of it laid out on white tablecloths with tiny paper napkins for all of us. You wouldn't have believed from the pristine state of the scrubbed room overlooking the main road to London that a man had tried to starve himself to death in it only a few weeks before.

It was hell on earth at first, the party, with everyone awkward and self-conscious. In the silence, Uncle Anwar, Oscar Wilde himself, made three attempts to jump-start the conversation, all attempts stalling. I examined the threadbare carpet. Even Helen, who looked around at everything with great sympathetic curiosity and could usually be relied upon for cheer and irritating opinion, said nothing but 'yum-yum' twice and looked out of the window.

Changez and Jamila sat apart, and although I tried to catch them looking at each other, I can guarantee that not a single surreptitious glance was exchanged by the future bed-mates. What would Changez make of his wife when he finally looked at her? The days of tight tops and mini-skirts for women were gone. Jamila was wearing what looked like several sacks: long skirts, perhaps three, one over the other, and a long smock in faded green beneath which the flat arcs of her braless breasts were visible to the slightly interested. She had on her usual pair of National Health glasses, and on her feet a rather unrelenting pair of Dr Martens in brown, which gave the impression that she was about to take up hill-walking. She was crazy about these clothes, delighted to have found an outfit she could wear every day, wanting, like a Chinese peasant, never to have to think about what to put on. A simple idea like this, so typical of Jamila, who had little physical vanity, did seem eccentric to other people, and certainly made me laugh. The one person it didn't seem eccentric to, because he didn't notice it, was her father. He really knew little about Jamila. If someone had asked him who she voted for, what the names of her women friends were, what she liked in life, he couldn't have answered. It was as if, in some strange way, it was beneath his dignity to take an interest in her. He didn't see her. There were just certain ways in which this woman who was his daughter had to behave.

Eventually four relatives of Anwar's turned up with more drink and food, and gifts of cloth and pots. One of the men gave Jamila a wig; there was a sandalwood garland for Changez. Soon the room was noisy and busy and animated.

Anwar was getting to know Changez. He didn't seem in the least displeased with him, and smiled and nodded and touched him constantly. Some time passed before Anwar noticed that his much-anticipated son-in-law wasn't the rippling physical specimen he'd expected. They weren't speaking English, so I didn't know exactly what was said, but Anwar, after a glance, followed by a concerned closer study, followed by a little step to one side for a better angle, pointed anxiously at Changez's arm.

Changez waggled the hand a bit and laughed without self-consciousness; Anwar tried to laugh too. Changez's left arm was withered in some way, and stuck on the end of the attenuated limb was a lump of hard flesh the size of a golf ball, a small fist, with only a tiny thumb projecting from the solid mass where there should have been nimble, shop-painting, box-carrying fingers. It looked as if Changez had stuck his hand into a fire and had had flesh, bone and sinew melted together. Though I knew a remarkable plumber with only a stump for a hand who worked for Uncle Ted, I couldn't see Changez decorating Anwar's shop with one arm. In fact, had he four Mohammed Ali arms I doubted if he'd know what to do with a paintbrush, or with a toothbrush for that matter.

If Anwar now perhaps had reason for entertaining minor reservations about Changez (though Changez seemed delighted by Anwar, and laughed at everything he said even when it was serious), this could be nothing compared to Jamila's antipathy. Did Changez have any idea of the reluctance with which his bride-to-be, now moving across to her bookshelf, picking up a book by Kate Millett, staring into it for a few minutes and replacing it after a reproachful and pitying glance from her mother, would be exchanging vows with him?

Jamila had phoned me the day after Helen and I fucked in Anerley Park to tell me of her decision. That morning I was so ecstatic about my triumph in seducing the dog-owner's daughter that I'd completely forgotten about Jamila's big decision. She sounded distant and cold as she told me she would marry the man her father had selected from millions, and that was the end of it. She would survive, she said. Not one more word on the subject would she tolerate.

I kept thinking to myself, Typical Jamila, that's exactly what she would do, as if this were something that happened every day. But she was marrying Changez out of perversity, I was sure of it. We lived in rebellious and unconventional times, after all. And Jamila was interested in anarchists and situationists and Weathermen, and cut all that stuff out of the papers and showed it to me. Marrying Changez would be, in her mind, a rebellion against rebellion, creative novelty itself. Everything in her life would be disrupted, experimented with. She claimed to be doing it only for Jeeta, but there was real, wilful contrariness in it, I suspected.

I sat next to Changez when we started to eat. Helen watched from across the room, unable to eat, virtually retching at the sight of Changez balancing a plate on his knee, garland trailing in his dal, as he ate with his good hand, nimbly using the fingers he had. Maybe he'd never used a knife and fork. Of course, Jamila would be entertained by that. She'd crow all over the place to her friends, 'Do you know my husband has never been in contact with cutlery before?'

But Changez looked so alone – and close up I could see bits of

82

bristle sticking out of his badly shaved face – that even I couldn't laugh at him in my usual way. And he spoke to me so kindly, and with such innocent enthusiasm, that I felt like saying to Jamila, Hey, he's not so bad!

'Will you take me on the road here to see one or two things that I might like to see?'

'Sure, whenever you like,' I replied.

'I also like to watch cricket. We can go perhaps to Lords. I have brought my own binoculars.'

'Excellent.'

'And visit bookshops? I hear there are many establishments in the Charing Cross Road.'

'Yes. What do you like to read?'

'The classics,' he said firmly. I saw that he had a pompous side to him, so certain he seemed in taste and judgement. 'You like classics too?'

'You don't mean that Greek shit? Virgil or Dante or Homo or something?'

'P. G. Wodehouse and Conan Doyle for me! Can you take me to Sherlock Holmes's house in Baker Street? I also like the Saint and Mickey Spillane. And Westerns! Anything with Randolph Scott in it! Or Gary Cooper! Or John Wayne!'

I said, to test him, 'There's lots of things we can do. And we can take Jamila with us.'

Without glancing at her, but filling his mouth with rice and peas until his cheeks bulged – he really was a greedy gobbler – he said, 'That would be much fun.'

'So you two pricks are big mates now,' Jamila hissed at me later. Anwar had reclaimed Changez and was patiently explaining to him about the shop, the wholesaler and the financial position. Changez stood there looking out of the window and scratching his arse, completely ignoring his father-in-law, who had no choice but to carry on with his explanation. As Anwar was talking Changez turned to him and said, 'I thought it would be much more freezing in England than this.'

Anwar was bewildered and irritated by this *non sequitur*.

'But I was speaking about the price of vegetables,' said Anwar.

'What for?' asked Changez in bewilderment. 'I am mainly a meat-eater.'

Anwar said nothing to this, but dismay, confusion and anger passed over his face. And he glanced down at Changez's duff hand again as if to reconfirm that his brother had really sent over a cripple as a husband for his only daughter.

'Changez seems all right to me,' I told Jamila. 'Likes books. Doesn't seem an overwhelming-sexual-urges type.'

'How do you know, clever dick? Why don't you marry him, then? You like men, after all.'

'Because you wanted to marry him.'

'I don't "want" anything but to live my life in peace.'

'You made your choice, Jammie.'

She was furious with me.

'Ah, pah! Whatever happens I'll be relying on you for support and concern.'

Thank God, I thought, as just then Dad turned up at the party. He'd come straight from work, and he wore his best bespoke Burton's suit, a yellow waistcoat with a watch on a chain (a present from Mum), and a striped tie in pink and blue with a knot as fat as a bar of soap. He looked like a budgerigar. Dad's hair was shining too, as he liked to put olive oil on it, convinced that this lubrication of the scalp banished baldness. Unfortunately, if you got too close to him you were tempted to look around for the source of the odour – perhaps there was an overdressed salad in the vicinity? But lately he'd been concealing this whiff with his favourite aftershave, Rampage. Dad was plumper than he'd ever been. He was turning into a porky little Buddha, but compared to everyone else in the room he was life itself, vibrant, irreverent and laughing. Beside him, Anwar had become an old man. Dad was also being magnanimous today; he reminded me of a smooth politician visiting a shabby constituency, smiling, kissing babies, shaking hands with relish – and departing as soon as he decently could.

Helen kept saying, 'Take me away from here, Karim,' and really getting on my nerves, so soon Dad and Helen and I went downstairs.

'What's going on?' I asked Helen. 'What are you so fed up about?'

'One of Anwar's relatives was behaving weirdly towards me,' she said.

Apparently, whenever she'd gone close to this man he'd shooed her away, recoiling from her and muttering, 'Pork, pork, pork, VD,

VD, white woman, white woman.' Apart from this, she was angry with Jamila for marrying Changez, the sight of whom made her feel ill. I told her to go to San Francisco.

Downstairs in the shop Anwar was now showing Changez around. As Anwar pointed and explained and waved at tins and packets and bottles and brushes, Changez nodded like a bright but naughty schoolboy humouring the eager curator of a museum but taking nothing in. Changez didn't seem ready to take over the running of Paradise Stores. Spotting me leaving, he hurried over and took my hand.

'Remember, bookshops, bookshops!'

He was sweating, and the way he held on to me indicated that he didn't want to be left alone.

'And please,' he said, 'call me by my nickname – Bubble.'

'Bubble?'

'Bubble. Yes, and yours?'

'Creamy.'

'Goodbye, Creamy.'

'Goodbye, Bubble.'

Outside, Helen had the Rover roaring and the radio on. I heard my favourite lines from *Abbey Road*: 'Soon we'll be away from here, step on the gas and wipe that tear away.' To my surprise Eva's car was also parked outside the library. And Dad was holding the door open. He was buoyant today, but also edgy and more authoritative than I'd seen him for ages, when mostly he'd been gloomy and sulky. It was as if he'd made up his mind about something yet was not sure if it was the right thing to do. So instead of being relaxed and content, he was tenser and less tolerant than ever.

'Get in,' he said, pointing to the back seat of Eva's car.

'What for? Where are we going?'

'Just get in. I'm your dad, aren't I? Haven't I always taken care of you?'

'No. And it's like I'm being taken prisoner. I said I'd be with Helen this evening.'

'But don't you want to be with Eva? You like Eva. And Charlie's waiting at home. He really wants to discuss one or two things with you.'

Eva smiled at me from the driver's seat. 'Kiss, kiss,' she said. I

85

knew I was going to be deceived. They're so stupid, grown-ups, thinking you can't see through every fucking thing they do.

I went to Helen and told her that something heavy was happening, I wasn't sure what it was, but I had to leave her now. She kissed me and drove away. All day I'd felt calm, though aware that everything in Jamila's life had changed; and now, on the same day, if I was right about the looks on the two faces in the car with me, the same thing was going to happen to me. I waved at Helen's car, I don't know why. But I never saw her again. I liked her, we were starting to go out, then all this happened and I never saw her again.

Sitting behind Eva and Dad in the car, watching their hands constantly fluttering towards each other, you didn't have to be a genius to see they were a couple. Here before me were two people in love, oh yes. And as Eva drove, Dad didn't take his eyes from her face.

This woman I barely knew, Eva, had stolen my father. But what did I really think of her? I hadn't even looked at her properly.

This new part of my life wasn't a woman who would seem attractive straight-on in a passport photograph. She had no conventional beauty, her features were not exquisitely proportioned and her face was a bit chubby. But she was lovely because the round face with the straight dyed-blonde hair, which fell over her forehead and into her eyes, was open. Her face was constantly in motion, and this was the source of her beauty. Her face registered the slightest feeling, concealing little. Sometimes she became childlike and you could see her at eight or seventeen or twenty-five. The different ages of her life seemed to exist simultaneously, as if she could move from age to age according to how she felt. There was no cold maturity about her, thank Christ. She could be pretty serious and honest, though, explaining hurt and pain as if we were all openly human like her, and not screwed-up and secretive and tricky. That time she'd told me how lonely and abandoned she felt when she was with her husband, those confessional words, 'lonely and abandoned', which usually would have me cringing all over the place, made me shiver.

When she was ecstatic, and she was often ecstatic, ecstasy flew from her face like the sun from a mirror. She was living outwardly, towards you, and her face was always watchable because she was rarely bored or dull. She didn't let the world bore her. And she was some talker, old Eva.

Her talk wasn't vague approbation or disapproval, some big show of emotion. I didn't say that. There were facts, solid and chewable as bread, in this feeling. She'd explained to me the origin of the Paisley pattern; I had the history of Notting Hill Gate, the use of a camera obscura by Vermeer, why Charles Lamb's sister murdered their mother, and a history of Tamla Motown. I loved this stuff; I wrote it down. Eva was unfolding the world for me. It was through her that I became interested in life.

Dad, I reckon, was slightly intimidated by her. Eva was cleverer than he was, and more capable of feeling. He hadn't encountered this much passion in a woman before. It was part of what made him want and love Eva. Yet this love, so compelling, so fascinating as it grew despite everything, had been leading to destruction.

I could see the erosion in the foundations of our family every day. Every day when Dad came home from work he went into the bedroom and didn't come out. Recently he'd encouraged Allie and me to talk to him. We sat in there with him and told him about school. I suspected he liked these ink-stained accounts because, while our voices filled the room like smoke, he could lie back concealed in its swathes and think of Eva. Or we sat with Mum and watched television, braving her constant irritation and sighs of self-pity. And all the time, like pipes dripping, weakening and preparing to burst in the attic, around the house hearts were slowly breaking while nothing was being said.

In some ways it was worse for little Allie, as he had no facts about anything. For him the house was filled with suffering and fluffed attempts to pretend that suffering didn't exist. But no one talked to him. No one said, Mum and Dad are unhappy together. He must have been more confused than any of us; or perhaps his ignorance prevented him from grasping just how bad things were. Whatever was happening at this time, we were all isolated from each other.

When we arrived at her house, Eva put her hand on my shoulder and told me to go upstairs to Charlie. 'Because I know that's what you want to do. Then come down. We have to discuss something important.'

As I went upstairs I thought how much I hated being shoved

around all over the place. Do this, do that, go here, go there. I would be leaving home pretty soon, I knew that. Why couldn't they get down to the important stuff right away? At the top of the stairs I turned for a moment and found out. Eva and my father were going into the front room, hand-in-hand, and they were reaching for each other low down, and clutching, tongues out, pressed against each other even before they'd got through the door. I heard it lock behind them. They couldn't even wait half an hour.

I poked my head through Charlie's trap-door. The place had changed a lot since last time. Charlie's poetry books, his sketches, his cowboy boots, were flung about. The cupboards and drawers were open as if he were packing. He was leaving and altering. For a start he'd given up being a hippie, which must have been a relief to the Fish, not only professionally but because it meant the Fish could play Charlie soul records – Otis Redding and all – the only music he liked. Now the Fish was sprawled in a black steel armchair, laughing as Charlie talked and walked up and down, pouting and playing with his hair. As Charlie paced, he picked up an old pair of frayed jeans or a wide-collared shirt with pink flowers on it, or a Barclay James Harvest album, and tossed it out of the skylight and into the garden below.

'It's ridiculous the way people are appointed to jobs,' Charlie was saying. 'Surely it should happen at random? People in the street must be approached and told that they are now editor of *The Times* for a month. Or that they are to be judges, or police commissioners, or toilet attendants. It has to be arbitrary. There can be no connection between the appointment and the person unless it is their utter unsuitability for the position. Don't you agree?'

'Without exception?' enquired the Fish, languidly.

'No. There are people who should be excluded from high position. These are people who run for buses and put their hands in their pockets to ensure their change doesn't jump out. There are other people who have sun-tans that leave white patches on their arms. These people should be excluded, because they'll be punished in special camps.'

Charlie then said to me, though I thought he hadn't noticed me, 'I'll just be down,' as if I'd announced that his taxi was waiting.

I must have looked wounded, because Charlie broke a little.

'Hey, little one,' he said. 'Come here. We might as well be mates. From what I hear we'll be seeing a lot of each other.'

So I clambered up through the hole and went to him. He bent forward to put his arms around me. He held me fondly, but it was a characteristic gesture, just as he was always telling people he loved them, using the same tone of voice with each of them. I wanted to smash through all that crap.

I reached round and got a good handful of his arse. There was plenty of it, too, and just perky enough for me. When, as predicted, he jumped in surprise, I whipped my hand through his legs, giving his whole beanbag a good tug. He was laughing and wincing even as he threw me across the room into his drum-kit.

I lay there, half crying and pretending not to be hurt, as Charlie continued to pace, flinging flowered clothes into the street below and discussing the possibility of a police force being set up to arrest and imprison rock guitarists who bent their knees while they played.

A few minutes later, downstairs, Eva was next to me on the sofa, bathing my forehead and whispering, 'You silly boys, you silly boys.' Charlie sat sheepishly opposite me and God was getting cranky next to him. Eva's shoes were off and Dad had removed his jacket and tie. He'd planned this summit carefully, and now the Zen of the entire thing had gone crazy, because just as Dad opened his mouth to start talking blood had started to drip into my lap from my nose as a result of Charlie chucking me into his drum-kit.

Dad started off in statesman-like fashion, as if he were addressing the United Nations, earnestly saying he'd come to love Eva over the time he'd known her and so on. But soon he took off from the earthly tediousness of the concrete for a glide in purer air. 'We cling to the past,' he said, 'to the old, because we are afraid. I've been afraid of hurting Eva, of hurting Margaret, and most of hurting myself.' This stuff was really getting on my nerves. 'Our lives become stale, they become set. We are afraid of the new, of anything that might make us grow or change.' All this was making my muscles feel slack and unused, and I wanted to sprint up the street just to feel myself alive again. 'But that is living death, not life, that is – '

This was enough for me. I interrupted. 'D'you ever think how boring all this stuff is?'

There was silence in the room, and concern. Fuck it. 'It's all vague and meaningless, Dad. Hot air, you know.' They watched me. 'How can people just talk because they like the sound of their own voices and never think of the people around them?'

'Please,' Eva begged, 'don't be so rude as to not let your father finish what he's started.'

'Right on,' Charlie said.

Dad said, and it must have cost him a lot to say so little after he'd been put down by me, 'I've decided I want to be with Eva.'

And they all turned and looked at me compassionately. 'What about us?' I asked.

'Yes, you'll be provided for financially and we'll see each other whenever you like. You love Eva and Charlie. Think, you're gaining a family.'

'And Mum? Is she gaining a family?'

Dad got up and put his jacket on. 'I'm going to speak to her right now.'

As we sat there, Dad went home to end our lives together. Eva and Charlie and I had a drink and talked about other things. I don't know what. I said I had to piss, but I ran out of the house and walked around the streets wondering what the fuck to do and trying to imagine what Dad was saying to Mum and how she was taking it. Then I got into a phone-box and made a reverse charges call to Auntie Jean, who was drunk and abusive as usual. So I just said what I intended to say and put the phone down. 'You might have to get over here, Auntie Jean. God – I mean, Dad – has decided to live with Eva.'

CHAPTER SEVEN

Life goes on tediously, nothing happens for months, and then one day everything, and I mean everything, goes fucking wild and berserk. When I got home Mum and Dad were in their bedroom together and poor little Allie was outside banging on the door like a five-year-old. I pulled him away and tried to get him upstairs in case he was traumatized for life, but he kicked me in the balls.

Almost immediately the heart-ambulance arrived: Auntie Jean and Uncle Ted. While Uncle Ted sat outside in the car Jean charged straight into the bedroom, pushing me aside as I tried to protect my parents' privacy. She shouted orders at me.

Within forty minutes Mum was ready to leave. Auntie Jean had packed for her while I packed for Allie. They assumed I'd go to Chislehurst with them, but I said I'd turn up later on my bike; I'd make my own arrangements. I knew I'd be going nowhere near them. What could be worse than moving to Chislehurst? Even for two days I wouldn't be able to bear the sight of Auntie Jean first thing in the morning, without her make-up on, her face blank as an egg, as she had prunes, kippers and cigarettes for breakfast and made me drink Typhoo tea. I knew she'd abuse Dad all day too. As it was, Allie was crying and yelling, 'Bugger off, you Buddhist bastard!' as he left with Mum and Jean.

So the three of them bundled out, their faces full of tears and fear and pain and anger and shouting. Dad yelled at them, 'Where are you all going? What are you leaving the house for? Just stay here!' but Jean just told him to shut his big gob.

The house was silent, as if no one had been there. Dad, who had been sitting on the stairs with his head in his hands, went into action. He wanted to get out too. He stuffed his shoes and ties and books into every plastic bag I could find before stopping himself, as he realized it was undignified to disfigure the house before deserting it.

'Forget it,' he said. 'Let's take nothing, eh?'

I liked that idea: it seemed aristocratic to me, just walking out empty-handed as if we were above all objects.

Eventually Dad phoned Eva to say the coast was clear. She came tentatively into the house, as warm and gentle as anything, and she took Dad out to the car. Then she asked me what I was going to do and I had to say I wanted to go with her. She didn't flinch as I expected her to. She just said, 'OK, get your things, it'll be lovely to have you. We're all going to have a terrific time together, you know that, don't you?'

So I got about twenty records, ten packets of tea, *Tropic of Cancer* and *On the Road*, and the plays of Tennessee Williams, and off I went to live with Eva. And Charlie.

That night Eva put me in her clean little spare room. Before getting into bed I went into the large bathroom beside her bedroom, where I hadn't been before. The bath was in the centre of the room, with an old-fashioned brass spigot. There were candles around the edge of it and an old aluminium bucket beside it. And on the oak shelves were rows of lipsticks and blushers, eye-make-up removers, cleansers, moisturizers, hair-sprays, creamy soaps for soft skin, sensitive skin and normal skin; soaps in exotic wrappings and pretty boxes; there were sweet-peas in a jam-jar and an egg-cup, rose-petals in Wedgwood saucers; there were bottles of perfume, cotton wool, conditioners, hair-bands, hair-slides and shampoos. It was confusing: such self-attention repelled me, and yet it represented a world of sensuality, of smell and touch, of indulgence and feeling, which aroused me like an unexpected caress as I undressed, lit the candles and got into the bath in this room of Eva's.

Later that night she came into my room in her kimono, bringing me a glass of champagne and carrying a book. I told her she looked happy and luminous, which made her look even more happy and luminous. Compliments were useful tools of the friendship trade, I told myself, but in her case it was true. She said, 'Thank you for saying that. I haven't been happy for a long time but now I think I'm going to be.'

'What's that book?' I said.

'I'm going to read to you,' she said, 'to help you appreciate the sound of good prose. And because you'll be reading to me in the next few months when I'm cooking and doing chores. You've got a good voice. Your dad said you've mentioned being an actor.'

'Yes.'

'Let's think about that, then.'

Eva sat down on the edge of the bed and read me *The Selfish Giant*, dramatizing all the characters and imitating a smug vicar at the sentimental end of the story. She didn't try overhard, she just wanted to let me know I was secure with her, that the break-up of my parents' marriage wasn't the worst thing that ever happened, and that she had enough love to cover us all. She was strong and confident now. She read for a long time, and I had the bonus of knowing my father was waiting impatiently to fuck her again on this night of nights which was really their honeymoon. I thanked her gratefully, and she said, 'But you're beautiful, and the beautiful should be given everything they want.'

'Hey, what about the ugly ones?'

'The ugly ones.' She poked her tongue out. 'It's their fault if they're ugly. They're to be blamed, not pitied.'

I laughed at this, but it made me think of where Charlie may have inherited some of his cruelty. When Eva had gone and I lay for the first time in the same house as Charlie and Eva and my father, I thought about the difference between the interesting people and the nice people. And how they can't always be identical. The interesting people you wanted to be with – their minds were unusual, you saw things freshly with them and all was not deadness and repetition. I longed to know what Eva made of things, what she thought of Jamila, say, and the marriage of Changez. I wanted her opinion. Eva could be snobby, that was obvious, but if I saw something, or heard a piece of music, or visited a place, I wouldn't be content until Eva had made me see it in a certain way. She came at things from an angle; she made connections. Then there were the nice people who weren't interesting, and you didn't want to know what they thought of anything. Like Mum, they were good and meek and deserved more love. But it was the interesting ones, like Eva with her hard, taking edge, who ended up with everything, and in bed with my father.

When Dad moved in with Eva, and Jamila and Changez moved into their flat, there were five places for me to stay: with Mum at Auntie Jean's; at our now empty house; with Dad and Eva; with Anwar and Jeeta; or with Changez and Jamila. I finally stopped going to school when Charlie did, and Eva arranged for me to go to a college where I could finish my A levels. This college seemed as if it was going to be the best thing that happened to me.

The teachers looked the same as the pupils and everyone was equal, ha, ha, though I made a fool of myself by calling the male teachers sir and females miss. It was the first time, too, that I'd been in a classroom with girls, and I got in with a bad bunch of women. The ceremony of innocence was well drowned as far as they were concerned. They laughed at me all the time, I don't know why; I suppose they thought I was immature. After all, I'd only just stopped doing my paper-round and I heard them talking about headlong stuff I never knew about before: abortions, heroin, Sylvia Plath, prostitution. These women were middle class but they'd broken away from their families. They were always touching each other; they fucked the lecturers and asked them for money for drugs. They cared little for themselves; they were in and out of hospital for drug addiction and overdoses and abortions. They tried to take care of each other and sometimes of me. They thought I was sweet and cute and pretty and everything, which I liked. I liked it all, because I was lonely for the first time in my life, and an itinerant.

I had a lot of spare time, and from leading a steady life in my bedroom with my radio, and with my parents downstairs, I now wandered among different houses and flats carrying my life-equipment in a big canvas bag and never washing my hair. I was not too unhappy, criss-crossing South London and the suburbs by bus, no one knowing where I was. Whenever someone – Mum, Dad, Ted – tried to locate me, I was always somewhere else, occasionally going to a lecture and then heading out to see Changez and Jamila.

I didn't want to be educated. It wasn't the right time of my life for concentration, it really wasn't. Dad was still convinced I was trying to be something – a lawyer, I'd told him recently, because even he knew that that doctor stuff was a wind-up. But I knew there'd have to come a time when I broke the news to him that the education system and I had split up. It would break his immigrant heart, too. But the spirit of the age among the people I knew manifested itself as general drift and idleness. We didn't want money. What for? We could get by, living off parents, friends or the State. And if we were going to be bored, and we were usually bored, rarely being self-motivated, we could at least be bored on our own terms, lying smashed on mattresses in ruined houses rather than working in the machine. I didn't want to work in a place where I couldn't wear my fur coat.

Anyway, there was plenty to observe – oh yes, I was interested in life. I was an eager witness to Eva and Dad's love, and even more fascinated by Changez and Jamila, who were, can you believe, living together in South London.

Jamila and Changez's flat, rented by Anwar, was a two-room box affair near the Catford dog track. It had minimal busted furniture, yellow walls and a gas fire. The one bedroom, which contained a double mattress covered by an Indian bedspread with swirling colours, was Jamila's room. At the end of the bed was a small card-table which Changez bought for her as a wedding present; I'd carried it back from a local junk shop. There was a Liberty-pattern tablecloth over it, and I bought Jamila a white vase in which there were always daffodils or roses. She kept her pens and pencils in a peanut-butter jar. Also on the table and piled up around her on the floor were her post-Miss Cutmore books: the 'classics' as she called them – Angela Davis, Baldwin, Malcolm X, Greer, Millett. You weren't supposed to stick anything on the walls, but Jamila had pinned up poems by Christina Rossetti, Plath, Shelley and other vegetarians, which she copied out of library books and read when she stretched her legs by taking a few steps around the tiny room. On a sticking-out piece of board nailed to the windowsill was her tape-recorder. From breakfast until the three of us cracked late-night beers, the place grooved to Aretha and the other mamas. Jamila never closed the door, so Changez and I drank and looked through at our Jamila's concentrating-so-hard profile, head bowed, as she read and sang and wrote in old school exercise books. Like me, she'd run right out on all that 'old, dull, white stuff' they taught you at school and college. But she wasn't lazy, she was educating herself. She knew what she wanted to learn and she knew where it was; she just had to shovel it all into her head. Watching Jamila sometimes made me think the world was divided into three sorts of people: those who knew what they wanted to do; those (the unhappiest) who never knew what their purpose in life was; and those who found out later on. I was in the last category, I reckoned, which didn't stop me wishing I'd been born into the first.

In the living room there were two armchairs and a table to eat takeaways off. Around it were two steel chairs with putrid white plastic on the seats. Beside it was a low camp-bed covered in brown blankets on which, from the first, Jamila insisted, Changez slept. There was no discussion of this, and Changez didn't demur at the crucial moment when something could – maybe – have been done. That was how it was going to be between them, just as she made him sleep on the floor beside their honeymoon bed in the Ritz.

While Jamila worked in her room, Changez lay joyously on the camp-bed, his good arm suspending a paperback above him, one of his 'specials', no doubt. 'This one is very extra-special,' he'd say, tossing aside yet another Spillane or James Hadley Chase or Harold Robbins. I think a lot of the big trouble which was to happen started with me giving Changez Harold Robbins to read, because it stimulated Changez in a way that Conan Doyle never did. If you think books don't change people, just look at Changez, because undreamed-of possibilities in the sex line suddenly occurred to him, a man recently married and completely celibate who saw Britain as we saw Sweden: as the goldmine of sexual opportunity.

But before all the sex trouble got properly into its swing there was all the other trouble brewing between Anwar and Changez. After all, Changez was needed in the shop even more urgently now that Anwar had so enfeebled himself on the Gandhi-diet in order to get Changez to Britain in the first place.

To start off Changez's career in the grocery business, Anwar instructed him to work on the till, where you could get by with only one arm and half a brain. And Anwar was very patient with Changez, and spoke to him like a four-year-old, which was the right thing to do. But Changez was far smarter than Anwar. He made sure he was hopeless at wrapping bread and giving change. He couldn't manage the arithmetic. There were queues at the till, until customers started walking out. Anwar suggested he come back to till-work another time. Anwar would find him something else to do to get him in the grocery mood.

So Changez's new job was to sit on a three-legged stool behind the vegetable section and watch for shop-lifters. It was elementary: you saw them stealing and you screamed, 'Put that back, you fucking thieving tom-cat!' But Anwar hadn't catered for the fact that Changez had mastered the supreme art of sleeping sitting up. Jamila told me that one day Anwar came into the shop and discovered

Changez snoring as he sat on his stool, while in front of his closed eyes an SL was shoving a jar of herrings down his trousers. Anwar blew up all over the place. He picked up a bunch of bananas and threw them at his son-in-law, hitting him so hard in the chest that Changez toppled off his stool and badly bruised his good arm. Changez lay writhing on the floor, unable to get up. Finally Princess Jeeta had to help Changez leave the shop. Anwar bellowed at Jeeta and Jamila and even yelled at me. I just laughed at Anwar, as we all did, but no one dared say the one true thing: it was all his own fault. I pitied him.

His despair became obvious. He was moody all the time, with a flashing temper, and when Changez was at home, nursing his bad arm, Anwar came to me as I worked in the store-room. He'd already lost any respect or hope he'd once had for Changez. 'What's that fucking fat useless bastard doing now?' he enquired. 'Is he better yet?' 'He's recuperating,' I said. 'I'll recuperate his fucking balls with a fucking flame-thrower!' said Uncle Anwar. 'Perhaps I will phone the National Front and give them Changez's name, eh? What a good idea, eh!'

Meanwhile Changez was getting better and better at lying on camp-beds, reading paperbacks and strolling around town with me. He was always up to any adventure that didn't involve working at tills or sitting on three-legged stools. And because he was slightly dim, or at least vulnerable and kind and easily led, being one of the few people I could mock and dominate with impunity, we became mates. He'd follow me where I fancied, as I avoided my education.

Unlike everyone else he thought me quite deviant. He was shocked when I took off my shirt in the street to get some damn sun on my tits. 'You are very daring and non-conformist, *yaar*,' he often said. 'And look how you dress, like a gypsy vagabond. What does your father say? Doesn't he discipline you very hard?'

'My father's too busy with the woman he ran off with,' I replied, 'to think about me too much.'

'Oh God, this whole country has gone sexually insane,' he said. 'Your father should go back home for some years and take you with him. Perhaps to a remote village.'

Changez's disgust at everyday things inspired me to show him South London. I wondered how long he'd take to get used to it, to become, in other words, corrupt. I was working on it. We wasted days and days dancing in the Pink Pussy Club, yawning at Fat Mattress at the Croydon Greyhound, ogling strippers on Sunday mornings in a pub, sleeping through Godard and Antonioni films, and enjoying the fighting at Millwall Football Ground, where I forced Changez to wear a bobble-hat over his face in case the lads saw he was a Paki and imagined I was one too.

Financially Changez was supported by Jamila, who paid for everything by working in the shop in the evenings. And I helped him out with money I got from Dad. Changez's brother sent him money, too, which was unusual, because it should have been the other way round as Changez made his way in the affluent West, but I was sure celebrations in India at Changez's departure were still taking place.

Jamila was soon in the felicitous position of neither liking nor disliking her husband. It amused her to think she carried on as if he weren't there. But late at night the two of them liked to play cards, and she'd ask him about India. He told her tales of run-away wives, too-small dowries, adultery among the rich of Bombay (which took many evenings) and, most delicious, political corruption. He'd obviously picked up a few tips from the paperbacks, because he spun these stories out like a kid pulling on chewing-gum. He was good at them, linking all the stories together with more gum and spit, reintroducing the characters with, 'You know that bad bad man who was caught naked in the bathing hut?', as in a wild soap opera, until he knew that at the end of her day spent sucking on dusty brain juice, her maddening mouth would inevitably say, 'Hey, Changez, husband or whatever you are, don't you know any more about that politician geezer that got thrown into jail?'

In turn he made the polite mistake of asking her what she believed socially and politically. One morning she laid the *Prison Notebooks* of Gramsci on his chest, not realizing that his addiction to paperbacks wasn't entirely undiscriminating. 'Why haven't you read this if you're so interested?' she challenged him weeks later.

'Because I prefer to hear it from your mouth.' And he did want to hear it from her mouth. He wanted to watch his wife's mouth move because it was a mouth he'd come to appreciate more and more. It was a mouth he wanted to get to know.

One day, while we were roaming around junk shops and the Paperback Exchange, Changez took my arm and forced me to face him, which was never a pleasant sight. He made himself say to me at last, after weeks of dithering like a frightened diver on a rock, 'D'you think my Jammie will ever go in bed with me? She is my wife, after all. I am suggesting no illegality. Please, you've known her all your life, what is your true and honest estimation of my chances in this respect?'

'Your wife? In bed with you?'

'Yes.'

'No chance.'

'What?'

'No way, Changez.'

He couldn't accept it. I elaborated. 'She wouldn't touch you with asbestos gloves on.'

'Why? Please be frank, as you have been until now on every other matter. Even vulgar, Karim, which is your wont.'

'You're too ugly for her.'

'Really? My face?'

'Your face. Your body. The whole lot. Yuk.'

'Yes?' At that moment I glimpsed myself in a shop window and was pleased with what I saw. I had no job, no education, and no prospects, but I looked pretty good, oh yes. 'Jamila's a quality person, you know that.'

'I would like to have children with my wife.'

I shook my head. 'Out of the question.'

This children issue was not trivial for Changez the Bubble. There had been a horrible incident recently which must have remained on his mind. Anwar asked Changez and me to wash the floor of the shop, thinking that perhaps I could successfully supervise him. Surely this couldn't go wrong? I was doing the scrubbing and Changez was miserably holding the bucket in the deserted shop and asking me if I had any more Harold Robbins novels he could borrow. Then Anwar turned up and stood there watching us work. Finally he made up his mind about something: he asked Changez about Jamila and how she was. He asked Changez if Jamila was 'expecting'.

'Expecting what?' said Changez.

'My bloody grandson!' said Anwar. Changez said nothing, but shuffled backwards, away from the fire of Anwar's blazing contempt, which was fuelled by bottomless disappointment.

'Surely,' said Anwar to me, 'surely there must be something between this donkey's legs?'

At this Changez started to explode from the centre of his vast stomach. Waves of anger jolted through him and his face seemed suddenly magnified while it flattened like a jellyfish. Even his bad arm visibly throbbed, until Bubble's whole body shuddered with fury and humiliation and incomprehension.

He shouted, 'Yes, there is more between this donkey's legs than there is between that donkey's ears!'

And he lunged at Anwar with a carrot that was lying to hand. Jeeta, who had heard everything, rushed over. Some strength or recklessness seemed to have been released in her by recent events; she had increased as Anwar had diminished. Her nose had become beaked and hawked, too. Now she placed the obstacle of her nose between Anwar and Changez so that neither could get at the other. And she gave Anwar a mouthful. I'd never heard her speak like this before. She was fearless. She could have shrivelled Gulliver with her breath. Anwar turned and went away, cursing. She sent Changez and me out.

Now Bubble, who hadn't had much time to reflect on his England-experience, was obviously starting to think over his position. Conjugal rights were being denied him; human rights were being suspended at times; unnecessary inconvenience was happening everywhere; abuse was flying around his head like a spit-shower – and he was an important man from a considerable Bombay family! What was going on? Action would be taken! But first things first. Changez was searching in his pockets for something. He eventually hoiked out a piece of paper with a phone-number on it. 'In that case – '

'In what case?'

'Of the ugliness you so helpfully mention. There is something I must do.'

Changez telephoned someone. It was very mysterious. Then I had to take him to a big detached house divided into flats. An old woman opened the door – she seemed to be expecting him – and as he went in he turned and instructed me to wait. So I stood around like a fool for twenty minutes. When he emerged I saw behind him at the door a small, black-haired, middle-aged Japanese woman in a red kimono.

'Her name is Shinko,' he told me happily as we walked back to the flat. The tail of Changez's shirt was sticking out of his unbuttoned fly like a small white flag. I decided not to inform him of this.

'A prostitute, eh?'

'Don't be not-nice! A friend now. Another friend in unfriendly cold England for me!' He looked at me with joy. 'She did business as described to the T by Harold Robbins! Karim, all my entire problems are solved! I can love my wife in the usual way and I can love Shinko in the unusual way! Lend me a pound, will you, please? I want to buy Jamila some chocolates!'

All this messing around with Changez I enjoyed, and I soon considered him part of my family, a permanent part of my life. But I had a real family to attend to – not Dad, who was preoccupied, but Mum. I rang her every day, but I hadn't seen her during the time I'd been living at Eva's; I couldn't face any of them in that house.

When I did decide to go to Chislehurst, the streets were quiet and uninhabited after South London, as if the area had been evacuated. The silence was ominous; it seemed piled up and ready to fall on me. Practically the first thing I saw when I got off the train and walked along those roads again was Hairy Back and his dog, the Great Dane. Hairy Back was smoking his pipe and laughing with a neighbour as he stood at his gate. I crossed the road and walked back to examine him. How could he stand there so innocently when he'd abused me? I suddenly felt nauseous with anger and humiliation – none of the things I'd felt at the time. I didn't know what to do. A powerful urge told me to return to the station and get on the train back to Jamila's place. So I stood there for at least five minutes, watching Hairy Back and wondering which way to go. But how could I have explained my actions to Mum, having promised to turn up and see her? I had to carry on walking.

I knew it did me good to be reminded of how much I loathed the suburbs, and that I had to continue my journey into London and a new life, ensuring I got away from people and streets like this.

Mum had taken to her bed in Jean's place on the day she left our house, and she hadn't got up since. But Ted was OK: I was looking forward to seeing him. He had completely changed, Allie told me; Ted had lost his life in order to find it. So Ted was Dad's triumph; he really was someone Dad had freed.

Uncle Ted had done absolutely nothing since the day Dad exorcized him as he sat with a record-player in his lap. Now Ted didn't have a bath or get up until eleven o'clock, when he read the paper until the pubs were open. The afternoons he spent out on long walks or in South London attending classes on meditation. In the evenings he refused to talk – this was a vow of silence – and once a week he fasted for a day. He was happy, or happier, apart from the fact that nothing in life had much meaning for him. But at least he recognized this now and was looking into it. Dad had told him to 'explore' this. Dad also told Ted that meaning could take years to emerge, but in the meantime he should live in the present, enjoy the sky, trees, flowers and the taste of good food, and perhaps fix a few things in Eva's house – maybe Dad's bedside light and tape-recorder – if he needed any practical therapy. Ted said he'd go fishing if he needed therapy. Anything too technical might catapult him into orbit again. 'When I see myself,' Ted said, 'I am lying in a hammock, just swinging, just swinging.'

Ted's whole hammock behaviour, his conversion to Ted-Buddhism, as Dad called it, incensed Auntie Jean. She wanted to cut down his swinging hammock. 'She's wild with him,' said Mum, with relish. This fight between Ted and Jean seemed to be her life's single pleasure, and who could blame her? Jean raged and argued, and even went so far as to attempt tenderness in her effort to get Ted back to ordinary but working unhappiness. After all, they now had no income. Ted used to boast, 'I've got ten men under me,' and now he had none. There was nothing under him but thin air and the abyss of bankruptcy. But Ted just smiled and said, 'This is my last chance to be happy. I can't muff it, Jeanie.' Once Auntie Jean did rip through to raw feeling by mentioning the numerous virtues of her former Tory boy, but Ted retaliated by saying (one evening during his vow of silence), 'That boy soon saw the light as far as you're concerned, didn't he?'

When I got to the house Ted was singing a pub song and he practically bundled me into a cupboard to discuss his favourite subject – Dad. 'How's yer father?' he said in a great whisper. 'Happy?' He went on dreamily, as if he were speaking of some Homeric adventure. 'He just upped and went off with that posh woman. It was incredible. I don't blame him. I envy him! We all want to do it, don't we? Just cut and run. But who does it? No one –

'cept your dad. I'd like to see him. Discuss it in detail. But it's against the law in this house to see him. You can't even talk about it.' As Auntie Jean entered the hall from the living room Ted pressed a finger to his lips. 'Don't say a word.' 'About what, Uncle?' 'About any bloody thing!'

Even today Auntie Jean was straight-backed and splendid in high heels and a dark-blue dress with a diamond brooch in the shape of a diving fish pinned to her front. Her nails were perfect little bright shells. She shone so brightly she could have been freshly painted; you were afraid that if you touched her you'd smudge something. She seemed ready to attend one of those cocktail parties where she smeared her lips on cheeks and glasses and cigarettes and napkins and biscuits and cocktail sticks until barely a foot of the room was not decorated in red. But there were no more parties in that house of the half-dead, just the old place containing one transformed and one broken person. Jean was tough and liked to drink; she would endure for a long while yet. But what would she do when she realized that, with things as they were, she was on a life sentence, not just a temporary suspension of essential pleasure?

'It's you, is it?' said Auntie Jean.

'I s'pose it is, yeah.'

'Where've you been?'

'At college. That's why I stay other places. To be near college.'

'Oh yes, I bet. Pull the other one, Karim.'

'Allie's here, isn't he?'

She turned away. 'Allie's a good boy, but he dresses up a lot, doesn't he?'

'Yeah, he was always one for the *outré*.'

'He's changing his clothes three times a day. It's girlish.'

'Very girlish.'

'I think he plucks his eyebrows too,' she said firmly.

'Well, he's hairy, Auntie Jean. That's why they all call him Coconut at school.'

'Men are supposed to be hairy, Karim. Hirsuteness is a characteristic of real men.'

'You've been a big detective lately, haven't you, Auntie Jean? Have you thought of applying for the police force?' I said, as I went upstairs. Good old Allie, I thought to myself.

I never bothered much about Allie, and most of the time I forgot I even had a brother. I didn't know him very well and I despised him for being well behaved and creeping around telling stories about me. I kept away from him so the rest of the family wouldn't find out what I was up to. But for once I was grateful he was around, both as company for Mum and as an irritant for Auntie Jean.

I'm probably not compassionate or anything, I bet I'm a real bastard inside and don't care for anyone, but I fucking hated treading up those stairs to Mum, especially with Jean at the bottom watching my every step. She probably had nothing else to do.

'If you was down here,' she said, 'I'd bloody slap you for your cheek.'

'What cheek?'

'The bloody cheek you've got inside of you. All of it.'

'Shut up, will you,' I said.

'Karim.' She nearly strangled on her own anger. 'Karim!'

'Get lost, Auntie Jean,' I said.

'Buddhist bastard,' she replied. 'Buddhists, the lot of you.'

I went in to Mum. I could hear Auntie Jean shouting at me but I couldn't make out anything she was saying.

Auntie Jean's spare room, in which Mum lay curled up in her pink nightie, her hair unbrushed, had one entire wall made of mirrored cupboards which were stuffed with old but glittering evening dresses from the perfumed days. Beside the bed were Ted's golf clubs and several pairs of dusty golfing shoes. They'd cleared nothing away for her. Allie told me on the phone that Ted fed her, coming in and saying, ' 'Ere, Marge, have a nice bit of fish with some bread and butter.' But he ended up eating it himself.

I was reluctant to kiss my mother, afraid that somehow her weakness and unhappiness would infect me. Naturally I didn't think for a minute that my life and spirit could stimulate her.

We sat for a while, saying little, until I started into a description of Changez's 'specials', his camp-bed and the bizarre spectacle of a man falling in love with his wife. But Mum soon lost interest. If other people's unhappiness couldn't cheer her up, nothing would. Her mind had turned to glass, and all life slid from its sheer aspect. I asked her to draw me.

'No, Karim, not today,' she sighed.

I went on and on at her: draw me, draw me, draw me, Mummy! I railed against her. I was pretty angry and everything. I didn't want her to give herself over to the view of life that underlay all this, the philosophy that pinned her to the shadow-corners of the world. For Mum, life was fundamentally hell. You went blind, you got raped, people forgot your birthday, Nixon got elected, your husband fled with a blonde from Beckenham, and then you got old, you couldn't walk and you died. Nothing good could come of things here below. While this view could equally have generated stoicism, in Mum's case it led to self-pity. So I was surprised when at last she started to draw me, her hand moving lightly over the page once more, her eyes flickering with some interest at last. I sat there as still as I could. When she pulled herself out of bed and went to the bathroom, instructing me not to look at the sketch, I got the chance to examine it.

'Sit still,' she moaned, when she'd returned and started again. 'I can't get your eyes right.'

How could I make her understand? Maybe I should say nothing. But I was a rationalist.

'Mum,' I said. 'You've been looking at me, your eldest son, Karim. But that picture – and it's a great picture, not too hairy – is of Dad, isn't it? That's his big nose and double chin. Those bags under his eyes are his suitcases – not mine. Mum, that's just not anything like my face.'

'Well, dear, fathers and sons come to resemble each other, don't they?' And she gave me a significant look. 'You both left me, didn't you?'

'I haven't left you,' I said. 'I'm here whenever you need me. I'm studying, that's all.'

'Yes, I know what you're studying.' It's funny how often my family were sarcastic about me and the things I was doing. She said, 'I'm all on my own. No one loves me.'

'Yes they do.'

'No, no one helps me. No one does anything to help me.'

'Mum, I love you,' I said. 'Even if I don't act like it all the time.'

'No,' she said.

I kissed her and held her and tried to get out of the house without saying goodbye to anyone. I crept downstairs and was outside and successfully making for the front gate when Ted sprinted around the side of the house and grabbed me. He must have been lurking, waiting.

'Tell yer dad we all appreciate what 'e's done. He's done a big bucketful for me!'

'All right, I'll do that,' I said, pulling away.

'Don't forget.'

'No, no.'

I almost ran back to South London, to Jamila's place. I made myself a pot of mint tea and sat silently at the living-room table. My mind was in turmoil. I tried to distract myself by concentrating on Jamila. She sat at her desk as usual, her face illuminated by the cheap reading light beside her. A big jar of purple wild flowers and eucalyptus stood on the top of a pile of library books. When you think of the people you adore there are usually moments you can choose – afternoons, whole weeks, perhaps – when they are at their best, when youth and wisdom, beauty and poise combine perfectly. And as Jamila sat there humming and reading, absorbed, with Changez's eyes also poring over her as he lay on his bed surrounded by 'specials' covered in fluff, with cricket magazines and half-eaten packets of biscuits around him, I felt this was Jamila's ultimate moment of herselfness. I, too, could have sat there like a fan watching an actress, like a lover watching his beloved, content not to be thinking about Mum and what we could do about her. Is there anything you can do about anyone?

Changez let me finish my tea; my anxiety dissipated a little. Then he looked at me.

'OK?' he said.

'OK what?'

Changez dragged his body from his camp-bed like someone trying to walk with five footballs under their arms. 'Come on.' He pulled me into the tiny kitchen.

'Listen, Karim,' he whispered. 'I must go out this afternoon.'

'Yeah?'

'Yes.'

He tried to move his pompous features significantly. Whatever he did gave me pleasure. Irritating him was one of the guaranteed delights of my life. 'Go out, then,' I said. 'There's no guard stopping you, is there?'

'Shhh. Out with my friend Shinko,' he said confidentially. 'She's taking me to the Tower of London. Then there's new positions I've been reading about, *yaar*. Pretty wild and all, with the woman on her

106

knees. The man behind. So you stay here and keep Jamila distracted.'

'Distract Jamila?' I laughed. 'Bubble, she doesn't care if you're here or not. She doesn't care where you are.'

'What?'

'Why should she, Changez?'

'OK, OK,' he said defensively, backing away. 'I see.'

I went on needling him. 'Speaking of positions, Changez, Anwar has been in the asking-after-your-health-position recently.' Fear and dismay came instantly into Changez's face. It was heaven to see. This wasn't his favourite subject. 'You look shit-scared, Changez.'

'That fucker, my father-in-law, will ruin my erection for the whole day,' he said. 'I better scoot.'

But I secured him by his stump and went on. 'I'm sick of him whining to me about you. You've got to do something about it.'

'That bastard, what does he think I am, his servant? I'm not a shopkeeper. Business isn't my best side, *yaar*, not my best. I'm the intellectual type, not one of those uneducated immigrant types who come here to slave all day and night and look dirty. Tell him to remember that.'

'OK, I'll tell him. But I warn you, he's going to write to your father and brother and tell them what a completely fat lazy arse you are, Changez. I'm telling you this with authority because he's made me typing monitor in the matter.'

He grasped my arm. Alarm tightened his features. 'For Christ's sake, no! Steal the letter if you can. Please.'

'I'll do what I can, Changez, because I love you as a brother.'

'Me too, eh?' he said affectionately.

It was hot, and I lay naked on my back with Jamila beside me on the bed. I'd opened all the windows in the flat, drenching the atmosphere in car fumes and the uproar of the unemployed arguing in the street. Jamila asked me to touch her and I rubbed her between the legs with Vaseline according to her instructions, like 'Harder' and 'More effort, please' and 'Yes, but you're making love not cleaning your teeth.' With my nose tickling her ear I asked, 'Don't you care for Changez at all?'

I think she was surprised that such a question could occur to me. 'He's sweet, Changez, it's true, the way he grunts with satisfaction as he reads, and bumbles around the place asking me if I want some keema. But I was compelled to marry him. I don't want him here. I don't see why I should care for him as well.'

'What if he loves you, Jammie?'

She sat up and looked at me. She thrust her hands at me and said passionately, 'Karim, this world is full of people needing sympathy and care, oppressed people, like our people in this racist country, who face violence every day. It is them I sympathize with, not my husband. In fact, he irritates me intensely sometimes. Fire Eater, the man's barely alive at all! It's pathetic!'

But as I painted her stomach and breasts in the little kisses I knew she loved, biting and nibbling her all over, trying to relax her, she was still pondering on Changez. She said, 'Basically he's just a parasitical, sexually frustrated man. That's what I think of him when I think of him at all.'

'Sexually frustrated? But that's where he's gone now. To see his regular whore! Shinko, she's called.'

'No! Really? Is it true?'

'Of course.'

'Tell me, tell me!'

So I told her about Changez's patron saint, Harold Robbins, about Shinko, and about the positions problem. This made us want to try numerous positions ourselves, as Shinko and Changez were no doubt doing as we spoke. Later, as we held each other, she said, 'But what about you, Karim? You're sad, aren't you?'

I was sad, it was true. How could I not be when I thought of Mum lying there in that bed day after day, completely wrecked by Dad having run off with another woman? Would she ever recover? She had great qualities, Mum, of charm and kindness and general decency, but would anyone ever appreciate them and not hurt her?

Then Jammie said, 'What are you going to do with your life now you've stopped going to college?'

'What? But I haven't stopped going. I just don't turn up for lectures that often. Let's not talk about it, it makes me depressed. What will you do now?'

She became fervent. 'Oh me, but I'm not hanging around, though it may look like it. I'm really preparing for something. I just don't know what it is yet. I just feel I have to know certain things and that one day they will be of great use to me in understanding the world.'

We made love again, and we must have been tired, because it can't have been less than two hours later that I woke up. I was shivering. Jamila was fast asleep with a sheet over her lower half. In a fog I crawled out of bed to pick up a blanket which had fallen on the floor, and as I did so I glanced through into the living room and made out, in the darkness, Changez lying on his camp-bed watching me. His face was expressionless; grave if anything, but mostly vacant. He looked as if he'd been lying there on his stomach for quite a while. I shut the bedroom door and dressed hurriedly, waking Jamila. I'd often wondered what I'd do in such a position, but it was simple. I scuttled out of the flat without looking at my friend, leaving husband and wife to each other and feeling I'd betrayed everyone – Changez, Mum and Dad, and myself.

CHAPTER EIGHT

'You do nothing,' said Dad. 'You're a bloody bum. You're destroy-ing yourself wantonly, d'you know that? It sickens my whole heart.'

'Don't shout at me, I can't stand it.'

'I've got to, boy, to get it into your thick head. How did you manage to fail all those exams? How is it possible to fail every single one?'

'It's easy. You don't show up for any of them.'

'Is that what you did?'

'Yes.'

'But why, Karim, especially as you pretended to me you were going off to take the damn exams. You left the house so full of the confidence I gave you. Now I see why,' he said bitterly. 'How could you do it?'

'Because I'm not in the right mood for studying. I'm too disturbed by all the stuff that's happening. You leaving Mum and all. It's a big deal. It affects my life.'

'Don't blame me if you've ruined your life,' he said. But his eyes filled with tears. 'Why? Why? Why? Don't interfere, Eva,' he said, as she came into the room, alarmed by our shouting. 'This boy is a complete dead loss. So what will you do, eh?'

'I want to think.'

'Think, you bloody fool! How can you think when you haven't got any brains?'

I knew this would happen; I was almost prepared for it. But this contempt was like a typhoon blowing away all my resources and possessions. I felt lower than I'd ever felt before. And then Dad ignored me. I couldn't sleep at Jamila's place any more for fear of having to face Changez. So I had to see Dad every day and have him deplore me. I don't know why he took it so fucking personally. Why did it have to bother him so much? It was as if he saw us as having one life between us. I was the second half, an extension of him, and instead of complementing him I'd thrown shit all over him.

So it was a big cheering surprise when I opened the front door of

Eva's house one day to find Uncle Ted standing there in his green overalls, a bag of tools hanging from his fist, smiling all over his chopped face. He strode into the hall and started to peer expertly at the walls and ceiling. Eva came out and greeted him as though he were an artist returning from barren exile, Rimbaud from Africa. She took his hands and they looked into each other's eyes.

Eva had heard from Dad what a poet among builders Ted was. How he'd changed and refused to go on and now was wasting his talent. This alerted Eva, and she arranged for them all to go out for supper. Later they went to a jazz club in the King's Road – Uncle Ted had never seen black walls before – where Eva slyly said to Dad, 'I think it's about time we moved to London, don't you?'

'I like the quiet of Beckenham, where no one bothers your balls,' said Dad, thinking that that was the end of the matter, as it would have been had he been talking to Mum.

But business was going on. Between jazz sets Eva made Ted an offer: come and make my house beautiful, Ted, we'll play swing records and drink margheritas at the same time. It won't be like doing a job. Ted jumped at the chance to work with Eva and Dad, partly out of nosiness – to see what freedom had made of Dad, and could perhaps make of Ted – and partly out of the returning appetite for labour. But he still had to break the news to Auntie Jean. That was the difficult bit.

Auntie Jean went into turmoil. Here was work, paid work, weeks of it, and Ted was delighted to do it. He was ready to start, except that the employer was Jean's enemy, a terrible, man-stealing, mutilated woman. Jean pondered on it for a day while we held our breath. Finally she solved the problem by agreeing to let Ted do it provided none of us told Mum and as long as Ted gave Jean a full report at the end of each day on what precisely was going on between Dad and Eva. We agreed to these conditions, and tried to think of salacious things for Ted to tell Jean.

Eva knew what she wanted: she wanted the whole house transformed, every inch of it, and she wanted energetic, industrious people around her. We got down to it immediately. With relief, I abandoned any pretence at being clever and became a mystic assistant labourer. I did the carrying and loading and smashing, Eva did the thinking, and Ted ensured her instructions were carried out. Dad fastidiously avoided the whole muck of building, once spitting an Arab curse at us: 'May you have the builders.' Ted replied with an obscurity he thought would delight Dad. 'Haroon, I'm kissing the joy as it flies,' he said, laying into a wall with a hammer.

The three of us worked together excellently, elated and playful. Eva had become eccentric: when a decision was needed Ted and I often had to wait while she retired upstairs and meditated on the exact shape of the conservatory or the dimensions of the kitchen. The way forward would emerge from her unconscious. This was not wildly different, I suppose, to what went on in a book I was reading, Edmund Gosse's *Father and Son*, in which the father would pray before any crucial decision and await God's direction.

Before lunch Eva had us traipse out into the garden, where we bent and stretched, and sat with our backs straight, and breathed through alternate nostrils before we ate our salads and fruit. Ted went in for it all with great, childlike alacrity. He took to the Cobra position as if it had been designed for him. Unlike me, he seemed to enjoy appearing foolish, thinking he had become a new, open person. Eva encouraged us to play, but she was a shrewd boss too. We laboured for her because we liked her, but she tolerated no lazy work: she was a perfectionist and she had taste, insisting on only the best materials, which was unusual in the suburbs, where Victorian or Edwardian houses were generally smashed open and stripped bare, only to be filled with chipboard and Formica.

Finally the house was painted white, every room. 'White is the only colour for a house,' Eva announced. There were polished dark wood floors and green blinds. Heavy wrought-iron black fireplaces were installed once more, to Ted's irritation, as he'd spent much of his working life tearing out fireplaces so women like my mother didn't have to get up early on freezing mornings to make up the fire on their knees.

When Auntie Jean slammed Uncle Ted's tea on the table at the end of each day – a meat pie and chips, or a nice bit of rump steak and tartar sauce (he hadn't the nerve yet to go vegetarian) – she sat opposite him with a stiff drink and demanded facts about Eva and Dad.

'So what did you tell her last night, Uncle Ted?' I'd ask him the next day as we worked. But what was there to tell? I couldn't imagine Ted contemplating the nature of Eva and Dad's taut happiness or telling of how they were always trying to pull each other's tracksuit bottoms down and playing games like seeing who could throw a lolly-stick in a bin the most times out of ten.

Perhaps he was more specific, speaking of what he usually saw when he came to work in the morning – Eva in her blue silk pyjamas and red robe shouting and laughing and giving orders to me for breakfast, and reading aloud from the papers. In the old days Mum and Dad took the *Daily Mirror*, that was all. Eva liked to sprinkle the house with about five papers and three magazines a day, skimming over *Vogue* and the *New Statesman* and the *Daily Express* before dumping the lot into the wastepaper basket beside the bed. Perhaps Ted told Jean of the walks the four of us took when Eva got tired of working; and the time Eva's feet hurt and she hailed a cab – absolute Roman decadence for Dad, Ted and me. We took a two-hour tour of South London with Eva drinking Guinness and hanging out the window cheering as we passed down the Old Kent Road, stopping beside the famous site of Dr Lal's surgery and the dance hall of love, where Mum met Dad and fell. But I doubted if Ted could say anything about all this joy and good times. It wouldn't be what Jean would want to hear. It wouldn't be of any use to her.

Obviously Ted and I weren't always around to scrutinize the intricate excitements of this new love, especially as Dad and Eva spent many evenings over the river in London proper, going to the theatre to see controversial plays, to German films or to lectures by Marxists, and to high-class parties. Eva's old friend Shadwell was starting to make his way as a theatre director, working as an assistant at the Royal Shakespeare Company, running workshops on Beckett and putting on plays by Artaud and new writers at fringe venues. Eva helped Shadwell out by designing one of these productions and making the costumes. This she loved, and it led to her, Dad and Shadwell going to dinners and parties with all kinds of (fairly) important people – not the sort we knew in the suburbs, but the real thing: people who really did write and direct plays and not just talk about it. Eva wanted to do more of this; she discussed furnishings and house decoration with the better-off ones – they were always buying new places in the country, these people, and she knew how to make herself useful.

How smart and glamorous they looked when they went off to London in the evenings, Dad in his suits and Eva with shawls and hats and expensive shoes and handbags. They glowed with happiness. And I'd walk around the empty house, or ring Mum for a chat; sometimes I'd lie on the floor in Charlie's attic and wonder what he was doing and what kind of good time he was having. Dad and Eva would come back late, and I'd get up to see them and hear, as they undressed, who'd said what to whom about the latest play, or novel, or sex-scandal. Eva would drink champagne and watch television in bed, which shocked me, and at least once a week she said she was determined to take us all to London for good. And Dad would talk about the play and say how the writer wasn't a patch on Chekhov. Chekhov was Dad's favourite all-time writer, and he always said Chekhov's plays and stories reminded him of India. I never understood this until I realized he meant that his characters' uselessness, indolence and longing were typical of the adults he knew when he was a child.

But one subject Jean and Ted must have discussed was money. It was even bothering me. We were haemorrhaging money on the house. Unlike Mum, who took scarcity for granted, Eva bought whatever she wanted. If she went into a shop and something caught her eye – a book of Matisse drawings, a record, Yin and Yang earrings, a Chinese hat – she bought it immediately. There was none of the agonizing and guilt over money we all went through. 'I deserve it,' she always said. 'I was unhappy before with my husband, and I won't be unhappy again.' Nothing would stop her. When I mentioned this profligacy to her one day as we were painting side by side, she dismissed me, saying, 'When we run out of money I'll get us some more.'

'Where from, Eva?'

'Haven't you noticed, Karim, the world's full of money! Haven't you noticed it sloshing around the country?'

'Yeah, I noticed it, Eva, but none of it's sloshing against our house.'

'When we need it I'll draw some of it over here.'

'She's right,' said Dad, somewhat magisterially, when I went to him later and told him what she'd said, trying to make him see how demented it was. 'You have to be in the correct frame of mind to draw masses of money to you.'

Coming from someone who'd obviously never been in the right frame of mind magnetically to attach anything but his salary to himself – money Anwar always referred to as 'unearned income' –

this seemed a bit rich. But love and Eva had unrolled the carpet of Dad's confidence, along which he now ebulliently danced. They made me feel conservative.

Dad started doing guru gigs again, once a week in the house, on Taoism and meditation, like before except that this time Eva insisted people paid to attend. Dad had a regular and earnest young crowd of head-bowers – students, psychologists, nurses, musicians – who adored him, some of whom rang and visited late at night in panic and fear, so dependent were they on his listening kindness. There was a waiting list to join his group. For these meetings I had to hoover the room, light the incense, greet the guests like a head waiter and serve them Indian sweets. Eva also insisted on Dad improving the service: she got him to consult esoteric library books early in the morning before work and asked him at breakfast, in a voice which must once have enquired of Charlie if he'd done his technical-drawing homework, 'And what did you learn this morning?'

Eva knew a man on the local paper, the same co-operative journalist who got Charlie on the front page of the *Bromley and Kentish Times*, and he interviewed Dad. Dad was photographed in his red waistcoat and Indian pyjamas sitting on a gold cushion. His commuter companions were impressed by this sudden fame, and Dad told me delightedly how they pointed him out to each other on Platform Two. To be recognized for some achievement in life lifted Dad immensely; before Eva he had begun to see himself as a failure and his life as a dismal thing. But the office, where he was an unelevated lazy Indian who had run away from his wife and children, there was disapproval from the clerks he worked with: there was mockery behind his back and in front of his face. On the picture in the newspaper a bubble was drawn protruding from his mouth saying, 'Dark mystery of life solved by dark charlatan – at tax-payers' expense.' Dad talked about leaving his job. Eva said he could do what he liked; she would support them both – on love, presumably.

I doubted whether Ted spoke to Auntie Jean of this, or of the other manifestations of love that filled our hours – of Eva, for example, imitating the numerous grunts, sighs, snorts and moans which punctuated Dad's conversation. Ted and I discovered her once in the ripped-out kitchen running through a symphony of his noises like a proud mother reproducing the first words of a child. Dad and Eva could discuss the most trivial things, like the nature of the people Dad met on the train, for hours, until I had to shout at them, 'What the fuck are you talking about!' They'd look at me in surprise, so enthralled had they been. I suppose it didn't matter what they said; the words themselves were a caress, an exchange of flowers and kisses. And Eva couldn't leave the house without returning and saying, 'Hey, Haroon, I found something you might like' – a book on Japanese gardens, a silk scarf, a Waterman's pen, an Ella Fitzgerald record and, once, a kite.

Watching this, I was developing my own angry theories of love. Surely love had to be something more generous than this high-spirited egotism-à-deux? In their hands love seemed a narrow-eyed, exclusive, selfish bastard, to enjoy itself at the expense of a woman who now lay in bed in Auntie Jean's house, her life unconsidered. Mum's wretchedness was the price Dad had chosen to pay for his happiness. How could he have done it?

To be fair to him, it was a wretchedness that haunted him. He and Eva argued about this: she thought him indulgent. But how could it honestly be otherwise? There were occasions when we were watching TV or just eating when waves of regret rippled across his face. Regret and guilt and pain just overwhelmed him. How badly he'd treated Mum, he told us. How much she'd given him, cared for him, loved him, and now he was sitting in Eva's house all cosy and radiant and looking forward to bed.

'I feel like a criminal,' he confessed innocently to Eva once, in a moment of forgetfulness, truth unfortunately sneaking through. 'You know, someone living happily on money he's committed grievous bodily harm to obtain.' Eva couldn't help herself crying out at him, and he couldn't see how suddenly and cruelly he'd wounded her. She was being unreasonable.

'But you don't want her! You weren't right for each other! You stultified each other. Weren't you together long enough to know that?'

'I could have done more,' he said. 'Made more effort to care. She didn't deserve to be hurt so. I don't believe in people leaving people.'

'This guilt and regret will ruin us!'

'It is part of me – '

'Please, please, clear it out of your mind.'

But how could he clear it out? It lay on him like water on a tin roof, rusting and rotting and corroding day after day. And though he was never to make such almost innocent remarks again, and though Eva and Dad continued to want to make love all the time, and I caught her giggling while she did idiotic things with him, like snipping the hair in his ears and nostrils with a huge pair of scissors, there were looks that escaped all possible policing, looks that made me think he was capable only of a corrupted happiness.

Perhaps it was in the hope of siphoning off this water that she put the beautiful white Ted-decorated house on the market as soon as it was finished. She'd decided to take Dad away. She would look for a flat in London. The suburbs were over: they were a leaving place. Perhaps Eva thought a change of location would stop him thinking about Mum. Once the three of us were in Eva's car in the High Street and Dad started to cry in the back. 'What is it?' I said. 'What's happened?'

'It was her,' he replied. 'I thought I saw your mother go into a shop. And she was alone. I don't want her to be alone.'

Dad didn't speak to Mum on the phone, and he didn't see her, knowing that this was for the best in the long run. Yet he had photographs of her in every jacket pocket, and they fell out of books at the wrong time and upset Eva; and when he asked me about Mum, Dad and I had to go into another room, away from Eva, as if we were discussing something disgraceful.

In packing up the house and moving us to London, Eva was also in pursuit of Charlie, who was only rarely around now. For him too, it was obviously true that our suburbs were a leaving place, the start of a life. After that you ratted or rotted. Charlie liked to sleep here and there, owning nothing, living nowhere permanent, screwing whoever he could; sometimes he even rehearsed and wrote songs. He lived this excess not yet in despair but in the excitement of increasing life. Occasionally I'd get up in the morning and there he'd be in the kitchen, eating furiously, as if he didn't know where his next grub was coming from, as if each day was an adventure that could end anywhere. And then he'd be gone.

Dad and Eva travelled to all Charlie's gigs, at art colleges, in pubs and at small festivals in muddy fields, Eva writhing and cheering all through them, beer in hand. Dad blinked at the back, disturbed by the noise and the crowd, the wild St Vitus dancing over young inert figures comatose in puddles of beer. He was disturbed by the grief, the stinking clothes, the bad trips, the fourteen-year-olds carted off in ambulances, the random unloving fucking and miserable escapes from family to squalid squats in Herne Hill. He'd much rather have advised a disciple – the earnest girl Fruitbat, perhaps, or her relentlessly smiling lover, Chogyam-Jones, who dressed in what looked like a Chinese carpet; their flattery was becoming necessary. But Dad accompanied Eva wherever she needed him. He was certainly enjoying life more than ever before, and when Eva finally announced that we were moving to London he admitted that it was the right thing to do.

As we packed Charlie's things in the attic, Dad and I talked about Charlie's problem: the fact was he knew the band didn't have an original sound. Their bauble was this striking singer-guitarist with exquisite cheekbones and girl's eyelashes, who was being asked to model clothes for magazines but not to play at the Albert Hall. Failure made Charlie arrogant. He developed the habit of carrying a book of poetry in his pocket, which he might open at any time for a swig of the sublime. It was an enraging affectation, worthy of an Oxford undergraduate, especially as Charlie might do it in the middle of a conversation, as he had done recently at a college gig: the Union President was talking to him when Charlie's hands reached into his side pocket, the book was extracted and opened, and the man's eyes popped in disbelief as Charlie imbibed a beakerful of the warm South.

What a confused boy he was. But from the start Eva had insisted he was talent itself, that he was beautiful and God had blown into his cock. He was Orson Welles – at least. Naturally, long knowledge of this divinity now pervaded his personality. He was proud, dismissive, elusive and selectively generous. He led others to assume that soon world-dazzling poetry would catapult from his head as it had from those of other English boys: Lennon, Jagger, Bowie. Like André Gide, who when young expected people to admire him for the books he would write in the future, Charlie came to love being appreciated in several high streets for his potential. But he earned this appreciation with his charm, which was often mistaken for ability. He could even charm himself, I reckoned.

What was this charm? How had it seduced me for so long? I would have done anything for Charlie, and was, in fact, even now sorting out twenty years' worth of his possessions. I wasn't alone in this vulnerability to him. Many others would say yes to him before he asked for anything. How did it work? I'd observed the varieties of charm. There were those who were merely ravishing, and they were the least talented. Then there were those who were powerful, but lacked other virtues. But at least power was self-created, unlike exquisite cheekbones. Further on were those who were compelling to listen to; and above them were those who could make you laugh, too. Others made you marvel at their cleverness and knowledge: this was an achievement as well as an entertainment.

Charlie had a pinch of all this; he was an all-round player. But his strength was his ability to make you marvel at yourself. The attention he gave you, when he gave you attention, was absolute. He knew how to look at you as if you were the only person who'd ever interested him. He asked about your life, and seemed to savour every moment of your conversation. He was excellent at listening, and did it without cynicism. The problem with this was that neurotics flocked to him. No one else would listen to them, but Charlie had done so once, say, and they couldn't forget him; perhaps he'd fucked them too. But Eva had to keep them away from him, saying if it was very urgent they could leave a note. And he'd escape the house by climbing over the back fence while they waited out the front all day.

After seeing it work for so long, I began to perceive Charlie's charm as a method of robbing houses by persuading the owners to invite you in and take their possessions. I was in no doubt: it was robbery; there were objects of yours he wanted. And he took them. It was false and manipulative and I admired it tremendously. I made notes on his techniques, for they worked, especially with girls.

Ultimately none of this was innocuous. No; Charlie was the cruellest and most lethal type of seducer. He extorted, not only sex, but love and loyalty, kindness and encouragement, before moving on. I too would gladly have exercised these master-skills, but there was one essential ingredient I lacked: Charlie's strong will and his massively forceful desire to possess whatever it was that took his fancy. Make no mistake, he was unusually ambitious. But he was getting nowhere and felt frustrated. He could see that it was getting late, and ultimately he was only in a rotten rock 'n' roll band called Mustn't Grumble which sounded like Hawkwind.

Charlie rarely saw his own father when he'd been a patient and sad character living with his mother. But when Charlie was staying at Eva's house he spent hours with my father, to whom he told the truth. Together they divined for Charlie's talent. Dad drew him maps to the unconscious; he suggested routes and speeds, clothing for the journey and how to sit at the wheel when approaching the dangerous interior. And for days and days, under the full moon of high expectation, Charlie laboured to wrench a fragment of beauty from his soul – in my view (and to my relief), to no avail. The songs were still shit.

It took me some time to work this out, for I still had such sympathy for Charlie that I couldn't look at him coolly. But when I had recognized his weakness – his desire to join a club called Genius – I knew I had him. If I wanted I could take some revenge on him, which would also – some puny power – be a bitter reproach to my own pointless life.

Sometimes I told Eva I wanted to be a photographer or an actor, or perhaps a journalist, preferably a foreign correspondent in a war zone, Cambodia or Belfast. I knew I hated authority and being ordered around. I liked working with Ted and Eva, and they let me come and go more or less as I wished. But my aim was to join Mustn't Grumble as a rhythm guitarist. I could play a little, after all. When I put this to Charlie he almost choked with laughter. 'But there is a job that's just right for you,' he said.

'Oh yeah, what is it?'

'Start Saturday,' he said.

And he gave me a job as Mustn't Grumble's occasional roadie. I was still a nothing, but I was in a good position to get at Charlie when the time was right.

And it was right one evening, at an art college gig where I was helping lug the gear to the van. I'd heard Dad and Eva in the bar analysing the performance as if it were Miles Davis's farewell appearance. Charlie strolled past me, his arm around a girl who had her tits hanging out, and he said, to make her laugh, 'Hurry up, Karim, you great girl's blouse, you friend of Dorothy. Bring my acid to the dressing room and don't be late.'

'But what's the hurry?' I said. 'You're not going anywhere – not as a band and not as a person.'

He looked at me uncertainly, fondling and patting his hair as usual, unsure if I was joking or not. 'What d'you mean?'

So: I had him. He'd walked right into it.

'What do I mean?'

'Yeah,' he said.

'To go somewhere you gotta be talented, Charlie. You got to have it upstairs.' I tapped my forehead. 'And on present evidence a back-door man like you hasn't got it up there. You're a looker and everything, a face, I'll concede that. But your work don't amaze me, and I need to be amazed. You know me. I need to be fucking staggered. And I'm not fucking staggered. Oh no.'

He looked at me for a while, thinking. The girl dragged at his arm. At last he said, 'I don't know about that. I'm breaking up the band anyway. What you've said isn't relevant.'

Charlie turned and walked out. The next day he disappeared again. There were no more gigs. Dad and I finished packing his things.

In bed before I went to sleep I fantasized about London and what I'd do there when the city belonged to me. There was a sound that London had. It was, I'm afraid, people in Hyde Park playing bongos with their hands; there was also the keyboard on the Doors's 'Light My Fire'. There were kids dressed in velvet cloaks who lived free lives; there were thousands of black people everywhere, so I wouldn't feel exposed; there were bookshops with racks of maga-zines printed without capital letters or the bourgeois disturbance of full stops; there were shops selling all the records you could desire; there were parties where girls and boys you didn't know took you upstairs and fucked you; there were all the drugs you could use. You see, I didn't ask much of life; this was the extent of my longing. But at least my goals were clear and I knew what I wanted. I was twenty. I was ready for anything.

PART TWO

In the City

CHAPTER NINE

The flat in West Kensington was really only three large, formerly elegant rooms, with ceilings so high that I often gaped at the room's proportions, as if I were in a derelict cathedral. But the ceiling was the most interesting part of the flat. The toilet was up the hall, with a broken window through which the wind whipped directly up your arse. The place had belonged to a Polish woman, who'd lived there as a child and then rented it to students for the past fifteen years. When she died Eva bought it as it was, furniture included. The rooms had ancient crusty mouldings and an iron-handled bell-pull for calling servants from the basement, now inhabited by Thin Lizzy's road manager, a man who had the misfortune, so Eva informed me, to have hair growing out of his shoulders. The sad walls, from which all colour had faded, were covered by dark cracked mirrors and big sooty paintings which disappeared one by one when we were out, though there were no other signs of burglary. Most puzzling of all was the fact that Eva wasn't perturbed by their disappearance. 'Hey, I think another picture's disappeared, Eva,' I'd say. 'Oh yes, space for other things,' she'd reply. Eventually she admitted to us that Charlie was stealing them to sell and we were not to mention it. 'At least he has initiative,' she said. 'Wasn't Jean Genet a thief?'

Within the three large rooms were partitions that made up other, smaller rooms, and the kitchen, which contained the bath. It was like a student flat, a wretched and dirty gaff with lino on the floor and large white dried flowers waving from the marble fireplace. The rooms' great spaces were interrupted by busted brown furniture. There wasn't even a bed for me; I slept on the sofa in the front room. Charlie, who also had nowhere to go, sometimes slept on the floor beside me.

Dad stood looking at the flat in disgust. Eva hadn't let him see it before; she just bought it quickly when we sold the house in Beckenham and had to get out. 'Oh my God,' Dad groaned, 'how have we come to live in such filth?'

He wouldn't even sit down, in case a spider jumped out of an armchair. Eva had to cover a chair in stapled-together plastic bags before it was hygienic enough for his arse. But Eva was happy. 'I can really do something with this,' she kept saying, striding around, as Dad turned pale; and there in the centre of the room she held him and kissed him again and again in case he lost his nerve and faith in her and longed to be with Mum. 'What d'you think?' said Dad, turning to me, his other worry. 'I love it,' I said, which pleased him. 'But will it be good for him?' he asked Eva. Eva said yes. 'I'll look after him,' she added, with a smile.

The city blew the windows of my brain wide open. But being in a place so bright, fast and brilliant made you vertiginous with possibility: it didn't necessarily help you grasp those possibilities. I still had no idea what I was going to do. I felt directionless and lost in the crowd. I couldn't yet see how the city worked, but I began to find out.

West Kensington itself was made up of rows of five-storey peeling stucco houses broken up into bed-sits that were mostly occupied by foreign students, itinerants and poor people who'd lived there for years. The District Line dived into the earth half-way along the Barons Court Road, to which it ran parallel, the trains heading for Charing Cross and then out into the East End, from where Uncle Ted had originally come. Unlike the suburbs, where no one of note – except H. G. Wells – had lived, here you couldn't get away from VIPs. Gandhi himself once had a room in West Kensington, and the notorious landlord Rachman kept a flat for the young Mandy Rice-Davies in the next street; Christine Keeler came for tea. IRA bombers stayed in tiny rooms and met in Hammersmith pubs, singing 'Arms for the IRA' at closing time. Mesrine had had a room by the tube station.

So this was London at last, and nothing gave me more pleasure than strolling around my new possession all day. London seemed like a house with five thousand rooms, all different; the kick was to work out how they connected, and eventually to walk through all of them. Towards Hammersmith was the river and its pubs, full of hollering middle-class voices; and there were the secluded gardens which fringed the river along Lower Mall and the shaded stroll along the towpath to Barnes. This part of West London seemed like the country to me, with none of the disadvantages, no cows or farmers.

Nearby was expensive Kensington, where rich ladies shopped, and a walk from that was Earls Court, with its baby-faced male and female whores arguing and shoving each other in the pubs; there were transvestites and addicts and many disoriented people and con-merchants. There were small hotels smelling of spunk and disinfectant, Australian travel agents, all-night shops run by dwarfish Bengalis, leather bars with fat moustached queens exchanging secret signals outside, and roaming strangers with no money and searching eyes. In Kensington nobody looked at you. In Earls Court everybody did, wondering what they could wrench from you.

But West Kensington was an area in between, where people stayed before moving up, or remained only because they were stuck. It was quieter, with few shops, not one of them interesting, and restaurants which opened with optimistic flourishes and invitations but where, after a few weeks, you could see the desolate owner standing in the doorway wondering where he'd gone wrong; his eyes told you the area wasn't going to revive in his lifetime. But Eva ignored all such eyes: this was where she reckoned she could do something. 'This place is going places,' she predicted, as we talked sitting around a paraffin heater, the sole source of warmth at the time, the top of which was draped with Dad's drying underpants.

Around the corner from the flat was a roaring famous bar and house of fights and dope called the Nashville. The front of it had oak beams and curved glass in the shape of a Wurlitzer jukebox. Every night the new groups blew West Kensington into the air.

As Eva had known, the location of the flat would always be a draw for Charlie, and when he turned up one evening to eat and sleep I said, 'Let's go to the Nashville.'

He looked at me warily and then nodded. He seemed keen enough to go, to investigate the latest bands and see what was happening in music. But there was a heaviness in his response. Later he tried to change his mind by saying to me, 'Don't you want to go somewhere quieter than that, where we can talk?' Charlie had avoided concerts and gigs for months. He was afraid of finding the London bands too good, as if he'd see a young group with such talent and promise that his own brittle hopes and aspirations would be exploded in a terrifying second of illumination and self-knowledge. Myself, I went to the Nashville every night and reckoned that Charlie's glory in South London was the most he'd ever get. In

London the kids looked fabulous; they dressed and walked and talked like little gods. We could have been from Bombay. We'd never catch up.

Predictably, I had to pay for Charlie. I did it willingly because I still loved his company so much, but I had little money. As property prices in London were moving upwards, Eva's shrewd plan was to decorate the flat as we had the last house, sell at a profit, and move on. But she was still meditating for hours and waiting for the voice of the flat to inform her of its favoured colour scheme. When word came, Ted and I would obey, and we'd get paid. Until then I was broke and Ted was left at home reminiscing with Mum about the war and trying to stop Jean from drinking.

Charlie was soon drunk. We were sitting in the small, side bar in the Nashville. I noticed that he was starting to smell. He didn't change his clothes too often, and when he did he just picked up whatever was around him – Eva's jumpers, Dad's waistcoats, and always my shirts, which he borrowed and I never saw again. He'd crash some party, see a better shirt in the closet, change into it, and leave mine behind. I'd started locking my shirts in a desk drawer every night, except that now I'd lost the key with all my Ben Shermans in there.

I'd been looking forward to telling Charlie how depressed and lonely I'd been since we moved to London. But before I'd managed a single moan, Charlie pre-empted me. 'I am suicidal,' he announced grandly, as if he were pregnant. He said he was circling in that round of despair where you don't care one iota what happens to you or anyone else.

A famous footballer with a famous perm was sitting next to Charlie listening to this. The Perm was soon taking pity on Charlie, as people tended to, and Charlie was asking him about the pressures of fame as if it were something that concerned him from day to day. 'What d'you do,' Charlie said, 'when the reporters won't leave you alone? When they're outside the window every morning?' 'It's all worth it,' the Perm replied. 'Sometimes I run out on to the pitch with an erection, I'm so excited.'

He bought Charlie, but not me, drinks. I wanted to get away from the Perm and talk to Charlie, but Charlie wasn't going anywhere. Luckily I'd had some speed earlier: when I was on blues I could get through anything. All the same I felt disappointed. Then, just as someone mentioned the band were preparing to go on next door, my luck changed. I saw Charlie suddenly jerk forward and vomit in the footballer's lap, before collapsing backwards off his stool. The Perm got excited. After all, he did have a pond consisting of Charlie's last Chinese meal steaming in his crotch. He'd told us earlier that he was planning on taking a woman to Tramp that night. Anyway, the Perm leapt up and booted Charlie a couple of times in the ear with those famous feet until the heavies pulled him away. I managed to heave Charlie into the main bar and prop him up against a wall. He was half unconscious and trying to stop himself crying. He knew what things had come to.

'Take it easy,' I told him. 'Keep away from people tonight.'

'I feel better, OK?'

'Good.'

'For the moment.'

'OK.'

I relaxed and looked around the dark room, at the end of which was a small stage with a drum-kit and mike-stand on it. Maybe I was just a provincial or something, but I began to see that I was among the strangest audience I'd seen in that place. There were the usual long-hairs and burned-out heads hanging at the back in velvet trousers or dirty jeans, patchwork boots and sheepskin coats, discussing bus fares to Fez, Barclay James Harvest and bread. That was the usual clientèle, the stoned inhabitants of local squats and basements.

But at the front of the place, near the stage, there were about thirty kids in ripped black clothes. And the clothes were full of safety-pins. Their hair was uniformly black, and cut short, seriously short, or if long it was spiky and rigid, sticking up and out and sideways, like a handful of needles, rather than hanging down. A hurricane would not have dislodged those styles. The girls were in rubber and leather and wore skin-tight skirts and holed black stockings, with white face-slap and bright-red lipstick. They snarled and bit people. Accompanying these kids were what appeared to be three extravagant South American transvestites in dresses, rouge and lipstick, one of whom had a used tampon on a piece of string around her neck. Charlie stirred restlessly as he leaned there. He hugged himself in self-pity as we took in this alien race dressed with an abandonment and originality we'd never imagined possible. I began to understand what London meant and what class of outrage we had to deal with. It certainly put us in proportion.

'What is this shit?' Charlie said. He was dismissive, but he was slightly breathless too; there was awe in his voice.

'Be cool, Charlie,' I said, continuing to examine the audience.

'Be cool? I'm fucked. I just got kicked in the balls by a footballer.'

'He's a famous footballer.'

'And look at the stage,' Charlie said. 'What rubbish is this? Why have you brought me out for this?'

'D'you wanna go, then?'

'Yes. All this is making me feel sick.'

'OK,' I said. 'Lean on my shoulder and we'll get you out of here. I don't like the look of it either. It's too weird.'

'Yeah, much too weird.'

'It's too much.'

'Yeah.'

But before we could move the band shambled on, young kids in clothes similar to the audience. The fans suddenly started to bounce up and down. As they pumped into the air and threw themselves sideways they screamed and spat at the band until the singer, a skinny little kid with carroty hair, dripped with saliva. He seemed to expect this, and merely abused the audience back, spitting at them, skidding over on to his arse once, and drinking and slouching around the stage as if he were in his living room. His purpose was not to be charismatic; he would be himself in whatever mundane way it took. The little kid wanted to be an anti-star, and I couldn't take my eyes off him. It must have been worse for Charlie.

'He's an idiot,' Charlie said.

'Yeah.'

'And I bet they can't play either. Look at those instruments. Where did they get them, a jumble sale?'

'Right,' I said.

'Unprofessional,' he said.

When the shambolic group finally started up, the music was thrashed out. It was more aggressive than anything I'd heard since early Who. This was no peace and love; here were no drum solos or effeminate synthesizers. Not a squeeze of anything 'progressive' or 'experimental' came from these pallid, vicious little council estate kids with hedgehog hair, howling about anarchy and hatred. No song lasted more than three minutes, and after each the carrot-haired kid cursed us to death. He seemed to be yelling directly at Charlie and me. I could feel Charlie getting tense beside me. I knew London was killing us as I heard, 'Fuck off, all you smelly old hippies! You fucking slags! You ugly fart-breaths! Fuck off to hell!' he shouted at us.

I didn't look at Charlie again, until the end. As the lights came up I saw he was standing up straight and alert, with cubes of dried vomit decorating his cheeks.

'Let's go,' I said.

We were numb; we didn't want to speak for fear of returning to our banal selves again. The wild kids bundled out. Charlie and I elbowed our way through the crowd. Then he stopped.

'What is it, Charlie?'

'I've got to get backstage and talk to those guys.'

I snorted. 'Why would they want to talk to you?'

I thought he'd hit me; but he took it well.

'Yeah, there's no reason why they should like me,' he said. 'If I saw me coming into the dressing room I'd have myself kicked out.'

We walked around West Kensington eating saveloy and chips drenched in vinegar and saturated with salt. People gathered in groups outside the burger place; others went to buy cigarettes from the Indian shop on the corner and then stood at the bus stop. In the pubs the bar staff put the chairs upside down on the tables and shouted, 'Hurry up now, please, thank you.' Outside the pub people argued about where to go next. The city at night intimidated me: the piss-heads, bums, derelicts and dealers shouted and looked for fights. Police vans cruised, and sometimes the law leapt out on to the street to grab kids by the hair and smash their heads against walls. The wrecked kids pissed into doorways.

Charlie was excited. 'That's it, that's it,' he said as we strolled. 'That's fucking it.' His voice was squeaky with rapture. 'The sixties have been given notice tonight. Those kids we saw have assassinated all hope. They're the fucking future.'

'Yeah, maybe, but we can't follow them,' I said casually.

'Why not?'

'Obviously we can't wear rubber and safety-pins and all. What would we look like? Sure, Charlie.'

'Why not, Karim? Why not, man?'

'It's not us.'

'But we've got to change. What are you saying? We shouldn't keep up? That suburban boys like us always know where it's at?'

'It would be artificial,' I said. 'We're not like them. We don't hate the way they do. We've got no reason to. We're not from the estates. We haven't been through what they have.'

He turned on me with one of his nastiest looks.

'You're not going anywhere, Karim. You're not doing anything with your life because as usual you're facing in the wrong direction and going the wrong way. But don't try and drag me down with you. I don't need your discouragement! Don't think I'm going to end up like you!'

'Like me?' I could hardly speak. 'What am I that you hate so much?' I managed to say.

But Charlie was looking across the street and not at me. Four kids from the Nashville, two girls and two boys, were piling into a car. They whooped and abused passers-by and fired water-pistols. The next thing I saw was Charlie sprinting through the traffic towards them. He dodged behind a bus and I thought he'd been knocked down. When he re-emerged he was ripping his shirt off – it was my shirt, too. At first I thought he was using it to wave at people, but then he bundled it up and threw it at a police car. Seconds later he'd leapt into car with the kids, his bare torso on someone's lap on the front seat. And the car took off up the North End Road before he'd got the door shut. Charlie was away to new adventures. I walked home.

A few days later Eva made an announcement. 'Karim,' she said. 'Let's start working together again. It's time. Ring Uncle Ted.'

'Great,' I said. 'At last.'

But there was one thing she wanted to do first. She had to give a flat-warming party. There was a theory of parties she said she wanted to try out. You invited people you thought would dislike each other and you watched them get along swingingly. For some reason I didn't believe her when she said this; I wasn't convinced that she was being straight. But whatever she was up to – and it was something – she spent days ticking and marking the party guest list, a thick, creamy piece of paper she kept with her at all times. She was unusually secretive about the whole thing and had intricate conversations with God-knows-who on the phone, and certainly wouldn't speak to Dad and me about what she was doing.

What I did know was that Shadwell was involved. It was his contacts she was using. They were conspirators. She flirted with him, used him, led him on and asked him favours. It bothered me, but Dad was unworried. He patronized Shadwell; he wasn't threatened. He took it for granted that people would fall in love with Eva.

But it was affecting Dad. For instance, he wanted to invite his meditation group to the party. Yet Eva insisted that no more than two of them come. She didn't want the new smooth crowd to think she was mixing with a bunch of basket-weavers from Bromley. So Chogyam-Jones and Fruitbat came, arriving an hour early, when Eva was still shaving her legs in the bath in the kitchen. Eva tolerated them since they paid for Dad's thoughts and therefore her dinner, but when they went into the bedroom to chant I heard her say to Dad, as she put on her yellow silk blouse for that brilliant evening, 'The future shouldn't contain too much of the past.' Later, just as the party was starting and Eva was discussing the origin of the word 'bohemian' with Dad, Fruitbat pulled out a handy pad and asked if she could write down something that Dad had said. The Buddha of suburbia nodded regally, while Eva looked as if she wanted to cut off Fruitbat's eyelids with a pair of scissors.

When this eagerly awaited party actually happened, it had been going forty minutes before Dad and I realized that we knew virtually no one there. Shadwell seemed to know everyone. He was standing at the door, greeting people as they came in, simpering and giggling and asking them how so-and-so was. He was being totally homosexual too, except that even that was a pose, a ruse, a way of self-presentation. And he was, as always, a picture of health, dressed in black rags and black boots and twitching maniacally. His face was white, his skin scrofulous, his teeth decaying.

Since I'd been living in the flat, Shadwell had been coming to see Eva at least once a week, during the day, when Dad was at the office. He and Eva went out on long walks together, or to the cinema at the ICA to see Scorsese films and exhibitions of dirty nappies. Eva made no effort to have us talk to each other, Shadwell and I; in fact I felt she wanted to discourage conversation. Whenever I saw her and Shadwell together they always looked pretty intense, as if they'd just had a fight or shared a lot of secrets.

Now, as the party fodder turned up in their glittering clothes, I began to see that Eva was using the evening not as a celebration but as her launch into London. She'd invited every theatre and film person she'd run into over the past few years, and a lot she hadn't. Many were Shadwell's acquaintances, people he'd met only once or twice. Every third-rate actor, assistant film director, weekend writer, part-time producer and their friends, if they had friends, slid on to our premises. As my darling new mother (whom I loved) moved radiantly about the room introducing Derek, who had just directed *Equus* at the Contact Theatre, to Bryan, who was a freelance journalist specializing in film, or Karen, who was a secretary at a literary agency, to Robert, who was a designer; as she spoke of the new Dylan album and what Riverside Studios was doing, I saw she wanted to scour that suburban stigma right off her body. She didn't realize it was in the blood and not on the skin; she didn't see there could be nothing more suburban than suburbanites repudiating themselves.

It was a relief when at last I saw someone I knew. From the window I spotted Jamila getting out of a cab, accompanied by a Japanese woman and Changez. I was delighted to see my friend's happy pudding face again, blinking up at the collapsing mansion in which our flat was located. As I caught his eye I realized how much I wanted to hold him in my arms again, and squeeze his rolls of fat. Except that I hadn't seen him since he lay on his camp-bed and watched me sleeping naked with his beloved wife, the woman I'd always characterized to him as 'sister'.

I'd spoken frequently to Jamila on the phone, of course, and apparently Changez – solid, stable, unshakeable Changez – had turned quite mad after the naked-on-the-bed incident. He'd railed at Jamila and accused her of adultery, incest, betrayal, whoredom, deceit, lesbianism, husband-hatred, frigidity, lying and callousness, as well as the usual things.

Jamila was equally fine and fierce that day, explaining just who her damn body belonged to. And anyway, it was none of his business: didn't he have a regular fuck? He could shove his hypocrisy up his fat arse! Changez, being at heart a traditional Muslim, explained the teachings of the Koran on this subject to her, and then, when words were not sufficient to convince her, he tried to give her a whack. But Jamila was not whackable. She gave

Changez a considerable backhander across his wobbling chops, which shut his mouth for a fortnight, during which he miserably carried his bruised jaw to his camp-bed – that raft in a storm – and didn't speak.

Now he shook hands with me and we held each other. I was slightly worried, I must admit, that he would knife me.

'How are you, Changez?'

'Looking good, looking good.'

'Yes?'

Without any hesitation he said, 'Let's not beat around any bushes. How can I forgive you for screwing my wife? Is that a nice thing to do to a friend, eh?'

I was ready for him.

'I've known Jammie all my life, *yaar*. Long-standing arrangement. She was always mine in so far as she was anyone's, and she's never been anyone's and never will be anyone's, you know. She's her own person.'

His sad face trembled as he shook his sincere, hurt head and sat down.

'You deceived me. It was a blow against the centre of my life. I couldn't take it. It was too much for me – it hit me hard, in the guts, Karim.'

What can you say when friends admit such hurt without vindictiveness or bitterness? I didn't ever want to aim a blow against the centre of his life.

'How are you two getting along anyway?' I asked, shifting the subject. I sat down beside him and we opened a Heineken each. Changez was thoughtful and serious.

'I've got to be realistic about adjustment. It's unusual for me, an Indian man, *vis-à-vis* the things that go on around my wife. Jamila makes me do shopping and washing and cleaning. And she has become friends with Shinko.'

'Shinko?'

He indicated the Japanese woman who had arrived with him. I looked at her; I did recognize her. Then it occurred to me who Shinko was – his prostitute friend, with whom he conjured Harold Robbins's positions. I was amazed. I could hardly speak, but I could snigger, for there they were, Changez's wife and his whore, chatting together about modern dance with Fruitbat.

I was puzzled. 'Is Shinko a friend of Jamila's, then?'

'Only recently, you complete cunt. Jamila made up her mind she didn't have sufficient women friends, so she went to call on Shinko's house. You told her about Shinko, after all, for no reason, gratis, thank you very much, I'll do the same for you some day. It was bloody embarrassing at first and all, I can tell you, as these two girls sat there right in front of my nose, but the girls it didn't phase out at all.'

'And what did you do?'

'Nothing! What could I do? They were instant friends! They were discussing all the subjects usually kept under the pillow. The penis here, the vagina there, the man on top, the woman here, there and everywhere. I just have to put up with all the humiliations that fall on my head in this great country! It's been difficult, too, since Anwar-saab has become insanely mad.'

'What are you on about, Changez? I don't know anything about this.'

He sat back, regarded me coolly and shrugged complacently.

'But what subject do you know about?'

'Eh?'

'You never go there, *yaar*, just as you avoid me now.'

'I see.'

'It makes you sad,' he said.

I nodded. It was true that I hadn't been to see Jeeta or Anwar for a long time, what with the moving and my depression and everything, and wanting to start a new life in London and know the city.

'Don't leave your own people behind, Karim.'

Before I had a chance to leave my own people and find out exactly how Anwar had gone insanely mad, Eva came over to me.

'Excuse me,' she said to Changez. 'Get up,' she said to me.

'I'm all right here,' I said.

She tugged me to my feet. 'God, Karim, won't you do anything for yourself?' Her eyes were bright with the thrill of things. As she talked she didn't stop looking around the room. 'Karim, darling, your big moment in life has arrived. There's someone here dying to meet you again, meet you properly. A man who will help you.'

She led me through the throng. 'By the way,' she murmured in my ear. 'Don't say anything arrogant or appear too egotistical.'

I was annoyed with her dragging me away from Changez. 'Why not?' I said.

'Let him talk,' she said.

She'd mentioned someone who would help me, but I saw only Shadwell ahead of me. 'Oh no,' I said, and tried to pull away. But she continued to haul me forward like a mother with a naughty child. 'Come on,' she said. 'It's your chance. Talk about the theatre.'

Shadwell didn't require much encouragement. It was easy to see that he was clever and well read, but he was also boring. Like many spectacular bores, his thoughts were catalogued and indexed. When I asked him a question he'd say, 'The answer to that is – in fact the several answers to that are . . . A.' And you'd get point A followed by points B and C, and on the one hand F, and on the other foot G, until you could see the whole alphabet stretching ahead, each letter a Sahara in itself to be crawled across. He was talking about the theatre and the writers he liked: Arden, Bond, Orton, Osborne, Wesker, each suffocated just by being in his mouth for a minute. I kept trying to get back to Changez's lugubrious face, which reclined morosely in his good hand as the guests filled the air around him with cultivated noises. I saw Changez's eyes fall caressingly on his wife's form and then rest on his prostitute's grooving hips as the two of them got down to Martha Reeves and the Vandellas. Then, spontaneously, Changez pushed himself up and danced with them, lifting each foot ponderously from the floor like a performing elephant, and sticking his elbows out as if he'd been asked, in a drama class, to be a flamingo. I wanted to dance with him and celebrate the renewal of our friendship. I crept away from Shadwell. But I caught Eva's eye. She glared at me.

'I can see you want to get away,' said Shadwell, 'to much more charismatic folk. But Eva tells me you're interested in acting.'

'Yes, for a long time, I suppose.'

'Well, are you or aren't you? Am I to be interested in you or not?'

'Yes, if you're interested.'

'Good, I am interested. I'd like you to do something for me. They've given me a theatre for a season. Will you come along and do a piece for me?'

'Yes,' I said. 'Yes, yes, I will.'

After the guests had gone, at three in the morning, as we sat among the debris and Chogyam and Fruitbat threw rubbish into plastic bags, I wanted to discuss Shadwell with Eva. I said he was boring as hell. Eva was already irritable; this Madame Verdurin of West London felt Dad and I hadn't appreciated the quality of her guests. 'Whose intelligence did you engage with this evening, Karim? You two behaved as if we were still in the sticks. And it is wicked, Karim, to mind Shadwell being dull. It's a misfortune, not a fault. Like being born with a nose like a turnip.'

'She's changed her tune,' I said to Dad. But he wasn't listening. He watched Eva all the time. Now he felt playful: he kept tickling the cushion next to him and saying, 'Come here, come here, little Eva, and let me tell you a secret.' They still played sickening games that I couldn't avoid, like putting sperm on each other's nose and calling one another Merkin and Muffin, for God's sake. Chogyam turned to Dad. 'What is your view on this matter of boredom?'

Dad cleared his throat and said that boring people were deliberately boring. It was a personality choice, and responsibility couldn't be avoided by saying they were like turnips. Bores wanted to narcotize you so you wouldn't be sensitive to them.

'Anyway,' Eva whispered, sitting beside Dad now and cradling his drowsy head as she looked up at me. 'Shadwell has a real theatre and for some reason he likes you. Let's see if we can land you a theatre job, eh? Is that what you want?'

I didn't know what to say. This was a chance, but I was frightened of taking it, frightened of exposing myself and failing. Unlike Charlie's, my will wasn't stronger than my misgivings.

'Make up your mind,' she said. 'I'll help you, Creamy, in any way you want.'

Over the next few weeks, with Eva directing me – which she loved – I prepared a Sam Shepard speech from *The Mad Dog Blues* for my audition with Shadwell. I'd never worked so hard at anything in my life; nor, once I'd started, had I wanted anything so badly. The speech began: 'I was on a Greyhound bus out of Carlsbad heading for Loving, New Mexico. Back to see my dad. After ten years. All duded out in a double-breasted suit with my shoes all shined. The driver calls "Loving" and I get off the bus . . .'

I knew what I was doing; I was thoroughly prepared; but that didn't mean that when the day came I wasn't in a state of nervous collapse. 'Are you familiar with *The Mad Dog Blues*?' I asked Shadwell, sure he would never have heard of it.

He was sitting in the front row of his theatre watching me, a notebook balanced on the leg of his rancid trousers. He nodded. 'Shepard is my man. And there are not many boys who would not want to be him, because A he is attractive, B he can write and act, C he can play the drums and D he is a wild boy and rebel.'

'Yes.'

'Now do *The Mad Dog Blues* for me, please. Brilliantly.'

Shadwell's theatre was a small wooden building like a large hut, in suburban North London. It had a tiny foyer but a wide stage, proper lights and about two hundred seats. They produced plays like *French without Tears*, the latest Ayckbourn or Frayn, or a panto. It was primarily an amateur place, but they did do three professional productions a year, mostly of plays on the school curriculum like *The Royal Hunt of the Sun*.

When I finished, Shadwell started to applaud with the tips of his fingers, as if scared his hands would give each other a disease. He climbed up on stage. 'Thank you, Karim.'

'You liked it, yeah?' I asked, out of breath.

'So much so that I want you to do it again.'

'What? Again? But I reckon that was my best shot, Mr Shadwell.'

He ignored me. He had an idea. 'Only this time two extra things will occur: A, a wasp will be buzzing around your head. And B, the wasp wants to sting you. Your motivation – and all actors love a bit of motivation – is to brush, push, fight it away, OK?'

'I'm not sure Sam Shepard would approve of this wasp business,' I said confidently. 'He really wouldn't.'

Shadwell turned and peered exaggeratedly into every cranny of the deserted theatre. 'But he's not fucking here, unless I've gone blind.'

And he went and sat down again, waiting for me to begin. I felt a complete wanker, waving at that wasp. But I wanted the part, whatever the part was. I couldn't face going back to that flat in West Kensington not knowing what to do with my life and having to be pleasant, and not being respected by anyone.

When I'd done with Shepard and the wasp, Shadwell put his arm round me. 'Well done! You deserve a coffee. Come on.'

He took me to a lorry driver's café next door. I felt elated, especially when he said, 'I'm looking for an actor just like you.'

My head rang with cheering bells. We sat down with our coffee. Shadwell put his elbow out half-way across the table in a puddle of tea, resting his cheek on the palm of his hand, and stared at me.

'Really?' I said enthusiastically. 'An actor like me in what way?'

'An actor who'll fit the part.'

'What part?' I asked.

He looked at me impatiently. 'The part in the book.'

I could be very direct at times. 'What book?'

'The book I asked you to read, Karim.'

'But you didn't.'

'I told Eva to tell you.'

'But Eva didn't tell me anything. I would have remembered.'

'Oh Christ. Oh God, I'm going mad. Karim, what the hell is that woman playing at?' And he held his head in his hands.

'Don't ask me,' I said. 'At least tell me what the book is. Maybe I can buy it today.'

'Stop being so rational,' he said. 'It's *The Jungle Book*. Kipling. You know it, of course.'

'Yeah, I've seen the film.'

'I'm sure.'

He could be a snooty bastard, old Shadwell, that was for sure. But I was going to keep myself under control whatever he said. Then his attitude changed completely. Instead of talking about the job he said some words to me in Punjabi or Urdu and looked as if he wanted to get into a big conversation about Ray or Tagore or something. To tell the truth, when he spoke it sounded like he was gargling.

'Well?' he said. He rattled off some more words. 'You don't understand?'

'No, not really.'

What could I say? I couldn't win. I knew he'd hate me for it.

'Your own language!'

'Yeah, well, I get a bit. The dirty words. I know when I'm being called a camel's rectum.'

'Of course. But your father speaks, doesn't he? He must do.'

Of course he speaks, I felt like saying. He speaks out of his mouth, unlike you, you fucking cunt bastard shithead.

'Yes, but not to me,' I said. 'It would be stupid. We wouldn't know what he was on about. Things are difficult enough as it is.'

Shadwell persisted. There seemed no way he was ever going to get off this subject.

'You've never been there, I suppose.'

'Where?'

Why was he being so bloody aggressive about it?

'You know where. Bombay, Delhi, Madras, Bangalore, Hyderabad, Trivandrum, Goa, the Punjab. You've never had that dust in your nostrils?'

'Never in my nostrils, no.'

'You must go,' he said, as if nobody had ever been there but him.

'I will, OK?'

'Yes, take a rucksack and see India, if it's the last thing you do in your life.'

'Right, Mr Shadwell.'

He lived in his own mind, he really did. He shook his head then and did a series of short barks in his throat. This was him laughing, I was certain. 'Ha, ha, ha, ha, ha!' he went. He said, 'What a breed of people two hundred years of imperialism has given birth to. If the pioneers from the East India Company could see you. What puzzlement there'd be. Everyone looks at you, I'm sure, and thinks: an Indian boy, how exotic, how interesting, what stories of aunties and elephants we'll hear now from him. And you're from Orpington.'

'Yeah.'

'Oh God, what a strange world. The immigrant is the Everyman of the twentieth century. Yes?'

'Mr Shadwell – ' I started.

'Eva can be a very difficult woman, you know.'

'Yeah?'

I breathed more easily now he'd changed the subject. 'The best women always are,' he went on. 'But she didn't give you the book. She's trying to protect you from your destiny, which is to be a half-caste in England. That must be complicated for you to accept – belonging nowhere, wanted nowhere. Racism. Do you find it difficult? Please tell me.'

He looked at me.

'I don't know,' I said defensively. 'Let's talk about acting.'

'Don't you know?' he persisted. 'Don't you really?'

I couldn't answer his questions. I could barely speak at all; the muscles in my face seemed to have gone rigid. I was shaking with embarrassment that he could talk to me in this way at all, as if he knew me, as if he had the right to question me. Fortunately he didn't wait for any reply.

He said, 'When I saw more of Eva than I do now, she was often unstable. Highly strung, we call it. Yes? She's been around, Eva, and she's seen a lot. One morning we woke up in Tangier, where I was visiting Paul Bowles – a famous homosexual writer – and she was suffocating. All her hair had dropped out in the night and she was choking on it.'

I just looked at him.

'Incredible, eh?'

'Incredible. It must have been psychological.' And I almost added that my hair would probably fall out if I had to spend too much time with him.

'But I don't want to talk about the past,' I said.

'Don't you?'

This stuff about him and Eva was really making me uncomfortable. I didn't want to know about it.

'OK,' he said at last. I breathed a sigh of relief. 'Happy with your father, is she?'

Christ, he was a nippy little questioner. He could have slain people with his questioning, except that he never listened to the answers. He didn't want answers but only the pleasure of his own voice.

'Let's hope it lasts, eh?' he said. 'Sceptical, eh?'

I shrugged. But now I had something to say. Off I went.

'I was in the Cubs. I remember it well. *The Jungle Book* is Baloo and Bagheera and all that, isn't it?'

'Correct. Ten out of ten. And?'

'And?'

'And Mowgli.'

'Oh yes, Mowgli.'

Shadwell searched my face for comment, a flinch or little sneer perhaps. 'You're just right for him,' he continued. 'In fact, you are Mowgli. You're dark-skinned, you're small and wiry, and you'll be sweet but wholesome in the costume. Not too pornographic, I hope. Certain critics will go for you. Oh yes. Ha, ha, ha, ha, ha!'

He jumped up as two young women carrying scripts came into the café. Shadwell embraced them, and they kissed him, apparently without revulsion. They talked to him with respect. This was my first indication of how desperate actors can get.

'I've found my Mowgli,' Shadwell told them, pointing down at me. 'I've found my little Mowgli at last. An unknown actor, just right and ready to break through.'

'Hallo,' one of the women said to me. 'I'm Roberta,' said the other.

'Hallo,' I said.

'Isn't he terrific?' Shadwell said.

The two women examined me. I was just perfect. I'd done it. I'd got a job.

CHAPTER TEN

That summer a lot happened quickly to both Charlie and me: big things to him; smaller but significant things to me. Although I didn't see Charlie for months, I rang Eva almost every day for a full report. And, of course, Charlie was on television and in the newspapers. Suddenly you couldn't get away from him and his blooming career. He'd done it. As for me, I had to wait the whole summer and into the late autumn for rehearsals of *The Jungle Book* to begin, so I went back to South London, happy in the knowledge that soon I'd be in a professional production and there'd be someone in the cast for me to fall in love with. I just knew that that was going to happen.

Allie had gone to Italy with his smart friends from school, looking at clothes in Milan, for God's sake. I didn't want Mum to be alone, now she'd left Ted and Jean, and moved back into our old house. Fortunately they'd given her the job back at the shoe shop, and she and I had to spend only evenings and weekends together. Mum was feeling much better, and she was active again, though she'd become very fat at Ted and Jean's.

She still didn't speak much, concealing pain and her wound from voices and trite expression. But I watched her transform the house from being their place – and it had been only a place, child-soiled, functional – into her home. She started to wear trousers for the first time, dieted, and let her hair grow. She bought a pine table from a junk shop and slowly sandpapered it down in the garden, and then sealed it, something she'd never done before, never even thought of doing before. I was surprised she even knew what sandpaper was; but I could be such a fool in not knowing people. There were shaky cane chairs to go with the table, which I carried home on my head, and there Mum sat hour after hour, doing calligraphy – Christmas and birthday cards on squares of lush paper. She cleaned as never before, with care and interest (this wasn't a chore now), getting on to her knees with a scrubbing brush and bowl of water, behind cupboards and along skirting boards. She washed down the walls and repainted doors smudged with our fingerprints. She repotted every plant in the house and started listening to opera.

Ted came by with plants. He loved shrubs, especially lilac bushes, which Jean had consequently banned from her garden, so he brought them to our place. He also came by with old radios and plates, jugs and silver candlesticks, anything he picked up on his roaming trips around South London while he waited for Eva to continue work on the new flat.

I read a lot, proper books like *Lost Illusions* and *The Red and the Black*, and went to bed early, in training for love and work. Although I was only a few miles away over the river, I missed the London I was getting to know and played games with myself like: if the secret police ordered you to live in the suburbs for the rest of your life, what would you do? Kill yourself? Read? Almost every night I had nightmares and sweats. It was sleeping under that childhood roof which did it. Whatever fear of the future I had, I would overcome it; it was nothing to my loathing of the past.

One morning rehearsals started. I said goodbye to Mum sadly, left South London and went to stay with Dad and Eva once more. And every day I ran from the tube to the rehearsal room. I was the last to leave at night. I loved the hard work and being with the ten other actors, in the pub, in the café, belonging to the group.

Shadwell had obviously spent many weekends on the Continent observing European theatre. He wanted a physical *Jungle Book* made of mime, voices and bodily invention. Props and costumes would be minimal. The jungle itself, its trees and swamps, the many animals, fires and huts, were to be fashioned from our bodies, movements, cries. Yet most of the actors he'd assembled hadn't worked in that way before. On the first day, when we all jogged five times around the rehearsal room to warm up, there were many exhausted lungs. One woman had worked only in radio – as a disc-jockey. One actor I became friendly with, Terry, had done only agit-prop before, touring the country in a van with a company called Vanguard in a music-hall pastiche about the miners' strike of 1972 called *Dig!* Now he found himself playing Kaa, the deaf snake known for the power of his hug. And Terry did look as if he had a powerful hug. He was going to spend the show hissing and flinging himself across the scaffolding arch which ran up the sides and across the top of the stage, and from which monkeys dangled, taunting Baloo the bear, who couldn't climb and groaned a lot. Terry was in his early forties, with a pale, handsome face – a quiet, generous, working-class Welsh man-boy. I liked him instantly, especially as he was a fitness fanatic and his body was solid and taut. I decided to seduce him, but without much hope of success.

I didn't clash with Shadwell until the second week, at the costume fitting. At the start, everyone was respectful towards him, listening carefully to his soporific explanations. But he soon became a joke to most of us, because not only was he pedantic and patronizing, he was also frightened of what he'd started and disliked suggestions for fear they implied that he was going wrong. One day he took me aside and left me with the designer, a nervous girl who always wore black. She carried a yellow scarf and had a jar of shit-brown cream in her hand, which she was trying to conceal behind her back.

'This is your costume, Mr Mowgli.'

I craned my neck to examine the contents of her hand.

'Where is my costume?'

'Take your clothes off, please.'

It turned out that on stage I would wear a loin-cloth and brown make-up, so that I resembled a turd in a bikini-bottom. I undressed. 'Please don't put this on me,' I said, shivering. 'Got to,' she said. 'Be a big boy.' As she covered me from toe to head in the brown muck I thought of Julien Sorel in *The Red and the Black*, dissimulating and silent for the sake of ambition, his pride often shattered, but beneath it all solid in his superiority. So I kept my mouth shut even as her hands lathered me in the colour of dirt. A few days later I did question Shadwell about the possibility of not being covered in shit for my début as a professional actor. Shadwell was concise for once.

'That's the fucking costume! When you so eagerly accepted your first-ever part did you think Mowgli would be wearing a kaftan? A Saint-Laurent suit?'

'But Mr Shadwell – Jeremy – I feel wrong in it. I feel that together we're making the world uglier.'

'You'll survive.'

He was right. But just when I was feeling at home in the loin-cloth and boot polish, and when I'd learned my lines before anyone else and was getting as competent as a little orang-utan on the scaffolding, I saw that our conflicts hadn't ended. Shadwell took me aside and said, 'A word about the accent, Karim. I think it should be an authentic accent.'

'What d'you mean authentic?'

'Where was our Mowgli born?'

'India.'

'Yes. Not Orpington. What accent do they have in India?'

'Indian accents.'

'Ten out of ten.'

'No, Jeremy. Please, no.'

'Karim, you have been cast for authenticity and not for experience.'

I could hardly believe it. Even when I did believe it we discussed it several times, but he wouldn't change his mind.

'Just try it,' he kept saying as we went outside the rehearsal room to argue. 'You're very conservative, Karim. Try it until you feel comfortable as a Bengali. You're supposed to be an actor, but I suspect you may just be an exhibitionist.'

'Jeremy, help me, I can't do this.'

He shook his head. I swear, my eyes were melting.

A few days passed without the accent being mentioned again. During this time Shadwell had me concentrate on the animal noises I was to make between the dialogue, so that when, for instance, I was talking to Kaa the slithering snake, who saves Mowgli's life, I had to hiss. Terry and I had to hiss together. When hissing, the thought of Dad lecturing to Ted and Jean at Carl and Marianne's was an aid. Being a human zoo was acceptable, provided the Indian accent was off the menu.

Next time it was mentioned the entire cast was present.

'Now do the accent,' Shadwell suddenly said. 'I trust you've been rehearsing at home.'

'Jeremy,' I pleaded. 'It's a political matter to me.'

He looked at me violently. The cast watched me too, most of them sympathetically. One of them, Boyd, had done EST and assertion-training, and primal therapy, and liked to hurl chairs across the room as an expression of spontaneous feeling. I wondered if he might not have some spontaneous feeling in my defence. But he said nothing. I looked towards Terry. As an active Trotskyite he encouraged me to speak of the prejudice and abuse I'd faced being the son of an Indian. In the evenings we talked of inequality, imperialism, white supremacy, and whether sexual experimentation was merely bourgeois indulgence or a contribution to the dissolution of established society. But now, like the others, Terry said nothing but stood there in his tracksuit waiting to slide hissingly across the floor once more. I thought: You prefer generalizations like 'after the revolution the workers will wake up filled with unbelievable joy' to standing up to fascists like Shadwell.

Shadwell spoke sternly. 'Karim, this is a talented and expensive group of highly trained actors. They are ready to work, hungry to act, full of love for their humble craft, keen, eager and centred. But you, only you I am afraid, yes, only you out of everyone here, are holding back the entire production. Are you going to make the appropriate concession this experienced director requires from you?'

I wanted to run out of the room, back to South London, where I belonged, out of which I had wrongly and arrogantly stepped. I hated Shadwell and everyone in the cast.

'Yes,' I said to Shadwell.

That night in the pub I didn't sit at the same table as the others but moved into the other bar with my pint and newspaper. I despised the other actors for not sticking up for me, and for sniggering at the accent when I finally did it. Terry left the group he was sitting with and joined me.

'Come on,' he said, 'have another drink. Don't take it so badly, it's always crap for actors.' 'Crap for actors' was his favourite expression. Everything always seemed to be crap for actors and you just had to put up with it – while the present corruption continued.

I asked if people like Shitwell, as we called him among other things, would shove me around after the revolution; whether there'd be theatre directors at all or whether we'd all get a turn at telling the others where to stand and what to wear. Terry didn't appear to have thought about this before and he puzzled over it, staring into his bitter and a bag of smoky bacon crisps.

'There will be theatre directors,' he said eventually. 'I think. But they'll be elected by the cast. If they are a pain the cast will throw them out and they'll return to the factory they came from.'

'Factory? How will we get people like Shadwell into factories in the first place?'

Terry looked shifty now; he was on sloping ground.

'He'll be required to do it.'

'Ah. By force?'

'There's no reason why the same people should do all the shit work, is there? I don't like the idea of people ordering other people to do work they wouldn't touch themselves.'

I liked Terry more than anyone I'd met for a long time, and we talked every day. But he did believe the working class – which he referred to as if it were a single-willed person – would do somewhat unlikely things. 'The working class will take care of those bastards very easily,' he said, referring to racist organizations. 'The working class is about to blow,' he said at other times. 'They've had enough of the Labour Party. They want the transformation of society now!' His talk made me think of the housing estates near Mum's house, where the 'working class' would have laughed in Terry's face – those, that is, who wouldn't have smacked him round the ear for calling them working class in the first place. I wanted to tell him that the proletariat of the suburbs did have strong class feeling. It was virulent and hate-filled and directed entirely at the people beneath them. But there were some things it was hopeless to discuss with him. I guessed that he didn't intervene in my dispute with Shadwell because he wanted the situation to deteriorate further. Terry didn't believe in social workers, left-wing politicians, radical lawyers, liberals or gradual improvement. He wanted things to get worse rather than better. When they were at their nadir there would be a transformation. So for things to get better they had to get worse; the worse they were the better they'd be in the future; they couldn't even start to get better before they'd started to go drastically downhill. This was how I interpreted his arguments. It exasperated him. He asked me to join the Party. He said I should join to prove that my commitment to the ending of injustice wasn't all hot air. I said I would sign up with pleasure on one condition. He had to kiss me. This, I said, would prove his commitment to overcoming his inbred bourgeois morality. He said that maybe I wasn't ready to join the Party just yet.

Terry's passion for equality appealed to my purer mind, and his hatred of existing authority appealed to my resentments. But although I hated inequality, it didn't mean I wanted to be treated like everyone else. I recognized that what I liked in Dad and Charlie was their insistence on standing apart. I liked the power they had and the attention they received. I liked the way people admired and indulged them. So despite the yellow scarf strangling my balls, the brown make-up, and even the accent, I relished being the pivot of the production.

I started to make little demands of Shagbadly. I required a longer rest; and could I be driven home by someone, as I felt so tired? I had to have Assam tea (with a touch of lapsang souchong) available at all times during rehearsal. Could that actor slide a little to the right; no, a little further. I began to see that I could ask for the things I needed. I gained confidence.

I spent little time at home now, so I was unable to be a detailed witness to the Great Love in the same account-keeping way as before. I did notice that Eva's absorption in the particulars of Dad's life had waned. They saw fewer Satyajit Ray films now, and went less to Indian restaurants; Eva gave up learning Urdu and listening to sitar music at breakfast. She had a new interest; she was launching a huge campaign. Eva was planning her assault on London.

At the flat there were drinks parties and little dinners every week, which irritated me, as I had to wait for everyone to finish filling the air with their thoughts on the latest novel before I could go to bed on the sofa. And often, after a day's rehearsal, I had to listen to Shadwell telling the dinner party how well his production of *The Jungle Book* was going, how 'expressionistic' it was. Fortunately Eva and Dad were often out, as Eva accepted all the numerous invitations she and Dad received from directors, novelists, editorial assistants, proof-readers, poufs, and whoever else it was she met.

I noticed that at these 'do's', as I still called them, to rile her, Eva was constructing an artistic persona for herself. People like her loved artists and anything 'artistic'; the word itself was a philtre; a whiff of the sublime accompanied its mention; it was an entrance to the uncontrolled and inspired. Her kind would do anything to append the heavenly word 'artist' to themselves. (They had to do it themselves – no one else would.) I heard Eva say once, 'I'm an artist, a designer, my team and I do houses.'

In the old days, when we were an ordinary suburban family, this pretentious and snobbish side of Eva amused Dad and me. And it had seemed, for a time, to be in retreat – perhaps because Dad was its grateful recipient. But now the show-off quotient was increasing daily. It was impossible to ignore. The problem was, Eva was not unsuccessful; she was not ignored by London once she started her assault. She was climbing ever higher, day by day. It was fantastic, the number of lunches, suppers, dinners, picnics, parties, receptions, champagne breakfasts, openings, closings, first nights, last nights and late nights these London people went to. They never stopped eating or talking or looking at people performing. As Eva started to take London, moving forward over the foreign fields of Islington, Chiswick and Wandsworth inch by inch, party by party, contact by contact, Dad thoroughly enjoyed himself. But he wouldn't recognize how important it all was to Eva. It was at a dinner party in the flat, when they were in the kitchen together fetching yogurt and raspberries, that I heard for the first time one of them turn on the other in anger. Eva said, 'For Christ's sake, can't you cut down on the bloody mysticism – we're not in Beckenham now. These are bright, intelligent people, they're used to argument, not assertion, to facts, not vapours!'

Dad threw back his head and laughed, not feeling the force of her criticism. 'Eva, don't you understand one plain thing? They have to let go of their rationality, of their interminable thinking and bothering over everything. They have control mania! It's only when we let go of life and allow our innate wisdom to flourish that we live!'

He picked up the desserts and hurried into the room, addressing the table in these terms, Eva becoming more furious until an intense discussion broke out about the importance of intuition in the breakthrough stage of science. The party flowered.

During this time Dad was discovering how much he liked other people. And, having no idea how important this or that person was, whether they worked for the BBC or the *TLS* or the BFI, he treated them all with equal condescension.

One night, after a rehearsal and drinks with Terry, I came into the flat to find Charlie getting dressed in Eva and Dad's bedroom, prancing in front of a full-length mirror which leaned against the partition wall. At first I didn't recognize him. After all, I'd seen only photographs of his new personality. His hair was dyed black now, and it was spiky. He wore, inside out, a slashed T-shirt with a red swastika hand-painted on it. His black trousers were held together by safety-pins, paperclips and needles. Over this he had a black mackintosh; there were five belts strapped around his waist and a sort of grey linen nappy attached to the back of his trousers. The bastard was wearing one of my green waistcoats, too. And Eva was weeping.

'What's the matter?' I said.

'Keep out of this,' said Charlie, sharply.

'Please, Charlie,' Eva implored him. 'Please take off the swastika. I don't care about anything else.'

'In that case I'll keep it on.'

'Charlie – '

'I've always hated your fucking nagging.'

'It's not nagging, it's for compassion.'

'Right. I won't be coming back here, Eva. You're such a drag now. It's your age. Is it the menopause that's making you like this?'

Beside Charlie on the floor was a pile of clothes from which he pulled jackets, macs and shirts before throwing them aside as unsuitable. He then applied black eye-liner. He walked out of the flat without looking at either of us. Eva screamed after him, 'Think of those who died in the camps! And don't expect me to be there tonight, you pig! Charlie, you can forget my support for ever!'

As arranged, I went to Charlie's gig that night, at a club in Soho. I took Eva with me. It didn't take much to persuade her to come and nothing would have prevented me from seeing precisely what it was that had turned my schoolfriend into what the *Daily Express* called 'a phenomena'. I even made sure we got there an hour early in order to take everything in. Even then the queue for the gig stretched around the block. Eva and I walked among the kids. Eva was excited and perplexed and intimidated by the crowd. 'How has Charlie done this?' she kept asking. 'We'll soon find out,' I said. 'Do their mothers know they're here?' she asked. 'Does he really know what he's doing, Karim?' Some of the kids were as young as twelve; most were about seventeen. They were dressed like Charlie, mostly in black. Some of them had orange- or blue-streaked hair, making them look like cockatoos. They elbowed and fought and gave each other tongue-sandwiches, and spat at passers-by and in each other's faces, there in the cold and rain of decaying London, with the indifferent police looking on. As a concession to the New Wave I wore a black shirt, black jeans, white socks and black suede shoes, but I knew I had uninteresting hair. Not that I was the only one:

some older men in 1960s expensive casual clothes, Fiorucci jeans and suede boots, with Cuban heels for Christ's sake, were chasing the band, hoping to sign them.

What, then, had Charlie done since that night in the Nashville? He'd got in with the punks and seen immediately what they were doing, what a renaissance this was in music. He'd changed the group's name to the Condemned and his own name to Charlie Hero. And as the mood of British music snapped from one paradigm to another, from lush Baroque to angry garage, he'd forced and battered Mustn't Grumble into becoming one of the hottest New Wave or punk bands around.

Eva's son was continually being chased by national papers, magazines and semioticians for quotes about the new nihilism, the new hopelessness and the new music which expressed it. Hero was to explain the despair of the young to the baffled but interested, which he did by spitting at journalists or just punching them. He had a smart head, Charlie; he learned that his success, like that of the other bands, was guaranteed by his ability to insult the media. Fortunately, Charlie had a talent for cruelty. These insults were published widely, as were his other assaults on hippies, love, the Queen, Mick Jagger, political activism and punk itself. 'We're shit,' he proclaimed one night on early evening television. 'Can't play, can't sing, can't write songs, and the shitty idiot people love us!' Two outraged parents were reported as having kicked in their TV screens at this. Eva even appeared in the *Daily Mirror* under the headline: 'PUNK MUM SAYS I'M PROUD OF MY SON!'

The Fish ensured that Charlie was in the news and firmly established as a Face. He was also ensuring that their first record, *The Bride of Christ*, would be out in a few weeks. Offence had already been caused. With luck the record would be vilified and banned, guaranteeing credibility and financial success. Charlie was well on his way at last.

That evening, as always, the Fish was polite and gentlemanly. He reassured Eva that he and Charlie knew exactly what they were doing. But she was anxious. She kissed the Fish and clutched his arm, and openly begged him, 'Please, please, don't let my son become a heroin addict. You've no idea how weak he is.'

The Fish got us a good position at the back of the club, where we stood on wooden beer crates holding on to each other as the floor seemed about to crack open with heat and stomping. I soon felt as if the entire audience were lying on top of me – and the band were still in the dressing room.

They came on. The place went berserk. The Condemned had thrown out everything of their former existence – their hair, clothes, music. They were unrecognizable.

And they were nervous, not quite at ease yet in their new clothes. They crashed through their set as if they were in a competition to see who could get through the most songs in the shortest time, sounding like an unrehearsed version of the group Charlie and I had seen in the Nashville. Charlie no longer played rhythm guitar but stood clutching a mike stand at the edge of the stage, howling at the kids, who pogoed like road drills, and spat and lobbed bottles until the stage was littered with broken glass. He got cut on the hand. Beside me, Eva gasped and covered her face. Then Charlie was smearing blood over his face and wiping it over the bass guitarist.

The rest of the Condemned were still nonentities, the clerks and Civil Servants of the music business. But Charlie was magnificent in his venom, his manufactured rage, his anger, his defiance. What power he had, what admiration he extorted, what looks there were in girls' eyes. He was brilliant: he'd assembled the right elements. It was a wonderful trick and disguise. The one flaw, I giggled to myself, was his milky and healthy white teeth, which, to me, betrayed everything else.

Then a riot started. Bottles flew, strangers punched each other and a tooth flew down Eva's cleavage. I had blood all over me. Girls passed out on the floor; ambulances were called. The Fish efficiently got us out.

I was thoughtful as we walked through Soho that night. Beside me, Eva, in her jeans and tennis shoes, stepped along lightly, trying to hum one of Charlie's songs and keep up with my fast pace. Eventually she took my arm. We were so easy with each other, we could have been going out together. We said nothing; I presumed she was speculating about Charlie's future. On my side, I burned with less envy of Charlie than I'd imagined I would. This was because one strong feeling dominated me: ambition. As yet it was unfocused. But I was completely impressed by Charlie's big con trick, by his having knocked on the door of opportunity and its opening up to him, its goods tumbling out. Now he could take what he wanted. Until this moment I'd felt incapable of operating effectively in the world; I didn't know how to do it; events tossed me about. Now I was beginning to see that it didn't necessarily have to be that way. My happiness and progress and education could depend on my own activity – as long as it was the right activity at the right time. My coming appearance in *The Jungle Book* was meagre in comparison with Charlie's triumph, but soon eyes would be on me; it was a start, and I felt strong and determined. It would lead upwards.

As we got into the car I looked at Eva and she smiled at me. I felt she hadn't been thinking about Charlie at all – except as an inspiration – but that, like me, she'd been dwelling on what she might do in the world. Driving us back home, Eva banged the steering wheel and sang, and yelled out of the window.

'Weren't they great? Isn't he a star, Karim!'

'Yeah, yeah!'

'They're going to be big, Karim, really huge. But Charlie will have to jettison that group. He can make it on his own, don't you think?'

'Yeah, but what will happen to them?'

'Those boys?' She waved them away. 'But our boy's going up. Up! Up!' She leaned over and kissed me on the cheek. 'And you too, OK?'

The dress rehearsal of *The Jungle Book* went well. We were all surprised by how smooth it was; no one forgot their lines, and technically all was fine. So we went into the first preview, in front of an audience, with plenty of confidence. The costumes were amusing and the audience applauded them. The naughty monkeys screeched their high-pitched calls as the Pack Council met to discuss the man cub's future. But as Shere Khan growled from the distance in his Hamlet's ghost voice, 'The cub is mine. Give him to me. What have the Free People to do with a man's cub?' I heard a cracking noise above me. Unprofessionally, I looked up, to see the iron net of the scaffolding bending, swaying and finally tipping towards me as bolts snapped and lights crashed down on to the floor of the stage. Voices in the audience shouted out warnings to us. Most of the front row jumped to their feet and fled up the aisle away from the danger. I deserted the play, as did the other actors on stage, and leapt into the audience. I landed on Shadwell, who was already on his feet screaming at the technicians. The play was abandoned for that night and the audience sent home. The rows were horrific, Shadwell a monster. Two other previews were cut. There was to be only one preview before the first night.

Naturally, I wanted Mum to be at the first night, and Dad too. But as they hadn't seen each other since the day they both left the house, I didn't think my début in *The Jungle Book* was the best time for a reunion. So I invited Mum, with Uncle Ted and Auntie Jean, to the preview. This time nothing went wrong. Afterwards, Uncle Ted, who had his suit and Brylcreem on, announced a treat. He would take us all out to Trader Vics at the Hilton Hotel. Mum had dressed up, and was looking all sweet in a blue dress with a bow at the front. She was cheerful, too; I'd forgotten how happy she could be. In a fit of unshyness she'd left the shoe shop and was working as a receptionist at a doctor's practice. She began to discuss illness with authority.

Mum wept with pride at my Mowgli. Jean, who hadn't wept since the death of Humphrey Bogart, laughed a great deal and was good-tempered and drunk.

'I thought it would be more amateur,' she kept saying, obviously surprised that I could be involved in anything that wasn't a total failure. 'But it was really professional! And fancy meeting all those television actors!'

The key to impressing Mum and Auntie Jean, and the best way to keep their tongues off the risible subject of my loin-cloth, which inevitably had them quaking with laughter, was to introduce them to the actors afterwards, telling them which sit-coms and police programmes they'd seen them in. After dinner we went dancing in a night club in the West End. I'd never seen Mum dance before, but she slipped out of her sandals and danced with Auntie Jean to the Jackson Five. It was a grand evening.

However, I imagined that the praise I received that night was merely to be a preview of the steaming sauna of appreciation that I'd receive after the first night. So after the opening I ran out of the dressing room to where Dad, in his red waistcoat, was waiting with all the others. None of them looked particularly cheerful. We walked up the street to a restaurant nearby, and still no one spoke to me. 'Well, Dad,' I asked, 'how did you enjoy yourself? Aren't you glad I didn't become a doctor?'

Like a fool, I'd forgotten that Dad thought honesty a virtue. He was a compassionate man, Dad, but never at the expense of drawing attention to his own opinions.

'Bloody half-cocked business,' he said. 'That bloody fucker Mr Kipling pretending to whity he knew something about India! And an awful performance by my boy looking like a Black and White Minstrel!'

Eva restrained Dad. 'Karim was assured,' she said firmly, patting my arm.

Fortunately, Changez had chuckled all through the show. 'Good entertainment,' he said. 'Take me again, eh?'

Before we sat down in the restaurant Jamila took me aside and kissed me on the mouth. I felt Changez's eyes on me.

'You looked wonderful,' she said, as if she were speaking to a ten-year-old after a school play. 'So innocent and young, showing off your pretty body, so thin and perfectly formed. But no doubt about it, the play is completely neo-fascist – '

'Jammie – '

'And it was disgusting, the accent and the shit you had smeared over you. You were just pandering to prejudices – '

'Jammie – '

'And clichés about Indians. And the accent – my God, how could you do it? I expect you're ashamed, aren't you?'

'I am, actually.'

But she didn't pity me; she mimicked my accent in the play. 'Actually, you've got no morality, have you? You'll get it later, I expect, when you can afford it.'

'You're going too far, Jamila,' I said, and turned my back on her. I went and sat with Changez.

The only other significant event of the evening was something that happened between Eva and Shadwell at the far end of the restaurant, beside the toilet. Shadwell was leaning back against the wall and Eva was angry with him, making hard gestures with her fists. Many bitter shades of disgust and pain and dejection passed over his face. At one point Eva turned and gesticulated towards me, as if she were taking him to task for something he'd done to me. Yes, Shadwell had let her down. But I knew that nothing would ever discourage him; he'd never give up wanting to be a director, and he'd never be any good.

So that was it. *The Jungle Book* was not mentioned again by any of them, as if they weren't ready to see me as an actor but preferred me in my old role as a useless boy. Yet the play did good business, especially with schools, and I started to relax on stage, and to enjoy acting. I sent up the accent and made the audience laugh by suddenly relapsing into cockney at odd times. 'Leave it out, Bagheera,' I'd say. I liked being recognized in the pub afterwards, and made myself conspicuous in case anyone wanted my autograph.

Sometimes Shadwell came in to watch the show, and one day he started being nice to me. I asked Terry why this was. 'I'm baffled too,' he said. Then Shadwell took me to Joe Allen's and offered me a part in his next production, which would be Molière's *Le Bourgeois Gentilhomme*. Terry, whose gentleness of heart so melted my own that I helped him sell his newspapers outside factories, on picket lines and outside East End tube stations at seven-thirty in the morning, was encouraging. 'Accept it,' he said. 'It'll do you good. 'Course, it's crap for actors, but it's experience for you.'

Unlike the other actors – they'd been in the business much longer than I had – I had no idea what work I could get. So I accepted. Shadwell and I embraced. Eva said nothing about it.

'What about you, Terry?' I asked one evening. 'Have you got any work lined up?'

'Oh yeah.'

'What?'

'Nothing precisely,' he said. 'But I'm waiting for the call.'

'What call?'

'I can't tell you that, Karim. But I can say confidently that the call is going to come.'

When I turned up at the theatre and Terry and I got changed next to each other, I frequently made a point of saying to him, 'Well, Terry, has the call come yet? Has Peter Brook rung?'

Or one of us would rush into the dressing room just before curtain-up and tell Terry there was someone who urgently needed to talk to him on the phone. Twice he fell for it, running half-dressed out of the room and instructing everyone to hold the show for a few minutes. He wasn't thrown by our malice. 'I'm not bothered by your childish games. I know the call's going to come. It's not something that makes me anxious at all. I'm going to wait patiently.'

One night, half-way through the run, the box-office manager excitedly rang through to us back-stage and said that the theatre director Matthew Pyke had booked a ticket for *The Jungle Book*. Within fifteen minutes everyone in the cast – apart from me – was talking about this. I'd never seen such chatter, nervousness and exhilaration in the dressing room before. But I did know how crucial such visits by hot directors were to actors, who worried constantly about their next job. *The Jungle Book* they'd forgotten about: it was in the past. Now they sat in the tiny dressing room, their washing hanging on the radiators, eating health food and tirelessly sending information and soft-focus photographs of themselves to directors, theatres, agents, TV companies and producers. And when agents or casting directors deigned to see the show, and stayed to the end, which was rare, the actors crowded around them afterwards, buying them drinks and roaring with laughter at anything they said. They ached to be remembered: upon such memories an actor's life depended.

This was why Pyke's appearance was so exciting. He was our most important visitor ever. He had his own company. You didn't have to go through him to get to someone who counted: he counted in his own right. But why had he come to see our pissy show? We couldn't work it out, although I noticed that Terry was being very cool about the whole thing.

Before the show some of us crowded into the tiny lighting box as Pyke, in his denim dungarees and white T-shirt – he still had long hair – took his seat. He was accompanied by his wife, Marlene, a middle-aged blonde. We watched him consult the programme, turning each page and examining our faces and the oblong patch of biography beneath the photographs.

The rest of the cast stood outside and waited for their turn to get a look at Pyke. I said nothing, but I had no idea who Pyke was and what he'd done. Was it plays? Films? Opera? Television? Was he American? At last I asked Terry; I knew he wouldn't be contemptuous of my ignorance. Terry eagerly gave me the whole picture; he seemed to know enough about Pyke to write his biography.

Pyke was the star of the flourishing alternative theatre scene; he was one of the most original directors around. He'd worked and taught at the Magic Theater in San Francisco; had therapy at the

Esalen Institute in Big Sur with Fritz Perls; worked in New York with Chaikin and La Mama. In London, with a couple of contemporaries from Cambridge, he started his own company, the Movable Theatre, for which he did two ravishing productions a year.

These productions played in London at the end of their well-meant journey around arts centres, youth clubs and studio theatres. Fashionable people attended the London opening: there were bright rock-stars, other actors like Terence Stamp, politicos like Tariq Ali, most of the ordinary acting profession, and even the public. Pyke's shows were also commended for their fantastic intermissions, dazzling occasions where the fashionable audience came dressed in such style they resembled Chinese peasants, industrial workers (boiler suits) or South American insurgents (berets).

Naturally Terry had hard-line views on all this, and as we changed for the show on that charged night he proclaimed them to the entire cast, as if he were addressing a meeting.

'Comrades, what is Pyke's stuff? What is it, after all – just think for a minute – but a lot of reformist and flatulent "left-wing" politics! It's plump actors pretending to be working class, when their fathers are neuro-surgeons. It's voluptuous actresses – even more beautiful than you all are – hand-picked and caressed by Pyke! Why do they always perform the whole show in the nude? Ask yourself these questions! It's fucking crap for actors, comrades. Absolute crap for actors!'

The other actors shouted Terry down.

'It's not crap for actors!' they cried. 'At least it's decent work after doing *The Jungle Bunny* and thrillers and beer commercials.'

Terry had taken off his trousers by now, and two women in the cast were looking through a gap in the curtain as he prepared to propagate his analysis of Pyke. Slowly he hung his trousers on a hanger, which he placed on the communal rail which ran through the dressing room. He liked girls looking at his muscly legs; he liked them hearing his muscly arguments, too.

'Oh yes,' he said. 'You're right. There's truth in what you say. It's better than fuck-all. Much better. That's why, comrades, I sent Pyke my particulars.'

Everyone groaned. But with Pyke to impress in the audience we had good reason to spring energetically over the scaffolding. The show was the best it had ever been, and its proper length, for once.

Recently we'd been taking ten minutes a night off it in order to have more time in the pub. After this show we changed quickly, without the usual bickering and jokes and attempts to pull each other's underpants off. Naturally I was the slowest, having the most to remove. There wasn't a working shower and I had to clean off my make-up with cold-cream and by splashing water from the sink over myself. Terry waited impatiently for me. When I'd finished and it was just the two of us left I put my arms around him and kissed his face.

'Come on,' he said. 'Let's move. Pyke's waiting for me.'

'Let's stay here for a while.'

'Why?'

I said, 'I'm thinking of joining the Party. I want to discuss various ideological problems I have.'

'Bollocks,' he said. He moved away from me. 'I'm not against this,' he said.

'What?'

'Touching.'

But he was against it.

'It's just that I have to think about my future right now. My call has come, Karim.'

'Yeah?' I said. 'Is this it? Is this the call?'

'Yeah, this is fucking it,' he said. 'Please. Come on.'

'Do up my buttons,' I said.

'Christ. You. You stupid boy. OK. Come on. Pyke's waiting for me.'

We hurried to the pub. I'd never seen Terry look so hopeful about anything before. I really wanted him to get the job.

Pyke was leaning against the bar with Marlene, sipping a half of lager. He didn't look the drinking type. Three of our company went up to him and chatted briefly. Pyke replied, but barely seemed bothered to move his lips. Then Shadwell came into the pub, saw Pyke, nodded contemptuously at us, and left. Instead of going over to Pyke, Terry led me to a corner table among the old men who drank alone every night, and there he calmly sucked his roll-ups as we sipped our usual pint with a whisky chaser.

'Pyke's not showing much interest in you,' I pointed out.

Terry was confident. 'He'll be over. He's very cold – you know what middle-class people are like. No feelings. I reckon he wants my working-class experience to give his puerile political ideas some authenticity.'

'Say no,' I advised him.

'I bloody might. Critics always say his work's "austere" or "puritanical" because he likes bare raked stages and theatres with their brickwork sticking out all over the place and no props. As if my mum and the working class like that. They want comfortable seats, french windows and sweets.'

Just then Pyke turned towards us and raised his glass a fraction of an inch. Terry smiled back.

' 'Course, Pykie's got his virtues. He's not self-promoting like those other cunt directors and conductors and producers who just live off other people's talent. He never does interviews and he never goes on telly. He's good like that. But,' said Terry darkly, leaning towards me, 'this is something you should know, if you're lucky enough to work with him one day.'

He told me that Pyke's private life wasn't a desert of austere and puritanical practices. If the inevitably deformed critics who admired his work – and the critics who sat with their faces pointing up at us did seem to have the countenances of gargoyles, while the aisles were crammed with their wheelchairs – knew of certain weaknesses – certain indulgences, let us say – they would see Pyke's work in a different light. 'Oh yes, a very different light.'

'What kind of light?'

'I can't tell you that.'

'But, Terry, surely we hide nothing from each other?'

'No, no, I can't say. Sorry.'

Terry didn't gossip. He believed that people were made by the impersonal forces of history, not by greed, malice and lust. And besides, Pyke was now walking straight towards us. Terry hurriedly stubbed out his roll-up, pushed his chair back and got up. His hand even went up to flatten his hair. He shook hands with Pyke. Then he introduced us to each other.

'Nice to see you, Terry,' Pyke said smoothly.

'Yeah, and you, and you.'

'You make an excellent snake.'

'Thank you. But thank God someone's doing some classy work in this crumby country, eh?'

'Who do you mean?'

'You, Matthew.'

'Oh yes. Me.'

'Yes.'

Pyke looked at me and smiled. 'Come and have a drink at the bar, Karim.'

'Me?'

'Why not?'

'OK. See you later, Terry,' I said.

As I got up Terry looked at me as if I'd just announced I had a private income. He sank back into his chair as Pyke and I walked away from the table, and tossed the whisky down his throat.

As Pyke got me a half of bitter I stood there regarding the rows of inverted bottles behind the barman's head, not looking at the other actors in the pub, who I knew were all staring at me. I meditated for a few seconds, concentrating on my breathing, immediately aware of how shallow it was. When we were set up with drinks, Pyke said, 'Tell me about yourself.'

I hesitated. I looked at Marlene, who was standing behind us, talking to an actor. 'I don't know where to begin.'

'Tell me something you think might interest me.'

And he looked at me with full concentration. I had no choice. I began to talk rapidly and at random. He said nothing. I went on. I thought: I am being psychoanalysed. I began to imagine that Pyke would understand everything I said. I was glad he was there; there were things it was necessary to say. So I told him things I'd never told anyone – how much I resented Dad for what he'd done to Mum, and how Mum had suffered, how painful the whole thing had been, though I was only now beginning to feel it.

The other actors, who were now gathered around Terry's table with jars of yellow beer in front of them, had turned their chairs around to watch me, as if I were a football match. They must have been amazed and resentful that Pyke wanted to listen to me, of all people, someone who was barely an actor. When I faltered as the realization hit me that it wasn't Mum who'd neglected me, but I who'd neglected Mum, Pyke said gently, 'I think you may like to be in my next production.'

I woke from my introspective dream and said, 'What kind of show will it be?'

I noticed that when Pyke was about to talk he put his head

thoughtfully to one side and looked away into the distance. He used his hands flirtatiously, slowly, not flapping or pointing but caressing and floating, as if wiping his flat hand inches from the surface of a painting. He said, 'I don't know.'

'What kind of part will it be?'

He shook his head regretfully.

'I'm afraid I can't begin to say.'

'How many people will be in it?'

There was a long pause. His hand, with the fingers splayed and taut, waved in front of his face.

'Don't ask me.'

'D'you know what you're doing?' I asked, more bravely.

'No.'

'Well, I don't know if I want to work in that vague kind of way. I'm inexperienced, you know.'

Pyke conceded. 'I think it may revolve around the only subject there is in England.'

'I see.'

'Yes.'

He looked at me as if I were sure of what this was.

'Class,' he said. 'Is that OK for you?'

'Yes, I think so.'

He touched me on the shoulder. 'Good. Thank you for joining us.' It was as if I were doing him a big favour.

I finished my drink, quickly said goodbye to the other actors and got out as fast as I could, not wanting to register their smirks and curiosity. I was walking across the car park when someone jumped on my back. It was Terry.

'Leave it out,' I said sternly, pushing him off.

'Oh yeah.'

There were no laughs in his face. He looked very low. He made me feel ashamed of my sudden happiness. I walked to the bus stop in silence with him beside me. It was cold, dark and raining.

'Has Pyke offered you a part?' he said at last.

'Yes.'

'Liar!'

I said nothing. 'Liar!' he said. I knew he was so incensed he couldn't control himself; I couldn't blame him for the fury which inhabited him. 'It can't be true, it can't be true,' he said.

Suddenly I shouted out into the night air. 'Yes, yes, yes, it is true!' And now the world had some tension in it; now it twanged and vibrated with meaning and possibility! 'Yes, yes, fucking yes!'

When I got to the theatre next day someone had laid a dirty red carpet from the dressing-room door to the spot where I normally changed. 'Can I help you off with your clothes?' one actor said. 'Can I have your autograph?' said another. I received daffodils, roses and an acting primer. The EST freak, Boyd, said, as he took off his trousers and shook his penis at me, 'If I weren't white and middle class I'd have been in Pyke's show now. Obviously mere talent gets you nowhere these days. Only the disadvantaged are going to succeed in seventies' England.'

For a few days I was too cowardly to tell Shadwell of Pyke's offer, and that I was not going to do the Molière. I was happy and didn't want the pleasure of anticipation soured by a row with him. So Shitvolumes started preparing his next show as if I were going to be in it, until one day, just before *The Jungle Book* was about to go up, he came into the dressing room.

'Jeremy,' I said, 'I think I'd better tell you something.'

We went into the communal lavatory, the only private space back-stage, and I broke the news to him. Shadwell nodded and said gently, 'You're being ungrateful, Karim. You shouldn't just bugger off, you know, it's not right. We all love you here, OK?'

'Please understand, Jeremy – Pyke's a big man. Very important. Surely there's a tide in the affairs of men which taken – '

Shadshit's voice suddenly rose to rehearsal pitch and he walked out of the toilet and into the dressing room. Behind us in the auditorium the show was about to begin, and the audience were in their seats. They could hear every syllable. I felt particularly ridiculous hurrying along behind him in my loin-cloth.

'What tide, you drowning prick?' he said. 'You haven't the experience to deal with Pyke. You'll be mincemeat within three days. You've got no idea what a tough fucking bastard Pyke is. He's charming, all right. All interesting people have charm. But he'll crucify you!'

'Why would he want to crucify a little person like me?' I said weakly. Boyd smirked and mouthed 'exactly' at Terry, who ignored him but seemed to be nodding in agreement with Shotbolt.

'For fun, you idiot! Because that's how people like that operate! They pretend they're democrats but they're little Lenins – '

Terry took offence at this. He glared at Shadwell and said, 'They should be so lucky!' But Shoddy was not to be deterred now he was going.

'They're cultural fascists and élitists who think they know better than anyone else how it is! They're paranoid, frightened people!'

Some of the others in the cast were laughing behind their hands like schoolkids when one of them is being castigated by Teacher. I walked towards the stage on my red carpet.

'I don't care what you say. I can look after myself.'

'Ha!' he shouted. 'We'll fucking see – you little parvenu!'

CHAPTER ELEVEN

Spring. Some time after I'd said goodbye to Bagheera, Baloo and the others, and get fucked to Shadwell, and didn't go to the last-night party, I was in a clean, bright rehearsal room with a polished wooden floor (so we could run around barefoot) in a church hall by the river, near Chelsea Bridge. There were six actors in Pyke's group, three men and three women. Two of us were officially 'black' (though truly I was more beige than anything). None of us was over thirty. Only one woman, pinched-face Carol, also from the suburbs (so I had her ambitious little number right away), had worked with Pyke before. There was a red-haired woman called Eleanor, in her early twenties, who seemed experienced and sensible, and unlike Carol didn't fancy herself as a bit of a star. And there was a nineteen-year-old black actress, Tracey, with firm but peculiar views. The other two men, Richard (gay) and Jon, were those solid, cynical, jobbing actors who'd been around the London fringe for years, acting in rooms above pubs for a share of the box-office, in basements, at festivals and in street theatre. They required little but a good part, a director who wasn't a fool or a dictator, and a comfortable pub near the venue with authentic beer. There was also a writer in the group, Louise Lawrence, an earnest and self-satisfied northern woman with thick glasses who said little but wrote down everything you said, especially if it was stupid.

At ten every morning I cycled into Chelsea, with Eva's mush-rooms-on-toast fuelling me, and rode around the hall with no hands – in celebration of life. I'd never been so enthusiastic about anything. This was my big chance, in more ways than one.

Pyke, in his shiny blue tracksuit, with his athletic body and greying hair, usually sat at a table with his feet on a chair. He was surrounded by laughing actors and the two stage-managers, ador-ing young women who were like his personal servants. The stage-managers looked after his newspapers, his orange juice, and planned his trips to New York. One of them carried his diary, the other his pencils and sharpener. His car (which Richard referred to as 'Pyke's Penis', as in 'Pyke's Penis is blocking the drive' or 'Pyke's Penis can do nought to sixty in thirty seconds') was a priority for them. And they spent many mornings on the phone arranging his dates with women.

The atmosphere Pyke created was in contrast to Shadwell's tense and chaotic rehearsals, which were essentially an imitation of how Shadwell thought geniuses worked. Pyke's morning began with breakfast and essential gossip around the table, the cruelty and extremity of which I'd never experienced before. My mother would never have let us talk about anyone like that. Pyke attacked other directors ('He couldn't direct air out of a puncture'); writers he didn't like ('I would gladly have handed him over to Stalin for re-education'); and critics ('His face would make pregnant women abort on sight'). After this we'd get up and play tag, or have piggy-back races, or play 'What's the time, Mr Wolf?'

None of this seemed like work to me, and I loved to think of what the suburban commuters in our street, who were paying for us through their taxes, would have made of a gang of grown-ups being pop-up toasters, surfboards and typewriters.

After lunch, to warm up again, Pyke had us play 'feely' games where we stood in the centre of a circle with our feet together and eyes closed and just let ourselves fall. Weak and relaxed, we'd be passed around the group. Everyone touched us; we embraced and kissed. This was how Pyke fused the group. It seemed to me during one of these games that Eleanor remained in my arms just that little bit longer than necessary.

On the fourth day, sitting there at ten in the morning with all of us gathered around him, Pyke played a game which disturbed me, which made me think there was a shadow side to him. Looking slyly around the group he said he would predict which of us would sleep together. He inspected each of us in turn and said, 'I think I know which way pleasure's course will run. I'll write down my predictions, and on the last night of the show I'll read them out. OK?'

During the second week the sun shone and we opened the doors. I wore an unbuttoned Hawaiian shirt which I sometimes knotted on my stomach. One of the stage-managers almost stopped breathing when she saw me, I'm not kidding. We each sat in what Pyke called 'the hot seat' with the group arranged in a staring semi-circle around us. Each of us had to tell the rest of the group the story of our life.

'Concentrate on the way you think your position in society has been fixed,' said Pyke.

Being sceptical and suspicious, the English sort to be embarrassed by such a Californian display of self, I found the life-stories – accounts of contradiction and wretchedness, confusion and intermittent happiness – oddly affecting. I giggled all through Lawrence's account of working in a San Francisco massage parlour (when she was stranded there), where the women were not allowed to proposition men directly in case they were cops. They had to say, 'Is there any other muscle you'd like relaxed, sir?' This was where Lawrence discovered socialism, for here, in a forest of pricks and pond of semen, 'I soon realized that nothing human was alien to me,' as she put it.

Richard talked about wanting to fuck only black men, and the clubs he cruised constantly in order to acquire them. And to Pyke's delight and my surprise Eleanor told of how she'd worked with a woman performance artist who persuaded her to extract the texts of poems – 'Cows' teeth like snowdrops bite the garlic grass' – from her vagina before reading them. The performance artist herself meanwhile had a microphone up her vagina and relayed the gurglings of her cunt to the audience. This was enough for me. I was hot on Eleanor's trail. For the time being I gave up on Terry.

Every few days I rang Jamila to give her a full account of cows' teeth like snowdrops, Pyke's Penis, San Francisco, Hawaii and pop-up toasters. Everyone else was encouraging: Eva, having heard of Pyke, was very impressed; and Dad was happy that I was working. The only person I was certain would urinate on my flame was Jamila.

So I explained the games and the reasoning behind them. 'Pyke's a shrewd man,' I told her. 'By having us expose ourselves he's made us vulnerable and dependent on each other. We're so close as a group it's incredible!'

'Pah. You're not close to each other. It's fake, just a technique.'

'I thought you believed in co-operation and all. Communist stuff like that.'

'Karim, shall I tell you what's been going on over here at the shop while you've been over there hugging strangers?'

'Why, what?'

'No, I'm not going to talk to you. Karim, you're basically a selfish person, uninterested in anyone else.'

'What?'

'Go back to being a tree.' And she put the phone down.

Soon, in the mornings, we stopped meeting at the rehearsal room: we all went our separate ways to research characters from different rungs of the social ladder. These people Louise Lawrence would eventually have to try and massage into the same play. In the afternoons we improvised around the characters and started to build scenes. Initially I thought I'd choose Charlie as my character, but Pyke discouraged me immediately. 'We need someone from your own background,' he said. 'Someone black.'

'Yeah?'

I didn't know anyone black, though I'd been at school with a Nigerian. But I wouldn't know where to find him. 'Who do you mean?' I asked.

'What about your family?' Pyke said. 'Uncles and aunts. They'll give the play a little variety. I bet they're fascinating.'

I thought for a few minutes.

'Any ideas?' he said.

'I've got just the thing,' I said.

'Excellent. I knew you'd be the right person to be in this show.'

After breakfast with Dad and Eva I cycled across the river, past the Oval cricket ground to Jeeta and Anwar's shop. I was beginning to think of Anwar as the character I'd play, and I wanted to see how he'd changed since the advent of Changez, who was such a disappointment that Anwar – who had been counting on being given a life-transfusion by a son – had become an old man, his natural course of decay being accelerated, not delayed, by the fresh element which had turned out to be not-so-fresh.

When I arrived Jeeta got up from behind the till and hugged me. I noticed how grubby and gloomy Paradise Stores looked now: paint was peeling from the walls, the shelves were dirty, the lino on the floor was curling and cracking, and several lights seemed to have failed, leaving the place tenebrous. Outside, in their old orange-boxes, even the vegetables looked forlorn, and Jeeta had grown tired of scrubbing off the racist graffiti which reappeared on the walls every time you removed it. Other shops in the area, all over London in fact, were modernizing rapidly, as ambitious Pakistanis and

Bengalis bought them up. Several brothers, say, would come to London; they'd get two jobs each, in an office during the day and a restaurant by night; they'd buy a shop, installing one brother as manager, with his wife behind the till. Then they'd get another shop and do the same, until a chain was established. Money flowed. But Anwar and Jeeta's shop had not changed in years. Business was slack. Everything was going wrong, but I didn't want to think about it. The play was too important.

I told Jeeta about the play and what I wanted – just to be around – knowing she'd barely understand or be interested. But she did have something to say.

'Whatever you do,' she said, 'if you're going to come here day after day, you must stop your uncle going out with his walking stick.'

'Why, Auntie Jeeta?'

'Karim, some thugs came here one day. They threw a pig's head through the shop window as I sat here.'

Jamila hadn't told me anything about this.

'Were you hurt?'

'A little cut. Blood here and there, Karim.'

'What did the police do?'

'They said it was another shop. A rival thing.'

'Bollocks.'

'Naughty boy, bad language.'

'Sorry, Auntie.'

'It made your uncle come very strange. He is roaming the streets every day with his stick, shouting at these white boys, "Beat me, white boy, if you want to!" ' And she blushed with shame and embarrassment. 'Go to him,' she said, and squeezed my hand.

I found Uncle Anwar upstairs in his pyjamas. He seemed to have shrunk in the past few months: his legs and body were emaciated, while his head remained the same size, perched on him like a globe on a walking stick.

'You bastard,' he said in greeting, 'where have you been?'

'I'm here with you every day now.'

He grunted his approbation and continued to watch television. He loved having me beside him, though he barely spoke and never asked me about myself. For a few weeks he'd been visiting the mosque regularly, and now I occasionally went with him. The mosque was a dilapidated terraced house nearby which smelled of bhuna gost. The floor was sprinkled with onion skins, and Moulvi Qamar-Uddin sat behind his desk surrounded by leather-bound books on Islam and a red telephone, stroking the beard which reached to his stomach. Anwar complained to the Moulvi that Allah had abandoned him despite regular prayers and a refusal to womanize. Hadn't he loved his wife and given her a shop, and now wasn't she refusing to go home to Bombay with him?

Anwar complained to me about Jeeta as we sat in the store-room like a couple of school truants. 'I want to go home now,' he said. 'I've had enough of this damn place.'

But as the days passed I watched Jeeta's progress. She certainly didn't want to go home. It was as if Jamila had educated her in possibility, the child being an example to the parent. The Princess wanted to get a licence to sell liquor on the premises; she wanted to sell newspapers and increase the stock. She could see how it was all done, but Anwar was impossible, you couldn't discuss anything with him. Like many Muslim men – beginning with the Prophet Mohammed himself, whose absolute statements, served up piping hot from God, inevitably gave rise to absolutism – Anwar thought he was right about everything. No doubt on any subject ever entered his head.

'Why don't you want to take up Jeeta's ideas?' I asked him.

'For what? What will I do with the profit? How many shoes can I wear? How many socks? How better will I eat? Thirty breakfasts instead of one?' And he always said, finally, 'Everything is perfect.'

'D'you believe that, Uncle?' I asked one day.

'No,' he replied. 'Everything gets worse.'

His Muslim fatalism – Allah was responsible for everything – depressed me. I was always glad to get away now. I had a far more exciting project heating up over the other side of the river. I had chosen Eleanor to fall in love with, and was making progress.

Almost every day after rehearsal Eleanor said, as I hoped she would, 'Are you coming over later, then, to keep me company?' And she watched my face anxiously, biting her nails and ripping the skin from around her fingernails with her teeth, and twisting her long red hair around her fingers.

From the start of rehearsal she had noticed my fear and inexperience, and offered consolation. Eleanor had already appeared in films, on TV and in the West End. I felt like a boy beside her, but there was something in her that needed me too, something weak rather than kind or passionate, as if I were a comfort during an illness, someone to touch, perhaps. As soon as I saw this weakness I closed in. I had never been seen with such a mature and beautiful woman before, and I encouraged her to go out with me so people would think we were a couple.

I started going to her flat in Ladbroke Grove, an area that was slowly being reconstituted by the rich, but where Rasta dope dealers still hung around outside the pubs; inside, they chopped up the hash on the table with their knives. There were also many punks around now, dressed, like Charlie, in ripped black. This was the acme of fashion. As soon as you got your clothes home you had to slash them with razor-blades. And there were the kids who were researchers and editors and the like: they'd been at Oxford together and they swooped up to wine bars in bright little red and blue Italian cars, afraid they would be broken into by the black kids, but too politically polite to acknowledge this.

But how stupid I was – how naïve. I was misled by my ignorance of London into thinking my Eleanor was less middle class than she turned out to be. She dressed roughly, wearing a lot of scarves, lived in Notting Hill and – sometimes – talked with a Catford accent. My mother would have been appalled by Eleanor's clothes and manners, and her saying 'shit' and 'fuck' every ten seconds. This wouldn't have perturbed Eva: she would have been disappointed and perplexed by Eleanor's concealment of her social origins and the way she took her 'connections' for granted. Eva would have given much to edge her body into the houses Eleanor had played in as a child.

Eleanor's father was American and owned a bank; her mother was a well-respected English portrait painter; one of her brothers was a university professor. Eleanor had been to country houses, to public school and Italy, and she knew many liberal families and people who'd flourished in the 1960s: painters, novelists, lecturers, young people called Candia, Emma, Jasper, Lucy, India, and grown-ups called Edward, Caroline, Francis, Douglas and Lady Luckham. Her mother was a friend of the Queen Mother, and when Ma'am turned up in her Bentley the local kids gathered round the car and cheered. One day Eleanor had to rush away from rehearsal because she was required by her mother to make up the numbers at a lunch for the Queen Mother. The voices and language of those people reminded me of Enid Blyton, and Bunter and Jennings, of nurseries and nannies and prep school, a world of total security that I'd thought existed only in books. They lacked all understanding of how much more than anyone else they had. I was frightened of their confidence, education, status, money, and I was beginning to see how important they were.

To my surprise, the people whose shabby houses I went to as I trailed around with Eleanor night after night, 'looking after her', were polite and kind and attentive to me, far more pleasant than the supercilious crowd Eva drew to her place. Eleanor's set, with their combination of class, culture and money, and their indifference to all three, was exactly the cocktail that intoxicated Eva's soul, but she could never get near it. This was unforced bohemia; this was what she sought; this was the apogee. However, I concealed this aspect of my social rise from Eva, saving it up for the perfect defensive or attacking occasion, though she and Dad had already heard that I'd set my sights on Eleanor. This was a relief to my father, I knew, who was so terrified that I might turn out to be gay that he could never bring himself to mention the matter. In his Muslim mind it was bad enough being a woman; being a man and denying your male sex was perverse and self-destructive, as well as everything else. When I could see Dad's mind brooding on the subject I was always sure to mention Mum – how she was, what she was doing – knowing that this powerful anguish was sure to banish the matter of my sexual orientation.

Eleanor was not without her eccentricities. She didn't like to go out unless the visits were fleeting and she could come and go at will. She never sat all the way through a dinner party, but arrived during it, eating a bag of sweets and walking around the room picking up various objects and enquiring into their history, before dragging me off after half an hour with a sudden desire to visit another party somewhere to talk to someone who was an expert on the Profumo affair.

Often we stayed in and she cooked. I was never one for education and vegetables, having been inoculated against both at school, but most nights Eleanor made me cabbage or broccoli or Brussels sprouts, steaming them and dunking them in frying butter and garlic for a few seconds. Another time we had red snapper, which tasted a little tough, like shark, in puff pastry with sour cream and parsley. We usually had a bottle of Chablis too. And none of this had I experienced before! Eleanor could sleep only if she was drunk, and I never cycled home before my baby was tucked up, half-cut, with a Jean Rhys or Antonia White to cheer her up. I would have preferred, of course, that I myself could be her nightcap.

It was clear that Eleanor had been to bed with a large and random collection of people, but when I suggested she go to bed with me, she said, 'I don't think we should, just at the moment, do you?' As a man I found this pretty fucking insulting. There were constant friendly caresses, and when things got too much (every few hours) she held me and cried, but the big caress was out.

I soon realized that Eleanor's main guardian and my main rival for her affection was a man called Heater. He was the local road-sweeper, a grossly fat and ugly sixteen-stone Scot in a donkey jacket whom Eleanor had taken up three years ago as a cause. He came round every night he wasn't at the theatre, and sat in the flat reading Balzac in translation and giving his bitter and big-mouthed opinion on the latest production of *Lear* or the *Ring*. He knew dozens of actors, especially the left-wing ones, of whom there were plenty at this political time. Heater was the only working-class person most of them had met. So he became a sort of symbol of the masses, and consequently received tickets to first nights and to the parties afterwards, having a busier social life than Cecil Beaton. He even popped in to dress rehearsals to give his opinion as 'a man in the street'. If you didn't adore Heater – and I hated every repulsive inch of him – and listen to him as the authentic voice of the proletariat, it was easy, if you were middle class (which meant you were born a criminal, having fallen at birth), to be seen by the comrades and their sympathizers as a snob, an élitist, a hypocrite, a proto-Goebbels.

I found myself competing with Heater for Eleanor's love. If I sat too close to her he glared at me; if I touched her casually his eyes would dilate and flare like gas rings. His purpose in life was to ensure Eleanor's happiness, which was harder work than road-sweeping, since she disliked herself so intensely. Yes, Eleanor loathed herself and yet required praise, which she then never believed. But she reported it to me, saying, 'D'you know what so-

and-so said this morning? He said, when he held me, that he loved the smell of me, he loved my skin and the way I made him laugh.'

When I discussed this aspect of Eleanor with my adviser, Jamila, she didn't let me down. 'Christ, Creamy Fire Eater, you one hundred per cent total prat, that's exactly what they're like, these people, actresses and such-like vain fools. The world burns and they comb their eyebrows. Or they try and put the burning world on the stage. It never occurs to them to dowse the flames. What are you getting into?'

'Love. I love her.'

'Ah.'

'But she won't even kiss me. What should I do?'

'Am I an agony aunt now?'

'Yes.'

'OK,' she said. 'Don't attempt kissing until I advise. Wait.'

Vain and self-obsessed Eleanor may have been, as Jamila said, but she didn't know how to care for herself either. She was tender only to others. She would buy me flowers and shirts and take me to the barber's; she would spend all day rehearsing and then feed Heater, listening all evening to him as he whined about his wasted life. 'Women are brought up to think of others,' she said, when I told her to protect herself more, to think of her own interests. 'When I start to think of myself I feel sick,' she said.

Lately, Heater had been taken up by a polymath theatre director with an interest in the deprived. Heater met Abbado and (once) Calvino at his house, where the polymath encouraged Heater to speak of knife fights, Glasgow poverty and general loucheness and violence. After dinner, Heater would open the windows and let in the stench of the real world. And Heater gave these satisfactions, as he knew he had to, like Clapton having to play 'Layla' every time he performed. But Heater got through the slashings quickly in order to bring up Beethoven's late quartets and something which bothered him in Huysmans.

One night Heater was at the Press night of *La Bohème* at Covent Garden, and Eleanor and I were sunk into her sofa all snug, watching television and drinking. This suited me: to be with just her, asking questions about the people whose houses we visited. They had histories, these top-drawers, and she told them as stories. Someone's grandfather had had an argument with Lytton Strachey;

someone else's father was a Labour peer who'd had an affair with a Conservative MP's wife; some other fortunate whore was an actress in a soon-to-be released film that everyone was going to a premiere of in Curzon Street. Someone else had written a novel about their former lover, and it was transparent who it was.

It must have been obvious that I wasn't listening to her today, though, because she turned to me and said, 'Hey, funny face, give me a kiss.' That got my attention. 'It's been so long for me, Karim, you know, I can hardly remember what lips feel like.'

'Like this,' I said.

It felt hot and wonderful, and we must have kissed for half an hour. I'm not exactly sure how long it lasted, because I soon paid no attention to what in my book should have been the kiss of a lifetime. I was thinking of other things. Oh yes, I was overwhelmed by angry thoughts, which pushed themselves to the front of my mind, not so much numbing my lips as detaching them from me, as if they were a pair of glasses, for instance.

In the past few weeks circumstances had made me discover what an ignoramus I was. Lately I'd been fortunate, and my life had changed quickly, but I'd reflected little on it. When I did think of myself in comparison with those in Eleanor's crowd, I became aware that I knew nothing; I was empty, an intellectual void. I didn't even know who Cromwell was, for God's sake. I knew nothing about zoology, geology, astronomy, languages, mathematics, physics.

Most of the kids I grew up with left school at sixteen, and they'd be in insurance now, or working as car-mechanics, or managers (radio and TV dept) in department stores. And I'd walked out of college without thinking twice about it, despite my father's admonitions. In the suburbs education wasn't considered a particular advantage, and certainly couldn't be seen as worthwhile in itself. Getting into business young was more important. But now I was among people who wrote books as naturally as we played football. What infuriated me – what made me loathe both them and myself – was their confidence and knowledge. The easy talk of art, theatre, architecture, travel; the languages, the vocabulary, knowing the way round a whole culture – it was invaluable and irreplaceable capital.

At my school they taught you a bit of French, but anyone who attempted to pronounce a word correctly was laughed down. On a trip to Calais we attacked a Frog behind a restaurant. By this ignorance we knew ourselves to be superior to the public-school kids, with their puky uniforms and leather briefcases, and Mummy and Daddy waiting outside in the car to pick them up. We were rougher; we disrupted all lessons; we were fighters; we never carried no effeminate briefcases since we never did no homework. We were proud of never learning anything except the names of footballers, the personnel of rock groups and the lyrics of 'I am the Walrus'. What idiots we were! How misinformed! Why didn't we understand that we were happily condemning ourselves to being nothing better than motor-mechanics? Why couldn't we see that? For Eleanor's crowd hard words and sophisticated ideas were in the air they breathed from birth, and this language was the currency that bought you the best of what the world could offer. But for us it could only ever be a second language, consciously acquired.

And where I could have been telling Eleanor about the time I got fucked by Hairy Back's Great Dane, it was her stories that had primacy, her stories that connected to an entire established world. It was as if I felt my past wasn't important enough, wasn't as substantial as hers, so I'd thrown it away. I never talked about Mum and Dad, or the suburbs, though I did talk about Charlie. Charlie was kudos. And once I practically stopped talking at all, my voice choking in my throat, when Eleanor said my accent was cute.

'What accent?' I managed to say.

'The way you talk, it's great.'

'But what way do I talk?'

She looked at me impatiently, as if I were playing some ridiculous game, until she saw I was serious.

'You've got a street voice, Karim. You're from South London – so that's how you speak. It's like cockney, only not so raw. It's not unusual. It's different to my voice, of course.'

Of course.

At that moment I resolved to lose my accent: whatever it was, it would go. I would speak like her. It wasn't difficult. I'd left my world; I had to, to get on. Not that I wanted to go back. I still craved adventure and the dreams I'd desired that night when I had my epiphany on Eva's toilet in Beckenham. But somehow I knew also that I was getting into deep water.

After the kiss, when I stood in the darkened room and looked out on the street, my knees gave way.

'Eleanor, I won't be able to cycle home,' I said. 'I think I've lost the use of my legs.'

She said, softly, 'I can't sleep with you tonight, baby, my head's all messed up, you've no idea. It's somewhere else and it's full of voices and songs and bad stuff. And I'm too much trouble for you. You know why, don't you?'

'Please tell me.'

She turned away. 'Another time. Or ask anyone. I'm sure they'll be happy to tell you, Karim.'

She kissed me goodnight at the door. I was not sad to go. I knew I'd be seeing her every day.

When we'd found the characters we wanted to play, Pyke had us present them to the rest of the group. Eleanor's was an upper-class English woman in her sixties who'd grown up in the Indian Raj, someone who believed herself to be part of Britain's greatness but was declining with it and becoming, to her consternation, sexually curious just as Britain became so. Eleanor did it brilliantly. When she acted she lost her hair-twiddling self-consciousness and became still, drawing us towards her as a low-voiced story-teller, adding just enough satirical top-spin to keep us guessing as to her attitude towards the character.

She finished to general approval and theatrical kisses. It was my turn. I got up and did Anwar. It was a monologue, saying who he was, what he was like, followed by an imitation of him raving in the street. I slipped into it easily, as I'd rehearsed so much at Eleanor's. I thought my work was as good as anyone's in the group, and for the first time I didn't feel myself to be lagging behind everyone else.

After tea we sat around to discuss the characters. For some reason, perhaps because she looked puzzled, Pyke said to Tracey, 'Why don't you tell us what you thought of Karim's character?'

Now although Tracey was hesitant, she did feel strongly. She was dignified and serious, not fashionable like a lot of middle-class kids who fancied themselves as actors. Tracey was respectable in the best suburban way, honest and kind and unpretentious, and she dressed like a secretary; but she was also bothered by things: she worried about what it meant to be a black woman. She seemed shy and ill at ease in the world, doing her best to disappear from a room without actually walking out. Yet when I saw her at a party with only black people present, she was completely different – extrovert, passionate, and dancing wildly. She'd been brought up by her mother, who worked as a cleaning woman. By some odd coincidence Tracey's mother was scrubbing the steps of a house near our rehearsal room one morning when we were exercising in the park. Pyke had invited her to talk to the group during her lunch-break.

Tracey usually said little, so when she did begin to talk about my Anwar the group listened but kept out of the discussion. This thing was suddenly between 'minorities'.

'Two things, Karim,' she said to me. 'Anwar's hunger-strike worries me. What you want to say hurts me. It really pains me! And I'm not sure that we should show it!'

'Really?'

'Yes.' She spoke to me as if all I required was a little sense. 'I'm afraid it shows black people – '

'Indian people – '

'Black and Asian people – '

'One old Indian man – '

'As being irrational, ridiculous, as being hysterical. And as being fanatical.'

'Fanatical?' I appealed to the High Court. Judge Pyke was listening carefully. 'It's not a fanatical hunger-strike. It's calmly intended blackmail.'

But Judge Pyke signalled for Tracey to go on.

'And that arranged marriage. It worries me. Karim, with respect, it worries me.'

I stared at her, saying nothing. She was very disturbed.

'Tell us exactly why it worries you,' Eleanor said, sympathetically.

'How can I even begin? Your picture is what white people already think of us. That we're funny, with strange habits and weird customs. To the white man we're already people without humanity, and then you go and have Anwar madly waving his stick at the white boys. I can't believe that anything like this could happen. You show us as unorganized aggressors. Why do you hate yourself and all black people so much, Karim?'

As she continued, I looked around the group. My Eleanor looked sceptical, but I could see the others were prepared to agree with Tracey. It was difficult to disagree with someone whose mother you'd found kneeling in front of a middle-class house with a bucket and mop.

'How can you be so reactionary?' she said.

'But this sounds like censorship.'

'We have to protect our culture at this time, Karim. Don't you agree?'

'No. Truth has a higher value.'

'Pah. Truth. Who defines it? What truth? It's white truth you're defending here. It's white truth we're discussing.'

I looked at Judge Pyke. But he liked to let things run. He thought conflict was creative.

Finally he said: 'Karim, you may have to rethink.'

'But I'm not sure I can.'

'Yes. Don't unnecessarily restrict your range either as an actor or as a person.'

'But Matthew, why must I do it?'

He looked at me coolly. 'Because I say so.' And added: 'You must start again.'

CHAPTER TWELVE

'Hey, Fatso, what's happening?'

'Same, same, big famous actor.' Changez sneezed into the dust-ghosts he'd raised. 'What big thing are you acting in now that we can come and laugh at?'

'Well, let me tell you, eh?'

I made a cup of banana and coconut tea from the several tins I carried at all times in case my host had only Typhoo. I especially needed my own resources at Changez's place, since he made tea by boiling milk, water, sugar, teabag and cardamom all together for fifteen minutes. 'Man's tea,' he called this, or, 'Top tea. Good for erections.'

Fortunately for me – and I didn't want her to hear my request to Changez – Jamila was out, having recently started work at a Black Women's Centre nearby, where she was researching into racial attacks on women. Changez was dusting, wearing Jamila's pink silk dressing-gown. Tubes of brown fat gurgled and swayed as he dabbed his duster at cobwebs the size of paperbacks. He liked Jamila's clothes: he'd always have on one of her jumpers or shirts, or he'd be sitting on his camp-bed in her overcoat with one of her scarves wrapped around his head and covering his ears, Indian fashion, making him look as if he had a toothache.

'I'm researching a play, Changez, looking all over for a character, and I'm thinking of basing mine on someone we both know. They're going to be privileged and everything to be represented. Bloody lucky.'

'Good, good. Jamila, eh?'

'No. You.'

'What? Me, hey?' Changez straightened himself suddenly and ran his fingers through his hair, as if he were about to be photographed.

'But I haven't shaved, *yaar*.'

'It's a terrific idea, isn't it? One of my best.'

'I'm proud to be a subject for a top drama,' he said. But his face clouded over. 'Hey, you won't show me in bad light, will you?'

'Bad light? Are you mad? I'll show you just as you are.'

At this assurance he seemed content. Now I'd secured his assent I changed the subject quickly.

'And Shinko? How is she, Changez?'

'Ah, same, same,' he said with satisfaction, pointing down at his penis. He knew I liked this subject; and as it was the only thing he could show off about we both got pleasure from the exchange.

'I have been in more positions than most men. I'm thinking of composing a manual. I like it very much from behind with the woman on her knees as if I am riding high a horse like John Wayne.'

'Doesn't Jamila object to that kind of thing?' I asked, observing him carefully and wondering how I'd portray the crippled arm. 'Prostitution and so on?'

'You've hit the nail exactly on the nose! At first they condemned me as a completely wrong man, a male exploiter pig – '

'No!'

'And for a few days I had to be exclusively masturbating twice a day. Shinko wanted to give up this game and become a gardener and all.'

'D'you think she'd be a good gardener?'

He shrugged. 'She has nimble fingers with weeds. But thank Christ Almighty in heaven, they realized Shinko was exploiting me. I was the victim and all, so it was soon back to business as usual.' Then Changez took my arm and looked into my eyes. He became unhappy. What a sentimental creature he was. 'Can I tell you something?' He looked into the distance – through the window and into the next-door neighbour's kitchen. 'We laugh at one or two things about my character, yes, but I'll tell you a not-laughing matter. I'd give up every position I've ever been in for five minutes to kiss my wife on her lips.'

Wife? What wife? My mind slid around at his words; until I remembered. I was always forgetting he was married to Jamila. 'Your wife still won't touch you, eh?'

He shook his head sadly and gulped. 'And you and she? Stuffing regularly?'

'No, no, for God's sake, Bubble, not since the time you watched us. It wouldn't be the same without you there.'

He grunted. 'So she's getting it absolutely nowhere at all?'

'Nowhere, man.'

'Good.'

'Yes. Women aren't like us. They don't have to have it all the time. They only want it if they like the guy. For us it doesn't matter who it is.'

But he didn't appear to be listening to my observations on the psychology of romance. He just turned and looked at me with great fire and determination, and these were not qualities that God had rained down upon him. He smashed his good fist down on the table and cried, 'I'll make her like me! I know I will, one day!'

'Changez,' I said seriously, 'please don't count on it. I've known Jamila all my life. Don't you see, she may never change towards you.'

'I do count on it! Otherwise my life is terminated. I will top myself off!'

'That's up to you but – '

'Of course I will do it. I will cut my throat.'

'What with?'

'A prick!'

He threw his cup and plate to the floor, pushed himself up and started to pace about the room. Usually his duff arm remained still and at his side, a useless trunk. But now, protruding from the folded-back sleeve of the pink dressing-gown, it stuck out in front of him and waved from side to side. Changez seemed to have become another person, reacting out of real pain rather than the ironic self-deprecation with which he usually regarded his strange life. When he looked at me, at his friend, it was with contempt, even as I strained on, trying to help the fat bastard.

'Changez, there are other women in the world. Maybe I can introduce you to some actresses – if you lose weight. I know dozens of them, and some of them are real luscious. They love screwing. Some of them want to help the black people and the Third World. They're the ones for you. I'll introduce.'

'You're a little English, with a yellowish face like the devil. The number of morals you have equals none! I have my wife. I love her and she will love me. I will wait until the day of dooms for her to – '

'That may be a long time.'

'I want her in my arms!'

'That's all I'm talking about, the time. And in the mean time you could be – '

'Fuck-all. I'm doing fuck-all until I get her. And one other matter. You can't be using my character in your acting business. No, no, no, definitely. And if you try and steal me I can't see how we can be friends to talk to each other again! Promise?'

I became frantic. What was this – censorship? 'Promise? You cunt! I can't fucking promise anything now! What are you talking about?' But it was like shouting at a rock. Something in him had solidified against me.

'You entered my wife,' he said. 'Now promise you won't enter me by the back door and portray me in your play.'

I was defeated. What could I say? 'OK, OK, I promise not to enter you,' I said half-heartedly.

'You love to belittle me, you love to laugh at me and call me a git to the side of my face. One day you will be laughing out of the other side of your neck with me. You will keep your promise?'

I nodded. I went.

I cycled like a maniac to Eleanor's flat. I had to discuss the situation with her. First I'd lost Anwar and now I was losing Changez. Without him my whole career would fall apart. Who else could I base my character on? I didn't know any other 'black' people. Pyke would sack me.

When I went into the hall of the house Heater was coming out. He blocked my way like a mountain of rags, and every time I tried to dodge around him I bumped into his stinking bulk.

'Christ, man, what are you doing, Heater?'

'She's got the dog,' he said. 'Off you run, little boy.'

'What fucking dog? A hot dog? Get out of the way, you bastard, she and I have business to attend to.'

'The black dog, she's got. Depression. So – not today, thank you. Come back another time.'

But I was too small and quick for Heater. I nipped past him, under his fetid arm, gave him a shove and was in Eleanor's place like a flash, locking the door behind me. I could hear him cussing me down behind the door.

'Go and clean dog turds from the street with your tongue, you working-class cunt!' I shouted.

I took in Eleanor's room, not recognizing it at first. There were clothes everywhere. The ironing-board was in the middle of the room and Eleanor, naked, was ironing a pile of clothes. As she pressed down hard with the iron, as if trying to force it through the board, she wept, and her tears fell on the clothes.

'Eleanor, what's the matter? Tell me, please. Has your agent rung with bad news?'

I went to her. Her dry lips moved, but she didn't want to talk. She went on moving the iron across the same patch of shirt. When she lifted the face of the iron I felt she wanted to place it on herself, on the back of her hand or arm. She was half mad.

I disconnected the iron and put my leather jacket over her shoulders. I asked her once more what the matter was, but she just shook her head, flinging her tears over me. I gave up asking stupid questions, and led her into the bedroom and put her to bed. She lay back and shut her eyes. I held her hand and sat there, looking around at the clothes flung about, the make-up and hairspray and lacquered boxes on the dresser, the silk cushion from Thailand with an elephant on it, the piles of books on the floor. On the table beside the bed was a gold-framed photograph of a black man in his mid-thirties, wearing a dark polo-neck sweater. He had short hair, looked athletic and was very handsome. I guessed that the picture had been taken four or five years ago.

I felt Eleanor wanted me there, not to say anything, but just not to go away. So as she went off to sleep, I settled down for a serious think about Changez. Eleanor I would consider later; at the moment there was nothing I could do.

If I defied Changez, if I started work on a character based on him, if I used the bastard, it meant that I was untrustworthy, a liar. But if I didn't use him it meant I had fuck-all to take to the group after the 'me-as-Anwar' fiasco. As I sat there I began to recognize that this was one of the first times in my life I'd been aware of having a moral dilemma. Before, I'd done exactly what I wanted; desire was my guide and I was inhibited by nothing but fear. But now, at the beginning of my twenties, something was growing in me. Just as my body had changed at puberty, now I was developing a sense of guilt, a sense not only of how I appeared to others, but of how I appeared to myself, especially in violating self-imposed prohibitions. Perhaps no one would know I'd based my character in the play on Changez; perhaps, later, Changez himself wouldn't mind, would be flattered. But I would always know what I had done, that I had chosen to be a liar, to deceive a friend, to use someone. What should I do? I had no idea. I ran over it again and again and could find no way out.

I looked at Eleanor to make sure she was sleeping. I thought I'd sneak off home and get Eva to do me some stir-fried vegetables in her wok. Build myself up. But when I stood up Eleanor was watching me, and she was smiling slightly, too.

'Hey, I'm glad you're here.'

'But I was planning on going and leaving you to sleep.'

'No, don't do that, darling.'

She patted the bed. 'Get in, Karim.' I was so pleased to see her looking cheerful that I obeyed instantly, getting in beside her, pulling up the covers and resting my head on the pillow next to her. 'Karim, you little idiot, take off your shoes and the rest of your clothes.'

She started to laugh as I pulled off my jeans, but before I'd got any further than my knees she was nibbling my cock, long before any of the foreplay which, as I'd been informed by the numerous sex manuals I'd devoured for years, was essential to celestial love-making. But then, Eleanor would do such things, I thought, as I lay there enjoying it. There was extremity in her soul. In certain states she might do anything. As it was, she always did whatever occurred to her, which was, admittedly, not difficult for someone in her position, coming from a background where the risk of failure was minimal; in fact, you had to work hard to fail in her world.

That's how it began, our sex life. And I was stunned by it; I'd never had such strong emotional and physical feeling before. I wanted to tell everyone that such regular live-fire through the veins was possible; for surely, if they knew of it, they'd be doing it all the time. What intoxication! During rehearsal, when I looked at her wearing a long blue and white skirt, sitting in a chair with her bare feet up on the seat, pressing the swathes of cloth down between her legs – and I told her to wear no underwear – my mouth flooded in anticipation. I'd get an erection and would have to flee the improvisation for the toilet, where I'd wank, thinking of her. When my smiles revealed that this was what I was doing, she'd join me. We began to think that all business buildings should have comfortable facilities, with flowers and music, for masturbation and love-making.

Physically, Eleanor wasn't coy like me; she didn't conceal desire; there was no shame. At any time she'd take my hand and lay it on her breasts, pressing my fingers around the nipple, which I rolled and pinched. Or she'd pull up her T-shirt and offer me her tit to suck, forcing it into my mouth with her fingers. Or she pushed my hand up her skirt, wanting to be touched. Sometimes we snorted coke, speed, or swallowed hash, and I stripped Eleanor on the sofa, pulling off each piece of clothing until she was naked, with her legs apart, while I was dressed. Eleanor was also the first person to illustrate the magic qualities of language during sex. Her whispers stole my breath away: she required a fucking, a stuffing, a sucking, a slapping, in this, that or the other way. Sex was different each time. It had a different pace, there were new caresses, kisses which lasted an hour, sudden copulations in odd places – behind garages or in trains – where we'd simply pull down our clothes. At other times sex lasted aeons, when I'd lie with my head between her legs lapping her cunt and rimming her as she held herself open for me with her fingers.

There were occasions when I looked at Eleanor and felt such love – her face and entire being seemed luminous – that I couldn't bear the strength of it and had to turn away. I didn't want to feel this deeply: the disturbance, the possession. Sex I loved; like drugs, it was play, headiness. I'd grown up with kids who taught me that sex was disgusting. It was smells, smut, embarrassment and horse laughs. But love was too powerful for me. Love swam right into the body, into the valves, muscles and bloodstream, while sex, the prick, was always outside. I did want then, in a part of myself, to dirty the love I felt, or, somehow, to extract it from the body.

I needn't have worried. My love was souring already. I was terrified Eleanor would tell me she had fallen for someone else, or would declare she was bored with me. Or I wasn't good enough for her. The usual.

Fear entered my life. It entered my work. In the suburbs there had been few things that seemed more petty than the fear everyone had of their neighbour's opinion. It was why my mother could never hang out the washing in the garden without combing her hair. I didn't give a shit about what those people thought; but now it was essential to me that Pyke and Tracey and the other others liked my acting. My status in the group was not high now, and I felt discouraged. I didn't even talk to Eva about what I was doing.

At night, at home, I was working on Changez's shambolic walk and crippled hand, and on the accent, which I knew would sound, to white ears, bizarre, funny and characteristic of India. I'd worked out a story for the Changez character (now called Tariq), eagerly arriving at Heathrow with his gnat-ridden suitcase, having been informed in Bombay by a race-track acquaintance that you merely had to whisper the word 'undress' in England and white women would start slipping out of their underwear.

If there were objections to my portrayal I would walk out of the rehearsal room and go home. Thus, in a spirit of bloody-minded defiance I prepared to perform my Tariq for the group. On the day, in that room by the river, the group sat in a half-circle to watch me. I tried not to look at Tracey, who sat leaning forward concentratedly. Richard and Jon sat back without expression. Eleanor smiled encouragingly at me. Pyke nodded, note-book on his knee; Louise Lawrence had her writing pad and five sharp pencils at the ready. And Carol sat in the lotus position, putting her head back and stretching unconcernedly.

When I finished there was silence. Everybody seemed to be waiting for someone else to speak. I looked around the faces: Eleanor was amused but Tracey had an objection coming on. Her arm was half-raised. I would have to leave. It was the thing I most dreaded, but I'd made up my mind. But somehow Pyke saw this coming too. He pointed at Louise, instructing her to start writing.

'There it is,' Pyke said. 'Tariq comes to England, meets an English journalist on the plane – played by Eleanor, no, by Carol. This is real quality, upper-class crumpet. He is briefly among the upper classes because of her, which gives us another area to examine! Girls fall for him all over the place because of his weakness and need to be mothered. So. We have class, race, fucking and farce. What more could you want as an evening's entertainment?'

Tracey's face was well and truly shut. I wanted to kiss Pyke.

'Well done,' he said to me.

Mostly the actors adored Matthew. After all, he was a complex, attractive man, and they owed him a bagful. Naturally, I was as sycophantic towards Pyke as the others, but underneath I was sceptical and liked to keep my distance. I put this scepticism down to my South London origins, where it was felt that anyone who had an artistic attitude – anyone, that is, who'd read more than fifty books, or could pronounce Mallarmé correctly or tell the difference between Camembert and Brie – was basically a charlatan, snob or fool.

I really wasn't too intimate with Pyke until one day my bike chain snapped and he started to drive me back from rehearsals in his sports car, a black machine with black leather seats which shot you along on your back about three inches above the surface of the road. There was a clear view of the sky through the open roof. This module had speakers in the doors to crash the Doors and anything by Jefferson Airplane over you. In the privacy of his own car Pyke liked to ruminate on sex at such length and in such detail that I felt that the telling of these stories was an integrally erotic aspect of the serious promiscuous life. Or perhaps it was because I'd been sexualized by Eleanor. Maybe my skin, eyes and body-tone shone with carnal awareness, teasing out sensual thoughts in others.

One of the first things Pyke said, the introduction to his character as it were, when we first began to talk, was this. 'When I was nineteen, Karim, I swore to dedicate myself to two things: to becoming a brilliant director and to sleeping with as many women as I could.'

I was surprised to find him naïve enough to boast of such desires. But, looking straight ahead of him as he drove, he talked of his hobbies: attending orgies and New York fuck-clubs; and of the pleasure of finding unusual locations for the usual act, and unusual people to perform it with.

For Marlene and Matthew, who were created by the 1960s and had the money and facilities to live out their fantasies in the 1970s, sex was both recreational and informative. 'We get to meet such interesting people,' Pyke said. 'Where else but in a New York fuck-club would you get to meet a hairdresser from Wisconsin?'

Marlene was the same. She was fucking a Labour MP and passing on to her dialectical friends gossip and information about the House of Commons and the rank machinations of the Labour Party.

One of Pyke's most recent adventures was with a policewoman, the fascination of which didn't lie in the woman's character – there was little of that – but in the uniform; and predominantly in the functioning of the Filth, the details of which she recounted to Pyke after fellatio. But Pyke was tiring of what he described as his 'legal period'. 'I'm on the look-out for a scientist – an astronomer or nuclear physicist. I feel too arts-based intellectually.'

With their poking into life's odd corners, Pyke and Marlene seemed to me to be more like intrepid journalists than swimmers in the sensual. Their desire to snuggle up to real life betrayed a basic separation from it. And their obsession with how the world worked just seemed another form of self-obsession. Not that I informed Pyke of this analysis: I merely listened with flared ears and panting lungs. I wanted to get closer to him. I was excited. The world was opening out. I'd never met anyone like this before.

During one of these truth sessions in the car after rehearsal, when I was exhaustedly happy with the feeling of having worked hard, Pyke turned to me with one of the generous smiles which I found so insidious. 'Hey, you should know I'm pleased with your contribution to the show. The character you've got going is going to be a big laugh. So I've decided to give you a very special present.'

The sky was passing at a tremendous rate. I looked at him in his clean white T-shirt and tracksuit bottoms. His arms were thin and his face had a mean and pinched look; he ran a lot. The soul music I insisted he played was turned up. He especially liked Smokey Robinson's 'Going to a Go Go', and when he liked something he wanted it again and again. But he hadn't known the Robinson tune before. I was thinking he wasn't as cool as he should have been when he pulled something so fucking cool I nearly froze to death and overheated at the same time.

There I was, talking away, saying, 'But you've been so kind to me already, Matthew, just giving me this job. Perhaps you don't realize what it means.'

'What d'you mean, don't realize?' he said, sharply.

'It's changed my life. Without you plucking me from nowhere I'd still be decorating houses.'

He grunted. 'Fuck that. That's not kind – it's just a job. Now, your present, that's really kind. Or, rather: who your present is. Who. Who.'

'Who?' We were starting to sound like a fucking owl chorus. 'Who is it?'

'It's Marlene.'

'Your wife's name is Marlene, isn't it?'

'Sure. If you want her, she's yours. She wants you.'

'Me? Really?'

'Yes.'

191

'She wants me? For what?'

'She says you're the kind of innocent boy that André Gide would have gone for. And, I s'pose, as Gide is no longer alive, you'll have to be satisfied with her, eh?'

I wasn't flattered.

'Matthew,' I said, 'I've never been so flattered in my life. It's incredible.'

'Yeah?' He smiled at me. 'From me to you, friend. A gift. A token of appreciation.'

I didn't want to seem ungrateful, but I knew I couldn't leave it there: I might find myself in an awkward spot in the future. Yet it wouldn't look too good if I turned down Pyke's gift. Actors all over the world would give their legs just to talk to him for five minutes, and here I was being invited to fuck his wife. I knew this was privilege. I knew the quality of what I was being given. I was full of appreciation, oh yes. But I had to be very careful. At the same time, in a part of me, in my cock to be precise, I was involved in his offer.

I said at last, 'You should know, Matthew, that I'm going out with Eleanor. I'm really keen on her. And she on me, I reckon.'

'Sure, I know that, Karim. I told Eleanor to go for you.'

'Yeah?'

He glanced at me and nodded.

'Thanks,' I said.

'Pleasure. You're very good for her. Calming. She was depressed for a long time after her last boyfriend knocked himself off in that terrible way.'

'Was she?'

'Wouldn't you be?'

'Yeah, man, I would.'

'Just awful,' he said. 'And what a man he was.'

'I know.'

'Handsome, talented, charismatic. Did you know him?' he asked.

'No.'

'I'm glad you two are together,' Pyke said, smiling at me.

I was devastated by this information about Eleanor. I considered what Pyke had just said, trying to fit it around what I knew of Eleanor and some of the things she'd told me about the past. Did her last boyfriend kill himself in some dreadful way? What way? When did it happen? Why hadn't she told me? Why hadn't anyone else told me? What was going on? I was about to ask Pyke about all this but it was too late for that. Pyke would think me an idiot for lying.

And Pyke wouldn't stop talking, though I only half heard him. The car had stopped outside West Kensington tube. The commuters piled out of the exit in a mass and virtually ran home. Now Pyke was writing something on a pad on his knee.

'Bring Eleanor along on Saturday. We're having some people round for supper. It'll be nice to see you both. I'm sure we can really get into something good.'

'I'm sure we can, too,' I said.

I struggled out of the car with Pyke's address in my hand.

When I got to the house, which was half ripped up since Ted had started work on it, Dad was sitting writing: he was working on a book about his childhood in India. Later he'd be doing a meditation class in a local hall. Eva was out. Sometimes I dreaded seeing Dad. If you weren't in the mood for him, or able to fend him off, his personality could club you down. He could start pinching your cheeks and tweaking your nose and stuff he thought was the funniest thing he'd ever seen. Or he'd pull up his jumper and slap out a tune on his bare stomach, urging you to guess whether it was 'Land of Hope and Glory' or 'The Mighty Quinn' in the Manfred Mann version. I swear he examined his pregnant gut five times a day, patting his belly, squeezing his tyres, discussing them with Eva as if they were the ninth wonder of the world, or trying to persuade her to bite them.

'Indian men have lower centres of gravity than Accidental men,' he claimed. 'We are more centred. We live from the correct place – the stomach. From the guts, not from the head.'

Eva endured it all; it made her laugh. But he wasn't my boyfriend. I'd also begun to see Dad not as my father but as a separate person with characteristics that were contingent. He was part of the world now, not the source of it; in one way, to my distress, he was just another individual. And ever since Eva had been working so hard, I'd begun to wonder at Dad's helplessness. He didn't know how to make a bed or how to wash and iron his clothes. He couldn't cook; he didn't even know how to make tea or coffee.

Recently, when I was lying down learning my lines, I'd asked Dad to make me some tea and toast. When eventually I followed him into the kitchen I saw that he'd cut open the teabag with scissors and poured the loose tea into a cup. He handled a piece of bread as if it were a rare object he'd obtained on an archaeological dig. Women had always looked after him, and he'd exploited them. I despised him for it now. I began to think that the admiration I'd had for him as a kid was baseless. What could he do? What qualities did he have? Why had he treated Mum as he had? I no longer wanted to be like him. I was angry. He'd let me down in some way.

'Come here, gloomy face,' he said to me now. 'How's the show?'

'Good.'

He started going on.

'Yes, but make sure they don't neglect you. Listen to me! Tell them you want the lead part or nothing. You can't climb down – you've already climbed up as a leading Mowgli actor in the theatre! You are the product of my number-one seed, aren't you?'

I imitated him. 'Number-one seed, number-one seed.' Then I said, 'Why don't you stop talking so much fucking crap, you wanker.' And went out.

I went to the Nashville, which was quiet at this time of day. I had a couple of pints of Ruddles and a bag of chicken-flavoured crisps, and sat there wondering why pubs had to be so gloomy, full of dark wood and heavy uncomfortable furniture, and lit by such crummy lighting you could barely see five yards through the poisoned air. I thought about Eleanor and kept wanting to cry out of pity for her. I also knew that if I sat in the pub long enough the feeling would pass. Eleanor obviously didn't want to talk about her last boyfriend, even if he had killed himself in some terrible way. She'd certainly never mentioned it directly to me. I'd been shut out of an important area of her life. It made me doubt how keen she really was on me.

In my life I was generally getting into some weird things; solid ground was moving beneath me. Take supper. I looked at the piece of paper on which Pyke had written his address. The word 'supper' itself confused and irritated me. They called everything by the wrong name, these London people. Dinner was lunch, tea was supper, breakfast was brunch, afters was pudding.

I had to discuss things with my friends. It would help me straighten out my head. But when, anxiously, I told Eva of the invitation to Pyke's (but not about his 'gift'), she had no insight into my fears and confusion. She thought it was a terrific chance. She knew precisely how elevated Pyke was, and she regarded me admiringly as if I'd won a swimming cup. 'You must invite Matthew over here some time in the next couple of weeks,' was her response. Next, I rang Jamila. She would be a different proposition. I was beginning to see how scared I was of her, of her 'sexuality', as they called fucking these days; of the power of her feelings and the strength of her opinions. Passion was at a premium in South London. 'Well?' I asked. 'What d'you think?'

'Oh, I don't know, Creamy. You always do what you want anyway. You listen to no one. But myself, I couldn't go to his place. I'm worried that they're taking you over, these people. You're moving away from the real world.'

'What real world? There is no real world, is there?'

She said patiently, 'Yes, the world of ordinary people and the shit they have to deal with – unemployment, bad housing, boredom. Soon you won't understand anything about the essential stuff.'

'But Jammie, they're shit-hot powerful people and all.' Then I made a mistake. 'Aren't you even curious to find out how the rich and successful live?'

She snorted and started laughing. 'I'm less interested in home furnishings than you, dear. And I don't want to be anywhere near those people, to be honest. Now, when are you coming to see us? I've got a big pot of real hot dal here that's going uneaten. Even Changez I won't let near it – I'm saving it for you, my old lover.'

'Thanks, Jammie,' I said.

On Friday night, at the end of the week's workshop, Pyke put his arms around Eleanor and me as we were leaving, kissed us both and said, 'See you tomorrow then, eh?'

'Yes,' I said. 'See you then.'

'We're looking forward to it,' he said.

'Me too,' I replied.

CHAPTER THIRTEEN

Sensational, I thought, looking across the carriage of the Bakerloo Line train at my face reflected in the opposite window. You little god. My feet danced and my fingers did the hand-jive to imaginary music – the Velvettes, 'He was Really Saying Something' – as the tube train rushed beneath my favourite city, my playground, my home. My baby was humming too. We'd changed at Piccadilly and were heading north-west, to Brainyville, London, a place as remote to me as Marseilles. What reason had I had to go to St John's Wood before? I looked fit and well; it must have been the vegetables. The press-ups and 'I must, I must increase my bust' exercises which Eva had recommended were also achieving their aim of sharpening my profile and increasing my confidence. I'd had a haircut at Sassoon in Sloane Street and my balls, recently talcum-powdered, were as fragrantly dusted and tasty as Turkish Delight. But my clothes were too big as usual, mainly because I was wearing one of Dad's dark-blue jackets and one of his Bond Street ties over a Ronettes T-shirt, with, obviously, no collar, and a pink jumper of Eva's on top of this. I was nervy, too, shaken up, I must admit, after Heater had threatened me with a carving knife in Eleanor's flat about an hour earlier, saying, 'You look after that woman, eh? If anything happens to her I'll kill ya!'

Eleanor sat beside me in a black suit and dark-red silk shirt with a high collar. She'd put her hair up, but a couple of ringlets had escaped, just right for me to slip my finger through. 'I've never seen you looking so beautiful,' I told her. I meant it. I couldn't stop kissing her face. I just wanted to hold her all day and stroke her, tickle her, play with her.

Up we strolled to the mansion, cheerful and excited. The house Pyke shared with Marlene had to be a four-storey place in a quiet street, with a recently watered front garden smothered in flowers, and two sports cars outside, the black and the blue. Then there was the incriminating basement in which lived the nanny who looked after Pyke's thirteen-year-old son by his first marriage.

I'd been briefed up to the hilt on all this by Terry, who investigated the crimes of the rich middle class with the vigour of a political Maigret. Terry was now employed; the call had come. He was playing a police sergeant in a police-station drama. This proved ideologically uncomfortable, since he'd always claimed the police were the fascist instrument of class rule. But now, as a policeman, he was pulling a ton of money, much more than I was, more than anyone else in the commune in which he lived, and he was constantly getting recognized in the street. He was also asked to open firework displays, judge play competitions and appear on celebrity game shows. In the street it was like walking around with Charlie, the way people called out to him and turned and stared, except that Terry's fans didn't know him as Terry Tapley, but as Sergeant Monty. These ironies made Sergeant Monty especially virulent about Pyke, the man who'd denied him the only job he'd really wanted.

Terry had taken me to a political meeting recently, after which, in the pub, a girl had spoken about life after the revolution. 'People will be reading Shakespeare on the bus and learning the clarinet!' she'd cried. Her commitment and hope impressed me; I wanted to do something myself. But Terry didn't think I was ready. He gave me a small task first. 'Keep an eye on Pyke for us,' he said, 'as you're so well in with him. His type are good for cash. There might be something up that street you can do one day. We'll let you know. But this time just look around – see what we might take him for when the time comes to call him in politically. In the short term you can help us by meeting his son.'

'Meeting his son? OK, Sergeant Monty.'

He went to slap my face.

'Don't call me that. And ask the boy – in front of all the guests – which school he goes to. And if it isn't one of the most expensive and exclusive in England, in the whole of the Western world for that matter, I'll change my name to Disraeli.'

'OK, Sergeant Monty – I mean, Disraeli. But I can't believe you're right about this. Pyke's radical, man.'

Terry snorted and laughed scornfully. 'Don't tell me about these fucking radicals. They're just liberals' – practically the worst thing, in his view, anybody could be. 'And their only use is in giving money to our party.'

It was the servant, a deferential Irish girl, who let us in. She brought Eleanor and me champagne and disappeared into the kitchen – to make 'supper', I presumed. She left us sitting nervously on the leather sofa. Pyke and Marlene were 'dressing', we'd been told. 'Undressing, more like,' I murmured. There was no one else there. The house was eerily quiet. Where the hell was everyone?

'Isn't it brilliant that Pyke's asked us over,' Eleanor said. 'D'you think it's supposed to be a secret? He doesn't usually hang out with actors, does he? I don't think he's invited anyone else from the cast, has he?'

'No.'

'Why us, then?'

'Because he loves us so much.'

'Well, whatever happens, we mustn't deny each other experience,' she said, in a haughty way, as if my whole purpose in life were to try and deny Eleanor experience. And she looked at me as if she wanted to press a hard grain of rice down the end of my penis.

'What experience?' I said, getting up and pacing around. She wouldn't reply, but sat there, smoking away. 'What experience?' I repeated. Now she was ruining my whole evening and I was getting more and more nervous. I seemed to know nothing, not even the facts of my girlfriend's life. 'Maybe the sort of experience you had with your last boyfriend? The one you loved so much. Is that what you mean?'

'Please don't talk about him,' she said softly. 'He's bloody dead.'

'That's not a reason not to talk about him.'

'It is to me.' She got up. 'I must go to the toilet.'

'Eleanor,' I cried for the first time in my life, but not the last. 'Eleanor, why don't we talk about this stuff?'

'But you don't know how to give. You don't understand other people. It would be dangerous for me to lay myself open to you.'

And off she went, leaving me that way.

I looked around. I was being a class detective. And Terry had seriously underestimated the sort of wealth we were dealing with here. I would have to have a word with him about the quality of his snooping sources. It was an impressive house, with dark-red and green walls and modern portraits hanging from them – a couple of Marlene, a photograph of her by Bailey – and 1960s furniture: low coffee tables with Caulfield and Bacon catalogues on them, and the two hard-back volumes of Michael Foot's biography of Nye Bevan. There were three couches in pastel shades, with Indian friezes on the wall above them; and a plaster sculpture with strings and lightbulbs, also attached to the wall: it looked like a large cunt. Leaning casually against another wall were three of Pyke's framed awards, and standing on the table were a couple of statuettes and a cut-glass bowl with Pyke's name on it. There were no posters or photographs from any of his productions. Apart from the awards, an outsider would have no clue to his profession.

Eleanor returned as the two Ms walked silkily down the wide staircase, Pyke in black jeans and black T-shirt, Marlene more exotic in a short white dress, bare arms and legs, and white ballet shoes. She was glamorous, Marlene, giving off a rough and uncompromising sexuality with her many smiles. But, as my mother would have said, she was no spring chicken.

The Irish maid served the four of us turkey salad and we sat and ate on our laps and drank more champagne. I was hungry, and had deliberately missed lunch in order to enjoy 'supper', but now I couldn't eat much. Marlene and Matthew didn't look as if food interested them either. I kept watching the door, expecting more people to turn up, but none did. Pyke had lied. He was quiet and distant tonight, as if he couldn't be bothered with the performance of conversation. He spoke only in murmured clichés, as if to underline the banality of the evening.

Marlene did most of the talking, and to keep silence at bay I asked so many questions I began to feel like a television interviewer. She told us of the separate entrances prostitutes had to the House of Commons; and as we ate our turkey there was the story of the Labour MP who liked to watch chickens being stabbed to death while he was having sex.

Marlene had some Thai sticks, and we were having an after-dinner joint when Percy, Pyke's son, came in, a pale and moody-looking boy with a shaved head, earrings and filthy clothes, far too rough and slovenly to be anything other than a member of the liberal middle class. My Terry antennae went up, trembling in anticipation.

'By the way,' Pyke said to the boy, 'd'you know who Karim's stepbrother is? It's Charlie Hero.'

The boy was suddenly riveted. He started to wave his body

around and ask questions. He had more life than his father. 'Hero's my hero. What's he like?'

I gave him a brief character-sketch. But I couldn't let Terry down. Now was my chance.

'What school d'you go to?'

'Westminster. And it's shit.'

'Yeah? Full of public-school types?'

'Full of media fuck-wits with parents who work at the BBC. I wanted to go to a comprehensive but these two wouldn't let me.'

He walked out of the room. And for the rest of the evening, from upstairs, we heard the muffled sound of the Condemned's first album, *The Bride of Christ*, playing again and again. When Percy had gone I gave Pyke and Marlene my most significant look, as if to say, 'You have betrayed the working class,' but neither of them noticed. They sat there smoking, looking utterly bored, as if this evening had already lasted a thousand years and nothing whatsoever could interest them or, more important, turn them on.

Except that suddenly Pyke got up, walked across the room and threw open the doors to the garden. He turned and nodded at Eleanor, who was talking to Marlene. Immediately, Eleanor broke off the conversation, got up and tripped out into the garden after Pyke. Marlene and I sat there. With the doors open the room grew rapidly cold, but the air smelled sweet, as if the earth were breathing perfume. What were they doing out there? Marlene behaved as if nothing had happened. Then she fetched herself another drink and came and sat beside me. She had her arm around me, which I pretended wasn't there. I tensed, though, and gave my opinions. I began to get the distinct impression that I was a marvellous person, what with concentrating on me and all. But there was something I had to know, something I felt sure she could help me with.

'Marlene, will you tell me something that no one's actually told me? Will you tell me what happened to Eleanor's boyfriend, Gene?'

She looked at me sympathetically, but with slight disbelief.

'Are you sure no one's told you?'

'Marlene, I know for sure that no one's told me nothing. It's driving me up the wall, too, I can tell you. Everyone acts as if it's some kind of ultimately big secret anyway. No one says anything. I'm being treated like a wanker.'

'It's not a secret, just raw and painful still for Eleanor. OK?' She shifted closer to me. 'Gene was a young West Indian actor. He was very talented and sensitive, thin and kind and raunchy, with this beautiful face. He knew a lot about poetry, which he'd declaim wonderfully aloud at parties. And African music was his speciality. He worked with Matthew once, a long time ago. Matthew says he was the best mime he ever met. But he never got the work he deserved. He emptied bed-pans in hospital programmes. He played criminals and taxi-drivers. He never played in Chekhov or Ibsen or Shakespeare, and he deserved to. He was better than a lot of people. So he was very angry about a lot of things. The police were always picking him up and giving him a going over. Taxis drove straight past him. People said there were no free tables in empty restaurants. He lived in a bad world in nice old England. One day when he didn't get into one of the bigger theatre companies, he couldn't take any more. He just freaked out. He took an overdose. Eleanor was working. She came home and found him dead. She was so young then.'

'I see.'

'That's all there is to it.'

Marlene and I sat there a while. I thought about Gene and what he'd been through; what they'd done to him; what he'd allowed to happen to himself. I saw that Marlene was scrutinizing me.

'Shall we have a kiss?' she said, after a while, stroking my face lightly.

I panicked. 'What?'

'Just a little kiss to start with, to see how we get along. Do I shock you?'

'Yes, because I thought you said kid, not kiss.'

'Perhaps that later, but now . . .'

She brought her face close to mine. There were wrinkles around her eyes; she was the oldest person I'd kissed. When we broke apart and I gulped back more champagne she raised her arms in a sudden dramatic gesture, like someone celebrating an athletics victory, and pulled off her dress. Her body was thin and brown, and when I touched it I was surprised by how warm she was, as if she'd been lightly toasted. It aroused me, and with my arousal came a little essential affection, but basically I was scared and I liked being scared.

The dope made me drowsy and held back sensation and reaction.

I don't know why, but the Thai sticks floated me back to the suburbs and Eva's house in Beckenham, the night I wore crushed velvet flares and Dad didn't know the way, and how I led him to the Three Tuns, where Kevin Ayers was playing and my friends that I loved were standing at the bar, having spent hours in their bedrooms preparing for the evening, their gladdest moment being when a pair of knowing eyes passed over their threads. Later, there was Charlie sitting at the top of the stairs, perfectly dressed, just observing. There were meditating advertising executives, and I crawled across the lawn to find my father was sitting on a garden bench, and Eva sitting on him, with horizontal hair. So I went to Charlie for comfort, and now his record was playing upstairs, and he was famous and admired, and I was an actor in a play in London, and I knew fashionable people and went to grand houses like this, and they accepted me and invited no one else and couldn't wait to make love to me. And there was my mother trembling with pain at her soul being betrayed, and the end of our family life and everything else starting from that night. And Gene was dead. He'd known poetry by heart and was angry and never got any work, and I wished I'd met him and seen his face. How could I ever replace him in Eleanor's eyes?

When I sat up I had to search my mind for a clue to where I was. I felt as if the lights in my mind had been turned off. But I did see a couple on the far side of the room, illuminated only by the light from the hall. And by the door an Irish girl stood as if by invitation, watching the strange couple kiss and rub their hands on each other. The man was pushing the woman back on the sofa. She had taken off the black suit and red shirt, for some reason, though she looked her loveliest in them.

Marlene and I tumbled on the floor. I had been in her already, and noticed odd things, like how she had strong muscles in her cunt, which she utilized to grip the end of my prick as professionally as my own pinkies. When she wanted to stop me moving inside her she merely flexed her cunt muscles and I was secured for life.

Later, when I looked up, the couple had separated and Pyke's body was carrying his erection in my direction, like a lorry sustaining a crane.

'That looks fun,' his voice said.

'Yes, it – '

But before I could complete the sentence, England's most interesting and radical theatre director was inserting his cock between my speaking lips. I could appreciate the privilege, but I didn't like it much: it seemed an imposition. He could have asked politely. So I gave his dick a South London swipe – not viciously, nor enough to have my part in the play reduced – but enough to give him a jolt. When I looked up for his reaction it was to see him murmuring his approval. Fortunately, Pyke pulled away from my face anyway. Something important was happening. His attention moved elsewhere.

Eleanor came over to Pyke; she came over to him quickly and passionately, as if he were of infinite value at this moment, as if she'd heard that he had a crucial message for her. She took his head in her hands as if it were a precious pot, and she kissed Pyke, pulling his somewhat corrugated lips towards her, as she'd pulled my head spontaneously towards her that morning when we were eating our grapefruit in the front room of her flat. His hand was between her legs now, his fingers up to the knuckle pushing inside her. As he frigged her she spoke to him in incantatory fashion. I strained to catch everything, and heard for my pains Eleanor whisper how much she wanted to fuck him, how she'd always wanted it since she first admired him and then spotted him in the foyer of a theatre – the ICA, was it, or was it the Royal Court, or the Open Space, or the Almost Free, or the Bush? – but anyway, however much she wanted him then, she was too intimidated by his renown, by his talent, by his status, to approach him; but at last she'd come to know him precisely the way she'd always wanted to know him.

Marlene was transfixed by all this. She moved around them for a better look. 'Oh yes, yes,' she was saying. 'It's so beautiful, so beautiful, I can't believe it.'

'Stop talking,' Pyke snapped, suddenly.

'But I can't believe it,' Marlene went on. 'Can you, Karim?'

'It's unbelievable,' I said.

This distracted Eleanor. She looked at me dreamily, and then at Pyke. She withdrew his fingers from her cunt and put them in my mouth.

'Don't let me have all the fun,' she said to Pyke, pleadingly. 'Please, why don't you two touch each other?'

Marlene nodded vigorously at this constructive suggestion.

'Yes?' Eleanor said. But it was difficult for me to reply with a mouthful of Pyke's fingers.

'Oh yes, yes,' said Marlene.

'Calm down,' said Pyke to her.

'I am calm,' Marlene said. She was also drunk.

'Christ,' said Pyke to Eleanor. 'Bloody Marlene.'

Marlene fell back on to the couch, naked, with her legs open.

'There's so much we can do tonight!' she cried. 'There's hours and hours of total pleasure ahead of us. We can do whatever we want. We've only just begun. Let me freshen our drinks and we'll get down to it. Now, Karim, I want you to put some ice up my cunt. Would you mind going to the fridge?'

CHAPTER FOURTEEN

I was in my usual state; I had no money. Things were so desperate it had become necessary for me to work. We were in the middle of a few weeks' break while Louise went away and tried to construct a single coherent drama around the improvisations and characters we'd created. The whole process of putting on a show with Pyke took months and months. We started in the early summer and now it was autumn. And anyway, Pyke had gone away to Boston to teach. 'We'll work on it for as long as it takes,' he said. 'It's the process and not the result that matters to me.' During this waiting time, instead of going on holiday like Carol, Tracey and Richard, I started to work as a wheel-barrow merchant – as I was called by Eva – on the transformation of the flat. Reluctantly, I started to shift the debris myself. It was hard, filthy work, so I was surprised when one night Eleanor suddenly said that she'd like to share the job with me. 'Please,' she said. 'I've got to get out of the house. Being here I start to think.'

Not wanting Eleanor to think, and wanting to draw her to me after that evening with Pyke (which we never discussed), I went to Eva and told her to employ Eleanor as well. 'Of course, she'll have to be paid the same as me. We're a co-operative,' I said.

By this time Eva had acquired a new sharpness, in all senses. She'd started to get as well organized as any managing director; she even walked more quickly; she was sleeker, crisper. There were lists of everything. No mystical vapours obscured the way things like clearing flats were actually done. Flowing and sensual intuition didn't mean practical foolishness. Eva spoke directly, without dishonesty. And this frightened people, especially plumbers, to whom it was a new idea. They'd never had anyone say to them, 'Now tell me exactly why it is you've made such a mess of this simple job? Do you always want to be fifth-rate? Is your work always shoddy?' She'd also added cachet to herself by being Charlie's mother. Twice she'd been interviewed by Sunday newspaper supplements.

Now she was getting sniffy with me. 'I can't afford to hire Eleanor too. Anyway, you told me she's mad,' she said.

'So are you.'

'Actors, Karim, are convivial company. They put on funny voices and do imitations. But they have no personality.'

'I'm an actor, Eva.'

'Oh yes, I forgot. So you are. But I don't think of you as one.'

'What are you saying?'

'Don't look so severe, darling. It's only that you don't have to throw yourself at the first woman to open her legs for you.'

'Eva!'

Since *The Jungle Bunny Book* I'd learned to fight back, though it cost me a lot to take on Eva. I didn't want to frighten off my new mummy. But I said, 'Eva, I won't work for you unless Eleanor does too.'

'All right, it's a deal, if you insist. The same wages for both of you. Except that now your wages are reduced by twenty-five per cent.'

So Eleanor and I did all the shitwork in that big roomful of white dust, ripping the place apart and tipping volcano-shaped piles of the past into skips outside. It was a busy time for Eva, too. She'd been commissioned to redesign the flat of a television producer who was away in America. This was Ted and Eva's first big outside job, so while Eleanor and I worked on our place, she and Ted would be at this other flat in Maida Vale, working on the plans. Eva and Dad slept there, as did I, occasionally.

While we worked, Eleanor and I listened to the new music, to the Clash, Generation X, the Condemned, the Adverts, the Pretenders and the Only Ones; and we drank wine and ate sausages carpeted with onions and lit up by mustard. At the end of the day we got the 28 bus to Notting Hill, always sitting at the front of the top deck as it cruised through the Kensington High Street traffic. I looked at the secretaries' legs down below and Eleanor worked out from the *Evening News* which play we'd see that night.

Back at her place we showered, put sugar-water in our hair so we looked like porcupines, and changed into black clothes. Sometimes I wore eye-liner and nail varnish. Off we went to the Bush, a tiny room above a pub in Shepherd's Bush, a theatre so small that those in the front row had their feet on the stage. The famous Royal Court Theatre in Sloane Square had plusher seats, and the plays were stuff to make your brain whirl, Caryl Churchill and Sam Shepard. Or we would go to the Royal Shakespeare Company's Warehouse in dark, run-down Covent Garden, sitting among students, Americans and Brainys from North London. As your buttocks were being punished on steel and plastic chairs you'd look across grey floorboards at minimal scenery, maybe four chairs and a kitchen table set among a plain of broken bottles and bomb-sites, a boiling world with dry ice floating over the choking audience. London, in other words. The actors wore clothes just like ours, only more expensive. The plays were three hours long, chaotic and bursting with anarchic and defiant images. The writers took it for granted that England, with its working class composed of slags, purple-nosed losers, and animals fed on pinball, pornography and junk-food, was disintegrating into terminal class-struggle. These were the science-fiction fantasies of Oxford-educated boys who never left the house. The middle class loved it.

Eleanor always emerged flushed and talkative. This was the kind of theatre she liked; this was where she wanted to work. She usually knew a few people in the audience, if not in the plays, and I always asked her to tell me how many among them she'd slept with. Whatever the number and whatever the play, sitting in the warm dark next to her inevitably gave me an erection, and at the interval she'd remove her tights so I could touch her the way she liked me to.

These were the best days: waking up and finding Eleanor hot as a pie; sometimes she'd sweated a puddle on her chest which seemed to have risen up through the width of her body as she slept. I remembered my father saying drunkenly to the Mayor at one of Auntie Jean's parties, as Mum nervously ate through most of a cake the size of a lady's hat, 'We little Indians love plump white women with fleshy thighs.' Perhaps I was living out his dreams as I embraced Eleanor's flesh, as I ran the palms of my hands lightly over her whole body, then kissed her awake and popped my tongue into her cunt as she opened her eyes. Half asleep, we'd love each other, but disturbing images would sometimes enter my head. Here we were, a fond and passionate pair, but to reach climax I found myself wondering what creatures men were that saw rapes, massacres, tortures, eviscerations at such moments of union. I was being tormented by devils. I kept feeling that terrible things would happen.

When Eleanor and I finished gutting the flat, and before Ted and Eva could get started on it, I spent some time with Jeeta and Jamila. All I wanted was to work in the shop in the evening and earn a bit of money. I didn't want to get myself involved in any serious disintegration. But things had changed a lot.

Uncle Anwar didn't sleep at all now. At night he sat on the edge of his chair, smoking and drinking un-Islamic drinks and thinking portentous thoughts, dreaming of other countries, lost houses, mothers, beaches. Anwar did no work in the shop, not even rewarding work like watching for shoplifters and shirtlifters. Jamila often found him drunk on the floor, rancid with unhappiness, when she went by to see her mother in the morning before work. Anwar's hunger-strike hadn't endeared him to his family, and now no one attended to him or enquired into the state of his cracking heart. 'Bury me in a pauper's grave,' he said to me. 'I've had it, Karim, boy.' 'Right you are, Uncle,' I said. And Princess Jeeta was becoming stronger and more wilful as Anwar declined; she appeared to be growing an iron nose like a hook with which she could lift heavy boxes of corned beef. She'd leave him drunk on the floor now, maybe wiping her feet on him as she passed through to raise the steel shutters on her domain of vegetables. It was Jamila who picked him up and put him in his chair, though they never spoke, looking at each other with bemused and angry love.

I began to see that Anwar's unhappiness wasn't only self-induced. There was a campaign against him. Since his attempt to starve himself to death, Princess Jeeta was, in her own way, starving her husband to death, but subtly, month by month. There was very definite but intangible deprivation. For example, she spoke to him, but only occasionally, and made sure not to laugh. He started to suffer the malnutrition of unalloyed seriousness. Someone to whom jokes are never told soon contracts enthusiasm deficiency. Jeeta cooked for him as before, but provided only plain food, the same every day, and long after the expected time, bringing it to him when he was asleep or about to pray. And the food was especially prepared to ensure constipation. Days went by without hope of relief. 'I am full of shit,' Anwar said to me. 'I feel as if I'm made of bloody concrete. Shit is blocking my ears, boy. It's shutting up my nose, it's seeping out through the pores of my fucking skin.'

When he spoke to Jeeta about the shit problem she said nothing, but the menu changed that day. His stomach was released, oh yes. And for weeks Anwar's shit didn't touch the sides of the toilet bowl; it would have shot through the eye of a needle. Princess Jeeta continued to ask Anwar's masterful advice, but only on the smallest things, like whether to stock sour cream or not. (Anwar said no, as their cream was usually sour anyway.) One day three men Jeeta had hired came in and ripped out the central block of shelves, thus creating more space in Paradise Stores. The men installed three low, long refrigerators, which stocked large quantities of frozen and chilled food, including sour cream; and Jeeta told Anwar nothing about this innovation until it happened. He must have walked downstairs into the shop and thought he was going mad when he saw it transformed.

At least once a week Princess Jeeta made slighting remarks about Changez, saying as she lifted a box, 'A good son-in-law would be doing this, instead of an old woman.' Or she pointed out babies and children to Anwar, and kissed them and gave their mothers free food, because she'd never have grandchildren now, so outstanding had been the choice of son-in-law by Anwar's brilliant brother in Bombay. To make things worse, once in a while, perhaps for a whole morning, she would be kind, loving and attentive to Anwar, and then, as the smiles returned to his face, she'd cut him dead for a week, until he had no idea where he stood or what was happening to him.

One day, on his way back from the mosque, Anwar descried through the snowstorm of his pain someone he only vaguely recognized, so long had it been since he'd seen him (and so fat had the person become), though mentally he stoned this figure to death every day, and referred to him, in front of me, as 'that fucking, bald, useless cripple'. It was Changez, and he was out shopping with Shinko, one of his favourite pastimes. They'd been to the Paperback Exchange and then to Catford's largest sex shop, the Lounge of Love, and Changez carried in his good arm a brown parcel containing newly acquired instruments of desire: red slitted knickers, stockings and suspenders, magazines called *Openings for Gentlemen* and *Citizen Cane*, and the star item, a large knobbly pink penis which, for a price, he intended to press into Shinko's jade gate as she called out 'Fuckmefuckmefuckmebigboybigboybigboy!'

On this unforgettable day Shinko carried with her a pineapple and a grapefruit, which she was intending to eat for her tea, had they not, later, rolled into the road and rotted forgotten in the gutter. As they plodded along in the English drizzle, Changez and Shinko, both loquacious and slow, discussed their respective homelands, India and Japan, which they missed desperately, but not enough to get on a plane and go there. And Changez, if I knew my Changez, would be abusing any Pakistanis and Indians he saw in the street. 'Look at that low-class person,' he'd say in a loud voice, stopping and pointing out one of his fellow countrymen – perhaps a waiter hurrying to work or an old man ambling to the day centre, or especially a group of Sikhs going to visit their accountant. 'Yes, they have souls, but the reason there is this bad racialism is because they are so dirty, so rough-looking, so bad-mannered. And they are wearing such strange clothes for the Englishman, turbans and all. To be accepted they must take up the English ways and forget their filthy villages! They must decide to be either here or there. Look how much here I am! And why doesn't that bugger over there look the Englishman in the eye! No wonder the Englishman will hit him!'

Suddenly a yell was heard all over Lewisham, all over Catford, and in Bromley. Changez, in the midst of a diatribe, and wearing unlaced Hush Puppies, turned as quickly as he could, which was not quickly at all, rather like a lorry in a cul-de-sac. But when he had manoeuvred from east to west he saw that his father-in-law, the man who had brought him to England, to Shinko, to Karim, to a camp-bed and Harold Robbins, was shuffling down the street towards him, his stick aloft, curses released from his mouth like mad dogs from a kennel. Changez immediately realized that these toothy dogs were not warnings or idle threats. No; the disappointed father-in-law was intending to crack his son-in-law over the loaf right now – and possibly club him to death. Shinko noticed that, surprisingly, Changez remained calm throughout. (And it was at this moment that her love for him was born.)

As Anwar smacked downwards with his stick, Changez lumbered to one side, just in time, withdrew the knobbly dildo from its paper-bag sheath, and with a Muslim warrior shout – at least, Shinko said it was a Muslim shout, but what would she know? – whacked my uncle smartly over the head with it. Uncle Anwar, who'd come from India to the Old Kent Road to lodge with a dentist, to jangle and gamble, to make his fortune and return home to build a house like my grandfather's on Juhu Beach, could never have guessed all those years ago that late in life he would be knocked unconscious by a sex-aid. No fortune-teller had predicted this. Kipling had written 'to each his own fear', but this was not Anwar's.

Anwar collapsed moaning on the pavement.

Shinko ran to a phone-box in which three boys had freshly urinated and called an ambulance. Later that day Changez was interviewed by the police and called immigrant, Paki, scum, wog, bastard and murderer, with the offending dildo on the table before him, as an *aide mémoire*. Changez's first impulse was to say that he was innocent, that the dildo had been planted on him by the police, since he knew such crimes occurred frequently. But even he knew better than to try to suggest to a white English jury that Constable McCrum had slipped a large pink sex-toy into the accused's pocket. Changez was held under consideration for assault.

Meanwhile Anwar, with a bandage around his head that made him look like the dying Trotsky, was in intensive care for a week. He'd had heart failure. Jamila and I and occasionally Princess Jeeta were at his bedside. But Jeeta could be cruel. 'Why do I want to see that black man?' she said one night, as we were on our way there on the bus.

I didn't know why, but Dad wouldn't go and see Anwar at all. Perhaps I felt more sentimental about Dad's past than he did himself, but I wanted to see the two men together again. 'Please go to the hospital,' I said.

'I don't want to give myself depression,' Dad replied fastidiously.

Dad had seriously fallen out with Anwar. They weren't speaking at all now. It was over the fact that Anwar thought Dad should never have left Mum. It was a corrupt thing to do. Have a mistress, Anwar said, and treat both women equally well, but never leave your wife. Anwar insisted that Eva was an immoral woman and that Dad had been seduced by the West, becoming as decadent and lacking in values as the rest of the society. He even listened to pop music, didn't he? 'He'll be eating pork pie next,' Anwar said. Naturally, all this infuriated Dad, who accepted the decadence and corruption line – he started using the word 'immoral' all the time – but not with reference to himself.

Only Eva could have got Dad out to see Anwar, but she was rarely at home anyway. Eva was working non-stop. They were a terrific couple, and good for each other, because Dad, with his ignorance of the world and plain arrogance, his 'You can do anything' approach, uninhibited by doubt or knowledge, gave Eva the support and confidence she'd always required. But of course, as she flourished she moved away from him. Eva was always out, and I knew Dad was thinking of Mum more than ever, and was probably idealizing her. He hadn't seen her, but they'd started to talk on the phone, whereas before I'd managed all their mutual business.

Anwar died, mumbling about Bombay, about the beach, about the boys at the Cathedral school, and calling for his mother. Jamila insisted he should be buried in a place she loved, a small grassy place where she often went to read, and gays to sunbathe and cruise. Anwar's body was washed by his friends at the nearby mosque, and five Indians in bright and clashing clothing brought the coffin to the graveside. One of the five men was simple, with a harelip; another had a little white beard. They opened the coffin lid and I went forward to join the queue filing past, always eager not to miss anything; but Dad held my arm as if I were a little boy, and refused to let me go as I pulled against his hand. 'You'll never forget it,' he said. 'Remember Uncle Anwar in other ways.'

'Which ways?'

'In his shop, for instance.'

'Really?'

'Stacking shelves,' he said sarcastically.

There was a minor row when one of the Indians pulled out a handy compass and announced that the hole hadn't been dug facing in the right direction, towards Mecca. The five Indians shifted the coffin a little and murmured verses from the Koran. All this reminded me of the time I was thrown out of a class at school for asking what people would be wearing in heaven. I thought I was one of the first people in history to find all religion childish and inexplicable.

But I did feel, looking at these strange creatures now – the Indians – that in some way these were my people, and that I'd spent my life denying or avoiding that fact. I felt ashamed and incomplete at the same time, as if half of me were missing, and as if I'd been colluding with my enemies, those whites who wanted Indians to be like them. Partly I blamed Dad for this. After all, like Anwar, for most of his life he'd never shown any interest in going back to India. He was always honest about this: he preferred England in every way. Things worked; it wasn't hot; you didn't see terrible things on the street that you could do nothing about. He wasn't proud of his past, but he wasn't unproud of it either; it just existed, and there wasn't any point in fetishizing it, as some liberals and Asian radicals liked to do. So if I wanted the additional personality bonus of an Indian past, I would have to create it.

When they lowered the coffin into the earth, and there seemed no crueller thing than life itself, Jamila staggered to one side, as if one leg had given way, fainting and almost collapsing on to the disappearing box. Changez, who had not taken his eyes from his wife all day, was instantly beside her, his feet plunging ankle-deep into mud, but with his arms around his wife at last, their bodies together, an ecstatic look on his face and, down below, I noticed, an erection. Rather inappropriate for a funeral, I thought, especially when you'd murdered the victim.

That night, when Jamila had put her mother to bed – and Jeeta had wanted to start work right away on reorganizing Paradise Stores – I raided the shop downstairs for the Newcastle Brown ale the three of us had recently taken to, and lugged the thick bottles upstairs to the flat. The place still contained, naturally, Anwar's possessions, as if he were away somewhere and would soon return. Pathetic possessions they were, too: slippers, cigarettes, stained waistcoats and several paintings of sunsets that Anwar thought were masterpieces and had left to me.

The three of us were tired but we weren't ready for sleep. Besides, Jamila and I had to look after the constantly weeping Changez, whom we referred to privately as the Dildo Killer. Outwardly the Dildo Killer was the most upset of us all – being the least English, I suppose – even though the victim, Anwar, had hated him and had got himself killed trying to reduce Changez's brain to mashed potato. Looking at Changez's regularly puckering and shuddering face, I could see that really it was Jamila he was upset about. The old man he was glad to be rid of. Changez was only terrified that Jamila would blame him for whacking her dad over the head and therefore love him less than she did already.

Jamila herself was quieter than usual, which made me nervous, because I had to do all the talking, but she was dignified and contained, vulnerable without crying everywhere. Her father had died at the wrong time, when there was much to be clarified and established. They hadn't even started to be grown-ups together. There was this piece of heaven, this little girl he'd carried around the shop on his shoulders; and then one day she was gone, replaced by a foreigner, an unco-operative woman he didn't know how to speak to. Being so confused, so weak, so in love, he chose strength and drove her away from himself. The last years he spent wondering where she'd gone, and slowly came to realize that she would never return, and that the husband he'd chosen for her was an idiot.

Wearing an inside-out sweatshirt and jeans once more, lying back on the rough orange sofa, Jamila put a bottle of Brown to her lips. Changez and I passed a bottle between us. Big Muslim *he* was, drinking on the day of a funeral. It was only with these two that I felt part of a family. The three of us were bound together by ties stronger than personality, and stronger than the liking or disliking of each other.

Jamila spoke slowly and thoughtfully. I wondered if she'd taken a couple of Valium. 'All of this has made me think about what I want in my life. I've been tired for a while of the way things have been. I've been conservative in a way that doesn't suit me. I'm leaving the flat. It's being returned to the landlord unless you' – she glanced at the Dildo Killer – 'want to pay the rent. I want to live somewhere else.'

The Killer looked terrified. He was being abandoned. He looked frantically between his two friends. His face was appalled. This, then, was how things happened. A few simple words were exchanged, and ever after it would all be different. One day you were in clover in your camp-bed, the next in shit up to your neck. She was being straightforward, Jamila, and the straightforward was not a method I preferred for myself. Changez had never accustomed himself to it either.

'Elsewhere where?' he managed to say.

'I want to try and live in another way. I've felt isolated.'

'I am there daily.'

'Changez, I want to live communally with a bunch of people – friends – in a large house they've bought in Peckham.'

She slid her hand over his as she broke the news. It was the first time I'd seen her touch her husband voluntarily.

'Jammie, what about Changez?' I asked.

'What would you like to do?' she asked him.

'Go with you. Go together, eh? Husband and wife, always together, despite our difficult characters, eh?'

'No.' She shook her head firmly, but with some sadness. 'Not necessarily.'

I butted in. 'Changez won't be able to survive alone, Jammie. And I'm going on tour soon. What'll happen to him, d'you think?'

She looked forcefully at both of us, but she addressed Changez.

'But that's for you to think about. Why don't you go back to your family in Bombay? They have a house there, you've told me. There is space, there are servants, chauffeurs.'

'But you are my wife.'

'Only legally,' she said gently.

'You will always be my wife. The legal is nothing, I understand that. But in my heart you are my Jamila.'

'Yes, well, Changez, you know it's never been like that.'

'I'm not going back,' he said flatly. 'Never. You won't make me.'

'I wouldn't make you do anything. You must do what suits you.'

Changez was less of a fool than I'd imagined. He'd observed his Jamila for a long time. He knew what to say. 'This is too Western for me,' he said. I thought for a moment he was even going to use the word 'Eurocentric' but he decided to keep it up his sleeve. 'Here, in this capitalism of the feelings no one cares for another person. Isn't that so?'

'Yes it is so,' Jamila admitted.

'Everyone is left to rot alone. No one will pick up another person when they are right down. This industrial system here is too hard for me. So I go down. All right,' he said loudly. 'I will try to make it alone.'

'What is it you really want, then?' she asked him.

He hesitated. He looked at her imploringly.

She said quickly, fatally, perhaps without thinking it through: 'Would you like to come with me?'

He nodded, unable to believe his hairy ears.

'Are you sure that's possible?'

'I don't know,' she said.

'Of course it's possible,' he said.

'Changez – '

'That's good,' I said. 'Excellent.'

'But I haven't thought about it.'

'We'll talk it over in time,' he said.

'But I'm not sure, Changez.'

'Jamila.'

'We won't be husband and wife – you know that'll never happen, don't you?' she said. 'In this house you'll have to take part in the communal life of the place.'

'I think he'll be superb communally, ol' Changez,' I said, since the Dildo Killer was weeping again, this time with relief. 'He'll help with washing the people's plates. He's a whizz with crockery and cutlery.'

She was stuck with him now. There was no way out. She said: 'But you'll have to pay your way, Changez. That's how I don't see it happening. My father paid the rent on our flat, but those days are gone. You'll have to support yourself.' And she added tentatively, 'You might have to work.'

This was too much. Changez looked at me anxiously.

'Exciting, huh?' I said.

We sat there, talking it over. He would go with her. She couldn't get out of it now.

As I watched Jamila I thought what a terrific person she'd become. She was low today, and she was often scornful of me anyway, the supercilious bitch, but I couldn't help seeing that there was in her a great depth of will, of delight in the world, and much energy for love. Her feminism, the sense of self and fight it engendered, the schemes and plans she had, the relationships – which she desired to take this form and not that form – the things she had made herself know, and all the understanding this gave, seemed to illuminate her tonight as she went forward, an Indian woman, to live a useful life in white England.

As I had some spare time before rehearsals started again I borrowed Ted's van and helped install Jamila and the Dildo Killer in their new house. Turning up with a truckful of paperbacks, the works of Conan Doyle and various sex-aids, I was surprised to see a big, double-fronted and detached place standing back from the main road, from which it was concealed by a thick hedge. There were rotting tarpaulins, old baths, disintegrating free magazines and sodden debris all over the garden; the stately house itself was cracking like an old painting. A pipe poured water down the walls. And three local skinheads, as respectable as Civil Servants, though one had a spider's web tattooed on his face, stood outside and jeered.

Inside, the place was full of the most eager and hard-working vegetarians I'd ever seen, earnest and humorous, with degrees in this and that, discussing Cage and Schumacher as they dragged out the cistern in their blue dungarees and boiler suits. Changez stood in front of a banner which read 'America, where are you now? Don't you care about your sons and daughters?' He looked like Oliver Hardy in a roomful of Paul Newmans, and was as frightened as a new boy at school. When someone hurried past him and said, 'Civilization has taken a wrong turn,' Changez looked as if he'd rather be anywhere than Utopia. I saw no tarot cards, though someone did say they were intending to 'make love to the garden'. I left Changez there and rushed home to add new touches to his character.

There were few jobs I relished as much as the invention of Changez/Tariq. With a beer and notebook on my desk, and concentrating for the first time since childhood on something that absorbed me, my thoughts raced: one idea pulled another behind it, like conjurer's handkerchiefs. I uncovered notions, connections, initiatives I didn't even know were present in my mind. I became more energetic and alive as I brushed in new colours and shades. I worked regularly and kept a journal; I saw that creation was an accretive process which couldn't be hurried, and which involved patience and, primarily, love. I felt more solid myself, and not as if my mind were just a kind of cinema for myriad impressions and emotions to flicker through. This was worth doing, this had meaning, this added up the elements of my life. And it was this that Pyke had taught me: what a creative life could be. So despite what he'd done to me, my admiration for him continued. I didn't blame him for anything; I was prepared to pay the price for his being a romantic, an experimenter. He had to pursue what he wanted to know and follow his feelings wherever they went, even as far as my arse and my girlfriend's cunt.

When I went back to the commune a few weeks later, to gather more ideas for Changez/Tariq and to see how Changez had settled in, I found the front garden had been cleared. There were piles of scaffolding ready to be erected around the house. There would be a new roof. Uncle Ted was advising on the renovation and had been over several times to help out.

I enjoyed seeing the vegetarians and their comrades working together, even if they did call each other comrade. I liked to stay late and drink with them, though they did go in for organic wine. And when he could persuade them to take off *Nashville Skyline*, Simon – the radical lawyer with short hair, tie and no beard, who seemed to run the place – played Charlie Mingus and the Mahavishnu Orchestra. He told me what jazz I might like because, to be frank, I'd become deadly bored with the new music I was hearing.

As we sat there they talked about how to construct this equitable society. I said nothing, for fear of appearing stupid; but I knew we had to have it. Unlike Terry's bunch, this lot didn't want power. The problem, said Simon, was how to overthrow, not those presently in power, but the whole principle of power-over.

Going home to Eva's, or back to Eleanor's for the night, I wished I could have stayed with Jamila and Changez. The newest ideas were passing through their house, I thought. But we were rehearsing a play, and Louise Lawrence had managed to compose a third of it. The opening was only weeks away. There was plenty to be done, and I was frightened.

CHAPTER FIFTEEN

It was while watching Pyke as he rehearsed in his familiar blue tracksuit, the tight bottoms of which hugged his arse like a cushion cover and outlined his little dick as he moved around the room, that I first began to suspect I'd been seriously let down. That prick, which had fucked me up the arse while Marlene cheered us on as if we were all-in wrestlers – and while Eleanor fixed herself a drink – had virtually ruptured me. Now, I began to be certain, the fucker was fucking me in other ways. I would look into it.

I watched him closely. He was a good director, because he liked other people, even when they were difficult. (He saw difficult people as puzzles to be solved.) Actors liked him because he knew that even they could discover for themselves the right way through a part if he gave them room. This flattered them, and actors love flattery. Pyke never got angry or shoved you in a direction you didn't want to go; his manipulations were subtle and effective. All the same, these were painful days for me. The others, especially Carol, often became angry, because I was slower and more stupid than they were. 'Karim's got all the right qualifications for an actor,' Carol said. 'No technique, no experience, no presence.'

So Pyke had to go over every line and move of the first scene with me. My greatest fear was that when the final script was delivered Lawrence and Pyke would have allowed me only a small part, and I'd be hanging around back-stage like a spare prick. But when Louise delivered the play I saw to my surprise that I had a cracker of a part. I couldn't wait to exhibit it.

What a strange business this acting is, Pyke said; you are trying to convince people that you're someone else, that this is not-me. The way to do it is this, he said: when in character, playing not-me, you have to be yourself. To make your not-self real you have to steal from your authentic self. A false stroke, a wrong note, anything pretended, and to the audience you are as obvious as a Catholic naked in a mosque. The closer you play to yourself the better. Paradox of paradoxes: to be someone else successfully you must be yourself! This I learned!

We went north in winter, touring the play around studio theatres and arts centres. We stayed in freezing hotels where the owners regarded their guests as little more than burglars, sleeping in unheated rooms with toilets up the hall, places without telephones where they refused to serve breakfast after eight. 'The way the English sleep and eat is enough to make you want to emigrate to Italy,' Eleanor said every day at breakfast. For Carol, all that mattered was playing in London; the north was Siberia, the people animals.

I was playing an immigrant fresh from a small Indian town. I insisted on assembling the costume myself: I knew I could do something apt. I wore high white platform boots, wide cherry flares that stuck to my arse like sweetpaper and flapped around my ankles, and a spotted shirt with a wide 'Concorde' collar flattened over my jacket lapels.

At the first performance, in front of an audience of twenty, as soon as I walked out on stage, farting with fear, there was laughter, uncertain at first, then from the belly as they took me in. As I continued, gusts of pleasure lifted me. I was a wretched and comic character. The other actors had the loaded lines, the many-syllabled political analysis, the flame-throwing attacks on pusillanimous Labour governments, but it was me the audience warmed to. They laughed at my jokes, which concerned the sexual ambition and humiliation of an Indian in England. Unfortunately, my major scenes were with Carol, who, after the first performance, started to look not-nicely across the stage at me. After the third performance, in the dressing room, she yelled, 'I can't act with this person – he's a pratt, not an actor!' And she ran to ring Pyke in London.

Matthew had driven back to London that afternoon. He'd gone all the way from Manchester to London to sleep with a brilliant woman barrister who'd defended bombers and freedom fighters. 'This is a superb opportunity, Karim,' he told me. 'After all, I've got the hang of the police, but the formal law, that pillar of our society, I want it beside me, on my very pillow.' And off he sped, leaving us to audiences and rain.

Perhaps Pyke was in bed discussing the fate of the Bradford Eight or the Leeds Six when Carol rang him. I imagined him being careful in his love-making with the barrister; he'd think of everything – champagne, hash, flowers – to ensure she thought highly and passionately of him. And now Carol was saying persuasively down the phone that I seemed to be in a different play to the others, a farce, perhaps. But, like most talented people who are successful with the public, Pyke was blessed with a vulgar streak. He supported me. 'Karim is the key to this play,' he told Carol.

When we arrived in London after visiting ten cities, we started to re-rehearse and prepare for previews at an arts centre in West London, not far from Eva's flat. It was a fashionable place, where the latest in international dance, sculpture, cinema and theatre was displayed. It was run by two highly strung aesthetes who had a purity and severity of taste that made Pyke look rococo in comparison. I sat around with them in the restaurant, eating bean-shoots and listening to talk of the new dance and an innovative form called 'performance'. I saw one 'performance'. This involved a man in a boiler suit pulling a piece of Camembert across a vast floor by a piece of string. Behind him two boys in black played guitars. It was called *Cheesepiece*. After, I heard people say, 'I liked the original image.' It was all an education. I'd never heard such venom expressed on subjects which I'd only ever considered lightly. To the aesthetes, as with Pyke (but much worse), the performance of an actor or the particular skill of a writer whose work I'd seen with Eleanor and thought of as 'promising' or 'a bit jejune', was as important as earthquakes or marriages. 'May they die of cancer,' they said of these authors. I also imagined they'd want to get together with Pyke and discuss Stanislavsky and Artaud and all, but they hated each other's guts. The two aesthetes barely mentioned the man whose show was rehearsing in their theatre, except in terms like 'that man who irons his jeans' or 'Caliban'. The two aesthetes were assisted by a fleet of exquisitely dressed middle-class girls whose fathers were television tycoons. It was an odd set-up: this was the subsidized theatre, and these were radical people, but it was as if everyone – the people who worked there, journalists, fans of the company, other directors and actors – wanted the answer to only one question: Is this play going to be successful or not?

To escape the mounting tension and anxiety, one Sunday morning I went to visit Changez at his new place. They were great people, the vegetarians, but I was nervous of how they would react when they found that Changez was a fat, useless bum, and that they would have to carry him.

At first I didn't recognize him. It was partly the environment in which he was now living. Old Bubble was sitting in the all-pine communal kitchen surrounded by plants and piles of radical newspapers. On the wall were posters advertising demonstrations against South Africa and Rhodesia, meetings, and holidays in Cuba and Albania. Changez had had his hair cut; his Flaubert moustache had been plucked from under his nose; and he was wearing a large grey boiler suit buttoned up to the throat. 'You look like a motor-mechanic,' I said. He beamed back at me. Among other things he was pleased that the assault case against him had been dropped, once it was certain that Anwar had died of a heart attack. 'I'm going to make the most of my life now, *yaar*,' he said.

Sitting at the table with Changez were Simon and a young, fair-haired girl, Sophie, who was eating muffins. She'd just returned from selling anarchist newspapers outside a factory.

When Changez offered, to my surprise, to go out to the shops for milk, I asked them how he was doing, whether everything was all right. Was he coping? I was aware that my tone of voice indicated that I thought of Changez as a minor mental patient. But Simon and Sophie liked Changez. Sophie referred to him once as a 'disabled immigrant', which, I suppose, the Dildo Killer was. Maybe this gave him credence in the house. He'd obviously had the sense not to talk at length about being from a family who owned racehorses. And he must have cut the many stories he used to tell me about the number of servants he'd been through, and his analysis of the qualities he reckoned were essential in a good servant, cook and sweeper.

'I love the communal life, Karim,' Changez said, when we went for a walk later that day. 'The family atmosphere is here without nagging aunties. Except for the meetings, *yaar*. They have them every five minutes. We have to sit time after time and discuss this thing and that thing, the garden, the cooking, the condition of England, the condition of Chile, the condition of Czechoslovakia. This is democracy gone berserk, *yaar*. Still, it's bloody amazing and everything, the nudity you see daily.'

'What nudity?'

'Full nudity. Complete nudity.'

'What kind of full and complete nudity?'

'There are five girls here, and only Simon and I representing the gentlemen's side. And the girls, on the communist principle of having no shame to hide, go completely without clothes, their breasts without brassieres! Their bushes without concealment!'

'Christ – '

'But I can't stay there – '

'What, after all that? Why not, Bubble? Look what I've fixed you up with! Think of the breasts without brassieres over breakfast!'

'Karim, it breaks my heart, *yaar*. But Jamila has started to yell with this nice boy, Simon. They are in the next room. Every night I hear them shaking the bed around. It blasts my bloody ears to Kingdom Coming.'

'That was bound to happen one day, Changez. I'll buy you some ear plugs if you like.' And I giggled to myself at the thought of Changez listening to the love of his life being shafted next door night after night. 'Or why don't you change rooms?'

He shook his head. 'I like to be near her. I like to hear her moving around. I am familiar with every sound she makes. At this moment she is sitting down. At that moment she is reading. I like to know.'

'You know, Changez, love can be very much like stupidity.'

'Love is love, and it is eternal. You don't have romantic love in the West any more. You just sing about it on the radio. No one really loves, here.'

'What about Eva and Dad?' I countered jauntily. 'That's romantic, isn't it?'

'That's adultery. That's pure evil.'

'Oh, I see.'

I was pleased to find Changez so cheerful. He seemed glad to have escaped lethargy into this new life, a life I'd never have imagined suiting him.

As we loafed around I saw how derelict and poor this end of the city – South London – really was, compared with the London I was living in. Here the unemployed were walking the streets with nowhere else to go, the men in dirty coats and the women in old shoes without stockings. As we walked and looked Changez talked of how much he liked English people, how polite and considerate they were. 'They're gentlemen. Especially the women. They don't try to do you down all the time like the Indians do.'

These gentlemen had unhealthy faces; their skin was grey. The housing estates looked like makeshift prison camps; dogs ran around; rubbish blew about; there was graffiti. Small trees had been planted with protective wire netting around them, but they'd all been snapped off anyway. The shops sold only inadequate and badly made clothes. Everything looked cheap and shabby, the worse for trying to be flash. Changez must have been thinking the same things as me. He said, 'Perhaps I feel at home here because it reminds me of Calcutta.'

When I said it was time for me to go, Changez's mood changed. From broodiness he snapped into businesslike attack, as if he'd worked out in advance what he wanted to say, and now was the time to deliver it.

'Now, tell me, Karim, you're not using my own character in your play, are you?'

'No, Changez. I told you already.'

'Yes, you laid your word of honour on the line.'

'Yes, I did. Right?'

He thought for a few seconds. 'But what does it stand for, ultimately, your word of honour?'

'Everything, man, every fucking thing, for God's sake! Christ, Changez, you're becoming fucking self-righteous, aren't you?'

He looked at me sternly, as if he didn't believe me, the bastard, and off he went to waddle around South London.

A few days later, after we'd started previewing the play in London, Jamila rang to tell me that Changez had been attacked under a railway bridge when coming back from a Shinko session. It was a typical South London winter evening – silent, dark, cold, foggy, damp – when this gang jumped out on Changez and called him a Paki, not realizing he was Indian. They planted their feet all over him and started to carve the initials of the National Front into his stomach with a razor blade. They fled because Changez let off the siren of his Muslim warrior's call, which could be heard in Buenos Aires. Naturally he was shocked; shit-scared and shaken up, Jamila said. But he hadn't been slow to take advantage of the kindness shown him by everyone. Sophie was now bringing him his breakfast in bed, and he'd been let off various cooking and washing-up duties. The police, who were getting sick of Changez, had suggested that he'd laid down under the railway bridge and inflicted the wound on himself, to discredit them.

The attack on Changez angered me, and I asked Jamila if I could do anything. Yes; these attacks were happening all the time. I should come with Jamila and her friends on a march the following Saturday. The National Front were parading through a nearby Asian district. There would be a fascist rally in the Town Hall; Asian shops would be attacked and lives threatened. Local people were scared. We couldn't stop it: we could only march and make our voices heard. I said I'd be there.

I hadn't been sleeping with Eleanor more than once a week recently. Nothing had been said, but she'd cooled towards me. I wasn't alarmed; after rehearsing I liked to go home and be frightened alone. I prepared myself for the opening by walking around the flat as Changez, not caricaturing him but getting behind his peculiar eyeballs. Robert de Niro would have been proud of me.

I took it for granted that Eleanor spent the evenings at parties with her friends. She often invited me, too, but I'd noticed that after a couple of hours with her crowd I felt heavy and listless. Life had offered these people its lips, but as they dragged from party to party, seeing the same faces and saying the same things night after night, I saw it was the kiss of death; I saw how much was enervated and useless in them. What passion or desire or hunger did they have as they lounged in their London living rooms? I told my political adviser, Sergeant Monty, that the ruling class weren't worth hating. He disagreed. 'Their complacency makes them worse,' he argued.

When I rang Eleanor and told her we should join the others in confronting the fascists, her attitude was strange, especially considering what had happened to Gene. She vacillated all over the place. On the one hand there was this shopping to do in Sainsbury's; on the other hand there was that person to visit in hospital. 'I'll see you at the demo, love,' she concluded. 'My head's a little messed up.' I put the phone down.

I knew what to do. I was supposed to be meeting Jamila, Changez, Simon, Sophie and the others at the house that morning. So what? I'd be late. I wouldn't miss the march; I'd just go straight there.

I waited an hour and caught the tube northwards, towards Pyke's. I went into the front garden of the house opposite his, sat down on a log and watched Pyke's house through a hole in the hedge. Time passed. It was getting late. I'd have to take a cab to the march. That would be OK, as long as Jamila didn't catch me getting out of a taxi. After three hours of waiting I saw Eleanor approach Pyke's house. What a genius I was: how right I'd been! Eleanor rang the bell and Pyke answered immediately. Not a kiss, or a stroke, or a smile – only the door shutting behind her. Then nothing. What did I expect? I stared at the closed door. What was I to do? This was something I hadn't thought about. The march and demonstration would be in full swing. Perhaps Pyke and Eleanor would be going on it. I'd wait for them; maybe declare myself, say I was passing, and get a lift to the march with them.

I waited another three hours. They must have been having a late lunch. It started to get dark. When Eleanor emerged I followed her to the tube and got into the carriage behind her, sitting opposite her in the train. She looked pretty surprised when she glanced up and saw me sitting there. 'What are you doing on the Bakerloo Line?' she asked.

Well, I wasn't in a defensive mood. I went and sat right next to her. Straight out, I asked her what she'd been doing at Pyke's, instead of throwing her body in front of fascists.

She threw back her hair, looked around the train as if for an escape and said she could say the same about me. She wouldn't look at me, but she wasn't defensive. 'Pyke attracts me,' she said. 'He's an exciting man. You may not have noticed, but there's so few of those around.'

'Will you carry on sleeping with him?'

'Yes, yes, whenever he asks me.'

'How long's it been going on?'

'Since that time . . . since that time we went over there for supper and you and Pyke did that stuff to each other.'

She rested her cheek against mine. The sweetness of her skin and entire aroma practically made me pass out.

'Oh, love,' I said.

She said, 'I want you to be with me, Karim, and I've done a lot for you. But I can't have people – men – telling me what to do. If Pyke wants me to be with him, then I must follow my desire. There's so much for him to teach me. And please, please, don't ever follow me around again.'

The doors of the train were closing, but I managed to nip through them. As I walked up the platform I resolved to break with Eleanor. I would have to see her every day at the theatre, but I'd never address her as a lover again. It was over, then, my first real love affair. There would be others. She preferred Pyke. Sweet Gene, her black lover, London's best mime, who emptied bed-pans in hospital soaps, killed himself because every day, by a look, a remark, an attitude, the English told him they hated him; they never let him forget they thought him a nigger, a slave, a lower being. And we pursued English roses as we pursued England; by possessing these prizes, this kindness and beauty, we stared defiantly into the eye of the Empire and all its self-regard – into the eye of Hairy Back, into the eye of the Great Fucking Dane. We became part of England and yet proudly stood outside it. But to be truly free we had to free ourselves of all bitterness and resentment, too. How was this possible when bitterness and resentment were generated afresh every day?

I'd send Eleanor a dignified note. Then I'd have to fall out of love with her. That was the rough part. Everything in life is organized around people falling in love with each other. Falling is easy; but no one tells you how to fall out of love. I didn't know where to begin.

For the rest of the day I wandered around Soho and sat through about ten porn films. For a week after that I must have gone into some kind of weird depression and sulk and social incapacity, because I cared nothing for what should have been the greatest evening of my life – the opening of the play.

In these days before the opening I didn't talk to the other actors. The intimacy Pyke had engendered now seemed like a drug which had temporarily given us the impression of affection and support but had now worn off, returning only in occasional flashbacks, like LSD. I took direction from Pyke but I didn't get in his car again. I'd admired him so much, his talent, daring and freedom from convention, but now I was confused. Hadn't he betrayed me? Or perhaps he was helping to educate me in the way the world worked. I didn't know. Anyway, Eleanor must have told him what had happened between us because he kept away from me and was merely polite. Marlene wrote to me once, saying, 'Where are you, sweetheart? Won't you come see me again, sweet Karim?' I didn't reply. I was sick of theatre people and the whole play; I was turning numb. What happened to me didn't seem to matter. Sometimes I felt angry, but most of the time I felt nothing; I'd never felt so much nothing before.

The dressing rooms were full of flowers and cards, and there were more kisses in an hour than in the whole of Paris in a day. There were TV and radio interviews, and a journalist asked me what the main events of my life had been. I was photographed several times beside barbed-wire. (I noticed that photographers seemed to love barbed-wire.) I was living intensely in my mind, trying to keep my eyes off Eleanor, trying not to hate the other actors too much.

Then, suddenly, this was it, the night of nights, and I was on stage alone in the full glare of the lights, with four hundred white English people looking at me. I do know that lines that sounded over-familiar and meaningless to me, and came out of my mouth with all the resonance of, 'Hallo, how are you today?' were invested with life and meaning by the audience, so much so that the evening was a triumph and I was – I have this on good authority, that of the critics – hilarious and honest. At last.

After the show I drank off a pint of Guinness in the dressing room and dragged myself out into the foyer. There I saw, right in front of me, a strange and unusual sight, especially as I'd invited no one to the opening.

If I'd been in a film I would have rubbed my eyes to indicate that I didn't believe what I was seeing. Mum and Dad were talking to each other and smiling. It's not what you expect of your parents. There, among the punk sophisticates and bow-ties and shiny shoes and bare-backed women, was Mum, wearing a blue and white dress, blue hat and brown sandals. Standing nearby was my brother, little Allie. All I could think was how small and shy my mum and dad looked, how grey-haired and fragile they were, and how the distance they were standing apart looked unnatural. You go all your life thinking of your parents as these crushing protective monsters with infinite power over you, and then there's a day when you turn round, catch them unexpectedly, and they're just weak, nervous people trying to get by with each other.

Eva came over to me with a drink and said, 'Yes, it's a happy sight, isn't it.' Eva and I stood there together and she talked about the play. 'It was about this country,' she said. 'About how callous and bereft of grace we've become. It blew away the self-myth of tolerant, decent England. It made the hair on the back of my neck stand up.

That's how I knew it was good. I judge all art by its effect on my neck.'

'I'm glad it did that, Eva,' I said. I could see she was in a bad state. I didn't know what to say. Anyway, Shadwell was lurking nearby, waiting for her to finish with me. And all the time Eva's eyes wouldn't keep still – not that they ever moved anywhere near Mum and Dad, though that would be their natural resting place. There they would devour. When she turned back to Shadwell he smiled at me and started to speak. 'I am ravished but resistant because . . .' he began. I looked at Mum and Dad once more. 'They still love each other, can't you see that?' I said to Eva. Or perhaps I didn't say it; perhaps I just thought it. Sometimes you can't tell when you've said something or just had it in your head.

I moved away, and found Terry standing at the bar with a woman who didn't look like the rest of the scented and parading first-nighters. Terry didn't introduce me to her. He didn't want to acknowledge her. He didn't shake my hand. So she said, 'I'm Yvonne, a friend of Matthew Pyke, and a police officer based in North London. Sergeant Monty and I' – and she giggled – 'were just discussing police procedures.'

'Were you, Terry?' I hadn't seen Terry looking like this before, this upset; he kept shaking his head as if he had water in his ears. He wouldn't look at me. I was worried about him. I touched the side of his head. 'What's wrong, Monty?'

'Don't call me that, you cunt. I'm not Monty. I am Terry and I am disturbed. I'll tell you what it is. I wish it had been me on that stage. It could have been me. I deserved it, OK? But it was you. OK? So why am I playing a fucking policeman?'

I moved away from him. He'd feel better tomorrow. But that wasn't the end of it. 'Hey, hey, where are you going?' he said. He was following me. 'There's something for you to do,' he said. 'Will you do it? You said you would.'

Forcibly, he led me to one side, away from everyone, so we wouldn't be overheard. He held my arm. He was hurting me. My arm was going numb. I didn't move away.

'It's now,' he said. 'We're giving you the call.'

'Not tonight,' I said.

'Not tonight? Why not tonight? What's tonight to you? A big deal?'

I shrugged. 'All right.'

I said I'd do it if I could. I knew what he was on about. I wasn't about to be a coward. I knew who to hate. He said, 'The Party requires funds right now. Go to two people and ask them for money.'

'How much?' I said.

'We'll leave that to you.'

I sniggered. 'Don't be stupid.'

'Watch your mouth,' he shouted. 'Just watch all that fucking lip!' Then he laughed and looked mockingly at me. This was a different Terry. 'As much as you can get.'

'So it's a test?'

'Hundreds,' he said. 'We want hundreds of pounds. Ask them. Push them. Rip them off. Steal their furniture. They can afford it. Get what you can. OK?'

'Yes.'

I walked away. I'd had enough. But he took my arm again, the same arm. 'Where the fuck are you going now?'

'What?' I said. 'Don't bring me down.'

He was angry, but I never got angry. I didn't care what happened.

'But how can you get the money if you don't know the names of the parties involved?'

'OK. What are the names?' I asked.

He jerked me around again until I was facing the wall. I could no longer see my parents; I could only see the wall and Terry. His teeth were clenched. 'It's class war,' he said.

'I know that.'

His voice dropped. 'Pyke is one. Eleanor is the other.'

I was astonished. 'But they're my friends.'

'Yeah, so they should be friendly.'

'Terry, no.'

'Yes, Karim.'

He turned away and looked around the crowded restaurant area. 'A nice bunch of people. Drink?'

'No.'

'Sure?'

I nodded.

'See you then, Karim.'

'Yeah.'

We separated. I walked about. I knew a lot of people but I hardly recognized them. Unfortunately, within a minute, I found myself standing in front of the one person I wanted to avoid – Changez. There would be debts to pay now. I was for it. I'd been so nervous about this that a couple of days earlier I'd tried to stop him coming, saying to Jamila, 'I don't think Changez will enjoy this evening.' 'In that case I must bring him,' she said, characteristically. Now Changez embraced me and slammed me on the back. 'Very good plays and top playing,' he said.

I looked at him suspiciously. I didn't feel at all well. I wanted to be somewhere else. I don't know why, I felt this was some kind of snide trick. I was for it. They were out to get me tonight.

'Yeah, you look happy, Changez. What's brought on this ecstasy?'

'But surely you will have guessed, my Jamila is expecting.' I looked at him blankly. 'We are having a baby.'

'Your baby?'

'You bloody fool, how could that be without sexual intercourse? You know very well I haven't had the extent of that privilege.'

'Exactly, dear Prudence. That's what I thought.'

'So by Simon she is expecting. But we will all share in it.'

'A communal baby?'

Changez grunted his agreement. 'Belonging to the entire family of friends. I've never been so happy.'

That was enough for me, thank you very much. I would piss off, go home. But before I could, Changez reached out his thick paw, the good hand. And I jumped back. Here we go, he's going to smash me, I thought, a fellow Indian in the foyer of a white theatre!

'Come a little closer, top actor,' he said. 'And listen to my criticism. I am glad in your part you kept it fundamentally autobiographical and didn't try the leap of invention into my character. You realized clearly that I am not a person who could be successfully impersonated. Your word of honour is honourable after all. Good.'

I was glad to see Jamila beside me; I hoped she'd change the subject. But who was that with her? Surely it was Simon? What had happened to his face? One of Simon's eyes was bandaged; the cheek below it was dressed; and half his head was wrapped in lint. Jamila looked grave, even when I congratulated her twice on the baby. She just eyed me steadily, as if I were some kind of criminal rapist. What was her fucking problem, that's what I wanted to know.

'What's your problem?'

'You weren't there,' she said. 'I couldn't believe it. You just didn't show up.'

Where wasn't I?

'Where?' I said.

'Do I have to remind you? At the demonstration, Karim.'

'I couldn't make it, Jammie. I was rehearsing. How was it? I hear it was effective and everything.'

'Other people from the cast of your play were there. Simon's a friend of Tracey's. She was there, right at the front.'

She looked at Simon. I looked at Simon. It was impossible to say what expression he had on his face, as so much of his face was a goner at the moment.

'That's how it was. A bottle in the face. Where are you going as a person, Karim?'

'Over there,' I said.

I was leaving, I was getting out, when Mum came up to me. She smiled and I kissed her. 'I love you so much,' she said.

'Wasn't I good, eh, Mum?'

'You weren't in a loin-cloth as usual,' she said. 'At least they let you wear your own clothes. But you're not an Indian. You've never been to India. You'd get diarrhoea the minute you stepped off that plane, I know you would.'

'Why don't you say it a bit louder,' I said. 'Aren't I part Indian?'

'What about me?' Mum said. 'Who gave birth to you? You're an Englishman, I'm glad to say.'

'I don't care,' I said. 'I'm an actor. It's a job.'

'Don't say that,' she said. 'Be what you are.'

'Oh yeah.'

She looked across at Dad, who was now with Eva. Eva was talking angrily to him. Dad looked sheepish, but he took it; he didn't answer back. He saw us and lowered his eyes. 'She's giving him a thick ear,' Mum said. 'Silly old cow – it'll do no good with a stubborn arse like him.'

'Go to the Ladies and blow your nose,' I said.

'I better,' she said.

At the door I stood on a chair and overlooked the crowd of

232

potential skeletons. In eighty years the lot of us would be dead. We lived, having no choice, as if that were not so, as if we were not alone, as if there would not come a moment when each of us would see that our lives were over, that we were driving without brakes towards a brick wall. Eva and Dad were still talking; Ted and Jean were talking; Marlene and Tracey were talking; Changez and Simon and Allie were talking; and none of them had much need for me now. Out I went.

In comparison with their fetid arses and poisonous talk, the night air was mild as milk. I opened my leather jacket and unbuttoned my fly and let my prick feel the wind. I walked towards the shitty river Thames, that tide of turds polluted with jerks who lived on boats and men who liked rowing. I got into this invigorating walking rhythm for a while, until I realized I was being followed by some kind of little creature whom I spotted a few yards behind me, walking calmly along with her hands in her pockets. I didn't give a fuck.

I wanted to think about Eleanor, and how painful it was to see her every day when all I wanted was to be back with her. I know I had hoped that my indifference would revive her interest in me, that she missed me and would ask me back to her place for more steamed cabbage and a last kiss of her thighs. But in my letter I'd asked her to keep away from me; that's exactly what she was doing, and it didn't seem to bother her. Perhaps I would try and talk to her one last time.

My curiosity about the person behind me was too much to bear, so further along the river I concealed myself in a pub doorway and jumped out, half naked, on the creature, shouting, 'Who are you? Why are you following me!' When I let her go she was unperturbed, unafraid and smiling.

'I admired your performance,' she said as we walked along. 'You made me laugh. I just wanted to tell you. And you have the nicest face. Those lips. Wow.'

'Yeah? You like me?'

'Yes, and I wanted to be with you a few minutes. You don't mind me following you, do you? I could see you wanted to leave. You looked terrified. Angry. What a state: phew. You don't want to be alone now, do you?'

'Don't worry about anything – it's good to have a friend.'

God, I sounded a fool. But she took my arm and we walked along the river, past William Morris's house and towards Hogarth's Tomb.

'It's odd that someone else had the same idea as me,' said the woman, whose name was Hilary.

'What idea?'

'To follow you,' she said.

I turned, and saw Heater standing there, not making any effort to conceal himself. I greeted him with a scream which rose from my stomach and flew across the air like a jet. Janov himself would have applauded.

'What d'you want, Heater! Why don't you fuck off and die of cancer, you fat, ugly, pseudy cunt?'

He adjusted his position so that he stood solidly with his feet apart, his weight evenly distributed. He was ready for me. He wanted to fight.

'I'm coming for you, Paki cunt! I don't like ya! An' you lot have been playing with my Eleanor. You an' that Pyke.'

Hilary took my hand. She was calm. 'Why don't we just run?' she said.

'That's a good idea,' I said. 'OK.'

'Let's go, then.'

I ran towards Heater and mounted him by stepping on his knee, grabbing him by the lapels and using the velocity to bounce my forehead against his nose in the way I'd been taught at school. Thank God for education. He wheeled away, holding his nose on to his face. Then Hilary and I were running and shouting; we were holding each other and kissing, and it seemed that blood was everywhere; it was just pouring off us. I'd forgotten that Heater had learned at school never to go anywhere without razor-blades sewn into the back of his lapels.

CHAPTER SIXTEEN

The theatre was full every night, and on Fridays and Saturdays, to our pleasure, people were turned away. We were going to do extra shows. The play was on my mind all day. How could it not be? It was a big event to get through every evening. It was impossible to do it and only half concentrate, as I saw one night, after finding myself stranded on stage, looking at Eleanor, having forgotten which act of the play we were in. I found that the best way to avoid having my day ruined by the show in the evening was to move the hours around, getting up at three or four in the afternoon so that the play took place in the morning, as it were, and you had hours afterwards in which to forget it.

After the show we went out into the restaurant area, where looks would linger on us. People pointed us out to each other. They bought us drinks; they felt privileged to meet us. They required us urgently at their parties, to spice them up. We went to them, turning up at midnight with our arms full of beer and wine. Once there we were offered drugs. I had sex with several women; all that was easier now. I got an agen., too. I was offered a small part in a television film, playing a taxi-driver. I had some money to play with. One night Pyke came by and asked us if we wanted to take the show to New York. There'd been an offer from a small but prestigious theatre there. Did we really want to go? 'Let me know if you can be bothered,' he said casually. 'It's up to you all.'

Pyke gave us some notes after the show, and then I asked him if I could visit him that weekend. He smiled and patted my arse. 'Any time,' he said. 'Why not?'

'Sit down,' he said when I got there, ready to ask him for money. An old woman in a pink nylon housecoat came into the room with a duster. 'Later, Mavis,' he said.

'Matthew – ' I began.

'Sit down while I take a shower,' he said. 'Are you in a big hurry?' And he went out again, leaving me alone in that room with the cunt sculpture. As before, I wandered around. I thought maybe I would steal something and Terry could sell it for the Party. Or it could be a kind of trophy. I looked at vases and picked up paperweights, but I had no idea what they were worth. I was about to put a paperweight in my pocket when Marlene came in, wearing shorts and a T-shirt. Her hands and arms were spotted with paint. She was decorating. Her flesh was sickly white now, I noticed. How had I kissed and licked it?

'It's you,' she said. She showed little of last time's enthusiasm. Presumably she'd gone off me. These people could go up and down. 'What are you up to?' she said. She came over to me. She brightened then. 'Give us a kiss, Karim.' She bent forward and closed her eyes. I kissed her lips lightly. She didn't open her eyes. 'That's not a kiss. When I'm kissed I want to stay kissed,' she said. Her tongue was in my mouth; her mouth was moving on mine; her hands were over me.

'Leave him alone, for Christ's sake, can't you?' said Pyke, coming back into the room. 'Where's that sandalwood body shampoo I like?'

She stood up. 'How should I know? I'm not vain. I'm not a fucking man. I don't use it.'

Pyke went through Marlene's bag; he went through various drawers, pulling things out. Marlene watched him, standing with her hands on her hips. She waited till he was at the door again before shouting at him, 'Why are you so arrogant? Don't talk to me as if I were some floozie actress. Why should I leave my Karim alone? You go out with his girlfriend.'

Pyke stood there and said, 'You can fuck him. I don't care. You know I don't care. Do exactly what you like, Marlene.'

'Fuck you,' said Marlene. 'Fuck freedom, too. Stick it up your arse.'

'Anyway, she's not his girlfriend,' said Pyke.

'She's not his girlfriend?' Marlene turned to me. 'Is it true?' She turned to Pyke. 'What have you done?' Pyke said nothing. 'He's broken it up, has he, Karim?'

'Yep,' I said. I got up. Marlene and Pyke looked at each other with hatred. I said, 'Matthew, I've just dropped by to ask you something. It's a small thing. It won't take long. Can we deal with it now?'

'I'll leave you two boys alone, then,' said Marlene, sarcastically.

'Where's my body shampoo?' Pyke asked. 'Really, where is it?'

236

'Fuck off,' Marlene said, going out.

'Well, well,' said Pyke to me, relaxing.

I asked him for the money. I told him what it was for. I asked him for three hundred pounds. 'For politics?' he asked. 'For the Party, is that it? Am I right?'

'Yes.'

'You?'

'Yes.'

'My, my, Karim. I must have made a mistake about you.'

I tried to be jaunty. 'Maybe you did.'

He looked at me seriously and with kindness, as if he were really seeing me. 'I didn't mean to put you down. I just didn't realize you were so committed.'

'I'm not, really,' I said. 'They just asked me to ask you.'

He fetched his cheque book. 'I bet they didn't tell you to say that.' He picked up his pen. 'So you're their postman. You're a vulnerable kid. Don't let them use you. Take a cheque.'

He was charming. He gave me a cheque for five hundred pounds. I could have talked to him all day, gossiping and chatting as we used to in his car. But once I'd got the money I left; he didn't particularly want me there and I didn't want to get into anything with Marlene. When I was going out the front door she ran down the stairs and called out, 'Karim, Karim,' and I heard Pyke say to her, 'He can't get away from you quick enough,' as I banged the door behind me.

I couldn't bring myself to visit Eleanor's flat again. So I asked her for money one night at the theatre. I found it hard to talk to her now. It was made more difficult because, while I put it to her, explaining this was business not love, she busied herself with things, with the many objects she had with her in the dressing room: books, cassettes, make-up, photographs, cards, letters, clothes. And she tried on a couple of hats, too, for God's sake. She did all this because she didn't want to face me, to sit and look straight at me now. But I also felt that she'd shut me out of her mind. I meant little to her; I hadn't been an important failure.

Not that I liked her much, either; but I didn't want to let her go. I didn't want to be pushed aside, dropped, discarded. Yet I had been. There it was. There was nothing I could do. So I just told her what I wanted. She nodded and held up a book. 'Have you read this?' she said. I didn't even look at it. I didn't want to get into books now. I asked her again for some money. It would help the Party; and they would change the things that needed changing.

She said, finally, 'No, I will not give you five hundred pounds.'

'Why not?'

'I've been thinking about Gene.'

'You're always thinking about Gene and – '

'Yes. So? Why not?'

'Forget it, Eleanor,' I said. 'Let's stick to this.'

'Gene was – '

I banged my hand on the table. I was getting fed up. And a line from Bob Dylan kept running through my head: 'Stuck Inside of Mobile with the Memphis Blues Again'.

'The Party. They need money. That's all it is. Nothing else. Nothing about Gene. Nothing about us.'

She insisted. 'I'm saying something. You're not listening to me.'

'You're rich, aren't you? Spread it around, darling.'

'You scornful bastard,' she said. 'Didn't we have a good time, you and I?'

'Yes, all right. I enjoyed myself. We went to the theatre. We screwed. And you went out with Pyke.'

She smiled at me then, and she said, 'This is the point. They are not a Party for black people. They are an all-honky thing, if you want to know. I'm not giving a bean to that kind of apartheid thing.'

'All right,' I said, getting up. 'Thanks anyway.'

'Karim.' She looked at me. She wanted to say something kind, so she said, 'Don't get bitter.'

On my day off I went to see Terry. He and his mates were squatting a house in Brixton. I got off the tube and walked north, as he'd instructed me, under the railway bridge I'd passed over on the train with Uncle Ted the time he slashed the seats; the time he said 'them blacks'. It was the same line my father travelled on to work all those years, with his blue dictionary in his briefcase.

These houses were built for another era, I thought, looking at Terry's place. They were five-storey places; they overlooked pretty parks; and they were rotting as this part of the city was rotting even as it flourished in the cracks. The kids here were wilder than anywhere else in London. The hair which Charlie had appropriated and elaborated on – black, spiky, sculptural, ornamental, evening-wear not work-wear – had moved on: to the Mohican. The girls and boys wore solid rainbows of hairy colour on their otherwise tonsured skulls. The black kids had dreadlocks half-way down their back, and walking sticks and running shoes. The girls wore trousers which tapered to above the ankle; the boys wore black bondage trousers with flaps and buckles and zips. The area was full of shebeens, squats, lesbian bars, gay pubs, drug pubs, drug organizations, advice centres, and the offices of various radical political organizations. There wasn't much work going on; people were hanging out; they asked you if you wanted black hash, which I did, but not from them.

The door of the house was open. The locks had been smashed. I went straight up and caught Terry at it. He was wearing shorts and a T-shirt; he was barefoot, and he was working on a long padded seat in front of a large window. He held a weighted bar behind his neck as he stood up and sat down, stood up and sat down, and watched rugby on a black and white TV. He looked at me in amazement. I hunted around for somewhere to sit, an unbroken chair or unstained cushion. It was a dirty place and Terry was a well-off actor. Before I'd sat down he had seized me and hugged me. He smelled good, of sweat.

'Hey, hey, it's you, it really is you, just turning up like this. Where you been?'

'Sergeant Monty,' I said.

'Where you been? Tell me. Where, Karim?'

'Raising money for you.'

'Yeah, really,' Terry said. 'I believe you.'

'Didn't you ask me to?'

'Yes, but – ' He rolled his eyes.

'You asked me to. You fucking ordered me. Didn't you? Are you saying you don't remember?'

'Remember? How could I fucking forget, Karim? That night. Wow. All that money and intelligence. Those smart people. University cunts. Fucking rich cunts. Fucking rot them. It can unsettle a boy like me.'

'Don't tell me,' I said.

He gestured with his hands and blew hard through his mouth. 'But I don't feel too pleased about it.'

He went off and made some tea, but it was Typhoo and the cup had brown stains on the outside. I put it aside and gave him Pyke's cheque. He glanced at it; he looked at me. 'Bloody good work. I thought you were joking. This is terrific. Well done, mate.'

'I only had to ask him. You know what liberals are like.'

'Yeah, they can afford it, the bastards.' He came over to me again after putting the cheque in his jacket pocket. 'Listen, there's other things you can do now for the Party.'

I said, 'I'm going to America with Pyke.'

'Fuck that. What for?' It was good to see Terry keen and eager again. 'This country's the place to be. It's on its knees. You can see that, can't you?'

'Yeah.'

' 'Course you can. Callaghan can't last. It'll be our turn.'

'America is OK.'

'Yeah. Great.' He punched me on the arm. 'Come on.' I felt he wanted to touch me or something. Kiss me. He said, 'Except it's a fascist, imperialist, racist shithole.'

'Yeah?'

'It's – '

I said, 'Sometimes I feel disgusted by your ignorance. Your fucking stupid blindness to things. America. Where do you think the gay militancy has come from?' Not that this helped my case. I thought a moment. He was listening, not yet sneering. 'The women's movement. Black rebellion. What are you talking about, Terry, when you talk about America? It's crap! Idiocy! Christ!'

'Don't shout at me. What am I saying? I'm saying I'll miss you, that's all! And I'm saying it's pretty damn weird, you an' Pyke being such big close friends after what he's done to you. Right? Right?'

'What's he done to me?' I said.

'You know. You were there.'

'I know? What is it? Tell me.'

'I've heard,' he said. 'Everybody talks.'

He turned away. He didn't want to say any more. Now I'd never know what they were saying about me and Pyke and what he'd done to me.

'Well,' I said. 'I don't care.'

'You don't care about anything,' he said. 'You're not attached to anything, not even to the Party. You don't love. Stay here and fight.'

I walked around the room. Terry's sleeping-bag was on the floor; there was a knife beside the bed. It was time to go. I wanted to loaf around this part of London. I wanted to ring Changez and have him walking beside me on his Charlie Chaplin feet. Terry was pacing; I was looking out the window trying to control myself. People who were only ever half right about things drove me mad. I hated the flood of opinion, the certainty, the easy talk about Cuba and Russia and the economy, because beneath the hard structure of words was an abyss of ignorance and not-knowing; and, in a sense, of not wanting to know. Fruitbat-Jones's lover, Chogyam-Rainbow-Jones, had a rule: he'd only talk about things he had practical experience of, things he'd directly known. It seemed to be a good rule.

I opened my mouth to tell Terry again what a fool I thought he was, how rigid in his way of seeing he could be, when he said, 'You can come and live here now that Eleanor's chucked you out. There's some good working-class girls in this squat. You won't go short.'

'I bet,' I said.

I went to him and put my hand between his legs. I didn't think he'd allow himself to like it too much; I didn't think he'd let me take his cock out, but I reckoned you should try it on with everyone you fancied, just in case. You never knew, they might like it, and if not, so what? Attractive people were a provocation in themselves, I found, when I was in this mood.

'Don't touch me, Karim,' he said.

I kept on rubbing him, pushing into his crotch, digging my nails into his balls, until I glanced up at his face. However angry I was with him, however much I wanted to humiliate Terry, I suddenly saw such humanity in his eyes, and in the way he tried to smile – such innocence in the way he wanted to understand me, and such possibility of pain, along with the implicit assumption that he wouldn't be harmed – that I pulled away. I went to the other side of the room. I sat staring at the wall. I thought about torture and gratuitous physical pain. How could it be possible to do such things when there'd be certain looks that would cry out to you from the human depths, making you feel so much pity you could weep for a year?

I went to him and shook his hand. He had no idea what was going on. I said, 'Terry, I'll see you.'

'When?' he asked, concerned.

'When I come back from America.'

He came to the door with me. He said goodbye, and then he said he was sorry. To be honest, I wouldn't have minded moving in with him and living in Brixton, but the time for that had probably passed. America was waiting.

CHAPTER SEVENTEEN

After the opening night in New York we got out of the theatre and were taken in taxis to an apartment building on Central Park South, near the Plaza Hotel. We were on the nine-hundredth floor or something, and one wall was solid glass, and there was a view over the park and to the north of Manhattan. There were servants with silver trays, and a black man played 'As Time Goes By' on the piano. I recognized various actors, and was told that agents and journalists and publishers were there too. Carol went from person to person introducing herself. Pyke stood on one spot, just off-centre of the room, where, gladly and graciously, he received unsolicited praise, and no doubt hoped to meet hairdressers from Wisconsin. Being English provincials, and resentfully afraid of capitalist contamination, Tracey, Richard and I skulked in a corner and were nervous. Eleanor enjoyed herself talking to a young film producer with his hair in a pigtail. Looking at her now, after saying only a few words to her for three months, I realized how little I knew her, understood her, liked her. I'd wanted her, but not wanted her. What had I been thinking about all the time I'd been with her? I resolved to talk to her after a few drinks.

The man who ran the theatre, Dr Bob, was a former academic and critic, an enthusiast for the 'ethnic arts'. His room in the theatre was full of Peruvian baskets, carved paddles, African drums and paintings. I knew he'd sensed I was looking into the abyss because as we rehearsed for the opening he said, 'Don't worry, I'll fix you up with some decent music,' as if he knew this was what I required to feel at home.

Now he sat Tracey and I in two somewhat exposed seats at the front of the room and hushed everyone behind us. They thought there was going to be a speech or announcement. Suddenly three dark-skinned men ran into the room, banging some sort of wooden hook on hand-held drums. Then a black man, wearing bright-pink trousers and naked from the waist up, started to fling himself, his arms outstretched, around the room. Two black women joined him, and fluttered away with their hands. Another man in sparkly trousers flew into the room, and the four of them did a kind of mating dance barely a foot from Tracey and me. And Dr Bob squatted in a corner yelling, 'Yeah' and 'Right on' as the Haitians danced. It made me feel like a colonial watching the natives perform. At the end there was rapturous applause and Dr Bob made us shake hands with all of them.

I didn't see Eleanor again that evening until most of the guests had gone and Eleanor, Richard, Carol and I were sitting around Pyke in a bedroom. Pyke was frisky and laughing. He was in New York with a successful show and was surrounded by admirers. What more could he want? And he was playing one of his favourite games. I could smell the danger. But if I left the room I'd be among strangers. So I stayed and took it, though I didn't feel up to it.

'Now,' he said, 'all of you – if you could fuck any one person in this apartment, who would it be?' And everyone was laughing, and looking around at each other, and justifying their choices, and trying to be daring and point at one another and say, 'You, you!' One glance told Pyke how volatile I was that night, so he excluded me. I nodded and smiled at him and said to Eleanor, 'Can we go outside to talk for a while?' but Pyke said, 'Just a minute, wait a while, I've got to read something.'

'Come on,' I said to Eleanor, but she held my arm. I knew what was going to happen. Pyke was getting out his notebook now. And he started to read out the predictions he'd written down when we first started to rehearse, in that room by the river where we were honest for the sake of the group. God, I was drunk, and I couldn't see why everyone was being so attentive to Pyke: it was as if Pyke were reading out reviews, not of the play, but of our personalities, clothes, beliefs – of us. Anyway, he read out stuff about Tracey and Carol, but I lay on my back on the floor and didn't listen; it wasn't interesting, anyway. 'Now, Karim,' he said. 'You'll be riveted by this.'

'How do you know?'

'I know.'

He started to read the stuff about me. The faces around him were looking at me and laughing. Why did they hate me so much? What had I done to them? Why wasn't I harder? Why did I feel so much?

'Karim is obviously looking for someone to fuck. Either a boy or a

244

girl: he doesn't mind, and that's all right. But he'd prefer a girl, because she will mother him. Therefore he's appraising all the crumpet in the group. Tracey is too spiky for him, too needy; Carol too ambitious; and Louise not his physical type. It'll be Eleanor. He thinks she's sweet, but she's not blown away by him. Anyway, she's still fucked-up over Gene, and feels responsible for his death. I'll have a word with her, tell her to take care of Karim, maybe get her to feed him, give him a bit of confidence. My prediction is that Eleanor will fuck him, it'll basically be a mercy fuck, but he'll fall hard for her and she'll be too kind to tell him the truth about anything. It will end in tears.'

I went into the other room. I wished I was in London; I just wanted to be away from all these people. I rang Charlie, who was living in New York, but he wasn't there. I'd spoken to him several times on the phone but not seen him as yet. Then Eleanor had her arm round me and she was holding me. I kept saying, 'Let's go, let's go somewhere, and we can be together.' She was looking at me pityingly and saying, no, no, she had to tell the truth, she'd be spending the night with Pyke, she wanted to know him as deeply as she could. 'That won't take a whole night,' I said. I saw Pyke coming out of the bedroom surrounded by the others, and I went to destroy him. But I didn't get a clean punch in. There was a tangle; I threw myself about; arms and legs were everywhere. But whose were they? I was in a frenzy, kicking and scratching and screaming. I wanted to chuck a chair through the glass window, because I wanted to be on the street watching it come through the window in slow motion. Then I seemed to be in a kind of box. I was staring up at polished wood and I couldn't move. I was pinned down. Almost certainly I was dead, thank God. I heard an American voice say, 'These English are animals. Their whole culture has fallen through the floor.'

Well, the cabs in New York City had these bullet-proof partitions to stop you killing the driver, and they had slidy seats, and I was practically on the floor. Thank God Charlie was with me. He had his arms around my chest and kept me from the floor. He refused to let me stop at a topless bar. What I did see were the Haitians walking down the street. I wound down the window, ordered the driver to slow down and shouted at them; 'Hey, guys, where are you going?'

'Stop it, Karim,' Charlie said gently.

'Come on, guys!' I yelled. 'Let's go somewhere! Let's enjoy America!'

Charlie told the driver to get going. But at least he was good-humoured and pleased to see me, even if, when we got out of the cab, I did want to lie down on the pavement and go to sleep.

Charlie had been at the show that night, but after the play he went out to dinner with a record producer and came on late to the party. On finding me passed out under the piano and surrounded by angry actors, he took me home. Tracey later told me she'd been loosening my shirt when she looked up and saw Charlie moving towards her. He was so beautiful, she said, that she burst into tears.

I woke up with a blanket around me in a lovely, bright room, not large, but with sofas, numerous old armchairs, an open fireplace, and a kitchen through the open partition doors. On the walls were framed posters for art exhibitions. There were books: it was a classy place, not the usual rock-star's hang-out. But then, I couldn't consider Charlie a rock-star. It didn't seem of his essence, but a temporary, borrowed persona.

I vomited three or four times before going upstairs to Charlie with coffee, and jam on toast. He was alone in bed. When I woke him there wasn't his usual snarl. He sat up smiling and kissed me. He said a lot of things I didn't believe were coming from his mouth.

'Welcome to New York. I know you feel like shit, but we're going to have fun like you've never known it. What a great city this is! Just think, we've been in the wrong place all these years. Now just go over there and put on that Lightnin' Hopkins record. Let's start off as we intend to go on!'

Charlie and I spent the day together walking around the Village, and had a milkshake thick with Italian ice-cream. A girl recognized him and came over to leave a note on the table. 'Thank you for giving your genius to the world,' she wrote. Her phone-number was on the bottom. Charlie nodded at her across the café. I'd forgotten how intimidating it was walking around with him. People recognized him everywhere, yet his hair was covered by a black woolly hat and he wore blue cotton overalls and workmen's boots.

I'd had no idea he was so famous in America. You'd turn a corner, and there was his face tacked to some demolition-site wall or on an illuminated hoarding. Charlie had done a tour of arenas and stadiums with his new band. He showed me the videos, but refused to sit in the room while I watched them. I could see why. On stage he wore black leather, silver buckles, chains and chokers, and by the end of the performance he was bare-chested, thin and white like Jagger, flinging his spidery figure like a malevolent basketball player across stages as wide as aircraft hangars. He appealed to the people who had the most disposable income, gays and young people, especially girls, and his album, *Kill For DaDa*, was still in the charts, months after it had been released.

But the menace was gone. The ferocity was already a travesty, and the music, of little distinction in itself, had lost its drama and attack when transported from England with its unemployment, strikes and class antagonism. What impressed me was that Charlie knew this. 'The music's feeble, OK? I'm no Bowie, don't think I don't know that. But I've got ideas between my ears. I can do good work in the future, Karim. This country gives me such optimism. People here believe you can do stuff. They don't bring you down all the time, like in England.'

So now he was renting this three-floor apartment in a brownstone on East 10th Street while he wrote the songs for his next album and learned the saxophone. In the morning, while snooping around, I'd noticed an empty and separate apartment at the top of the house. As I stood there with my coat on, ready to walk to the theatre and sad to leave him – he seemed so generous and charmed to be with me – I said; 'Charlie, me and the whole cast, we're all living in this big apartment. And I can't bear to see Eleanor every day. It breaks my heart.'

Charlie didn't hesitate. 'I'd be 'appy to 'ave you 'ere. Move in tonight.'

'Great. Thanks, man.'

I walked down the street, laughing, amused that here in America Charlie had acquired this cockney accent when my first memory of him at school was that he'd cried after being mocked by the stinking gypsy kids for talking so posh. Certainly, I'd never heard anyone talk like that before. Now he was going in for cockney rhyming slang, too. 'I'm just off for a pony,' he'd say. Pony and trap – crap. Or he was going to wear his winter whistle. Whistle and flute – suit. He was selling Englishness, and getting a lot of money for it.

A few days later I moved in with him. During most of the day

Charlie was around the house, giving interviews to journalists from all over the world, being photographed, trying on clothes, and reading. Sometimes there'd be young Californian girls lying around the place listening to Nick Lowe, Ian Dury and especially Elvis Costello. I spoke to these girls only when spoken to, since I found their combination of beauty, experience, vacuity and cruelty harrowing.

But there were three or four smart serious New York women, publishers, film critics, professors at Columbia, Sufis who did whirling dances and so on, whom he listened to for hours before he slept with them, later getting up to make urgent notes on their conversation, which he would then repeat to other people in the next few days. 'They're educating me, man,' he said about these besotted women, with whom he discussed international politics, South American literature, dance, and the ability of alcohol to induce mystical states. In New York he wasn't ashamed of his ignorance: he wanted to learn; he wanted to stop lying and bluffing.

As I wandered about the flat and heard him learning about Le Corbusier, I could see that fame, success and wealth really agreed with him. He was less anxious, bitter and moody than I'd ever known him. Now that he was elevated, he no longer looked up and envied. He could set aside ambition and become human. He was going to act in a film and then a stage play. He met prominent people; he travelled to learn. Life was glorious.

'Let me tell you something, Karim,' he said at breakfast, which was when we talked, his present girlfriend being in bed. 'There was a day when I fell in love for the first time. I knew this was the big one. I was staying in a house in Santa Monica after doing some gigs in LA and San Francisco.' (What magical names these were to me.) 'The house had five terraces on the side of a steep, lush hill. I'd been for a swim in this pool, from which a flunkey had recently fished all leaves with a net. I was drying myself and talking on the phone to Eva in West Kensington. The wife of a famous actor whose house it was came out to me and handed me the keys to her motorcycle. A Harley. It was then I knew I loved money. Money and everything it could buy. I never wanted to be without money again because it could buy me a life like this every day.'

'Time and money are the best, Charlie. But if you're not careful they'll fertilize weirdness, indulgence, greed. Money can cut the cord between you and ordinary living. There you are, looking down on the world, thinking you understand it, that you're just like them, when you've got no idea, none at all. Because at the centre of people's lives are worries about money and how to deal with work.'

'I enjoy these conversations,' he said. 'They make me think. Thank God, I'm not indulgent myself.'

Charlie was fit. Every day at eleven a taxi took him to Central Park, where he ran for an hour; then he went to the gym for another hour. For days at a time he ate only peculiar things like pulses, bean-shoots and tofu, and I had to scoff hamburgers on the stoop in the snow because, as he said, 'I won't have the animal within these walls.' Every Thursday night his drug-dealer would call by. This was more of the civilization he'd espied in Santa Monica, Charlie figured. Especially the way this ex-NYU film student came by with his Pandora's Box and threw it open on top of Charlie's MOMA catalogue. Charlie would lick a finger and point to this amount of grass, that amount of coke, a few uppers, some downers and some smack for us to snort.

The play didn't last long in New York, a month only, because Eleanor had to start shooting a small part in the big film she'd landed. The play wasn't doing sufficient business for us to cast another actress in Eleanor's role; and anyway, Pyke had gone off to San Francisco to teach.

When the others went back to London I ripped up my ticket and stayed in New York. There was nothing for me to do in London, and my aimlessness would be eyeballed by my father, who would use it as evidence that I should have become a doctor; or, at least, that I should visit a doctor. In New York I could be a walking stagnancy without restraint.

I liked walking around the city, going to restaurants with Charlie, doing his shopping (I bought him cars and property), answering the phone and sitting around with British musicians who were passing through. We were two English boys in America, the land where the music came from, with Mick Jagger, John Lennon and Johnny Rotten living round the corner. This was the dream come true.

All the same, my depression and self-hatred, my desire to mutilate myself with broken bottles, and numbness and crying fits, my inability to get out of bed for days and days, the feeling of the world moving in to crush me, went on and on. But I knew I wouldn't go mad, even if that release, that letting-go, was a freedom I desired. I was waiting for myself to heal.

I began to wonder why I was so strong – what it was that held me together. I thought it was that I'd inherited from Dad a strong survival instinct. Dad had always felt superior to the British: this was the legacy of his Indian childhood – political anger turning into scorn and contempt. For him in India the British were ridiculous, stiff, unconfident, rule-bound. And he'd made me feel that we couldn't allow ourselves the shame of failure in front of these people. You couldn't let the ex-colonialists see you on your knees, for that was where they expected you to be. They were exhausted now; their Empire was gone; their day was done and it was our turn. I didn't want Dad to see me like this, because he wouldn't be able to understand why I'd made such a mess of things when the conditions had been good, the time so opportune, for advancement.

Charlie gave me money when I needed it, and he encouraged me to stay in New York. But after six months I told him it was time to go. I was afraid he found me a burden, a nuisance, a parasite, though he'd never complained. But now he was insistent and paternal. 'Karim, you stay here with me where you belong. There's a lotta bastards out there. You got everything you need, haven't you?'

'Sure I have.'

'What's your problem, then?'

'None,' I said. 'It's just that I – '

'That's fine. Let's go shopping for clothes, OK?'

He didn't want me to leave. It was eerie, our growing dependency on each other. He liked having me there as a witness, I suspected. With other people he was restrained, enigmatic, laconic; he had the magazine virtues and wore jeans well. But he liked to tell me everything in the old schoolboy way. With me, he could be dazzled by the people he met, the places he was invited, the gifts that were thrown at him. It was I, Karim, who saw him stepping into the stretch-limo; it was I who saw him sitting in the Russian Tea Room with movie-stars, famous writers and film producers. It was I who saw him going upstairs with women, in debate with intellectuals, and being photographed for Italian *Vogue*. And only I could appreciate how far he'd come from his original state in Beckenham. It was as if, without me there to celebrate it all, Charlie's progress had little meaning. In other words, I was a full-length mirror, but a mirror that could remember.

My original impression that Charlie had been released by success was wrong, too: there was much about Charlie I wasn't able to see, because I didn't want to. Charlie liked to quote Milton's 'O dark, dark, dark'; and Charlie was dark, miserable, angry. I soon learned that fame and success in Britain and America meant different things. In Britain it was considered vulgar to parade yourself, whereas in America fame was an absolute value, higher than money. The relatives of the famous were famous – yes, it was hereditary: the children of stars were little stars too. And fame gained you goods that mere money couldn't obtain. Fame was something that Charlie had desired from the moment he stuck the revered face of Brian Jones to his bedroom wall. But having obtained it, he soon found he couldn't shut it off when he grew tired of it. He'd sit with me in a restaurant saying nothing for an hour, and then shout, 'Why are people staring at me when I'm trying to eat my food! That woman with the powder puff on her head, she can fuck off!' The demands on him were constant. The Fish ensured that Charlie remained in the public eye by appearing on chat shows and at openings and galleries where he had to be funny and iconoclastic. One night I turned up late to a party and there he was, leaning at the bar looking gloomy and fed up, since the hostess demanded that he be photographed with her. Charlie wasn't beginning to come to terms with it at all: he hadn't the grace.

Two things happened that finally made me want to get back to England and out of Charlie's life. One day when we were coming back from the recording studio, a man came up to us in the street. 'I'm a journalist,' he said, with an English accent. He was about forty, with no breath, hair or cheeks to speak of. He stank of booze and looked desperate. 'You know me, Tony Bell. I worked for the *Mirror* in London. I have to have an interview. Let's make a time. I'm good, you know. I can even tell the truth.'

Charlie strode away. The journalist was wretched and shameless. He ran alongside us, in the road.

'I won't leave you alone,' he panted. 'It's people like me who put your name about in the first place. I even interviewed your bloody mother.'

He grasped Charlie's arm. That was the fatal move. Charlie chopped down on him, but the man held on. Charlie hit him with a playground punch on the side of the head, and the man went down, stunned, on to his knees, waving his arms like someone begging forgiveness. Charlie hadn't exhausted his anger. He kicked the man in the chest, and when he fell to one side and grabbed at Charlie's legs Charlie stamped on his hand. The man lived nearby. I had to see him at least once a week on the street, carrying his groceries with his good hand.

The other reason for my wanting to leave New York was sexual. Charlie liked to experiment. From the time we'd been at school, where we'd discuss which of the menstruating dinner ladies we wanted to perform cunnilingus on (and none of them was under sixty), we wanted to fuck women, as many as possible. And like people who'd been reared in a time of scarcity and rationing, neither of us could forget the longing we'd had for sex, or the difficulty we once had in obtaining it. So we grabbed arbitrarily at the women who offered themselves.

One morning, as we had bagels and granola and OJs on the rocks in a nearby café, and talked about our crummy school as if it were Eton, Charlie said there were sexual things he'd been thinking about, sexual bents he wanted to try. 'I'm going for the ultimate experience,' he said. 'Maybe you'd be interested in looking in too, eh?'

'If you like.'

'If you like? I'm offering you something, man, and you say if you like. You used to be up for anything.' He looked at me contemptuously. 'Your little brown buttocks would happily pump away for hours at any rancid hole, pushing aside toadstools and fungus and – '

'I'm still up for anything.'

'Yeah, but you're miserable.'

'I don't know what I'm doing,' I said.

'Listen.' He leaned towards me and tapped the table. 'It's only by pushing ourselves to the limits that we learn about ourselves. That's where I'm going, to the edge. Look at Kerouac and all those guys.'

'Yeah, look at them. So what, Charlie?'

'Anyway,' he said. 'I'm talking. Let me finish. We're going the whole way. Tonight.'

So that night at twelve a woman named Frankie came over. I went down to let her in while Charlie hastily put on the Velvet Underground's first record – it had taken us half an hour to decide on the evening's music. Frankie had short, cropped hair, a bony white face, and a bad tooth, and she was young, in her early twenties, with a soft rich voice and a sudden laugh. She wore a black shirt and black pants. When I asked her, 'What do you do?', I sounded like a drip-dry at one of Eva's Beckenham evenings so long ago. I discovered that Frankie was a dancer, a performer, a player of the electric cello. At one point she said, 'Bondage interests me. Pain as play. A deep human love of pain. There is desire for pain, yes?'

Apparently we would find out if there was desire for pain. I glanced at Charlie, trying to kindle some shared amusement at this, but he sat forward and nodded keenly at her. When he got up I got up too. Frankie took my arm. She was holding Charlie's hand, too. 'Maybe you two would like to get into each other, eh?'

I looked at Charlie, recalling the night in Beckenham I tried to kiss him and he turned his face away. How he wanted me – he let me touch him – but refused to acknowledge it, as if he could remove himself from the act while remaining there. Dad had seen some of this. It was the night, too, that I saw Dad screwing Eva on the lawn, an act which was my introduction to serious betrayal, lying, deceit and heart-following. Tonight Charlie's face was open, warm; there was no rejection in it, only enthusiasm. He waited for me to speak. I never thought he would look at me like this.

We went upstairs, where Charlie had prepared the room. It was dark, illuminated only by candles, one on each side of the bed, and three on the bookshelves. For some reason the music was Gregorian chanting. We'd discussed this for hours. He didn't want anything he could listen to when he was being tortured. Charlie removed his clothes. He was thinner than I'd ever seen him, muscly, taut. Frankie put her head back and he kissed her. I stood there, and then I cleared my throat. 'Are you both sure you want me here and everything?'

'Why not?' said Frankie, looking at me over her shoulder. 'What d'you mean?'

'Are you sure you want spectators at this thing?'

'It's only sex,' she said. 'He's not having an operation.'

'Oh yes, OK, but – '

'Sit down, Karim, for God's sake,' said Charlie. 'Stop farting about. You're not in Beckenham now.'

'I know that.'

'Well then, can't you stop standing there and looking so English?'

'What d'you mean, English?'

'So shocked, so self-righteous and moral, so loveless and incapable of dancing. They are narrow, the English. It is a Kingdom of Prejudice over there. Don't be like it!'

'Charlie's so intense,' Frankie said.

'I'll make myself at home, then,' I said. 'Don't mind me.'

'We won't,' said Charlie irritably.

I settled myself into an armchair under the curtained window, the darkest place in the room, where I hoped I'd be forgotten. Frankie stripped to her tattoos and they caressed each other in the orthodox way. She was skinny, Frankie, and it looked rather like going to bed with an umbrella. But I sipped my pina colada, and even as I sweated under the indignity of my situation I considered how rare it was to see another couple's copulation. How educational it could be! What knowledge of caresses, positions, attitudes, could be gleaned from practical example! I would recommend it to anyone.

Frankie's hold-all was beside the bed, and from it she produced four leather bands, which she secured to Charlie's wrists and ankles. Then she roped him to the broad, heavy bed, before pressing a dark handkerchief into his mouth. After more fumbling in the bag, out came what looked like a dead bat. It was a leather hood with a zipper in the front of it. Frankie pulled this over Charlie's head and, on her knees, tied it at the back, pursing her lips in concentration, as if she were sewing on a button. And now it wasn't Charlie: it was a body with a sack over its head, half of its humanity gone, ready for execution.

Frankie kissed and licked and sucked him like a lover as she sat on him. I could see him relaxing. I could also see her reaching for a candle and holding it over him, tilting it over his chest until the wax fell and hit him. He jumped and grunted at this, so suddenly that I laughed out loud. That would teach him not to stamp on people's hands. Then she tipped wax all over him – stomach, thighs, feet, prick. This was where, had it been me with hot wax sizzling on my scrotum, I would have gone through the roof. Charlie obviously had the same impulse: he struggled and rocked the bed, none of which stopped her passing the flame of the candle over his genitals. Charlie had said to me in the afternoon, 'We must make sure I'm properly secured. I don't want to escape. What is it Rimbaud said? "I am degrading myself as much as possible. It is a question of reaching the unknown by the derangement of all the senses." Those French poets have a lot to be responsible for. I'm going the whole way.'

And all the time, as he voyaged to the unknown, she moved over him with her lips whispering encouragement, 'Ummmm . . . that feels good. Hey, you like that, eh? Be positive, be positive. What about this? This is delicious! And what about this, this is really intense, Charlie, I know you're getting into it, eh?' she said as she virtually turned his prick into a hotdog. Christ, I thought, what would Eva say if she could see her son and myself right now?

These ponderings were interrupted by what I could see and Charlie couldn't. She extracted two wooden pegs from her bag, and as she bit one nipple she trapped the other with the peg, which I noticed had a large and pretty efficient-looking spring on it. She followed this with a peg on the other nipple. 'Relax, relax,' she was saying, but a little urgently I thought, as if afraid she'd gone too far. Charlie's back was arched, and he seemed to be squealing through his ears. But as she spoke he did relax slowly and submit to the pain, which was, after all, exactly what he had wanted. Frankie left him then, as he was, and went away for a few minutes to let him come to terms with desire and self-inflicted suffering. When she returned I was examining my own thoughts. And it was at this moment, as she blew out a candle, lubricated it and forced it up his arse, that I realized I didn't love Charlie any more. I didn't care either for or about him. He didn't interest me at all. I'd moved beyond him, discovering myself through what I rejected. He seemed merely foolish to me.

I got up. It surprised me to see that Charlie was not only still alive but still hard. I ascertained this by moving around to the side of the bed for a seat in the front stalls, where I squatted to watch her sit on him and fuck him, indicating as she did so that I should remove the pegs from his dugs as he came. I was glad to be of assistance.

What an excellent evening it was, marred only by Frankie losing one of her contact lenses. 'Jesus fucking Christ,' she said, 'it's my only pair.' So Charlie, Frankie and I had to hunt around on the floor on our hands and knees for half an hour. 'We've got to rip up the floorboards,' said Frankie at last. 'Is there a wrench in the place?'

'You could use my prick,' said Charlie.

He gave her money and got rid of her.

After this I decided to fly back to London. My agent had rung and said I was up for an important audition. She'd said it was the most important audition of my life, which was obviously a reason for not attending. But it was also the only audition my agent had sent me up for, so I thought I should reward her with an appearance.

I knew Charlie wouldn't want me to leave New York, and it took me a couple of days to gather the courage to broach the subject. When I told him, he laughed, as if I had an ulterior motive and really wanted money or something. Immediately he asked me to work full-time for him. 'I've been meaning to ask you for a while,' he said. 'We'll mix business with pleasure. I'll talk to the Fish about your salary. It'll be fat. You'll be a little brown fat-cat. OK, little one?'

'I don't think so, big one. I'm going to London.'

'What are you talking about? You're going to London, you say. But I'm going on a world tour. LA, Sydney, Toronto. I want you to be there with me.'

'I want to look for work in London.'

He became angry. 'It's stupid to leave just when things are starting to happen here. You're a good friend to me. A good assistant. You get things done.'

'Please give me the money to go. I'm asking you to help me out. It's what I want.'

'What you want, eh?'

He walked up and down the room, and talked like a professor conducting a seminar with students he'd never met before.

'England's decrepit. No one believes in anything. Here, it's money and success. But people are motivated. They do things. England's a nice place if you're rich, but otherwise it's a fucking swamp of prejudice, class confusion, the whole thing. Nothing works over there. And no one works – '

'Charlie – '

'That's why I'm definitely not letting you go. If you can make it here, why go anywhere else? What's the point? You can get anything you want in America. And what do you want? Say what you want!'

'Charlie, I'm asking you – '

'I can hear you asking me, man! I can hear you pleading! But I must save you.'

That was that. He sat down and said no more. The next day, when in retaliation I said nothing, Charlie suddenly blurted out, 'OK, OK, if it means so much to you, I'll buy you a return ticket to London, but you've got to promise to come back.'

I promised. He shook his head at me. 'You won't like it, I'm telling you now.'

CHAPTER EIGHTEEN

So on Charlie's money, with a gram of coke as a leaving present and his warning on my mind, I flew back to London. I was glad to be doing it: I missed my parents and Eva. Though I spoke to them on the phone, I wanted to see their faces again. I wanted to argue with Dad. Eva had hinted that significant events were going to take place. 'What are they?' I asked her all the time. 'I can't tell you unless you're here,' she said, teasingly. I had no idea what she was talking about.

On the flight to London I had a painful toothache, and on my first day in England I arranged to go to the dentist. I walked around Chelsea, happy to be back in London, relieved to rest my eyes on something old again. It was beautiful around Cheyne Walk, those little houses smothered in flowers with blue plaques on the front wall. It was terrific as long as you didn't have to hear the voices of the people who lived there.

As the dentist's nurse led me to the dentist's chair and I nodded at him in greeting, he said, in a South African accent, 'Does he speak English?'

'A few words,' I said.

I walked around Central London and saw that the town was being ripped apart; the rotten was being replaced by the new, and the new was ugly. The gift of creating beauty had been lost somewhere. The ugliness was in the people, too. Londoners seemed to hate each other.

I met Terry for a drink while he was rehearsing more episodes of his Sergeant Monty series. He barely had time to see me, what with picketing and demonstrating and supporting various strikes. When we did talk it was about the state of the country.

'You may have noticed, Karim, that England's had it. It's coming apart. Resistance has brought it to a standstill. The Government were defeated in the vote last night. There'll be an election. The chickens are coming home to die. It's either us or the rise of the Right.'

Terry had predicted the last forty crises out of twenty, but the bitter, fractured country was in turmoil: there were strikes, marches, wage-claims. 'We've got to seize control,' he said. 'The people want strength and a new direction.' He thought there was going to be a revolution; he cared about nothing else.

The next day I talked to the producers and casting people of the soap opera I was being considered for. I had to see them in an office they'd rented for the week in Soho. But I didn't want to talk to them, even if I'd flown from America to do so. Pyke had taken care with his art or craft – nothing shoddy got on stage; his whole life was tied up with the quality of what he did. But five minutes told me that these were trashy, jumped-up people in fluffy sweaters. They spoke as if they were working on something by Sophocles. Then they asked me to run around the office in an improvisation set in a fish and chip shop – an argument over a piece of cod which led to boiling fat being tipped over someone's arm – with a couple of hack actors who'd already been cast. They were boring people; I'd be with them for months if I got the job.

At last I got away. I went back to the Fish's flat, which I was borrowing, an impersonal but comfortable place a bit like an hotel. I was sitting there, wondering whether I should pack up my things and move permanently to New York to work for Charlie, when the phone rang. My agent said, 'Good news. They've rung to say you've got the part.'

'That's good,' I said.

'It's the best,' she replied.

But it took two days for the meaning of the offer to sink in. What was it exactly? I was being given a part in a new soap opera which would tangle with the latest contemporary issues: they meant abortions and racist attacks, the stuff that people lived through but that never got on TV. If I accepted the offer I'd play the rebellious student son of an Indian shopkeeper. Millions watched those things. I would have a lot of money. I would be recognized all over the country. My life would change overnight.

When I was certain I'd got the job, and had accepted the part, I decided to visit Dad and Eva with the news. I thought for an hour about what to wear, and inspected myself from several angles in four mirrors before, during and after dressing casually but not roughly. I didn't want to look like a bank teller, but neither did I want to expose the remains of my unhappiness and depression. I wore a black cashmere sweater, grey cords – this was lush, thick corduroy, which hung properly and didn't crease – and black American loafers.

Outside Dad and Eva's house a couple were getting out of a taxi. A young man with spiky hair was carrying several black cases of photographic equipment and a large lamp. He was accompanied by a smart, middle-aged woman in an expensive beige mac. To the woman's irritation the photographer gesticulated at me as I walked up the steps and rang Eva's bell. The man called out a question. 'Are you Charlie Hero's manager?'

'His brother,' I replied.

Eva came to the door. She was confused for a moment by the three of us arriving at once. And she didn't recognize me at first: I must have changed, but I didn't know how. I felt older, I knew that. Eva told me to wait in the hall a minute. So there I stood, leafing through the mail and thinking it had been a mistake to leave America. I'd turn down the soap opera job and go back. When she'd shaken hands with the other two visitors and sat them in the flat, she came to me, arms outstretched, and kissed and hugged me.

'It's good to see you again, Eva. You've no idea how much I missed you,' I said.

'Why are you talking like this?' she said. 'Have you forgotten how to talk to your own family?'

'I'm feeling a little strange, Eva.'

'All right, love, I understand.'

'I know you do. That's why I came back.'

'Your dad will be pleased to see you,' she said. 'He misses you more than any of us miss each other. Do you see? It breaks his heart for you to be away. I tell him Charlie is taking care of you.'

'Does that reassure him?'

'No. Is Charlie a heroin addict?'

'How can you ask these questions, Eva?'

'Tell me on the nose.'

'No,' I said. 'Eva, what's going on? Who are these ridiculous people?'

She lowered her voice. 'Not now. I'm being interviewed about the flat for *Furnishings* magazine. I want to sell this place and move on.

They're taking photographs and talking to me. Why did you have to come today of all days?'

'Which day would you have preferred?'

'Stop it,' she warned me. 'You're our prodigal son. Don't spoil it.'

She led me into the room where I used to sleep on the floor. The photographer was unpacking his cases. I was shocked by Dad's appearance as he got up to embrace me. 'Hallo, boy,' he said. He wore a thick white collar around his neck, which pressed his chins up around his jaw. 'My neck is paining me no bloody end,' he explained, grimacing. 'This sanitary towel takes the weight off my brains. They push down on my spine.'

I thought of how, when I was a kid, Dad always out-ran me as we charged across the park towards the swimming pool. When we wrestled on the floor he always pinned me down, sitting on my chest and making me say I'd obey him always. Now he couldn't move without flinching. I'd become the powerful one; I couldn't fight him – and I wanted to fight him – without destroying him in one blow. It was a saddening disappointment.

In contrast, Eva looked fresh and businesslike, in a short skirt, black stockings and flat shoes. Her hair was expensively cut and dyed, her scent was lovely. There was nothing suburban about her; she'd risen above herself to become a glorious middle-aged woman, clever and graceful. Yes, I'd always loved her, and not always as a stepmother, either. I'd been passionate about her, and still was.

She took the journalist on a tour of the flat, and, holding my hand, led me around with them. 'You come and look at what we've done,' she said to me. 'Try and admire it, Mr Cynical.'

I did admire it. The place was larger than before. Various storerooms and much of the broad hallway had been incorporated, and the rooms opened out. She and Ted had worked hard.

'As you can see, it's very feminine in the English manner,' she said to the journalist as we looked over the cream carpets, gardenia paintwork, wooden shutters, English country-house armchairs and cane tables. There were baskets of dried flowers in the kitchen and coconut matting on the floor. 'It's soft but not cluttered,' she went on. 'Not that this is my favourite look.'

'I see,' said the journalist.

'Personally, I'd like something more Japanese.'

'Japanese, eh?'

'But I want to be able to work in a number of styles.'

'Like a good hairdresser,' said the journalist. Eva couldn't help herself: she gave the woman a fierce look before recomposing her face. I laughed aloud.

The photographer rearranged the furniture and photographed objects only in the places where they had not been initially positioned. He photographed Eva only in poses which she found uncomfortable and in which she looked unnatural. She pushed her fingers back through her hair a hundred times, and pouted and opened her eyes wide as if her lids had been pinned back. And all the while she talked to the journalist about the transformation of the flat from its original dereliction into this example of the creative use of space. She made it sound like the construction of Notre Dame. She didn't say she was intending to put the flat on the market as soon as the article came out, using the piece as a lever to get a higher price. When the journalist asked her, 'And what is your philosophy of life?' Eva behaved as if this enquiry were precisely the sort of thing she expected to be asked in the course of discussing interior decoration.

'My philosophy of life.'

Eva glanced at Dad. Normally such a question would be an excuse for him to speak for an hour on Taoism and its relation to Zen. But he said nothing. He just turned his face away. Eva went and sat beside him on the arm of the sofa, and, with a gesture both affectionate and impersonal, she stroked his cheek. The caress was tender. She looked at him with affection. She always wanted to please him. She still loves him, I thought. And I was glad he was being cared for. But something occurred to me: did he love her? I wasn't sure. I would observe them.

Eva was confident and proud and calm. She had plenty to say; she'd thought things over for many years; at last ideas were beginning to cohere in her mind. She had a world-view, though 'paradigm' would be a word she'd favour.

'Before I met this man,' she said. 'I had no courage and little faith. I'd had cancer. One breast was removed. I rarely talk about it.' The journalist nodded, respecting this confidence. 'But I wanted to live. And now I have contracts in that drawer for several jobs. I am beginning to feel I can do anything – with the aid of techniques like meditation, self-awareness and yoga. Perhaps a little chanting to slow the mind down. You see, I have come to believe in self-help, individual initiative, the love of what you do, and the full development of all individuals. I am constantly disappointed by how little we expect of ourselves and of the world.'

She looked hard at the photographer. He shifted in his seat; his mouth opened and closed twice. He almost spoke. Was she addressing him? Did he expect too little of himself? But she was off again.

'We have to empower ourselves. Look at those people who live on sordid housing estates. They expect others – the Government – to do everything for them. They are only half human, because only half active. We have to find a way to enable them to grow. Individual human flourishing isn't something that either socialism or conservatism caters for.'

The journalist nodded at Eva. Eva smiled at her. But Eva hadn't finished; more thoughts were occurring to her. She hadn't talked like this before, not with this clarity. The tape was running. The photographer leaned forward and whispered in the journalist's ear. 'Don't forget to ask about Hero,' I heard him say.

'No comment about that,' Eva said. She wanted to go on. The fatuity of the question didn't irritate her: she just wanted to continue developing her theme. Her thoughts seemed to surprise her. 'I think I – ' she began.

As Eva opened her mouth, the journalist lifted herself up and twisted her body around to Dad, cutting Eva out. 'You have been complimented, sir. Any comment? Does this philosophy mean much to you?'

I liked seeing Eva dominate. After all, Dad was often pompous, a little household tyrant, and he'd humiliated me so frequently as a kid that I felt it did him good to be in this position. However, it didn't yield me the pleasure it could have. Dad was not chirpy today; he wasn't even showing off. He spoke slowly, looking straight ahead at the journalist.

'I have lived in the West for most of my life, and I will die here, yet I remain to all intents and purposes an Indian man. I will never be anything but an Indian. When I was young we saw the Englishman as a superior being.'

'Really?' said the journalist, with a little pleasure.

'Oh, yes,' Dad said. 'And we laughed in his white face for it. But we could see that his was a great achievement. And this society you have created in the West is the richest there has been in the history of the world. There is money, yes, there are washing-up bowls. There is domination of nature and the Third World. There is domination all round. And the science is most advanced. You have the bombs you need to make yourself feel safe. Yet there is something missing.'

'Yes?' enquired the journalist, with less pleasure than before. 'Please tell us what we are missing.'

'You see, miss, there has been no deepening in culture, no accumulation of wisdom, no increase in the way of the spirit. There is a body and mind, you see. Definite. We know that. But there is a soul, too.'

The photographer snorted. The journalist hushed him, but he said, 'Whatever you mean by that.'

'Whatever I mean by that,' said Dad, his eyes sparkling with mischief.

The journalist looked at the photographer. She didn't reproach him; she just wanted to get out. None of this would go into the article, and they were wasting their time.

'What's the point of even discussing the soul?' the photographer said.

Dad continued. 'This failure, this great hole in your way of life, defeats me. But ultimately, it will defeat you.'

After this, he said no more. Eva and I looked at him and waited, but he'd done. The journalist switched the cassette-player off and put the tapes in her bag. She said, 'Eva, that marvellous chair, tell me – where did you get it?'

'Has Charlie sat on it?' said the photographer. He was now confused, and angry with Dad.

The pair of them got up to leave. 'I'm afraid it's time,' said the journalist, and headed rapidly for the door. Before she got there it was thrown open, and Uncle Ted, all out of breath and wide-eyed in anticipation, charged into the room. 'Where are you going?' he said to the journalist, who looked blankly at this hairless madman in a demob suit with a pack of beers in his hand.

'To Hampstead.'

'Hampstead?' said Ted. He jabbed at his underwater watch. 'I'm not late, maybe a little. My wife fell down the stairs and hurt herself.'

'Is she all right?' Eva said with concern.

'She's in a right bad state, she really is.' Ted sat down, looked around at all of us, nodding at me, and addressed the journalist. His distress possessed him; he wasn't ashamed of it. He said, 'I pity my wife, Jean.'

'Ted – ' Eva tried to interrupt him.

'She deserves all our pity,' he said.

'Really?' said the journalist, dismissively.

'Yes, yes! How do we become that way? How does it happen? One day we're children, our faces are bright and open. We want to know how machines work. We are in love with polar bears. The next day we're throwing ourselves down the stairs, drunk and weeping. Our lives are over. We hate life and we hate death.' He turned to the photographer. 'Eva said you'd want to photograph us together. I'm her partner. We do everything together. Don't you want to ask me any questions about our working methods? They're quite unique. They could be an example to others.'

'Sadly, we must be off,' said the tight-arsed scribbler.

'Never mind,' said Eva, touching Ted lightly on the arm.

'You're a bloody fool, Ted,' said Dad, laughing at him.

'No, I'm not,' Ted said firmly. He knew he was not a fool; no one could convince him he was.

Uncle Ted was glad to see me, and I him. We had plenty to say. His depression had cleared; he was like he was before, when I was a kid, salty and enthusiastic. But the violence was gone, the way he used to look at everyone the first time he met them, as if they meant to harm him and he'd have to harm them first.

'My work, I love it, son,' he said. 'I could have talked about that to the newspapers. I was going half mad, you remember? Eva saved me.'

'Dad saved you.'

'I want to save other people from leading untrue lives. D'you live an untrue life, Creamy?'

'Yes,' I said.

'Whatever you do, don't bloody lie to yourself. Don't – '

Eva came back in and said to him, 'We must go.'

Ted gestured at Dad. 'I need to talk, Haroon. I need you to listen to me! Yes?'

'No,' said Eva. 'We've got to work. Come on.'

So Ted and Eva went off to discuss a job with a client in Chelsea. 'Have a pint with me later this week,' Ted said.

When they'd gone Dad asked me to cook him cheese on toast. 'But make it not too floppy,' he said.

'Haven't you eaten, then?'

That's all it took to get him started. He said, 'Eva doesn't look after me now. She's too busy. I'll never get used to this new woman business. Sometimes I hate her. I know I shouldn't say it. I can't bear her near me but hate it when she's not here. I've never felt like this before. What's happening to me?'

'Don't ask me, Dad.'

I didn't want to leave him but I'd agreed to visit Mum. 'I have to go,' I said.

'Listen to just one thing more,' he said.

'What is it?'

'I'm leaving my job. I've given my notice. The years I've wasted in that job.' He threw up his hands. 'Now I'm going to teach and think and listen. I want to discuss how we live our lives, what our values are, what kind of people we've become and what we can be if we want. I aim to encourage people to think, to contemplate, to just let go their obsessions. In which school is this valuable meditation taught? I want to help others contemplate the deeper wisdom of themselves which is often concealed in the rush of everyday life. I want to live intensely my own life! Good, eh?'

'It's the best thing I've heard you say,' I said gently.

'Don't you think so?' My father's enthusiasm was high. 'What reveries I've been having recently. Moments when the universe of opposites is reconciled. What intuitions of a deeper life! Don't you think there should be a place for free spirits like me, wise old fools like the sophists and Zen teachers, wandering drunkenly around discussing philosophy, psychology and how to live? We foreclose on reality prematurely, Karim. Our minds are richer and wider than we ever imagine! I will point these obvious things out to young people who have lost themselves.'

'Excellent.'

'Karim, this is the meaning of my life.'

I put my jacket on and left him. He watched me walk down the street; I was sure he was still talking to me as I went. I got the bus down through South London. I was in a nervous state emotionally.

At the house I found Allie getting dressed to Cole Porter songs. 'Mum's not here yet,' he said. She hadn't come home from the health centre where she was now working as a receptionist for three doctors.

I could see he'd become pretty zooty, little Allie. His clothes were Italian and immaculate, daring and colourful without being vulgar, and all expensive and just right: the zips fitted, the seams were straight, and the socks were perfect – you can always tell a quality dresser by the socks. He didn't even look out of place sitting there on Mum's fake leather sofa, the flowery pouf in front of him, his shoes resting on Mum's Oxfam rug like jewels on toilet paper. Some people know how to do things, and I was glad to see that my brother was one of them. Allie had money, too; he was working for a clothes designer. He and I talked like grown-ups; we had to. But we were shy and slightly embarrassed all the same. Allie's ironic attitude changed when I told him about the soap opera job. I didn't make much of it: I talked like I was doing them a favour by being in it. Allie jumped up and clapped his hands. 'That's great! What brilliant news. Well done, Karim!' I couldn't understand it: Allie went on and on about it as if it meant something.

'It's not like you to be so keen,' I said suspiciously when he came back from ringing his friends and telling them about my job. 'What's gone wrong with your head, Allie? Are you putting me on?'

'No, no, honest. That last play you did, with Pyke directing, it was good, even entertaining once or twice.'

'Yeah?'

He paused, perhaps fearing that his praise had been too warm. 'It was good – but hippie.'

'Hippie? What was hippie about it?'

'It was idealistic. The politics got on my nerves. We all hate whingeing lefties, don't we?'

'Do we? What for?'

'Oh yeah. Their clothes look like rags. And I hate people who go on all the time about being black, and how persecuted they were at school, and how someone spat at them once. You know: self-pity.'

'Shouldn't they – I mean, we – talk about it, Allie?'

'Talk about it? God, no.' Clearly he was on to a subject he liked. 'They should shut up and get on with their lives. At least the blacks have a history of slavery. The Indians were kicked out of Uganda.

There was reason for bitterness. But no one put people like you and me in camps, and no one will. We can't be lumped in with them, thank God. We should be just as grateful we haven't got white skin either. I don't like the look of white skin, it – '

'Allie, I visited a dentist the other day who – '

'Creamy, let's put your teeth aside for a minute and – '

'Allie – '

'Let me say that we come from privilege. We can't pretend we're some kind of shitted-on oppressed people. Let's just make the best of ourselves.' He looked at me like a Sunday school teacher telling you not to let yourself down. I liked him now; I wanted to know him; but the things he was saying were strange. 'So congratulations, big brother. A soap opera, that's something to crow about. Television's the only medium I like.'

I screwed up my face.

'Karim, I hate the theatre even more than I hate opera. It's so – ' He searched for the wrong word. 'So make-believe. But listen, Creamy, there's something you should know about Mum.'

I looked at him as if he were going to say she had cancer or something. 'Since their divorce came through she's been seeing a man. Jimmy. It's been going on for four months or so. It's a big shock, OK, I know that. But we just have to accept it and not take the piss, if that's possible.'

'Allie – '

He sat there all cool. 'Don't ask me a lot of bloody questions, Karim. I can't tell you about him because I haven't met him and I'm not allowed to.'

'Why not?'

'And nor are you, OK? He's seen pictures of us aged ten or something, but no older. Jimmy doesn't know Mum's exact age. She thinks he'd be shocked and put off to discover she had sons as old as us. So we have to keep a pretty absent profile.'

'Christ, Allie.'

'There you are.'

I sighed. 'Good for her. She deserves it.'

'Jimmy's OK. He's respectable, he's employed, he doesn't put his prick around.' Then this admiring look came over him again, and he shook his head and whistled. 'A soap opera, eh? That's class.'

'You know,' I said. 'After Mum and Dad broke up, everything went crazy. I didn't know where I was.'

He was looking at me. I felt guilty that I'd never discussed his feelings about this. 'Don't talk about it now,' he said. 'I can't take it either. I know too well what you mean.'

He smiled reassuringly.

'All right,' I said.

Then he leaned towards me and said venomously, 'I don't see Dad. When I miss him I speak to him on the phone. I don't have much time for people who run away from their wife and kids. I don't blame you for going with him – you were young. But Dad was selfish. And what about him giving up his job? Don't you think he's insane? He'll have no money. Eva will have to support him. Therefore Eva will have to support Mum. Isn't that grotesque? And Mum hates her. We'll all be parasites on her!'

'Allie – '

'What will he be doing, St Francis of Assisi, discussing life, death and marriage – on which he's a world expert – with idiots who'll think he's a pompous old bore? God, Karim, what happens to people when they start to get old?'

'Don't you understand anything?'

'Understand what?'

'Oh, Allie, how stupid can you be? Don't you see the way things happen?'

He looked hurt and deflated then: it wasn't difficult to do that to him, he was so unsure of himself. I couldn't think how to apologize and return to our former understanding.

He murmured, 'But I've not looked at it from another point of view.'

Just then I heard a key in the door. A new sound, yet it was a noise I'd heard every day for years when Mum came home from the shop to get our tea. It was her now. I went out and hugged her. She was pleased to see me, but not that pleased, once she'd ascertained that I hadn't been killed, and had a job. She was in a hurry. 'A friend's coming round later,' she said without a blush, as Allie and I winked at each other. While she showered and dressed, we dusted and vacuumed the front room. 'Better do the stairs, too,' Allie said.

Mum spent ages preparing herself, and Allie told her what jewellery to wear, and the right shoes and everything. This was a woman who never used to have more than one bath a week. When we first moved into the house, in the late-1950s, there wasn't even a bathroom. Dad used to sit with his knees up in a tin tub in the front room, and Allie and I ran to and fro with jugs of water heated on the stove.

Now Allie and I hung around the house as long as possible to torment Mum with the idea that Jimmy might turn up and see that we were both about forty years old. She was saying, 'Haven't you two lads got anywhere to go?' when the front door bell rang. Poor Mum froze. I never thought she'd go as far as this, but she said, 'You two go out the back door.' She almost shoved us out into the garden and locked the door behind us. Allie and I hung around giggling and throwing a tennis ball at each other. Then we went round to the front of the house and peeped through the black outlined squares of the 'Georgian' windows she'd had installed, making the front of the house resemble a crossword puzzle.

And there was Jimmy, our father's replacement, sitting on the sofa with Mum. He was a pale man and an Englishman. This was a surprise: somehow I'd expected an Indian to be sitting with her, and when there wasn't I felt disappointed in her, as if she'd let us down. She must have had enough of Indians. Jimmy was in his late thirties, earnest, and dressed plainly in a grey suit. He was lower middle class like us, but handsome and clever-looking: the sort who'd know the names of all the actors in Vincent Minnelli films, and would go on television quizzes to prove it. Mum was opening a present he'd brought when she looked up and saw her two sons peering through the net curtains at her. She blushed and panicked, but in seconds she collected her dignity and ignored us. We slunk off.

I didn't want to go home right away, so Allie took me to a new club in Covent Garden designed by a friend of his. How London had moved on in ten months. No hippies or punks: instead, everyone was smartly dressed, and the men had short hair, white shirts and baggy trousers held up by braces. It was like being in a room full of George Orwell lookalikes, except that Orwell would have eschewed earrings. Allie told me they were fashion designers, photographers, graphic artists, shop designers and so on, young and talented. Allie's girlfriend was a model, a thin black girl who said nothing except that being in a soap opera could only lead to better things. I looked around for someone to pick up, but was so lonely I knew they'd smell it on me. I wasn't indifferent enough for seduction.

I said goodbye to Allie and went back to the Fish's. I sat there in his cavernous flat for a while; I walked around; I listened to a Captain Beefheart track, 'Dropout Boogie', until it drove me mad; I sat down again; and then I went out.

I drifted around the late streets for an hour, until I got lost and hailed a cab. I told the driver to take me to South London, but first, hurrying now, I got him to drive me back to the flat. He waited while I went in and searched the Fish's place for a gift for Changez and Jamila. I would make up with them. I did love them; I would show them how much by giving them a huge tablecloth belonging to the Fish. On the way I stopped off to get an Indian take-away to extra-appease them, in case they were still cross with me about anything. We drove past Princess Jeeta's shop, which at night was grilled, barred and shuttered. I thought of her lying upstairs asleep. Thank God I have an interesting life, I said to myself.

At the commune I rang the bell, and after five minutes Changez came to the door. Behind him the place was silent, and there was no sign of naked political discussion. Changez held a baby in his arms.

'It's one-thirty in the morning, *yaar*,' was what he said in greeting, after all this time. He turned back into the house, and I followed him, feeling like a dog about to be kicked. In the shabby living room, with its filing cabinets and old sofa, I saw to my relief that Changez was unchanged, and I wouldn't have to take any shit from him. He hadn't become bourgeois and self-respecting. There was jam on his nose, he wore the bulging boiler suit with books poking from numerous pockets, and, I suspected, looking at him closely, he was developing full female breasts. 'Here's a present,' I said, offering the tablecloth. 'All the way from America.'

'Shhh . . . ' he replied, indicating the baby buried in blankets. 'This is the daughter of the house, Leila Kollontai, and she's asleep at last. Our baby. Top naughty.' He sniffed the air. 'Is take-away in the offing?'

'Absolutely.'

'Dal and all? Kebabs?'

'Yeah.'

'From the top curry house on the corner?'

'Exactly.'

'But they become cold dramatically. Open, open!'

'Wait.'

I flapped the tablecloth and started to remove various papers, dirty plates and a head of Lenin from the table. But Changez was eager to get at the food, and insisted we fling the Fish's tablecloth on top of everything else. 'Hungry, eh?' I said, as he sat down and plucked the slithery leaking cartons from the bag.

'I'm on bloody dole, Karim. Full-time I am eating potatoes. If I'm not dodgy they'll find me a job. How can I work and look after Leila Kollontai?'

'Where is everyone else?'

'Mr Simon the father is away in America. He's been long gone, lecturing on the history of the future. He's a big man, *yaar*, though you didn't appreciate.'

'And Jamila?' I said hesitantly. 'I've missed her.'

'She's here, intact and all, upstairs. But she won't be happy to talk to you, no, no, no, no. She'll be happy to barbecue your balls and eat them with peas. Are you remaining long?'

'Bubble, you fat fucker, what are you talking about? It's me, Creamy Jeans, your only friend, and I've come all the way to the swamp of South London to see you.'

He shook his head, handed me Leila Kollontai, who had a plump face and olive skin, and ripped the lids from the cartons. He started to press lumps of spinach into his mouth with his fingers, after sprinkling red chilli powder over it. Changez didn't like any food he could taste.

I said, airily, 'I've been in America, putting on political theatre.' I went into what I'd been doing, and boasted about the parties I'd been to, the people I'd met and the magazines I'd been interviewed for. He ignored me and filled his bulging face. As I went on, he said suddenly, 'You're in bloody shit, Karim. And what are you going to do about it? Jammie won't forgive you for not putting your face in it at the demonstration. That's the thing you should be worried about, *yaar*.'

I was stung. We fell silent. Changez seemed uninterested in anything I had to say. I was forced to ask him about himself. 'You must be pleased, eh, now Simon's away and you've got Jamila to yourself full-time. Any progress?'

'We are all progressing. There is another woman coming in close here.'

'Where?'

'No, no. Jamila's friend, you fool.'

'Jamila's got a woman friend? Am I hearing you right?' I said.

'Loud and clear. Jammie loves two people, that's all. It's simple to grasp. She loves Simon, but he's not here. She loves Joanna, and Joanna is here. She has told me.'

I stared at him in wonderment. How could he have had any idea, when he kicked off from Bombay, of the convoluted involvements ahead of him? 'How d'you feel about this?'

'Eh?' He was uncomfortable. It was as if he wanted no more said; the subject was closed. This was how he squared things in his mind, and it was good enough for him. 'Me? Precisely what questions are you asking?' And he could have added, 'If you insist on asking such questions.'

I said, 'I am asking how you, Changez, you with your background of prejudice against practically the whole world, are coping with being married to a lesbian.'

The question shook him more than I had the sense to see it would. He fought for words. At last he said, from beneath his eyebrows, 'I'm not, am I?'

Now I was confused. 'I don't bloody know,' I said. 'I thought you said they loved each other.'

'Yes, love! I am all for love,' he declared. 'All in this house are trying to love each other!'

'Good.'

'Aren't you all for love?' he asked, as if wishing firmly to establish this common ground.

'Yes.'

'So, then?' he said. 'Whatever Jamila does is all right by me. I am not a tyrant fascist, as you know. I have no prejudice except against Pakistanis, which is normal. So what is your point, Karim? What are you labouring to – '

Just then the door opened and Jamila came in. She looked thinner and older, her cheeks were slightly hollow and her eyes more lined, but there was something quicker, lighter and less serious in her now; she seemed to laugh more easily. She sang a reggae song and danced a few steps towards Leila and back. Jamila was accompanied

273

by a woman who looked nineteen but I guessed was older, in her late twenties. She had a fresh, open face, with good skin. Her short hair was streaked with blue, and she wore a red and black workman's shirt and jeans. As Jamila pirouetted the woman laughed and clapped her hands. She was introduced to me as Joanna, and she smiled at me and then stared, making me wonder what I'd done.

'Hallo, Karim,' Jamila said, and moved away as I rose to hold her. She took Leila Kollontai and asked if the baby had been all right. She kissed and rocked her. As Jammie and Changez talked I became aware of a new tone between them. I listened carefully. What was it? It was gentle respect; they were speaking to each other without condescension or suspicion, as equals. How things had changed!

Meanwhile, Joanna was saying to me, 'Haven't I seen you before?'

'I don't think we've met.'

'No, you're right. But I'm sure we've seen each other somewhere.' Puzzled, she continued to look at me.

'He's a big famous actor,' Jamila put in. 'Aren't you, dear?'

Joanna punched the air. 'That's it. I saw the play you were in. I loved it, too. You were great in it. Really funny.' She turned to Changez. 'You liked it too, didn't you? I remember you persuaded me to go and see it. You said it was accurate.'

'No, I don't think I liked it as much as I said,' Changez murmured. 'What I remember of it has left little permanent trace in my memory. It was white people's thing, wasn't it, Jammie?' And Changez looked at Jamila as if for approval, but she was breast-feeding the kid.

Fortunately, Joanna wasn't put off by that fat bastard, Changez. 'I admired your performance,' she said.

'What do you do?'

'I'm a film-maker,' she said. 'Jamila and I are making a documentary together.' Then she turned to Changez. 'We should crash, Jammie and I', she said. 'Wouldn't it be great if there was grapefruit and toast for breakfast again.'

'Oh yes,' said Changez, with an ebullient face but darting, worried eyes. 'Don't you worry, there will be, for you and Jamila at nine on the dot.'

'Thank you.'

Joanna kissed Changez then. When she'd turned away, he wiped his cheek. Jamila gave Leila Kollontai to Changez and, offering Joanna her hand, she went off. I watched them go before turning to Changez. He wouldn't look at me now. He was angry; he was staring and shaking his head.

'What's the matter?' I said.

'You make me think about too many things.'

'Sorry.'

'Go upstairs and sleep in the room at the end of the hall. I must change Leila. She has mucked herself.'

I felt too tired to walk upstairs, so when Changez went out I lay down behind the sofa, pulling a blanket over me. The floor was hard; I couldn't sleep. The world was swaying about like a hammock with my body on it. I counted my breaths and became aware of the rise and fall of my stomach, the hiss of my breath in my nostrils, my forehead relaxing. But, as in many of my meditation attempts, I was soon thinking of sex and other things. How stolidly contented Changez seemed at last. There was no vacillation in his love; it was true, it was absolute, he knew what he felt. And Jamila seemed content to be loved in this way. She could do what she wanted and Changez would always put her first; he loved her more than he loved himself.

I awoke cold and cramped, not sure where I was. Instead of getting up I stayed on the floor. I could hear voices. It was Changez and Jamila, who'd obviously come back into the room and had been talking for a while as Jamila tried to put Leila to sleep. They had plenty to say to each other, as they discussed Leila's wind, the house, the date of Simon's return – and where he'd sleep – and Joanna's documentary.

I went back to sleep. When I woke up again Jamila was getting ready for bed. 'I'm going up,' she said. 'Get some sleep yourself, sweetie. Oh, and Leila is out of nappies.'

'Yes, the little naughty has made her clothes all filthy, too. I'll wash them first thing tomorrow at the laundrette.'

'And mine? There's just a few things. And Joanna's leggings? Could you – '

'Leave me in complete control. Colonel Changez.'

'Thank you,' Jamila said. 'Colonel Changez.'

'Main thing is, I'm mighty bloody glad you're eating well,' Changez said. His voice was high and strained; he was talking quickly, as if he thought the moment he shut his mouth she'd go away. 'I'm giving you only healthy food from now on. Jamila, think: there will be top grapefruit and special warm bread for breakfast. Top fresh sardines for lunch with fresh bread, followed by pears and soft cheese – '

He bored her, he knew he bored her, but he couldn't stop. She tried to interrupt. 'Changez, I – '

'Auntie Jeeta is selling good food now, since I converted her to new lines.' His voice rose. 'She is old-fashioned, but I am saying follow the latest trends which I am discovering in magazines. She is becoming enthusiastic with my guidance. She walks naughty Leila in the park while I organize shop!' He was almost yelling. 'I am installing mirrors for the detection of criminals!'

'Excellent, Changez. Please don't shout. My father would be proud of you. You're – '

There was movement. I heard Jamila say, 'What are you doing?'

'My heart is beating,' he said. 'I will kiss you goodnight.'

'OK.'

There was a sucking noise, followed by a complacent, 'Good-night, Changez. Thanks for looking after Leila today.'

'Kiss me, Jamila. Kiss my lips.'

'Um. Changez – ' There were physical sounds. I could feel his bulk in the room. It was like listening to a radio play. Was he grabbing her? Was she fighting him off? Should I intervene? 'Thanks, Changez, that's enough kissing. Haven't you been ser-viced by Shinko lately?'

Changez was panting. I could imagine his tongue hanging out; the exertion of assault was too much for him.

'Karim stirred me up, Jammie. I've got to explain this to you. That little devil bugger – '

'What's he been saying?' Jamila asked with a laugh. 'He's got problems, we all know that. But he's a sweet boy, too, isn't he, his little hands pawing things, his eyebrows fluttering about – '

'He's got tremendous personal problems, as you say quite rightly. I am beginning to think he is totally perverted too, the way he likes to squeeze my body. I explain to him, what am I, an orange? I say – '

'Changez, it's late and – '

'Yes, yes, but Karim for once was saying something with mean-ing.'

'Really?'

Changez was desperate to say this, but he paused for a few seconds and held his breath, unsure whether he was making a mistake or not. Jamila waited for him.

'He said you're a female lesbian type and all. Jamila, I couldn't believe my hearing. Rubbish, you bastard, I told him. I was ready to blow him off the earth. That's not my wife, is it?'

Jamila sighed. 'I didn't want to have this conversation now.'

'That's not what you can be doing with Joanna, is it?'

'It's true at the moment that Joanna and I are very close – very fond of each other.'

'Fond?'

'I can't think that I've liked anyone as much for a long time. I'm sure you know how it is – you meet someone and you want to be with them, you want to know them deeply. It's passion, I suppose, and it's wonderful. That's how I feel, Changez. I'm sorry if it – '

He shouted, 'What's wrong with your only husband here and available that you are turning to perversion? Am I the one single normal person left in England now?'

'Don't start. Please, I'm so tired. I'm so happy at last. Try and accept it, Bubble.'

'And all you here in this house, you good types, talk of the prejudice against this Yid and that black burglar bastard, this Paki and that poor woman.'

'Changez, this is offensive, this is – '

'But what about ugly bastards? What about us? What about our rights to be kissed?'

'You are kissed, Changez.'

'After the exchange of pounds sterling only!'

'Please, let's go to bed. There are plenty of people who will kiss you. But not me, I'm afraid. Not me. You were imposed on me by my father.'

'Yes, I am not wanted.'

'But you're not ugly inside, Changez, if you want that patronizing assurance.'

He was only half listening; and he was far from exhausted.

'Yes, inside I look like Shashi Kapoor, I know that for sure,' he said, beating his hand on his knee. 'But some people are really ugly pig-faces, and they have a terrible time and all. I'm beginning a national campaign to stop this prejudice. But it should start stopping with you, here in this damn house of the holy socialists!'

There was more noise, but more sartorial than physical this time. 'Look,' he said. 'Look, look, aren't I a man at least?'

'Oh, cover it up. I'm not saying it isn't exquisite. God, Changez, some of your attitudes to women are antique. You've got to sort yourself out. The world is moving on.'

'Touch it. Give yourself a holiday.'

She snorted. 'If I need a holiday I'll go to Cuba.'

'Touch it, touch it, or – '

'Let me warn you,' she said. And not once did she raise her voice or show any sign of fear. There was irony, of course, as always with Jamila, but complete control, too. 'Anyone can be removed from this house by a democratic vote. Where would you go then, Bombay?'

'Jamila, wife, take me in,' he moaned.

'Let's clear the table and take it into the kitchen,' she said softly. 'Come on, Colonel Changez. You need rest.'

'Jamila, I beg you – '

'And I wouldn't let Joanna catch you waving that mushroom about. As it is, she suspects all men of being rapists, and seeing you doing that she'd know it was true.'

'I want love. Help me – '

Jamila continued in her detached way. 'If Joanna saw you doing this – '

'Why should she see? For a change it's just you and me together for a few precious moments. I never see my own wife alone.'

I was shifting about uncomfortably. This voyeur stuff was getting to be too much for me. In the past I'd been happy to look in on others' love-making. I'd virtually watched it more than I'd done it; I'd found it educational, it showed solidarity with friends, and so on. But now, as I lay there behind the sofa, I knew my mind required more fodder – bigger ideas, new interests. Eva was right; we didn't demand enough of ourselves and of life. I would demand; I would get up and demand. I was about to declare myself when Jamila suddenly said, 'What was that noise?'

'What?'

She lowered her voice. 'It sounded like a fart coming from behind the sofa.'

'A fart?'

I sat up and looked over the top of the sofa. 'It's only me,' I said. 'I was trying to sleep. I didn't hear a thing.'

'You bastard,' said Changez, becoming even more agitated. 'Jamila, I am calling the police on this damn snooper! Let me dial 999 immediately!'

He was trembling and puffing and spitting even as he secured his trousers. He shouted, 'You have always mocked my love for Jamila. You have always wanted to stand between us.'

In fact, it was Jamila who stood between Changez and me to stop him attacking me. She escorted me upstairs to a room where I could lock the door, safe from Changez's anger. In the morning I got up early and tiptoed through the sleeping house to the front door. On my way there I heard Leila Kollontai start to cry, and then I heard Changez talking softly to her in Urdu.

A few days later I went to see Dad again. There he was, sitting in one of Eva's armchairs in his pyjamas, with a pallid young man on the floor in front of him. The man was intense, weepy, despairing. Dad was saying: 'Yes, yes, this whole business of living is very difficult.'

Apparently these kids from Dad's classes were always turning up at the flat, and he had to deal with them. This he considered to be 'compassionate activity'. He was now saying that, for the sake of 'harmony', each day of your life had to contain three elements: scholarship, compassionate activity and meditation. Dad was teaching this several times a week at a nearby Yoga Centre. I'd always imagined that Dad's guru business would eventually fall off in London, but it was clear now that he would never lack employment while the city was full of lonely, unhappy, unconfident people who required guidance, support and pity.

Eva took me into the kitchen to show me some soup-bowls. She'd also bought a Titian print of a young man with long hair who looked like Charlie when he was at school. Long-stemmed tulips and daffodils sat in jugs on the table. 'I'm so happy,' Eva told me as she showed me things. 'But I'm in a hurry. They've got to do something about death. It's ridiculous to die so young. I want to live to be one hundred and fifty. It's only now that I'm getting anywhere.'

Later, I sat down with Dad. His flesh was heavy, marked, and fatty now, the upper half of his face composed of flaccid pouches sewn together in a sort of tier under the eyes, unfolding one by one like an Italian terrace down his cheeks.

'You've told me nothing of what's happening in your life,' he said. I wanted to stagger him with my soap opera news. But when I want to stagger people I usually can't; staggered is the last thing they are. 'I'm in a soap opera,' I said, in Changez's voice. 'Top pay. Top job. Top person.'

'Don't always laugh in my face like an idiot,' Dad said.

'But I'm not. I wasn't.'

'You're still a liar too, I see.'

'Dad – '

'At least you're doing something visible at last and not bumming,' he said.

I flushed with anger and humiliation. No, no, no, I wanted to shout. We're misunderstanding each other again! But it was impossible to clarify. Maybe you never stop feeling like an eight-year-old in front of your parents. You resolve to be your mature self, to react in this considered way rather than that elemental way, to breathe evenly from the bottom of your stomach and to see your parents as equals, but within five minutes your intentions are blown to hell, and you're babbling and screaming in rage like an angry child.

I could barely speak, until Dad asked me the question which was so difficult for him and yet was the only thing in the world he wanted to know.

'How's your mum?' he said.

I told him she was well, better than I'd seen her for years, good-tempered and active and optimistic and all. 'Good God,' he said quickly. 'How can that possibly be? She was always the world's sweetest but most miserable woman.'

'Yes, but she's seeing someone – a man – now.'

'A man? What kind of a man? Are you sure?'

He couldn't stop asking questions. 'Who is he? What's he like? How old is he? What does he do?'

I chose my words carefully. I had to, since I'd noticed that Eva was behind Dad, in the doorway. She stood there casually, as if we were discussing our favourite films. She hadn't the taste to turn away. She wanted to know exactly what was going on. She didn't want any secrets within her domain.

Mum's boyfriend was not remarkable, I said to Dad. At least, he was no Beethoven. But he was young and he cared for her. Dad couldn't believe it was so simple; none of it satisfied him. He said, 'D'you think – of course, you don't know this, how could you, it's none of your business, it's none of mine, but you might have guessed, or heard it from Allie or from her, especially with your great big nose poking into other people's businesses non-stop – do you think he's kissing her?'

'Yes.'

'Are you sure?'

'Oh yeah, I'm sure of it. And he's injected her with new life, he really has. It's terrific, eh?'

This practically assassinated him there and then. 'Nothing will ever be the same again,' he said.

'How could it be?'

'You don't know what you're talking about,' he said, and he turned his face away. Then he saw Eva. He was afraid of her, I could see.

'My love,' he said.

'What are you doing, Haroon?' she said angrily. 'How can you even think like this?'

'I'm not thinking like it,' Dad said.

'Stupid, it's stupid to regret anything.'

'I don't.'

'Yes, you do, you see. And you won't even acknowledge it.'

'Please, Eva, not now.'

He sat there trying not to mind her, but the resentment was going deep. All the same, I was surprised by him. Was it only now, after all this time, that he realized the decision to leave our mother was irrevocable? Perhaps only now could he believe it wasn't a joke or game or experiment, that Mum wasn't waiting at home for him with curry and chapatis in the oven and the electric blanket on.

That evening I said I'd take Dad, Eva, Allie and his girlfriend out to dinner to celebrate my new job and Dad giving up his. 'What a good idea,' said Eva. 'Maybe I'll make an announcement, too.'

I rang Jammie at the commune and invited her and Changez to join us. Changez took the phone from her and said he'd come out if he could but wasn't sure about Jamila, because of naughty Leila.

And anyway, they'd been out at the polling booths all day, working for the Labour Party at the election.

We got dressed up, and Eva persuaded Dad into his Nehru jacket, collarless and buttoned up to the throat like a Beatle jacket, only longer. The waiters would think he was an ambassador or a prince, or something. She was so proud of him, too, and kept picking stray hairs off his trousers, and the more bad-tempered he looked, because of everything being wrong, the more she kissed him. We took a taxi to the most expensive place I knew, in Soho. I paid for everything with the money I'd got by trading in the ticket to New York.

The restaurant was on three floors, with duck-egg blue walls, a piano and a blond boy in evening dress playing it. The people were dazzling; they were rich; they were loud. Eva, to her pleasure, knew four people there, and a middle-aged queen with a red face and pot-belly said, 'Here's my address, Eva. Come to dinner on Sunday and see my four Labradors. Have you heard of so-and-so?' he added, mentioning a famous film director. 'He'll be there. And he's looking for someone to do up his place in France.'

Eva talked to him about her work and the job she was currently doing, designing and decorating a country house. She and Ted would have to stay in a cottage in the grounds for a while. It was the biggest thing they'd been asked to do. She was going to employ several people to help her, but they would only be self-aware types, she said. 'Self-aware but not self-conscious, I hope,' said the queen.

Inevitably, little Allie knew some other people there, three models, and they came over to our table. We had a small party, and by the end of it everyone in the place seemed to have been told I was going to be on television, and who was going to be the next Prime Minister. It was the latter that made them especially ecstatic. It was good to see Dad and Allie together again. Dad made a special effort with him and kept kissing him and asking him questions, but Allie kept his distance; he was very confused and he'd never liked Eva.

To my relief, at midnight Changez turned up in his boiler suit, along with Shinko. Changez embraced Dad and me and Allie, and showed us photographs of Leila. She couldn't have had a more indulgent uncle than Changez. 'If only you'd brought Jamila,' I said. Shinko was very attentive to Changez. She spoke of his care for Leila and his work on Princess Jeeta's shop, while he ignored her and brayed his loud opinions on the arrangement of items in a shop – the exact location of sweets in relation to bread – even as she praised him to others.

He ate massively, ol' Changez, and I encouraged him to have two helpings of coconut ice-cream, which he ate as if it were about to be taken from him. 'Have anything you like,' I said to all of them. 'D'you want dessert, d'you want coffee?' I began to enjoy my own generosity; I felt the pleasure of pleasing others, especially as this was accompanied by money-power. I was paying for them; they were grateful, they had to be; and they could no longer see me as a failure. I wanted to do more of this. It was as if I'd suddenly discovered something I was good at, and I wanted to practise it non-stop.

When everyone was there, and nicely drunk and laughing, Eva stood up and knocked on the table. She was smiling and caressing the back of Dad's head as she strained to be heard. She said, 'Can I have some quiet. Some quiet, please, for a few minutes. Everyone – please!'

There was quiet. Everyone looked at her. Dad beamed around the table.

'There's an announcement I must make,' she said.

'For God's sake make it, then,' Dad said.

'I can't,' she said. She bent to his ear. 'Is it still true?' she whispered.

'Say it,' he said, ignoring the question. 'Eva, everyone's waiting.'

She stood up, put her hands together and was about to speak when she turned to Dad once more. 'I can't, Haroon.'

'Say it, say it,' we said.

'All right. Pull yourself together, Eva. We are getting married. Yes, we're getting married. We met, fell in love, and now we're getting married. In two months' time. OK? You're all invited.'

She sat down abruptly, and Dad put his arm around her. She was speaking to him, but by now we were roaring our approval and banging the table and pouring more drinks. I raised a toast to them, and everyone cheered and clapped. It was a great, unsullied event. After this there were hours of congratulation and drinking and so many people around our table I didn't have to talk much. I could think about the past and what I'd been through as I'd struggled to locate myself and learn what the heart is. Perhaps in the future I would live more deeply.

And so I sat in the centre of this old city that I loved, which itself sat at the bottom of a tiny island. I was surrounded by people I loved, and I felt happy and miserable at the same time. I thought of what a mess everything had been, but that it wouldn't always be that way.